VAMPIRE GIRL PROBLEMS:
Twice Bitten: Book Two

CRYSTAL-RAIN LOVE

ACKNOWLEDGMENTS

Special thanks to Christle Gray for letting me bounce things off you and being there for me during the whole process of creating this book.
Thanks, "Big Rome" for agreeing to let me model the toughest human bodyguard a vampire could have off of you... and letting me poke fun at you just a little bit.

ONE

I was awakened by the warm caress of soft lips just under my ear and a searching hand wandering down my hip. He gripped the hem of my T-shirt and started pulling it up, his intent to undress me. The moment the bunched material reached the underside of the bra covering my meager breasts, my hand shot out, covering his. My entire body stiffened, frozen in fear.

"Danni. It's just me."

I took a deep breath, more for the calming effect than an actual need to intake air, and turned to face him. With piercing blue eyes that shone like deep sapphire, a perfect nose, dark, expressive brows and lips that could drive a woman to madness, Rider Knight wasn't just anything. He was everything. He was too much, and far out of my league. He was inhumanly perfect.

"I don't know whether to be flattered or offended," he murmured before kissing the tip of my nose. He propped himself up with his elbow and gazed down at me. He was naked, had already been that way when I'd entered his room the night before and found him lying under the sheets, sheets that had spilled away enough for me to fully take in his hard, lean but muscular chest now. More perfection. He grinned the cocky grin that let me know he was in my head, listening as I oohed and ahhed over his beauty. "Beauty?" He grimaced. "Pick another word, one with testicles."

"Like you have to worry about masculinity," I muttered. He was a perfect specimen of everything a man should be. "I've lost count how many times I've asked you to stay out of my head."

"About as many times as I've told you I can't help it when you're projecting your thoughts." He released the hem of my shirt and used that hand to cup my bottom, pulling me in close against him and his complete nakedness. "You seem to lose focus when you're scared. Why are you scared now? It's only you and me here. You know I would never hurt you."

I bit my lip as heat flooded my face. While I'd only had sex once in my life and that had been some time ago, it wasn't a physical pain I feared from him. It was the humiliation, the inevitable disappointment he would feel. He was a master vampire, something I was still learning all the details about. I knew he was powerful, so very powerful. I'd seen him throw a man into a wall without so much as lifting a finger. And he was old. I didn't know exactly how old because a vampire's age was a carefully guarded secret. I was still struggling to understand that as well, but there'd been a moment after Rider had killed his own brother to protect me that I'd somehow dipped into his mind and saw his memories. Just from what I'd seen that night in that quick flash, I knew he'd been around for centuries. I couldn't even imagine how many women he'd been with in such a long span of time, but I could imagine how horribly I would measure up to their beauty and experience.

"Danni." He closed his eyes and took a deep breath through his nose, releasing it slowly. It wasn't the first time he'd done this with me. I was trying his patience. "Do you remember what I told you last night?"

I started to roll over, away from eyes I knew would be too powerful to turn away from once they reopened, but he stopped me with just a fraction of the strength contained in just one of his arms. I looked into his open eyes and nodded.

"What did I tell you?"

"You said you love me."

"Do you believe me?"

I wanted to. I wanted to so very badly, but I couldn't bring myself to accept that this man would want me, this strong, gorgeous, amazing man who saved my life, not once, but multiple times. For starters, we hadn't known each other long enough. I couldn't fathom a man who'd been alive for centuries falling in love so quickly with someone as unremarkable as me. Then there was the fact I was the only vampire he'd sired and the deep fear that it was that bond he actually felt, that he'd confused it with romantic love.

"I'm not confusing anything," he said. "Get out of your own head, Danni. Quit overanalyzing everything, searching every word I say to you for a crack. Just feel."

"Feel what?"

"This." He covered my mouth with his own, pressed his tongue deep inside as he rolled me onto my back and lowered himself into the cradle of my hips. My thighs automatically locked in place, closing around his hips like a vise. "Danni," he said against my lips as he ran his hand down my thigh. "Relax. You've got me in a scissors here. Just let go."

"I don't know how."

"Relax." His tongue delved into my mouth again, rolled around, starting a trail of fire that went through my body right down to the place he was trying to get inside, but my legs were stone. My heart raced, my body warmed, but as his tongue teased me into a frenzy and his hands explored beneath my shirt, my brain went into overdrive. I struggled to recall what the magazines said to do. I'd had a subscription to *Cosmopolitan* for years and devoured every issue like I was studying for an exam, so when I found myself in a situation like this, I'd know what to do to please a man. Why couldn't I remember any of it? The more I tried to think what I should do, the more I froze, until suddenly my legs were squeezing Rider's body like a ThighMaster and my fingers were locked into his shoulder blades. "Babe, relax," he said, kissing a trail from my mouth to my neck while his hands fondled my breasts through my bra. "You don't have to do anything. Just relax and I'll do everything."

"That's not what the magazines say," I blurted out, not bothering to hide the fact I'd been studying magazines for sex tips. There was too much activity in my brain for me to even contemplate the thought of locking down my thoughts from him anyway. Suddenly I recalled a conversation I'd had with Rider about him intruding upon my private thoughts, and he'd warned me that I projected so loud others in his nest could pick up on my thoughts too. "Oh no," I cried out, slapping my hands over my eyes as if that could hide me from the world. "We're above the bar and all your vampires are down there and can probably hear everything going on in my head. Now they all know I'm the only idiot woman in the world who'd have Rider Knight naked on top of her and instead of doing the reverse donkey cowgirl, I've got you locked inches away from the promised land."

I felt a vibration against my neck and looked down to see Rider shaking with laughter. "You're laughing at me!"

He propped himself up, allowing enough space so he could wipe his wet eyes on his arm. "How exactly does one do the reverse donkey cowgirl?"

"I don't know. I don't know anything, but I'm sure plenty of your admirers do and would be glad to show you, since I'm such a failure."

"Yeah, I'm pretty sure it's not a real thing, but if I ever learn it, I promise it'll be with you." He started to roll off me, but my legs were still clamped around him. "Okay, I'm done. Release."

"You don't want to be with me anymore."

"I desire to be inside you far greater than I've ever desired to be in any other woman on this earth, Danni, but not like this. You're not ready and if I have to force my way in, it would be wrong." He pushed his hands under me and scooped me up as he sat back, bringing me with him so I straddled him on the edge of the bed. He ran his thumb along my bottom lip as his mouth curved into a soft smile. "I'm not laughing at you. You amuse me. It's a major reason why I feel the way I feel about you."

"I'm a joke to you."

"No, not even close. You're a ray of sunshine and a warm, beautiful light in a world that has been dark for far too long." He cupped my face in both his hands and looked me deep in the eyes. "I won't lie to you and say I haven't been with a lot of women. I have, I've been around a long time, but in all that time I have never been with anyone who makes me smile like you do. Even when you're flinging barbs at me with that wicked sharp tongue of yours, you put joy in my heart. You've talked to Eliza, you know that a lot of the vampires in my nest were created by sires who abused them. Siring a vampire doesn't create a feeling of instant love. What I feel for you has nothing to do with the fact that I sired you. A lot of vampires are arrogant enough to tell their fledglings that they created them. I am not so arrogant to think that. I only gave you a second chance at life. I am not talented enough to create someone as wonderful as you, Danni Keller. You are a treasure and damn it, one day you're going to realize it."

Wow. What could I even say to that? At a loss for words, I wrapped my arms around Rider's shoulders and held him close. He held me back even tighter, resting his head against mine. With the bond between us, I didn't really need to say a word. I sent my feelings out to him, not sure how I did it, but when he kissed my temple, I knew he'd gotten the message.

"Get dressed. I'm going to go downstairs, wrap some things up with the business, and you and I are going on a trip, someplace where you will feel comfortable."

"You can do that?" I asked in surprise. Rider was the master of the city, which from what I've gathered means he runs the whole supernatural community in the Louisville area, as well as owning The Midnight Rider, the name of the bar beneath us, and his own security company which I realized I didn't even know the name of. The other vampires deferred to him, all out of respect, but whether that respect came from love or fear depended on the vampire in question. I knew he had shapeshifters working for him as well, and at least one witch he'd called in to help me out of a jam.

"I have good people I can leave in charge for a spell. We're just taking a short trip, a romantic getaway. I think it's deserved after all that has happened."

A lot had definitely happened. After a rough day at work, I'd come into the bar six weeks ago with every intention of getting drunk and hooking up with someone random, anyone who would get my mind off my boss. I'd been obsessed with the good-looking, extremely rich Dex Prince, member of the Prince family and heir to the family businesses, one of which was the advertising company I worked for. That particular day I'd lost an account and Dex had made a remark about my lack of sex appeal. When my co-worker, Gina, suggested we meet up at The Midnight Rider for drinks, I hadn't needed any convincing.

Little had I known that Gina had already been seduced by an incubus without her knowledge, coerced into sending me to that very bar that very night so the incubus in question, Selander Ryan, could attack me in the alley behind it. Rider had saved my life that night, but he'd done so by biting me as well, transitioning my turn so that instead of becoming a succubus, I'd become a vampire like him. Actually, I became a hybrid. I had the vampire fangs, but they secreted succubus venom. Sunlight was a bitch to deal with and I learned the hard way that most human food isn't for newly turned vampire consumption. I also drank blood, lots of blood. I didn't make it a week before I accidentally killed a guy who'd stumbled out of a bar and made the mistake of asking me to suck him while I was thirsty. I sucked him all right, just not where or how he'd wanted. Rider covered his death up for me and placed people from his security company all around me to protect me from Selander Ryan, who invaded my dreams and even used my advertising company to promote a fragrance his company, Nocturnal, Inc. had created. He and Rider were in a power struggle over me. They each had bitten me. They each felt I was theirs, although whereas Selander Ryan thought I was his to control, Rider thought I was his to protect. As if that wasn't enough to deal with, I also had a hunter after me. Rider had struck a deal with the Quimby line of hunters centuries ago, and throughout the ages, every Quimby hunter honored the deal and did not hunt any vampire under Rider's protection. Barnaby Quimby broke that deal by targeting me, stating the fact I was a hybrid canceled the pact out. Rider killed him shortly after the hunter had made the mistake of shooting an arrow at me. He then killed a man in his employ and allowed others in his nest to kill a woman in his employ, both of whom had betrayed him by allowing Barnaby Quimby access into Rider's garage, where he'd tried to take me out.

While Rider and his people had been protecting me from Selander Ryan and Barnaby Quimby, I'd been denying my feelings for Rider and trying to maintain as much of a normal life as I could. That included dating my hot boss, who I'd fantasized about for years. He turned out to be a huge bastard I'd had to kill to prevent being raped when he decided he didn't like being refused. Rider had cleaned that mess up for me as well. Well, he'd called in Rihanna, a sassy witch, to do the actual cleaning up, but he'd been there for me and he'd walked me out of Dex's penthouse and right into the final fight between him and Selander Ryan.

They'd both bitten me and they'd both been capable of controlling me. Rider had chosen not to, refusing to dominate a person in such a manner, but Selander had simply kept his cards hidden. He waited until that night, after he and Rider's people engaged in a full on battle to show how much control he had over me. He raised me in the air with only his mind and twisted my neck, ready to snap it in front of Rider, to kill what Rider held dear, but I chose that moment to accept Rider as my master, voiding out the power of Selander Ryan's bite. He could no longer kill me with his mind, but he could kill me with his hands. He moved to do so and Rider, cloaked in the mysterious golden glow of his own power, reached into Selander Ryan's chest and ripped out the incubus's heart.

He had saved my life yet another time, and it was in that moment I tumbled into his mind and saw his very long life play out in a series of memories starting from his childhood. It was within that moment that I learned he had killed his own brother to spare my life, an evil brother he'd fought countless times over the centuries but always refrained from delivering that final blow until it came to the choice between his life and mine.

He'd seen me safely home and left. I didn't reach out to him. I didn't know if he'd want me to after the intrusion. I'd not just read his mind, I'd witnessed the most private, painful moments of his life. I'd witnessed him discovering his brother had become an incubus and changed their mother into a succubus. I'd witnessed him being turned into a vampire, and I'd witnessed him killing his mother because her stepson had turned her into a creature she would despise, and it was the only way Rider knew how to save her. I witnessed him promise his mother that he would find a way to protect his brother, who only shared a father with him, but his mother loved both boys as if they were both from her own body.

And I witnessed him kill that half-brother in full living color.

I quit my job two weeks later, continued seeing Eliza, the vampire counselor Rider had set me up with. I got bagged blood from Nannette, a vampire nurse I'd also met through Rider. I drank the gross bagged blood instead of getting it fresh from Rider. I didn't dare drink from a human after I'd killed the first man I'd tried that with. I accepted Rider as my master the night he'd killed Ryan, and I'd felt a powerful surge the moment I did, as I became fully his, but I still feared the possibility of succubus remnants. More specifically, I feared I might still have the venom in my bite, venom that caused men to lose their minds with lust the second I plunged my teeth into them. Rider was a powerful vampire, strong enough to control himself when I bit him, which is why I only fed from him. The two times I'd bitten humans had been disastrous and resulted in their deaths at my hands.

I was separated from him for four weeks between the night he killed Selander Ryan and last night when I'd found myself on the street in front of the bar and he'd sensed me, and welcomed me inside to find him lying in his bed, naked, his eyes heavy from extreme tiredness but inability to sleep. The portrait of his mother he kept over the chrome bar at the left side of his bed had been taken down as if he could no longer bear to look at her, or maybe he felt her accusing eyes on him. He'd reassured me that killing his brother, or half-brother, was the only way to save him and that he didn't hold any of it against me. He told me he loved me shortly before daybreak. We were both so tired we went to sleep as the sun rose, his arms wrapped around me as I drifted into a dreamless, peaceful sleep.

"Yeah, I guess we do deserve a nice, quiet getaway," I said, hoping all the troubles we'd had would stay behind us. My legs finally unfrozen, I moved off him, allowing him to rise from the bed in all his naked glory and cross the room to remove pants from his dresser. I watched him dress, not the slightest bit concerned he was on display, and hoped to someday gain a fraction of the confidence he had. I hoped the day would come soon because one of the troubles that plagued us was my own damn insecurity. He'd told me as much himself and although he'd shown great patience with me, I knew it was only a matter of time before patience gave out. Of all the ways I could lose him, I couldn't stand the thought of losing him by not loving myself enough. "So, where are we going?"

"It's a surprise." He pulled a black T-shirt over his head and winked at me.

"You're not going to ask if I need to take time off work?"

"No."

"You know I quit my job, don't you?"

"Of course."

"So you've still had security on me these past four weeks, tracking my every move?"

He walked back to the bed and leaned down, caging me between his arms as he kissed me. "Of course."

I suppose I could have been angry with Rider for secretly having his security team on me during the time we were apart, but honestly, it would be like screaming at a wall. If Rider wanted me protected, he was going to protect me, whether or not I requested his help. I used to think of it as an ownership. He'd created me. I was his property. He protected his investment. Over time, I'd realized it wasn't about that at all. He gave me a second chance at life because he didn't want me to die, and he still didn't. He protected me because he wanted me safe. I didn't need to ask for his protection. It was just there, and I had the feeling it always would be. He didn't feel he'd created me, or that he owned me, but he did have feelings for me and would be hurt if I was hurt. So I let him slide.

"Are we there yet?" I asked for the hundredth time since Rider had backed his Ferrari out of the garage attached to the bar and set forth on our getaway adventure. He smiled at me, catching on pretty quickly to the joke. Apparently mimicking an annoying child wasn't going to get me any information, so I settled in and watched the scenery flow by as we traveled the expressway. My ears started to ring as we climbed higher in the mountains and I paid closer attention to the signs we passed, wondering if he was taking me to my favorite place in the world, somewhere I'd visited often with my father as a child. Life had been simpler when he was around. My mother was nicer, my sister and I weren't competing for anything, and I had a great man in my life who loved me just for me. It was something that as I grew older, I'd started thinking I'd never have again. I looked over at Rider and thought maybe, just maybe, I still could. I just had to learn how to let him.

"Almost there," Rider said, taking one hand off the steering wheel to pick mine up and drop a kiss on my knuckles. My mouth dropped open as we exited the expressway and I recognized the turns we took and the billboards that increased in size and number as we approached the Parkway. We were in Pigeon Forge, Tennessee. Rider had brought me to my favorite place in the entire world, a place that, for some reason, had always felt more like home to me than my actual home.

"This is my favorite place in the whole freaking universe," I said as we reached the Parkway and traveled toward Gatlinburg. "How did you know? I haven't been here in years and I know I haven't thought about it around you."

"You kind of did," he said softly, both hands back on the steering wheel and his watchful gaze on the tourist-packed road. "When Ryan attacked you and I bit you to counter his bite. When you were fighting between the two bites, while you were burning with fever from the turning and going in and out of consciousness, you were talking out of your head, and at one point, I believe you were talking with your father."

I felt my eyes grow wet just from the thought of talking to my father during that time. I wondered had I been hallucinating him or had I been so close to death I'd actually seen him. "What did I say?"

"You were thrashing around in the bed so hard I could hardly hold you, then you cried out 'Take me back there, Daddy, back to the place where I was happy. Take me back to the painted forest in the clouds' and you calmed down. While you rested, I looked through that big scrapbook on your dresser and I saw a picture of you on your father's shoulders while here on vacation. The trees were so many different colors and I could see the clouds so close it looked like your little arms could touch them. I knew this was the place you wanted to go, and I told myself that if you survived the turn, I would bring you here."

The dam broke loose and tears poured from my eyes as I sobbed uncontrollably. I knew exactly what picture he'd seen and how incredibly happy I'd been on that trip. During the time I'd turned I'd spoken to him so horribly, accused him of rape and kidnapping in addition to drugging me, and he'd been helping me the whole time and had planned this trip because he knew it was a place that would make me happy.

"Damn." Rider looked over at me, pain in his eyes. "I'm sorry, Danni, maybe I shouldn't have done this. Was I out of line?"

"No. No," I said after hiccupping a sob. I shook my head and squeezed his arm. "I'm just really touched that you would think to bring me here. This is the best gift ever. Truly, it is." I looked over at him and saw the confusion and worry etched across his face. He had the power to fling people across rooms with just his mind, yet he looked absolutely scared to death he'd done something wrong. It made me laugh until fresh tears sprung from my eyes and I searched his glove compartment for a tissue.

"First, I make you cry, then I make you laugh. Neither time do I have a clue why. Even with the ability to read your mind, I don't think I'll ever have you fully figured out."

"Good," I said, drying my tears with Kleenex. "At least our relationship will never go stale."

"I have no doubt about that," he said as he took a turn that led us away from the Parkway and we wound up narrow, curving roads that took us farther up into the mountains. At one point, it seemed I could lower my window, reach out and grab a cloud if I wanted.

"I've never been to this area," I said as the ground leveled out and he slowly crept forward, using his night vision and the soft glow of the moon to find a group of cabins set back from the road.

"Hotels along the Parkway aren't the best places for the privacy our kind requires. We'll be staying in a cabin here. It's secluded and right within the forest you love." He parked the car and one by one, large, shadowy figures appeared on the hill before us.

"Um, Rider?" I gripped his arm tight.

"It's okay." He placed his free hand over the one I clenched his arm with. "You were worried about members of the nest hearing your thoughts, so I left our main security detail back home. We still need protection, especially during the daylight hours, so I've made arrangements. Let's get out and I'll introduce you to the Smoky Mountain Wolf Pack."

TWO

Rider opened my door and offered me his arm. I gladly took it, hoping holding on to him would cover my nervousness. I'd met other vampires, and these weren't the first shifters I'd seen. During the battle between Rider and Selander, I'd watched one of Rider's employees shift into a tiger and *eat* a man. He'd been wiping down the bar when I'd walked into The Midnight Rider last night. This wolf pack had a very different vibe, maybe because they weren't part of Rider's regular crew.

A young man with a nose piercing, shaggy rainbow-colored hair and a wrinkled Pink Floyd T-shirt trotted down the hill. "I'll get your bags," he said, passing us. Rider clicked a button on his key fob, opening the trunk.

"We have bags?" I looked behind us and watched the man pull two suitcases from the trunk. "I didn't pack anything."

"I had some things packed for you."

"But I was at your place. I have nothing there."

"I may have bought some things for you last week."

"Really?"

We'd climbed the stone steps built into the hill and were now before the large group of mostly male, mostly muscular, and mostly scary shifters. Even the two women I saw looked pretty formidable, but maybe that was because of the death glares they sent my way.

"Mr. Knight." The man in front, the largest of all, greeted Rider. He had dark honey-colored hair that touched down to his shoulders, olive green eyes that reflected the moonlight, and hands that could probably crush bowling balls. I didn't even want to imagine what his biceps could do.

"Mr. Grey." Rider nodded.

"If his first name is Christian, I'm out of here," I blurted without thinking. This got a barely suppressed grin from Rider and a full, hearty laugh from the man before us.

"I like her," the burly man said. "Most women want my first name to be Christian. They're disappointed when they find out it isn't, and that I'm not into whips and chains. Finding a suitable mate has become increasingly more tedious since those damn books came out, but I suppose it could be worse. I have a cousin named Jacob." He spread his arms wide. "Welcome to The Cloud Top. You will be staying in the guest house, and although your privacy will be respected, you will be protected by some of my finest guards. No one will enter your cabin unless requested or, of course, if there is the threat of danger. There will always be two guards in front, two in back, and the entire area is protected at all times. Daniel will be at your beck and call for anything you may need," he continued, nodding his head toward the man who'd retrieved our suitcases as he now passed us going up the hill and continued on away with our things. "He's the one we discussed," he added, voice lower, before turning. "Follow me."

We followed the man toward a large two-story cabin as the rest of the group eyed us curiously and broke off to do whatever it was that they did. "This is the guest house," he announced as he went up the porch, past a wolf standing guard. An actual wolf, not a man but a large gray wolf with very watchful, intelligent eyes.

"Is that a shifter?" I asked Rider. He nodded, and we followed our host inside the cabin.

It was beautiful. Hard-wood floors, a large kitchen in marble and chrome, a spacious living area with a pool that was half indoor, half outside on the deck, with a partition that could be opened in-between. The entire back wall was glass, but we were quickly informed that although we could see outside, no one could see in. A winding staircase took us upstairs to the master bedroom with a king-sized bed that looked out through another completely glass wall offering a beautiful view of the mountaintops and lush, colorful forest below. I caught movement and realized I could see a large waterfall as well.

Daniel was in the room, dropping off our luggage. "No worries," he said. "No one can see in, so feel free to get your—"

"Daniel!" Our host barked out the young man's name from the bathroom and other bedroom he was showing Rider from the hall.

Daniel laughed softly and exited the room. I stayed inside the master bedroom, standing before the glass wall, enjoying the view. Even at night, I saw so many beautiful colors. The Great Smoky Mountains National Park was like a living painting. I couldn't imagine a more beautiful sight.

"I can," Rider said softly, reading my mind as he approached quietly from behind. He wrapped his arms around my waist and pulled me back against his chest as I heard the door downstairs close. "You standing here before it all."

"This is perfect. You can't get this view from within the city." I thought about the looks I'd received from the two women. "Are you sure we're safe here? You didn't bring any of your own security team. How do you know you can trust these people? I thought werewolves and vampires didn't usually mix."

"You can't believe everything from books or movies," he answered with a gentle laugh. "Good Lord, one woman said we sparkle. Can you imagine me sparkling like a damn pixie? I'd gladly die before suffering that indignation."

I laughed at the ridiculous image of Rider sparkling that popped into my head and turned toward him. "You're definitely not a sparkler, but you are pretty amazing. Thank you for this."

"My pleasure. I enjoy seeing you happy." He kissed me, slow and sweet. "We still have quite a few hours before dawn. What did you want to do?"

I glanced at the big, inviting bed covered in silk sheets. "I thought you brought me here to..."

"I brought you here to a place you feel comfortable and safe, to shake off the taint of all the bad crap that has happened since my half-brother attacked you, a place we can begin something fresh. I don't expect anything from you and I'm not making demands. When you're ready for that, you know I'm here."

"Did I mention you're amazing?"

"Yeah," he answered, "but it never gets old."

I kissed him and turned toward the windows, but the luggage caught my eye. "You shopped for me?"

"Yeah..." He raked a hand through his hair. "It might seem weird, but I missed you and I couldn't bring myself to just drop in after what you'd seen. I was out and saw some things in a window, imagined them on you, then next thing I knew I was in the store shopping for you."

"And you just happened to have everything in a suitcase?"

"I knew eventually one of us would come to the other. Lord knows I couldn't stay away from you much longer. If you hadn't been outside the bar last night, I probably wouldn't have lasted much longer before I just drove by, shoved you into the car and brought you here. I always intended to bring you here."

I walked over to the two suitcases resting on the edge

of the bed and ran my fingers over the golden charm shaped like a heart on the zipper of one. "I assume this one is mine?"

Rider nodded. "You don't have to wear anything you don't like. We can shop while here too. I checked some tourism websites and they have a lot of places to shop for clothes, shoes, and anything else you can imagine."

I smiled as I unzipped the suitcase. Rider was a generous man, from what I'd seen. I'd had around the clock security since I'd been turned, even when I wasn't with him, and he'd set me up a blood account for which I had yet to receive a bill. Then there was the money I'd seen him shell out to pay a witch to clean up the bloody mess I'd made of my former boss. I didn't want him to spend any more money on me, especially when I wasn't sure what he had available or how big of a dent I'd put in his finances. He had a Harley, an expensive-looking SUV and a Ferrari, owned the bar and his own security company, but he lived in that small room over the bar so despite the large bills he'd had in his wallet the night he'd paid Rihanna for the clean-up I wasn't so sure he was exactly rolling in money.

"I'd be completely satisfied just enjoying the scenery and getting to know each other better," I said as I opened the suitcase and immediately noticed a flimsy pair of underwear. A picked up the scrap of silk, noting the ribbon ties on the sides that I imagined were supposed to keep the little bit of material over my goodies. "Oh my. I guess if I wore these you'd know me better, like... all of me."

Rider grinned. "Those might have been a bit more for me than for you."

"I see." I picked up a lacy pink bra and noted the size on the tag. 34A. "You got my size right."

"Of course. I've seen you naked, Danni, and I have every inch of you emblazoned into my brain, which is why I don't understand why you're so shy about letting me see you. I already have, and I found no flaws. I'm not going to find any flaws because they don't exist."

Heat flooded my face as I recalled waking up during the turn to find myself completely naked in Rider's arms. I didn't exactly feel sexy about it, but there were the other times I'd fed from him and my clothes had mysteriously started to come off. Those moments were sexy, until I'd become aware of my body on display, insecurity struck, and I ran away. He certainly hadn't seemed repulsed by my small breasts. Although there was the succubus venom to consider. Every time I drank from him, I'd been injecting the venom into his bloodstream, filling him up with what was basically a liquid aphrodisiac. I probably lost it the night Selander Ryan died, actually before he even died, when I gave myself over completely to Rider by declaring him my one and only master.

"Can you spare any blood?" I asked him.

"Yeah. Are you hungry?" He moved toward me, raising his shirt.

Oh yes, I thought as he pulled the shirt over his head, revealing more lean muscle for my eyes to feast on. I pushed the suitcases off the bed and grabbed him by the waistband, shoving him down onto the edge so I could straddle him.

"Danni?"

"I need to see if I still have the venom," I explained, lowering myself onto him. I traced my finger over the pulse point I found in his neck, watching, mesmerized, as I felt his heartbeat flutter just under his golden skin.

He clamped his hand around my nape and pulled me in for a deep kiss that warmed me from the inside out. I'd been shaking with nerves, but by the time he moved his lips away from mine, those shakes were from something much different. "Go ahead. Do it."

I looked into his dark blue eyes, saw the hunger brewing inside, and kissed him back as he grew hard beneath me. I shifted my hips, rubbing against him and eliciting a throaty moan I swallowed with a smile before pulling away to whisper kisses down his jaw and into the hollow of his neck. His pelvis lifted under me repeatedly as he gripped my hips and held me tight against him, simulating what he wanted to do inside me. My body flooded with heat knowing he was with me, that he wanted to be in me, and I hadn't even given him any venom yet. I rolled my tongue over the pulse point in his neck once, twice, three times, then sank my now descended fangs into his flesh. His blood rolled over my tongue, his power filling me. It was so much better than bagged blood, and as he thrust upward against me even harder, his fingers digging into my hips, I knew the venom remained and was feeding his desire for me. Part of me hurt and would always hurt, wondering if it was the venom he craved, but at least I knew that no matter what I did wrong, he would enjoy being with me and come back for more. Maybe I wouldn't lose him after all, and wasn't that what mattered?

I'd been more curious about the venom than hungry for the blood, no matter how delicious it was, so I took a few more sips and licked the wound, sealing his skin. Before I lost my nerve, I pulled my shirt over my head and discarded my bra.

"Sweet Demon Baby Lucifer," Rider said softly, taking me in with eyes that were dilated with lust and had darkened to a shade of blue I couldn't put a name to.

"I thought the expression was Sweet Baby Jesus."

"I don't dare say His name now with the thoughts of what I want to do to you currently in my head. He might smite my horny ass before I get to this promised land you spoke of."

I laughed until I cried, Rider joining in. The hot, wicked fog of lust that had been accumulating between us shattered and something totally different filled my body. It was still warm and still drew me to Rider, but it wasn't impatient and hungry. It was ... safe, welcoming... It was home.

"It's love," Rider said, flipping me onto my back and using his hands and mouth on every inch of me, and despite a few moments when I worried whether I was appealing enough, I didn't run away. And neither did he. A while later, as he moved in and out of me, he whispered, "Danni, I have to tell you something."

I braced myself for the worst. "What?"

"You don't have the venom."

I woke to the feel of Rider's fingers gently stroking my arm as I lay with my head on his chest, one leg draped across his waist and my hand resting just below one of his perfectly sculpted pecs.

"Good evening."

"Good evening? You sound like a vampire." His chest rumbled with silent laughter underneath me. "I don't remember falling asleep. I thought we were going to watch the sunrise."

"You zonked out just as it started. Understandably, you were exhausted, and very well sated."

"Was I?" I propped myself up on my elbow to find him smiling at me, just as I'd expected, and kissed him good morning, or what passed for our morning. "I do recall doing a lot of ... stuff. Several times."

"We never got around to that reverse donkey cowgirl thing though."

"Ugh." I groaned, plopping back down to hide my face against his chest, now rumbling again with laughter.

"No, no, I've been thinking about it since I woke up. We need to figure it out."

"No, we don't." My words came out muffled, my face still buried in his chest.

"But you wanted to do it. Reverse means backward and I'm thinking if a cowgirl is involved, there'd be some riding involved too."

"Stop it."

"You'd obviously be the cowgirl, so we'll have to start with you on top, but there's the donkey part. Am I the donkey?"

"Yes, you're definitely the jackass," I said, poking his ribs. "Now stop."

"Interesting you should say jackass, because I was just thinking that ass is another word for donkey. Danni Keller, is it a butt thing you wanted to do with me? You kinky little vixen, I never saw that coming." He barely got the words out around his laughing.

"Did you see this coming?" I asked, grabbing a pillow to pelt him repeatedly as he continued to laugh.

After a few good hits, he grabbed my wrists and held them up in the air, causing the sheet to fall away from my body. I was on complete naked display over him. "Very nice."

I dropped the pillow and gathered the sheet around me. "Really?"

"Baby steps," I said. "It's different being naked while doing naked things and being naked while … not doing naked things."

"Naked things?" He bit his lip but couldn't hold the laughter back from his eyes.

"It's nice that I can amuse you so much. It really is. I'm so happy I can be the entertainment factor in your life."

"Really? You sound a little miffed about it. Maybe we should do some naked things to get you back in your happy place. I hear there's this naked thing called the reverse donkey cowgirl."

"You're never going to let me forget that, are you?"

"Probably not. I'm kind of an asshole."

"I can see that," I said as he sat up and settled me on his lap. "I should ban you from all naked activities until you learn to be nicer."

"Ban me, you ban yourself," he teased. "I think you kind of liked all those things we did last night."

"Kind of," I said. "A little bit."

"Mmmhmm, just a little bit? There were a lot of rounds for just a little bit."

"There were," I agreed. "I really don't have the succubus venom anymore?"

"You really don't." He kissed me and moved a lock of hair out of my face. "I told you that you didn't need the venom to turn me on."

"I thought I'd still possibly have it," I murmured, something niggling me. I'd felt the surge of Rider's power the moment I'd accepted him as my only master, but something still felt different about me. I didn't feel like I was one hundred percent vampire, but what did I know? I'd only been one for less than two months. "So... everything was good last night?"

"No," Rider said, shaking his head before his mouth turned into a warm smile. "Good is a completely inadequate word for last night."

I leaned in to kiss him but caught sight of something large and dark flying past the glass wall out of the corner of my eye. "What the—?"

"What?"

"I just saw an impossibly large bird fly across the glass wall," I said, moving off of Rider as I bundled the sheet tighter around me. "There!" I said, pointing as it came around again from the other side, obviously flying in a circle around the cabin. My mouth dropped open as I realized what I was looking at was definitely not a bird. It had wings but no feathers and was the size of a small plane. A plane with scales and big, yellow eyes. "I thought I was awake, but obviously I'm still asleep because this is a very weird dream."

"No, it's not a dream," Rider said, pulling me into the crook of his arm as we rested with our backs against the multitude of pillows piled against the headboard. "That's a dragon."

THREE

I looked at him and he used a finger to tip my jaw up, closing my gaping mouth, and lowered my arm, which was still pointing out the window. "A dragon?"

He nodded.

"Dragons aren't real."

"Six weeks ago, you didn't think vampires or werewolves were real."

"But we're still people. That's a gigantic, flying dinosaur!"

Rider laughed. "Actually, he's a pretty normal-sized guy when he's not flying around like that. I wasn't expecting him to be so big."

"Wait. That's a shifter, and you knew he was here?"

"When I made arrangements for this cabin, part of the deal was that I take Daniel back with us. A national forest isn't the best place for a fire-breathing dragon."

"Daniel?" I gawked. "The rainbow-haired kid?"

"He's not that much younger than you."

"He seemed young." I shook my head. "We're taking him back with us?"

"That was the deal," Rider said, as the giant dragon flew around the cabin again.

"Why is he flying around the cabin? Can he see us?" I tightened my grip on the sheet covering me. "What's he up to?"

"I was told he's a bit of a wise-ass. He can't see in, but he's probably enjoying making you think he can."

"How do you know he can't? He's a dragon. Maybe he has special dragon sight and this special glass doesn't block anything from him."

Rider sighed and grabbed a remote from the nightstand. He studied it for a moment before pushing a button that caused dark drapes to cover the glass section of the room. "There. Problem solved. Would you like me to kick his ass?"

"No." I looked down at the suitcases I'd shoved off the bed the previous night. "I guess I should get dressed."

"No reverse donkey cowgirl?"

"No reverse donkey cowgirl. No cowgirl anything if you keep teasing me. The donkey will be neutered."

"Message received."

Rider actually hadn't done a bad job of buying clothes for me. Other than the risqué underclothes, he'd bought me a few fitted T-shirts and jeans that molded perfectly to my body. It was almost scary how well he knew my sizes. I selected a royal blue T-shirt and light denim jeans, and after showering—alone, despite a bit of protest—took the stairs to the first floor where I found Rider leaning back against the kitchen counter with his arms folded, in the midst of discussion with Grey. They both stopped talking as I descended the stairs and looked my way.

"Ma'am." Grey dipped his head, nodding his greeting. "Enjoying your stay so far?"

"Very much." I smiled as I reached the two of them. "This cabin is great, and it's a beautiful spot."

"I was just telling Rider about the waterfall. There's a ledge that enables you to actually walk behind the fall without getting wet. It's a big tourist draw, but they aren't allowed in that area after sunset. The two of you can have it all to yourselves. It's quite stunning at night when the moon hits the water at just the right angle."

"That sounds wonderful." I looked at Rider, who was dressed in another black T-shirt and jeans. "Did you want to see that?"

"I'll go wherever you want to go," he said, sliding his arm around my waist. "Did you want to go into the city before it gets too late and everything starts shutting down?"

I thought about it. "A lot of what I liked to do in the city involved eating and I can't really do that anymore. We should go out in the daytime tomorrow though, maybe go to the aquarium and some shops. Maybe a few rides at Dollywood?"

"Can you go outside in the daylight for that amount of time?" Grey asked, frowning.

"We have special sunscreen," Rider explained. "We won't stay outside in broad daylight any longer than necessary, but with the sunscreen, we'll be all right going from building to building. We'll enter the theme park later so we don't endure the worst of the sun. The ride lines should be shorter by then anyway. We'll need some of your people for security. We won't be at full strength."

"Of course. Anything you need. I'll have a pair of wolves shadowing you to the waterfall as well, just in case. We know the area better than you. They'll keep a respectful distance. As I stated before, Daniel is at your beck and call. He'll be nearby as well, watching the area from an aerial view. When he goes up high enough, he looks like a really big bird to any humans who might catch sight of him from below."

"Do you have a lot of dragons in your pack?" I asked.

"I don't have any dragons in my pack. Daniel is new to this area. He's been passed around from a few other places and we're still looking for somewhere that's a good fit for a fire-breathing wise-ass with an authority problem." He clapped one of his meaty hands on Rider's shoulder. "Good luck, brother. With your record for straightening out strays, I'm hoping you're just what he needs."

"You are aware that my methods aren't always gentle?"

Grey barked out a deep, throaty laugh. "Yeah, of all the words I've heard to describe you, gentle isn't one of them, and it's not like I haven't rung the twerp's bell a few times. Honestly, I'm sending him off to you, so no one from my pack kills him. He likes to push buttons."

The dragon shifter in question walked through the front door, grinning. "Good morning, Mister and Mrs. Dracula."

"Daniel!" Grey stepped toward the shifter, but Rider reached out, halting the large werewolf by placing the back of his hand against the man's massive chest. Judging by his own grin, he wasn't insulted.

"I got this," he said. "It appears Daniel is testing the waters, feeling out his new employer."

"Is that what we're calling it?" Daniel asked. "And here I thought people applied for jobs before they got new employers. Maybe the term you're looking for is owner."

"I was being friendly," Rider said, stepping closer to Daniel with his hands clasped behind his back. "I understand you're new here and still looking for a place to belong," he said as he circled the dragon shifter. "Maybe jokes and attitude are the tools you use to help you cope, but they are tools which, if used wrong, can get you seriously hurt."

Daniel chuckled. "Is this the part where I'm supposed to cower in fear at the thought of what you'll do to punish me if I mouth off too much? If Red Rover over there's giant ass hasn't knocked the chip off my shoulder, I'm not going to worry too much about you. Sure, you can bite me, but you'll have to catch me first. I fly, you know, and I breathe fire. I hear vampires are very flamma—" Daniel flew back into the wall, knocking a framed painting of a group of wolves off it before he slid down to the floor. He looked up at Rider, who remained standing with his hands still clasped behind his back. "How did you do that?"

"It seems you don't know as much as you think you know about vampires," Rider said. "You damn sure don't know much about me. I'm a very fair man but I don't take well to threats. If you threaten me or anyone under my protection with fire, you will be the one to burn. Do you understand?"

"Yeah, I understand," the man said as he stood and rotated his arm. He glared at Grey and opened the door, mumbling, "I'll be outside when you're ready to leave."

"He's really not a bad guy," Grey said, shoulders shaking with his deep, rumbling laughter. "He just likes to see how far he can push people. He likes it a little too much. It was pretty damn fun watching it backfire on him just then."

"How many packs have passed him around?"

Grey shrugged. "Quite a few. He's stubborn as hell and honestly, I don't think he wants to fit in. That's why I thought you might be able to handle him. You've taken in quite a few rogue wolves and other assorted shifters. They seem to do well under you."

"I don't think he'll be much trouble now. Can't fault the guy for testing me out. I would have done the same thing." Rider moved to the door and motioned me over. "Come on, babe. Let's go check out this waterfall."

"Was it necessary to hurt the man?" I asked Rider as we hiked the trail leading to the waterfall hand in hand. Every once in a while I caught glimpses of shifters in wolf form traveling parallel to us through the trees, allowing us to have the path to ourselves while they stayed just close enough to offer protection if needed. I wasn't sure Rider would even need their help if something happened, but I supposed it was like a political thing. If a vampire was killed while visiting a wolf pack's territory, his people might demand blood in retribution, so the wolf pack made sure there were no incidents.

"Absolutely," Rider answered, giving my hand a squeeze. "Grey told me enough about Daniel for me to know he's got an attitude problem. I knew he'd try to feel me out, and it was best I let him know right away that I'm not someone he can keep pushing. It's better I show him a little of what I can do now than wait for him to go too damn far later and have to deal with him like I did with James and Marie."

Now it was my turn to squeeze Rider's hand as I remembered the night he lost two of his people after they'd betrayed him, all because they felt he'd placed my protection over their own welfare. "Is it necessary for him to be ruled over by someone? He seems like he just wants to be free."

"He is free," Rider said gruffly. "Long story short, he's not from here. He's from another realm where—"

"Realm?" I stopped walking, forcing Rider to stop as well.

"Yes," he said, looking back at me. "Another realm."

"*Realm?*"

He frowned. "I feel like we've had this discussion before. No, wait. I'm thinking of a scene from *Thor.*"

I shook my head. "Can you explain this other realm thing, please?"

"I'm trying to. You cut me off." He tugged on my hand and we started walking again. "I don't know much about it, but apparently the entire werewolf race started there, or more accurately, it started from a woman who was cast out of that realm and into our realm. For a long time, it was just werewolves that came from there, but while she was in this realm, some bad shit was happening in the realm she came from. People were being punished by being forced to take the form of animals, including dragons, gargoyles and unicorns."

"You're joking," I said as I tried to imagine such a thing.

"You've seen Daniel. Is a gargoyle or unicorn much harder to imagine than a huge, fire-breathing dragon?"

"I guess not, but how did they get here? Wait, are they here? Unicorns?"

Rider frowned at me. "You can't have one as a pet."

"I wasn't going to ask for one!"

He grinned. "There are all kinds of shifters here now. There always have been a lot of different shifters, but the dragons, gargoyles and unicorns are new. They were prisoners in the other realm. They came here in search of The White Wolf, the woman who'd first been punished like them and cast out of the realm. From what I've been told, she helped them overthrow the tyrant who had punished them, but many of them chose to stay in this realm rather than stay there. Apparently, the way the vile woman turned them into shifters was to somehow use magic along with killing the animal whose form she gave the prisoners. Unicorns are sacred there, gargoyles and dragons are also well loved. Many people in that realm see the shifters as killers who slaughtered innocent animals."

"But they didn't do it to themselves."

"Yeah, I guess the truth doesn't matter to some people. They believe what they want. Anyway, Daniel is a prisoner there even if he was freed from the physical prison he was in. He's a prisoner of people's hatred. Here, he has a chance at living freely without everyone looking at him as a vile animal killer. However, that doesn't mean he can just do as he pleases. You know yourself that shifters aren't common knowledge here, and for good reason. The supernatural community has to work together for self-preservation. We can't have a giant dragon flying around unchecked."

"I suppose not."

Rider looked at me. "You think I'm unfair?"

"No." I shook my head. "You don't have to look out

for Daniel at all. I know you do whatever it takes to protect your people, and from what I've seen, anyone in need of your help. I just wish there didn't have to be so much violence."

He kissed my hand. "Me too, sweetheart, me too, but the violence I give out is a lot less than the violence that could happen if I didn't."

"Does it have to be that way?"

"Sadly, yes. I didn't become master of the city by turning the other cheek or waiting for enemies to strike my home. I try to be fair and noble, but for every vampire with a conscience, there's a dozen who just don't give a damn about anyone but themselves. The same goes for shapeshifters, witches—you name it. To survive, you can't show weakness. I won't do Daniel any favors by babying him. He needs to be strong, and he needs to learn respect so he can gain it himself. If I'm hard on him, it's for his own good and the good of our people. I treat everyone under my care the same way."

"You don't treat me that way."

"You're not just someone under my employ," he said softly, raising my hand to the center of his chest. "You're in here. You're different."

I smiled, touched, but self-doubt whispered in my head. "How did I manage to get in there? Word around the bar is women practically give themselves to you."

"Word around the bar?"

"The night Barnaby Quimby attacked me and you found out you'd been betrayed by James and Marie, I heard you ask one of your men if there'd been any complaints from anyone else about your leadership. I recall him commenting that the only complaints were from women you weren't sleeping with and I believe he said this was usual, so apparently there's a line for you and those in back get upset." The minute I started talking, I wanted to slap myself, but the words of self-sabotage just kept tumbling out.

"A line?" He grinned, but it was tight. "You're fishing for something."

"I'm just making conversation," I said, sliding my fingers out of his and moving ahead as the waterfall came into view. It was tall and beautiful. As Grey had said, it truly was a sight to behold when the moonlight hit it just right.

"Hell of a conversation." Rider followed me onto the ledge behind the waterfall and wrapped his arms around my waist from behind. "Whatever questions you have floating around in that mind of yours, ask them," he said, resting his chin on the top of my head as we watched the water flow in front of us.

"You're not going to just read my mind?"

"You're not projecting your thoughts. You are, however, projecting a feeling I don't like. This is supposed to be a happy place for you."

"I am happy."

"If you were happy, you wouldn't need to tell me. I'd feel it. What I'm feeling from you right now is not happiness." He found a place to sit on the ledge and pulled me onto his lap. "Spit it out, Danni, What's wrong?"

"Nothing's wrong," I lied, chastising myself internally for allowing my self-doubt to creep in and ruin what should be a romantic evening away with my new boyfriend. Instead of enjoying the moment, I was thinking ahead to what would happen when we returned and wondering how long it would take for the happy bubble I'd woken up in to burst.

"You mentioned women at the bar being unhappy and said something about a line. Sounded kind of jealous, or worse, like maybe you don't trust me."

"It's not about trust."

"Then what's it about?"

"I don't know. Belief?"

"And what the hell does that mean?" His nostrils flared and the slightest trace of irritation entered his voice.

"What makes me so special when there's a line of women ready to peel their clothes off for you when we get back home?"

"Really?"

"Really."

"For starters, the fact that you're not in that line."

I blinked. "What?"

"Danni, I know there's a bunch of women back in Louisville that I could have with nothing more than a look. There always has been and if I was an insecure man I'd eat it up, but I'm not an insecure man, and I'm not a fool. I know they don't want me. They want to be with a man in my position. They're in lust with the power I have. Just because they're willing to sleep with me doesn't mean I have to give them the satisfaction. You heard Rome tell me the women were unhappy I wasn't sleeping with them. Wasn't, as in was not, as in what could you possibly be upset about? The fact that they exist?"

"Yes," I mumbled.

"What, do you want me to kill them or something?"

"Of course not."

"Well, I can't really help other women being attracted to me, just like you can't help men being attracted to you."

Oh, yeah. Men were just breaking down doors to get to me. "You've slept with some of them."

"Past tense. Purely physical. Doesn't matter."

"And it matters with me?"

"You really have to ask that?" His eyes grew dark, and an indentation formed in his cheek from where he grit his teeth so tight. Of course he was angry. He'd killed his brother to save my life, and I was giving him shit.

"I'm sorry. I don't know why I'm like this."

"I do. You need to get your mother's voice out of your head."

I sighed heavily and watched the waterfall. He was right. I knew it, but I couldn't just cut off what was left of my family, even if they constantly criticized me. Saying that to him didn't feel right though, not when I knew he'd had to kill his, so I continued watching the waterfall and wished I'd never opened my mouth and let my stupidity roll right on out.

"I love you because you didn't just peel off your clothes for me," he said softly against my ear a short while later. "I love you because I couldn't get you with a wink or even a single kiss. I love you because when you're not making me laugh you're frustrating the hell out of me, because you terrify and worry me and I never quite know whether I want to kiss you or throttle you but I wouldn't dare lay a finger on you to hurt you because seeing you hurt would kill me. I love you because if I treat you bad you'll tell me to go to Hell and you'll mean it. I love you because you're genuine and you're a struggle and you make me feel something worth feeling and I haven't had that in a very long time. Don't cry."

It was too late. I wiped away the silent tears cascading down my cheeks.

"Dude, I'm gonna hurl."

We looked over to see Daniel in human form, standing outside the waterfall.

"You ever hear of privacy?" Rider asked as we stood.

"You ever hear of Dr. Phil? I've watched his show a lot over the past few weeks. You might want to give him a call and see if he can help you out with your issues."

"I'm going to kill him now," Rider muttered, stepping forward as I pulled on his arm to stop him.

"Hey, I was just gonna ask if you wanted your picture taken under the falls," Daniel said. "I didn't know you were back here being all cutesie-pukesy."

"I'm going to kill him now," Rider repeated.

"No, you're not," I told him, still holding his arm. "You're going to play nice for me."

He looked down at me. "You owe me then." He lowered his voice. "I want the reverse monkey cowboy thing."

"Uh, it was reverse donkey cowgirl," I whispered. "I'm not sure, but I think you might have just said you want wild ape sex with a guy."

His eyes narrowed. "Shit. You set me up to say that."

"I did no such thing."

"Now I really deserve the other thing."

"Yeah, not going to happen."

"Fine. I'm killing the dragon." He turned back toward Daniel.

"I'm wearing that little scrappy thing with the ribbons on the sides though," I advised him, bringing him to a halt before he turned and lifted me over his shoulder. "What are you doing?"

"What's it look like, woman? I'm taking you back to the cabin to untie some ribbons," he said, as he moved toward the side of the waterfall. "Fly away, dragon-boy, before I knock the scales off your ass."

I yawned as I opened my eyes and stretched, working out the kinks caused by some very creative making up the night before. I'd fallen asleep with my head on Rider's chest again, his arm draped around me. I looked at the clock on the nightstand by his side of the bed and saw it was early morning, earlier than we'd planned to start the day but I figured since I'd awakened I might as well get him up too and we could enjoy the early morning colors in the forest before making our way into the city.

"Hey." I nudged him. "Wake up, sleepy-head."

"He always was a late sleeper when we were kids," a familiar voice that sent a chill skating down my spine said from behind me, close enough I felt his breath on the nape of my neck. I turned around and came face to face with Selander Ryan.

"Hello, Danni. Miss me?"

FOUR

"Danni? Danni!"

I became aware of someone screaming while my body shook and an army infiltrated the surrounding area.

"Danni! What's wrong?"

I looked into Rider's wide, alarmed eyes and blinked. Okay, so it was me doing the god-awful screaming. He was trying to shake me out of whatever fit I was having, and the army was our security detail, bounding up the stairs. Rider covered my unmentionables with the bedsheet just before the first couple of werewolves stopped in our doorway. "What's going on?" a large man asked, his eyes accessing the room quickly.

"Nothing," Rider said, waving them away. "She just had a bad dream."

"Shit," the man muttered, gesturing for his other men to follow him out. "False alarm."

"What the hell did she dream about? Giant killer garlic?"

"Shut up, Daniel," the man snapped, and I heard scuffling before their footsteps thunked heavily back down the stairs.

"It wasn't a dream," I said as I calmed enough to speak

actual words instead of just screaming my head off. "He was here."

"Who?" Rider asked, pushing a lock of hair that had gotten stuck in a trail of tears away from my face. "No one's here."

"Selander Ryan," I cried. "Selander Ryan was here in this bed with us. He was right next to me. I felt his breath on the back of my neck and I looked right into his eyes."

"Danni, it was just a nightmare."

"I've had nightmares. This wasn't just a nightmare. He was here."

"No, he wasn't." Rider wrapped me in his arms and rubbed my back while making soothing noises. "He's gone. He can't hurt you. It was just a bad dream."

"Then why is your heart beating so fast?" I asked, as I not only heard the rapid beating, but felt its hectic rhythm against my chest.

"You scared me," he explained a moment later. "Waking to you screaming is not something I wish to go through again."

I pulled back and took a good look into his eyes and they still reflected more concern than what should come from a loved one having a bad dream. "There's more to it than just that. When I visited Selander Ryan in my dreams while you were in my apartment, you knew it. You sensed him. You sensed him now. Don't lie to me about this, Rider."

"I've never lied to you. I never will lie to you."

"Good. Now… Did you or did you not sense Selander Ryan when I started screaming?"

"Danni, I'm your sire. I'm going to feel anything you feel that strongly."

"Did. You. Sense. Him?"

"I did, but it came from you. You just had a really intense nightmare."

"I know he was here."

"Danni." He held my face in his hands and looked me

square in the eyes. "He's dead."

"How can you be sure?"

"How can I be sure? Danni, I reached into his chest, pulled out his freaking heart and crushed it with my own bare hand. That's how I can be sure. You were there. You saw it! He is dead. Gone. Finished. He's over."

The alarm clock on the nightstand blared, and we both jumped. With a nervous laugh at our reaction, Rider pressed the button to silence it. "You wanted to get up earlier today and do some stuff in the city. Why don't you take a relaxing bath to calm down, get dressed, and we'll go down the mountain and revisit some of the places you liked to visit with your father? It'll take your mind off this."

If only it were so easy, I thought. I still felt Selander Ryan's warm breath along the back of my neck. If he was still able to invade my dreams after having his heart ripped from his chest and crushed into smithereens, he could get me anywhere, like maybe in a bathtub. I imagined being pulled under the water and bit my lip to keep from crying. "I don't want to be alone. Will you come with me?"

"Of course I'm coming with—Oh, wait, you mean, take a bath with you? After I all but whined to shower with you last night and you wouldn't let me because you didn't want me to see you naked without a sheet over you?" He grinned, but it quickly faded. "Man, you must really be shaken up."

"I really am. No sex stuff. I just really need you with me right now and I'm honestly too scared to care what I look like naked. I never thought I'd say that, but there it is. Will you stay with me?"

"Of course. Whatever you need." He kissed my forehead. "Always."

We drove down to the trailheads outside of the area owned by the wolf pack, the trails the tourists used, and visited a few more waterfalls before driving the scenic Cades Cove loop, watching out for black bears and deer. I tried to focus on the natural beauty the area was known for, but Selander Ryan stayed in the back of my mind the entire time. I kept imagining him jumping out from behind bushes or appearing right behind me as he had in the bed earlier, and from the way Rider would occasionally squeeze my hand while stealing sideways glances, I knew he was picking up on it. I tried telling myself I was in my favorite place in the world with a wonderful man who would never let anyone hurt me, but I couldn't completely shake away the feeling that I was right, that what had happened was more than just a dream.

Daniel and two more of Grey's men followed us wherever we went in a black sports car and joined us when we stopped and got out to do things. I didn't recognize the werewolves to know if they were part of the security who'd responded when I'd awakened screaming that morning, but Daniel had been and he eyed me curiously.

"Let's get out of the sun," Rider said after we got off a rollercoaster at Dollywood and guided me toward the side of an ice creamery with an overhang that cast a fair amount of shade. He caressed my cheek while studying me. "Babe, you're too pale for my liking. I think you handled the sun better when you were a hybrid."

I had. Since the night Selander Ryan had died—which I hoped was accurate—I really hadn't spent much time out in the daylight like I had before when I'd belonged to both him and Rider. I hadn't realized it was harder for me to bear now, regardless of the sunscreen, but the line for the rollercoaster had been mostly out in the open and slow moving. It had zapped my strength pretty well. "It's hitting me harder today. Maybe we should just go back to the cabin and rest until nightfall."

"We can do that if you really want, but after we get a good day's sleep tomorrow, we're heading back home. Now's the time to squeeze in anything else you want to do.

I'll do whatever you want to do, but either way, you need blood now."

"Is she going to be all right?" Daniel asked, moving past the two werewolf guards to stand at my side. He looked at me with genuine concern.

"She needs blood," Rider explained, looking around. "I'll cast a shadow here to hide us, Danni, and you can take what you need."

"I'm not feeding from you," I said, shaking my head. "Not now. We're both weaker in the day and you haven't fed since we left Louisville. If something happens, you need to be at full strength."

"I'm fine. You're not. You need to feed now."

I looked past him to the shops across from us. "And what will you do for me if I drink?"

Frowning, Rider turned to see what I was looking at. "Oh, come on," he groaned, seeing the Old Time Photo shop. I'd tried to get him to go into two earlier, before we'd visited Dollywood and he'd adamantly refused to have his picture taken in a ridiculous get-up. "I've already gotten on rollercoasters with screaming brats and suffered through traffic at Cades Cove just to look at bears. Pick something else."

"Dude," Daniel laughed. "If you do that, I'll let her drink *my* blood."

"Can we drink shifter blood?" I asked.

"Yeah," Rider answered, narrowing his eyes on Daniel. "It's stronger than human blood, so isn't that bad of an idea."

"Plus, you won't lose any strength feeding me," I advised. "All you have to do is put on a—"

"I'm not putting on overalls and chewing on a piece of wheat."

"You don't have to be a hillbilly. You can be a gangster or an outlaw."

"You could always be a flapper," Daniel suggested.

"I could always ram a stick up your ass, spin you over a

campfire, and see if dragons taste like chicken," Rider snapped, causing the werewolves to erupt into a fit of laughter.

"Damn, dude. Why you gotta make it all personal and violent?" Daniel placed his hand over his heart as if shocked and offended.

"I'm not so sure I want his blood in your system," Rider told me, glaring at Daniel as he spoke.

"Let's just go back to the cabin then," I said, pouting as I leaned against the side of the ice creamery. "I can always come back again later after I've built up more tolerance for the sun. However long that will take. I'm sure some of the places I want to go will still be here. The shops I wanted to go to are probably online. I mean, I guess it's not that big of a deal if I can't view the art in the portrait shop up close and I don't have to smell the soaps in that little handcrafted soap store. I can just guess which ones I'll like as I place them in my online shopping cart."

"Oh for chrissakes, fine. I'll put on a ridiculous costume and take the damn picture if you'll feed, but I hope you realize my balls are shrinking just from agreeing to this."

"Yay!" I clapped my hands with as much energy as I could muster. "I promise I'll make sure they grow big and heavy again when we get back to the cabin."

"Daaayum, dude," Daniel said. "If that's why you're taking the picture, I don't even got any jokes on you, just respect."

"Oh, shut up," Rider growled, moving Daniel and me toward the rear of the ice creamery. "I'll cast enough shadow to hide you. Give her your wrist, Dragon-Breath, and let her drink as much as she needs."

Daniel blanched a little. "I'm not going to die from this, am I?"

"No, if you die, it'll be from running your mouth, and I'll be the one doing the killing," Rider assured him.

"You know, it's almost fascinating how you go from

41

zero to murder in under a second like that." Daniel held out his arm, offering his wrist to me. "Bon appétit," he muttered. "In full disclosure, I ate pasta last night. There might have been garlic in the sauce."

"That's not a problem," I said, as Rider shook his head in irritation and gathered enough shadow to hide us from any humans who might look our way.

"Okay, that's a cool trick," Daniel said, admiring the shadow cover as I took his arm. He shook a little, and I was thankful. If he was shaking, he wouldn't notice that I was shaking a little bit too. The only time I'd drank from a living source other than Rider was when I'd killed a man. I'd been fueled by anger. Drinking from someone other than Rider while not angry was a new experience for me. I had a moment of fear, recalling how the succubus venom had turned men into rutting animals I'd had to put down, but Rider had assured me I no longer had it in my bite. Selander Ryan was dead. The venom was gone with him. I took a deep breath and bit through the flesh in Daniel's wrist, knowing the sooner I got it over with, the sooner Rider could quit wasting his energy casting the shadow around us. I knew the older a vampire was, the less often blood was needed, but I also knew time spent awake during the day took a toll and he'd fed me our first night in the cabin. I didn't want him expending energy longer than necessary. Even if my brain told me Selander Ryan was dead, even if I'd seen him die with my own two eyes, my quivering heart had doubts. I wanted Rider in full fighting form if his evil half-brother had somehow managed to crawl his way up from Hell just to screw with us, which sounded very much like something he would do.

Daniel's blood slowly spilled out onto my tongue, not as thin as blood I got from Rider. It didn't pack as powerful of a wallop as Rider's blood either, but it was stronger than human and far better than bagged blood even though it had a slightly spicy taste to it, which was different from anything I'd experienced before. Daniel's blood seemed warmer too. Then again, maybe knowing I was drinking from a dragon shifter was putting thoughts in my head. He'd stopped shaking, but his heart rate increased, which seemed to help pump the blood out faster. I figured his heartbeat was in overdrive because the poor guy was scared I was going to suck him dry after he'd so generously offered to feed me so I only drank until my eyelids no longer felt heavy and I licked his wrist, sealing the wound I'd made there. "Thank you."

"No problem," Daniel said softly, running his thumb over his wrist as if searching for a scar. He blinked a few times and wavered a bit as Rider released the shadows he'd been cloaking us with.

"Go sit over there," Rider ordered him, nodding his head toward an empty spot at a group of small outside dining tables that had been set up close to a small building offering grab and go food options before turning toward the werewolves. "Get him something to eat, something with protein."

One of the werewolves got in line to order while the other made sure Daniel got somewhere to sit. He walked on his own and seemed fine, but he was paler than before I'd drank from him. I really didn't think I'd taken that much.

"Will he be all right?"

"He should be fine," Rider assured me. "You didn't take all that much. He probably didn't eat well this morning before we left and we haven't stopped anywhere to eat, so they haven't either. I didn't think about that. If you're concerned, we can stay with him."

"Nice try." I narrowed my eyes. "You're not getting out of taking the picture with me. I risked drinking from a dragon to get that picture. For all I know, I could have charred my insides."

"He breathes fire, he doesn't bleed it." Rider sighed in disgust. "Let's get this damn humiliation over with while the wolves are busy with Daniel. I'm not doing this with an audience."

I took Rider's offered hand and crossed over to the Old Time Photo shop. A portly man with a thick mustache stood from behind the counter and greeted us as we walked in. "Welcome, folks! Honeymooners?"

"No." I shook my head, suddenly feeling a little sad as I wondered if a future with Rider would ever involve marriage. I pushed the thought away. We were just beginning our relationship. It was ridiculous to even think of marriage yet.

"Not yet anyway, eh?" He winked at me before swinging his arm out to show off the various framed pictures on the walls. "As you can see, we have a few options for you. Hillbillies in a washtub."

"No hillbillies," Rider said gruffly.

"All righty then. We got gangsters and flappers, outlaws and floozies, cowboys and cowgirls." He paused and frowned at Rider. "Geez, fella. It isn't that bad. My cousin works at a shop in California. They have vampires and slayers there. At least with this you get to be a tough guy with a gun instead of a pansy-assed vampire with a crap load of glitter tossed all over you."

I slapped a hand over my mouth before a laugh could escape, but I couldn't stop the snort as Rider closed his eyes, pinched the bridge of his nose, and muttered a very colorful string of curses.

"I just want you to know that if anyone ever sees this picture and gives me any shit for this, it's going to be your fault when I remove their spine through their throat," Rider told me later as he stepped out of the changing room wearing the gangster costume.

"Oh, come on, you look really handsome," I told him.

"Please. I didn't wear this crap the entire time it was in style," he growled, keeping his voice low enough that the photographer couldn't hear. "I can't believe I escaped it all those years just to look like this big of a douchebag now."

"Well, how do I look?" I asked as I secured the

feathered headpiece and did a twirl, the fringe along the brightly colored dress twirling right along with me.

"It's a trap," the photographer warned Rider in a horrible stage-whisper as he fiddled with the camera.

"I'm not answering on grounds that I want and deserve sex for doing this."

I sighed. "Whatever. Can I have the gun? I'd really like to be the one doing the shooting."

"And I'd like to be the one getting shot," Rider muttered, handing me a gun. "Here. Put me out of my misery."

"It's just a prop," the photographer advised.

"Pity," Rider said.

Rider parked the Ferrari at the Cloud Top just after nightfall and cut the engine. "You sure there's not anything else you want to do?" he asked.

The moment the sun went down, we'd gotten an energy boost, and the night was still young, but I'd visited the places I'd remembered from previous trips. I'd bought some tacky souvenirs, a gorgeous painting of a beautiful waterfall, and I'd been like a kid in a candy store at the handcrafted soap shop. Rider had indulged all my wants and desires, no matter how silly, even if he'd been uncomfortable with most everything we'd done.

"I'm good for the night." I leaned over, held his face in my hands, and kissed him. "Thank you for today."

"Don't thank me," he said, resting his forehead against mine. "I was kind of an ass."

"Hey guys!" The door on my side of the car opened and Daniel leaned down to look in at us. "Need any help with your bags?"

"I guess we're getting out now," I muttered.

"I guess so," Rider grumbled back, "and the bags are staying in the car," he told Daniel as he got out on his side while I exited my side, using the hand up Daniel offered.

He walked around the car and pressed the button on his key fob to activate the alarm system as he reached my side and glared at Daniel's hand on mine until the younger man let go. "I might not fly, but if you go near those bags trying to see that picture, I'll be in your face before you can blink. You might as well forget the picture exists because you're never going to see it, and if you tell anyone about it when we take you home with us, I will yank out your tongue and whip you senseless with it."

"Geez, man. Have you been drinking from bodybuilders or something? You might want to consider giving them a piss test because I think you're getting their roid rage."

Rider stepped forward, murder or at least a good beating in his eyes, so I placed myself between him and the wisecracking shifter. "Thanks for the blood today, Daniel. I think you should go now."

He looked down at me and smiled. "Any time."

"Is he going to make it back home with us in one piece?" I asked Rider after Daniel walked away. "You seem to be just a step away from throttling him every time he speaks."

"Yeah, we need to talk about that and some other things," Rider said, leading me toward the guest cabin. A sinking feeling started in my gut and by the time we reached the cabin and closed the front door behind us, it felt as though my entire stomach had fallen out.

"What things?" I asked, hating the tremble I heard in my voice. I didn't want to appear weak, but experience had taught me that 'We need to talk' usually came before something really bad.

"Please, sit down." Rider gestured toward the sofa, and my legs felt boneless as I plopped down onto the cushions. He sat on the coffee table in front of me and took my hands. "Danni, this time we've spent together here at The Cloud Top has been wonderful, but when we go back home—"

46

"Are you breaking up with me?" I asked, or more accurately, screeched as I came up off the sofa to glare down at him. To his credit, his eyes widened in what looked like genuine surprise. It only angered me more. How dare he act surprised!

"What? Why? Wait." He fumbled over words as he stood and reached for me but I was already on the move, pacing out of his reach, my footfalls loud and far more forceful than necessary, but if I didn't stomp I'd pummel him with my hands which were already balled into fists.

"I don't believe this. I don't freaking believe it!" Now my hands were uncurled and striking the air as I waved my arms around like a crazy person, punctuating each sentence with a fling of a limb. "You bring me to my happy place to seduce me, make me think this is the start of a wonderful new relationship with a really great guy, and then you dump me after getting what you want? Why? Because of a stupid picture your uptight ass didn't want to take?!"

"Hey, there's no need for name-calling," Rider said. "Would you just calm down? I'm not dumping you."

"Then what are you doing? Why else would you start a conversation off like that? What could you possibly be leading up to?" I quit pacing, folded my arms, and watched him expectantly. "Well?"

"You know how I feel about you, Danni. I don't want to ever see you hurt, so when we get back home, things have to be different. I'm not saying we can't be together, we just—"

"No!" I shook my head and willed the tears burning the back of my eyes not to fall. "I'm not listening to this right now." I moved for the door and Rider came after me.

"Do not follow me!" I yelled at him as I yanked the door open, stopping long enough to point at him and issue a stern warning. "Follow me and you'll be going back home without your testicles!"

I slammed the door closed behind me and barreled

down the porch steps, past the werewolf guards awkwardly trying to act like they hadn't just heard the big, bad vampire guest of honor getting threatened by his less scary vampire … lover? Entertainment? What was I anyway? I wondered that as I stormed toward the trail that would lead me to the waterfall I'd visited with Rider when he'd told me why he loved me. Or I supposed when he'd lied to me, but that couldn't be right. He'd killed his brother for me, hadn't he?

"Hey Danni!" Daniel called out as I passed him and a couple of shifters talking. "Hey, are you all right?"

I held my hand up, palm out, in the universal sign for leave me the hell alone as I passed and continued on to the trail. I didn't know why I wanted to go to the waterfall where Rider had said such beautiful things while my heart was cracking in half and my mind was scrambling to try to make sense of everything. He'd killed his brother to save my life. That had to mean something, but what was with the crap about things having to be different when we go back home? Was it about the picture or did his attitude about the picture stem from him being in a bad mood all day because he'd been thinking about how to kick me to the curb? He couldn't even wait until we got back home. He had to do it here, in Pigeon Forge, my favorite place in the world. He knew it was my favorite place. That was why he'd brought me.

"He brought you here so you'd have sex with him," I told myself as I flexed my hands, wishing I had a punching bag in front of me. "And your dumb ass not only slept with him, you trusted him and made yourself vulnerable. You know you're not the type of woman men keep around. Stupid, stupid, stupid!"

The waterfall came into view ahead, and I marched toward it, chewing the inside of my cheek. I would not cry, even if I was alone. He could pop up at any time, and I refused to let him see how hurt I was.

I heard rustling behind me and spun around, arm

reflexively drawn back, hand curled into a ball. It wasn't Rider. A slender woman with long auburn hair stepped forward, her nostrils flaring as her mouth curved into a wicked grin.

"What are you planning on doing with that?" she asked.

"I thought you were someone else," I said, lowering my fist. I turned to continue on to the waterfall and she quickly rounded me and planted herself firmly in my path with her hands loose at her sides, her head lowered and her narrowed gaze locked on to mine. "I'm going to the waterfall," I said. "You're in my way."

"You're in my way," she said, her tone carrying a threat. "Don't think we're stupid and don't see what you're trying to do here. Grey is a werewolf. He will mate with one of us, not some trashy vampire bitch."

Hold on. I shook my head and blinked as I took a moment to try to figure out what the woman was talking about. All I knew for sure was I wasn't in the mood for some woman with an attitude standing in my way. "Look, honey, I don't know what your deal is, but I came here with someone and I'm leaving with someone. That someone isn't Grey. I don't know how y'all do your mating business and frankly, I don't care. Now get out of my way."

"You talk big for someone who has to have security to protect you from nightmares," she said. "Your security isn't here now, and I don't like your tone."

"What a coincidence. I don't like yours either, and I don't need security to handle you in the mood I'm in right now." I knew she was a wolf, and I might be new to the paranormal world, but it didn't take a genius to figure out werewolves or any shifters, for that matter, were tough. I was a vampire, but more than that, I was pissed. I'd take my chances. In my current mood, I didn't even care if I won or lost the fight. I just wanted blood. "Move out of my way."

"What are you going to do if I don't?"

"Well, bitch, I guess I'll just have to knock the fleas off your ass."

FIVE

"Oh, no you did not just say that to me."

"Pretty sure I just fucking did."

"Do you know who the hell you're talking to?"

"Some rabid bitch standing in my way?" I asked. "So far, you've only puffed your chest out and talked some shit," I said. "I didn't take crap from trash-talking bullies in high school when I was just a scrawny kid and I'm damn sure not doing it now that I can rip your throat out with my teeth so either move the fuck out of my way or come at me, Canine Barbie."

"Your death wish is my command," the woman said as she launched herself at me, claws extended. Not literally. Still in human form, she swiped at my face as I ducked and delivered a pretty solid punch to her stomach. She hunched over, but before I could do more, she'd grabbed a handful of my hair and yanked hard enough for my head to whip back.

"Really?" I swiped my leg out, knocking her off balance, and pinned her to the ground with my knee as I delivered a punch to her face. "You're a werewolf and you're yanking hair? You're a disgrace to paranormal women everywhere!" I punched her again, loving the sound of her nose breaking. I definitely punched harder since turning into a vampire. Okay, so maybe Rider had taught me how to throw a solid punch, but I wasn't about to give him any credit. "And 'Your death wish is my command' as a threat? I'm from Louisville, Kentucky, home of Muhammad Ali. You'll have to do a lot better than that weak-ass line!"

"How about I just do this?" She grabbed my arms and rolled over, flipping me onto my back before rearing back with a pretty meaty looking fist. That wasn't saying a lot. All fists looked big and meaty when they were coming toward your face.

A second before she could connect her knuckles to my face, I grabbed her beneath her armpits and flung her over my head before quickly getting to my feet and turning toward the place she'd landed five feet away. "You done?" I asked as she rose to a crouch.

"You're not bloody and broken yet," she growled, shifting into a rather large red wolf.

"I can't stand to see an animal hurt but I know you're under all that fur and so help me if you make me fight you in that form I'm going to really be pissed and I'm going to beat you that much harder."

The wolf hunkered down, snarled, and launched herself in the air, jaws open and ready to dine on vampire meat.

"Oh, you mangy fucking bitch," I growled as I ducked under the wolf, grabbed its tail with both hands and started banging it against trees. "I. Fucking. Told. You. This. Would. Only. Make. Me. Madder," I yelled, enunciating each individual word by slamming her body into another tree. One thin tree snapped, and I started slamming her into the ground, ignoring her yelps. I'd warned her I wasn't in the mood. I'd warned her not to come at me like that. I'd already been mad when I'd set out on the trail and she'd only worsened my temper. I couldn't stop. "I'll fucking kill you!" I screamed, continuing to slam her body into the ground over and over. I became aware of pounding feet and the air shifting over me as if a large plane flew overhead and still I continuously slammed the woman into the ground.

"Danni, stop!"

I didn't stop. I couldn't stop. Rider's voice only made me angrier. I couldn't remember the last time I'd been so angry, and I knew something was strange about that and something was very, very wrong with me, but I didn't care. I only wanted to hurt someone until I no longer hurt, and as far as I was concerned, the woman had volunteered to be the punching bag I very much needed.

"Danni!"

I was grabbed around the waist and pulled away from the wolf as another set of hands grabbed her tail and yanked her free of my grasp. "That bitch still has breath left in her lungs!" I yelled, lunging for the battered wolf.

"Danni, stop, damn it!" I froze, not because I wanted to, but because I'd been made to. My body shook with rage as I stared into Rider's eyes, knowing he was using his power as my sire to control my body. "I don't want to control you," he said, his voice softer but no less angry, "but you're not giving me a choice now. What the hell are you trying to do, start a vampire-werewolf war?"

"She started it," I said.

"Your woman is right," I heard Grey say as Rider's control over me started to fade. He slowly released his mental hold over me, but kept his arms around my middle as a precaution. I turned to see the woman had shifted back to her human form. Her nose was clearly broken, her eyes bruised, and various cuts marred her body and her clothes. Grey's foot was on her neck.

"Get the hell off her like that!"

"Danni!" Rider growled my name in warning. "Werewolves handle pack business their own way. It's not our place."

Grey threw his head back and laughed, quickly joined in by the other shifters I'd just noticed around us. Even

Daniel was there and I realized he was the change I'd felt in the wind over my head while I'd been slamming the woman into the ground. He grinned, but didn't laugh. He didn't appear amused by whatever had caused the hearty laughter from the wolves. He looked as if he'd been amused by the whole incident and knowing he had a reputation for starting crap, I'd probably made his night, entertainment wise.

"They're laughing," I said.

"I know," Rider replied.

"Is that a good thing or a bad thing?"

"I have no idea." Rider released me and planted his feet in what I recognized as his fighting stance.

"I am not putting my weight on her," Grey explained, wiping his eyes. "Shannon has forgotten her place and needs to remember her place is under my heel. I apologize for this attack. I gave a direct order for no harm to come to either of you while my guests at The Cloud Top and Shannon has chosen to disobey and bring shame to our pack. She will be punished, and to show how sorry I am for this incident, I will rescind our deal. You do not have to take Daniel back with you. You owe us nothing for the use of our land."

I looked over at Daniel and noticed how quickly his grin turned into a frown. He lowered his gaze, but not before I'd seen the disappointment in his eyes.

"Daniel leaves with us," I said. "That was the deal. There is no reason not to honor it. This woman tried me and she got her ass handed to her. We're even."

Daniel looked up at me, a small smile tugging at the corners of his mouth as Grey again roared with laughter. "If you want him, you can gladly take him."

"Good. Thank you for the use of your cabin. We're leaving now."

"Danni."

"I said we're leaving now!" I snapped at Rider before turning and going back down the trail. I'd wanted to sit by the waterfall and think, but there was no way that was happening now. As shifters stepped out of my way, parting like the Red Sea, I knew I wouldn't get any quiet time to work out the hurt and confusion in my mind. Rider was angry at me. I'd been attacked out of the blue, and who knew what the other wolves thought of me? It was time to go home since the place I'd always found peace in was now anything but.

"A woman with such spirit must make for a lot of excitement," I heard Grey say. "Tell me she has a sister."

"Yes," Rider answered, "but I like you too much to unleash that hell-beast on you."

I seethed in anger as the men laughed and continued marching back toward the cabin to pack. He had a lot of nerve calling my sister a hell-beast, considering I was pretty sure his half-brother was down in the fiery pit roasting marshmallows with Hitler.

We'd been driving in uncomfortable silence for three hours before Rider erupted into laughter. It started out as a silent, full body vibration and grew in sound and intensity until tears streamed from his eyes and he placed a hand over his stomach as if it were cramping.

"What is so amusing?" I asked.

"You went full Hulk versus Loki on that werewolf." Rider wiped his eyes, still laughing. "It was straight out of *The Avengers*."

"Oh, it's funny now?" I asked. "You didn't seem so amused when you were using your sire power over me."

"Yeah, now that I know you're safe from retribution, it's hilarious. Luckily, Grey was pissed off at his wolf for starting the whole thing. Danni, I'm glad you defended yourself and beat the hell out of that woman for attacking you, but you were out of control." He looked at me, all humor gone from his eyes. "I'm sorry I used my power over you. I never wanted to do that. I don't want to ever do it again, but if it will save your life, I *will* do it again."

"I hardly needed you saving my life," I snapped. "I was winning that fight all by myself."

"No, you'd already won the damn fight. I told you to stop, and you didn't. You don't listen to me and it's a problem, which was exactly what I was trying to discuss with you earlier and you—"

"Discuss? Is that what you call it when you make demands and expect me to just follow them? Is that what it's called when you just tell me how things are going to be?"

"You're right. We don't have discussions. We can't have a discussion when one party refuses to just listen for once. Honestly, Danni, other than stopping you from *killing* someone, have I ever used my sire power over you to force you to do anything against your will?"

I folded my arms and set my gaze on the view from outside the passenger side window, catching sight of Daniel's truck behind us in the side-view mirror. "No," I conceded. "You haven't."

"Have I ever hurt you?"

I continued looking out the window, watching mile markers pass by as the backs of my eyes burned. I inhaled deeply, exhaled. "There are all kinds of ways you can hurt a person. What's changing when we get back home?"

He reached over, attempted to hold my hand, but I refused to unfold my arms. Giving up, he placed his hand on my knee but sighed and removed it when I stiffened. "I couldn't sleep the four weeks we were apart after the night Ryan died. Each day that passed without talking to you was torture. I couldn't break up with you if I wanted to, Danni. I need you in my life. Hell, maybe I need you more than you need me. Maybe that's why you're always being so difficult, pushing me away."

"I'm not pushing you away."

"You are constantly looking for a reason to run. You ran off tonight instead of just talking with me."

"I needed time to think about what you'd said."

"I hadn't even said anything yet! You wouldn't let me. You heard less than a dozen words and assumed the worst in me, and boom, there you went."

"Pardon me if I couldn't just stand there and listen to you tell me…" I paused. He'd just said he couldn't break up with me if he wanted to. He'd said he needed me in his life. Damn it. "What were you going to tell me?" I asked, voice low.

"Wait. You mean you don't already know? You actually want me to say what I'm thinking instead of guessing the worst possible thing?"

"Don't be an ass. Just tell me."

"I don't know if I should while driving. How do I know your stubborn, foolish ass won't jump out of the car and skin yourself all over the expressway?"

"I'm wearing the Ralph Lauren jeans you bought me. I'd never jump out of a moving vehicle in these."

He laughed, shaking his head. "Lord help me, but I adore you. I'm not leaving you, Danni, and I'll do everything in my power to keep you with me, but things have to change. I love you just the way you are, but I'm responsible for a lot of people. To stay in control of the supernatural community, I must have their respect. When I first turned you, it didn't seem that strange for me to have so much security on you. You were co-sired by my archnemesis, so it made sense to watch you in order to get to him, but—"

"I'm sorry. Archnemesis?"

"Yes." Rider frowned.

"Archnemesis?"

"Yes, that's what I said."

"Why? Who the heck says archnemesis? I've never even heard of that word outside of a comic book."

Rider's jaw popped. "Are you through? I'm trying to have a serious conversation."

"Go ahead, Batman." I gestured for him to continue.

"Didn't mean to get your tights in a bunch."

He let out a heavy, irritated sigh. "This is what I'm talking about. I love that you speak your mind and ninety-five percent of the time I find you amusing even when you're driving me crazy, but when we are in front of other people, *my people*, you can't give me attitude. Sometimes you have to just listen to me and do what I say."

"I'm sorry." I clenched my fists. "It sounded like you just sat there and told me I have to follow your command like you own me."

"That's not what I said."

"It's what I just heard."

"Damn it, Danni, I'm trying to keep you safe."

"From what? According to you, Selander Ryan is definitely dead, and you killed Barnaby Quimby."

"Do you think that's the end of all threats against you and now everything's going to be all blue skies and rainbows? You just fought a werewolf! There's always something else out there that can hurt you, maybe even kill you, especially when—" He clenched his jaw and gripped the steering wheel tighter.

"Especially when what?"

"Especially when you mean the world to me," he said, a bit softer. "You're my weakness. There are other vampires out there who would love to control my territory. There are others who know I've killed ones just like them and freed their fledglings, vampires who know I'll do the same to them. They would do anything to stop me before I discover them. You saw with James and Marie that despite what I've done for those in my nest, there will be traitors. Now that Selander Ryan is gone, I have no reason to give to protect you other than the fact I care about you so much. Loving you is putting a target on you and if you would listen to me, and just do the simple things I ask you to do, I wouldn't need so much security on you. You kicked that werewolf's ass. You're not weak. You're needy, but not weak."

"Hey!"

"You are needy, Danni. You know you are. I'm not insulting you, I'm just painting a clear picture for you. You pick apart every single thing I do or say, looking for some horrible hidden meaning. You're jealous of women I'm not even sleeping with. You need constant reassurance that I want you and only you, and I would love to give that to you every single time you need it, but I can't. That's why I took you to Pigeon Forge. I knew you loved it and would be comfortable there, maybe comfortable enough to really listen to me. We needed the alone time because we won't get it as much back home, definitely not as openly." He raked a hand through his hair and took a moment, seeming to sort out his thoughts. "I need you to believe that I care about you and to trust me enough to know that if I tell you to do something, it's for your protection and the protection of our community. I need you to give me the same level of respect as anyone else in my nest. Give me hell in private if you want, but I have to be the boss in front of my people. If they see me as weak, I will lose their respect. If I lose their respect, I lose the foundation I've worked my ass off building. My territory is one of the better ones. The vampires in my nest, the shifters under my employ, they have good lives. They have freedom. If I lose my territory to someone else, everyone loses." He placed his hand on my knee and squeezed. "I need you to understand that I love you when I'm not able to say the words out loud. To believe your happiness means a lot to me when it might seem like it means nothing."

"So you're saying we can only be together in secret?" I asked, my words tight as I tried to understand just what exactly he was saying. So far, all I'd heard was a bunch of 'nobody can know we're together' crap.

"No, I'm not explaining this well at all."

"Yeah, I hope that's the case because if you're saying you're ashamed of me, I'm going to seriously reconsider jumping out of this car and ruining these jeans. No, screw that. I'm going to shove you out of the car."

"I could actually see you do that." Rider laughed and grabbed my hand, raised it to kiss my knuckles. "Everyone will know about us. Everyone will know you are mine. What they won't know is how much control *you* actually have over *me*."

I just sat there, blinking, for a good moment. "It sounded like you said I have control over you."

"Never in a million years would I have put on a ridiculous costume and taken that picture with anyone else," he said, shaking his head as he laughed. "Never would I allow anyone to tell me not to hurt someone. No one questions me and walks away unscathed. No one." He looked at me. "Except you."

"And that's a problem?"

"Yes. The world can know you're mine, but they can't know I belong to you."

"What does that mean, exactly?" I asked as we pulled off the expressway, almost home.

He sighed. "It means that silly picture we took is for your eyes only. It means if Daniel mentions it to anyone or gives me any attitude, I'm going to knock him on his ass, even if it makes you angry with me. It means we know Pigeon Forge was a romantic getaway but my people will think the purpose of the trip was to bring back new muscle and you were there because you're the woman I want in my bed. They can know I enjoy your company, they just can't know what I'd do for you. That's a piece of information that cannot get in my enemies' hands."

"Daniel is the muscle?" I asked, a little surprised. He'd never seemed very impressed with him, and in human form, the guy wasn't as intimidating as Rider or Grey's men.

"He can turn into a dragon and breathe fire. Whether he's a pain in the ass or not, he's kind of awesome. Just don't tell the little punk I said that."

I smiled, but I was back to a frown in a blink. My

amazing new boyfriend was in love with me, but I couldn't tell anyone? It wasn't the relationship I wanted, and that really sucked, because he was definitely the man I wanted.

"I'm sorry I opened my mouth tonight. I shouldn't have said anything until we were on our way back. We'd still be there now. You would have had one more beautiful, romantic night in the place you love."

"One more night of a fake relationship," I said softly.

"This isn't fake," Rider said, as he pulled the Ferrari into the garage attached to the bar and cut the engine. He turned toward me and rubbed his thumb over my cheek. "I meant every word I said to you at the waterfall. I love you."

"In private."

"I'm sorry," he whispered. Even in the privacy of his car, in the garage with no one around, he whispered. "Rome, Tony, Nannette and Eliza are my most trusted associates and the closest thing I have to friends. They know how I feel about you, but are wise enough not to speak of it. Grey knows you're very special to me. You're not a dirty secret, Danni. I promise you that if it was safe to do so, I'd scream my love for you from the top of this building. Please trust me."

I looked at him, opened my mouth, but couldn't say the words. Trust wasn't easy for me. The first guy I'd slept with made fun of me to his friends afterward. I'd been ridiculed by my mother and grandmother since my teens, when it became clear I'd never have the perfect body my sister had. I'd heard over and over again from them that I didn't have what it took to get a man for the long haul, and the more Rider had spoken, the more their words had haunted me. Maybe he did love me in his own way, but if loving me was seen as a danger, what was the point? I might be a vampire, but I still wanted the happily ever after. I wanted wedding bells. I couldn't see Rider giving up his territory for that so either he'd have to eventually be willing to take the risk of revealing to his enemies that he cared for someone or I was going to have to settle for hearing the words "I love you" in private.

Or I was going to have to leave the man I loved and settle for someone willing to care about me in front of the world. I opened my door and stepped out. Rider usually opened my door for me, but I saw no point waiting for him to act like a gentleman now. Maybe that had changed, too. If so, I didn't want to know yet. I'd learned more than enough for one night.

Rider exited his side of the car, grabbed our bags, and led me out of the garage, through the hall and up the stairs to what I'd started considering his inner sanctum. It was basically a bedroom with a bar on one side, a chaise on the other. He had a closet, a large dresser, and a door on the right led to a private bathroom. A flatscreen TV rose out of the bar with the click of a button and that was pretty much it for entertainment. That and the entertainment that took place in the large bed. It wasn't a home.

"You could have dropped me off at my apartment," I said as Rider lowered the bags to the floor.

"Why would I do that?"

"It's where I live."

"I sleep better with you next to me."

I looked at the bed. "Good thing this is just a bedroom. I guess you don't need anything else for me."

"It's not like that, Danni." He stepped closer and tipped my chin up. "This is just a bedroom because it's all I ever needed here. This has always just been a place I sleep during the day. You're the only person who's ever stayed here with me. It's safe. The door is spelled so no one can get in unless I want them to, and several of my people are always downstairs in the bar. Your apartment building is more complicated to secure." He stepped away, ran a hand through his hair, then turned back to me. "I could buy you a house."

I looked up at him. "You'd buy me a house?"

"I'll buy you one right now if it'll put a smile on your

face."

I shook my head, suddenly sadder than I had been when I'd watched Pigeon Forge disappear behind us on our way out. Houses were for families, or at least married couples. "You can't buy smiles, not from me."

With a sadness in his eyes that nearly drew an apology from me despite the fact I'd said nothing wrong, Rider kissed my forehead and sighed. "I was going to go check in with my staff and feed. I hate to leave you here unhappy. Is there anything I can do to make you smile?"

"No," I said, a smile seeming absolutely unfathomable at the moment. "I have a lot to think about. Just go."

SIX

He left. The jerk just walked out the door and left me all alone in his stupid room over the bar with nothing to do but watch TV and digest the conversation we'd had, and what a suck-ass conversation it was. The more I thought about it, the more I wanted to cry. The more I wanted to cry, the more I wanted to punch something. Someone. *Him.*

I sat on the bed, watching some cupcake competition on the TV, and that made me angry. I couldn't even eat cupcakes anymore. Sure, I could eat again eventually, but I was upset now. I needed the cupcakes now. And cookies, and doughnuts, and cake. Lots of cake. What did upset people do if they couldn't stuff their faces with heaps of fattening, sweet, unhealthy food? What kind of sick, twisted asshole made it so vampires couldn't eat without getting sick after first turning? Did they not realize how upsetting it was to turn? No one needed cupcakes and doughnuts more than a newly turned vampire! I started crying and I couldn't tell if it was because of Rider or because I really needed a chocolate cupcake. Or a dozen chocolate cupcakes.

Thor: The Dark World came on the TV, reminding me of

Rider's *Avengers* comment. I wiped away my tears, took a deep breath, and turned the TV off. Normally, I wouldn't miss seeing Chris Hemsworth in all his shirtless glory, but I wasn't in the mood for sexy men. Sexy men were jackasses. I was too worked up to even attempt trying to sleep before sunrise and I didn't want to hang around in Rider's room with nothing to do but obsess over everything he'd said to me while knowing he was off somewhere drinking blood from one of the former hookers he paid for the service. I found my purse and left the room. I still had time to make it home before sunrise.

I took the stairs down and opened the door leading to the bar, figuring I'd exit through it. I didn't know the code for the garage and that appeared to be the only back way out. It was late night or extremely early morning, depending on how you looked at time, but the bar was still pretty full. I felt a variety of energies as I stepped onto the floor. I knew the bar was full of vampires, shifters, maybe even a witch or two mixed in with the oblivious humans who had no idea who or what they were mingling with. I didn't feel any need to warn them. Rider would never allow any human to come to harm in his bar. Even I was attacked outside of it. Selander Ryan wasn't dumb enough to try anything inside.

I started toward the front door, ignoring the curious look I received from the Asian tiger shifter manning the bar. I didn't know his name, but he'd been there the night Rider killed Selander Ryan. Rome, a very large black man who worked for Rider, stood at the door with his extremely muscular arms crossed, surveying the room. His gaze met mine and held. It unnerved me. I didn't sense any kind of supernatural vibe from Rome, but still wouldn't want to fight him. I could probably fit both my arms inside just one of his muscles. The way he looked at me, I wasn't sure I was going to get out the front door without a challenge.

"Hey."

I looked over to see Daniel sitting in a dark booth by himself, a binder stuffed with papers on the table in front of him.

"Hey." I stopped my trek toward the door and walked over to the table. "Everything going all right?"

"Yeah. I just have this gigantic pile of information to get through." He gestured toward the binder. "Thanks for speaking up to Grey earlier. I really didn't want to stay at The Cloud Top any longer. Beautiful area, but hanging with the wolf pack was getting old. Want to sit?"

I glanced over at Rome, noted I was still under his watchful eye, and slid into the opposite side of the booth. "Sure. It's no big deal. I got the impression you weren't happy there."

"Yeah, I kinda get the impression you aren't happy at all." He frowned. "Maybe it's just the tear tracks staining your face."

I swiped at my cheeks. "It's been a rough night. I'm fine."

"Sorry about Shannon. She's a bitch. You slammed the hell out of her." He laughed. "That was awesome. I was told your boyfriend was the guy not to piss off, but I might be more afraid of you."

"I'm normally not like that," I advised, recalling how strange it had felt slamming the woman into the ground over and over, how it hadn't seemed like me even while I was doing it. It hadn't been my first fight, but it had been unusually brutal. "Something just came over me. I lost control."

"Maybe you shouldn't drink from me again."

I looked him in the eye and he dropped his gaze. "Is there something I should know about your blood?"

"I have a temper issue," he said, leaning back in the seat before meeting my gaze. "I don't know that it would affect my blood, but you did drink from me prior to the fight. Since I've been a dragon shifter, I've had a few rage moments myself. Just to be safe, I probably shouldn't be a main source."

"I usually drink bagged blood, or straight from Rider."

"Do you act differently after drinking from him than when you drink the bagged blood?"

"Not that I can recall," I answered. "His blood packs a pretty powerful punch, even more than yours, but both are way better than bagged. I don't think his has ever changed my personality or made me violent." It possibly made me horny, I thought, realizing how drawn I've been to Rider every time I've drank from him. I wasn't drawn to Daniel or the other two men I drank from, so I figured what turned me on about drinking from Rider was the fact that he himself turned me on. Just being close to the man, having my mouth on him, was enough to make me want him. I hoped. He said drinking blood wasn't a sexual thing. If it was, I definitely didn't want him drinking from any other women.

"Maybe it was just a fluke then." Daniel shrugged. "Either way, she got what she deserved. She'd been talking shit since you showed up, trying to convince the other women you were after Grey. He's the pack leader, and every female wolf in the area is after him to be chosen as his mate. He's been incredibly picky so far and some of them are fearing he'll fall for a human and turn her or choose another type of shifter. When you arrived, Shannon thought he might try a vampire."

"I was with Rider."

"Having a boyfriend hasn't stopped women from going after Grey before."

"I'm not that kind of woman, and I'm not sure Rider is what you'd call a boyfriend," I said, remembering him once laughing at my use of the word and the comment that he hadn't been anyone's *boyfriend* for a very long time.

"Boyfriend, lover, whatever." Daniel looked around the bar. "The first thing I was told was not to screw with him, and definitely don't screw with his woman. Whatever you two are, it's more than friends."

"He's my sire."

"He's more than that."

Unsure what to say to that, I nodded my head toward the binder. "What is all that?"

"It's like an employee manual," Daniel answered. "I haven't been assigned anywhere just yet, waiting on that to come from the big man himself, but these are all the rules and policies, and general information like where I'm going to live. I'm guessing you didn't get one."

"I'm not one of Rider's employees." I sighed. "I actually quit my job a couple weeks ago. I need to find another soon before all my savings is lost on rent."

"You don't live with Rider?"

"No. I have my own place."

"Well, I doubt he'll let you go homeless, so I wouldn't worry about the job search too much. You could always work for him, couldn't you?"

"I'm not a bodyguard and the first time I came into a bar, it was this one and I ended up getting attacked by an incubus and was saved by getting turned into a vampire. I'm not a big fan of bars."

Daniel laughed. "I guess not. Yet you're sitting here in one with me, the same one."

"Yeah, well, I guess company is everything. You know, all I've heard about you is that you're a wisecracking jerk. You don't seem that bad to me."

"Uh, thanks... for that." Daniel smiled, and it was a nice smile. "My attitude depends on who or what I'm dealing with, I guess. You're good company too. You have a nice vibe."

I smiled, for the moment letting go of the horrible conversation with Rider and the sadness that had clung to me since it began. "I was told you come from another realm. I didn't even know there were other realms. I thought it sucked turning into a vampire, but you're in a whole different world. That has to be hard."

"We were given a mountain of information to go

through when we decided to stay," he explained. "Imortians speak the language you call English, so at least we didn't have a communication barrier. The biggest difference between Imortia and here is that in Imortia we celebrate magic. Here it is hidden. Unicorns and dragons are just animals there, however they are highly revered animals. Here, they are thought to be fairytale creatures. We don't have vampires there, and although shifters came from Imortia, they are the product of foul magic. Many of us chose to come here rather than face the judging eyes of those who don't care that we did not choose to be what we now are."

"I can understand that," I said. "I chose to be a vampire, but only because it was choose to become a vampire or die. Honestly, I didn't think it was real, even after I turned. Sometimes I think I made the wrong choice, like tonight. I had a full crying fit because I can't eat food until I build up a tolerance and I really need a damn cupcake."

Daniel laughed. "Well, I'm glad you made the choice you did. You're not nearly as ghoulish as I expected a vampire to be. You're actually pretty damn cute, and if today was any indication, I think I'm going to like being around you. As soon as you build up your tolerance for food again, I'll make sure you get a cupcake, just as a token of appreciation for not leaving me there with Grey."

I felt the heat of a blush climbing my neck and ducked my head. I'd never been good with compliments, even though I craved them. "Would you have really been stuck there? Couldn't you go off on your own? I know not all shifters are part of a pack. Rider has some working for him, and they follow his command, not a pack leader."

"Although all the werewolves here now originated from Zaira, a woman who was banished from Imortia, the majority of shifters who came here when I did were not wolves. Our queen at the time, Fairuza, was an evil bitch. She turned us into dragons, unicorns, gargoyles, all manner of large cat, anacondas… you name it. A sort of temporary agency was established to welcome us, educate us on this realm, and put us into jobs. Many of the shifters were able to do their own thing, but no one wanted to let a fire-breathing dragon loose without supervision. I've been bumped around all over, from one wolf pack to another, looking for a place that works. I'm hoping this is it."

"You didn't seem like you wanted to come here when we first arrived there. You tested Rider."

"And he showed me who he was. I think it best to find out early on who I'm dealing with."

"And after that demonstration, you wanted to come here?"

"No. I thought he was an arrogant jackass," Daniel answered with more honesty than he should in the presence of Rider's people. I looked around, but other than Rome's watchful eye on me, I didn't detect anyone paying us much attention.

"So, what made you change your mind?"

"You woke up screaming from a nightmare. I figure anyone who has that reaction to a dream must still be pretty vulnerable, pretty human. I also noticed the way Rider watched you. That man stayed on constant alert for any danger your way, and when a guy like him, with that big of a stick up his ass, is willing to take what I can safely assume was an embarrassingly goofy picture just to make someone else happy he can't be that big of a dick. I figure working for him won't be so bad. So what did you dream about anyway? That was some serious screaming."

Just bringing up the nightmare reminded me of the terrifyingly realistic sensation of Selander Ryan's breath on the back of my neck. I barely suppressed a shiver. "I'd rather not talk about it."

"All right." Daniel nodded and pushed the binder aside. "What would you like to talk about? This thing is boring me to tears. I've had more than my fill of information since coming to this realm. My brain needs a break from soaking it all in."

"Tell me more about Imortia," I suggested. "You said there was a queen. Is there a king?"

"When the queen chooses to marry, there is a king. Fairuza liked having a lot of men and was known to punish those who refused her advances or dared find another woman attractive."

"So the queen is the ruler of Imortia, even if there is a king?"

"Yes. Another difference between Imortia and this realm is that women were never seen as inferior to men there. Women harness magic with greater skill than men and are usually the ones to be born with it to begin with. Since magic is celebrated and considered a great gift in Imortia, women have always been in control."

"What other differences are there?" I asked, genuinely curious.

"The Imortian people come in a wide variety of skin tones. Some are light, some are dark. Some have blue eyes, some have brown, and some have purple, a color very rare here. No one cares, maybe because we don't have countries or states. We are all Imortian. Learning this realm's history was very jarring. I don't think I will ever understand the concept of racism, not how it came to be and definitely not how it still exists. It is mind-blowingly ridiculous, not to mention horrifically vile."

"I can't argue with you there," I said. "I actually grew up in a pretty racist home, but fortunately I had my father's influence. He judged people by who they were, not what shade of skin they possessed. I don't want to know how I might have turned out if I hadn't had him."

"He's gone now?"

I nodded. "Cancer."

"Something else horrible about this realm. It sounds like a particularly brutal disease."

I glanced at the binder, ready to change the subject. I'd already been emotional when I'd come down to the bar.

Talking about my father would definitely produce a storm of tears. "So they gave you a place to stay? You didn't get a choice?"

"Yeah, an apartment they said was recently vacated by the last person stupid enough to betray your boyfriend. I gather that person didn't leave breathing?"

"No. If Rider trusts you and you betray him, it doesn't end pretty," I warned Daniel. "He's not a bad guy. Two of his employees helped a hunter try to kill me. That's why they died."

Daniel nodded his understanding. "Good thing for me, I think you're too cute to kill."

I'm pretty sure I blanched a little. "I wouldn't be saying that either."

"Just an innocent compliment. He's that jealous?"

"Rider Knight has no need to be jealous," I said, laughing at the concept. "However, he is …"

"Possessive?"

"Protective," I quickly corrected him, my back straighter, hackles raised. I had probably used the same word to describe Rider before. I'd used a lot of words to describe him and plenty weren't the most flattering of choices, but I didn't like someone else calling him anything not one hundred percent positive. "So, back to Imortia. What do people do there? Do you have television shows, movies? Any other realm rock bands I might want to listen to?"

Daniel laughed, shaking his head. "Imortia is a very different place than this realm. We don't even have television sets, let alone shows to watch. We do enjoy plays and live music, but music is always live, never recorded."

"Seriously? What do you do when there's not a play or someone performing live?"

"Imortia is similar to many of the places in your fairytales. There is the queen and her staff. There are healers and seers, warriors and witches. The people work hard from sunup to sundown and if they get time to relax, that can be spent playing instruments, singing, reading, or going for a hike through the winding falls. One of my favorite things to do as a kid was play hide and seek with the twinkle fairies."

"Twinkle fairies?"

"They're tiny, magical beings that fly and at night they're like shooting stars."

"You're kidding me."

"Danni, you're sitting across from a guy who can breathe fire. Are twinkle fairies really that hard to believe?"

"I haven't actually seen you breathe fire," I teased him. "That could just be a rumor to make you seem like a badass."

"Maybe it is." He shrugged, but his grin gave him away.

"Does it hurt?"

"No. When I shift into a dragon, I still have my mind and emotions, but physically, I am the dragon. My throat is coated for protection, so breathing fire doesn't harm me at all. As for the shift itself, I don't feel a thing. There are other types of shifters who do hurt and they shred their clothes in the process, winding up naked when they shift back. That's got to suck."

"Why the difference?"

"My type of shifter was born of magic. Although we take on the physical body of the animal whose spirit we share, magic creates the change. A part of that magic is we get to maintain our decency. Well, those who had any decency to begin with." He winked.

We continued talking, Daniel describing the beauty of Imortia to me and telling funny stories of things that had happened there or with the various wolf packs he'd been with since leaving. I told him a little about myself, and about the night I'd been attacked and everything that had led to the night Selander Ryan had been killed, omitting the two men I'd killed before that happened, and the images I'd seen in Rider's mind after he'd crushed Ryan's heart. He was the first person I'd truly talked openly to about what had happened since turning. Eliza didn't count. She was a counselor, and Rider was my sire. Daniel was the first person I felt I could talk to like a friend without worrying I'd say too much and get thrown in the wacky bin.

About an hour passed before the whole vibe in the bar turned dark. I didn't even need to turn around to see that Rider had returned, but I did. I watched him walk from the back door, past the bar, headed straight for our table. As I watched him, I watched the people around him react. The bartender's body tensed, ready should he be needed. The human women cast admiring glances his way, one going so far as to fan herself. A woman I suspected to be a vampire sat at the bar, rolling her gaze up and down Rider's body before turning to stare daggers into me. I cast a quick glance at Rome to see him standing at attention. I was pretty sure he wasn't even breathing.

Rider walked right to our table, his face a hard mask, and stopped. "Go upstairs. Now," he commanded in a tone that brooked no room for negotiation. *Please*, he added softly through our mental link, although anyone looking at his face wouldn't have had a clue he'd done so.

Realizing all eyes in the bar, at least those belonging to nonhumans who knew who Rider was and who I was to him, were on us, I grabbed my purse and slid out of the booth. "Good luck with your new job," I told Daniel, offering what I hoped was a calming smile as he sat on his side of the booth, looking up at Rider with an expression that said he wasn't happy with the tone he'd used with me. I hoped his unhappiness didn't go any further than the look. Surely, he knew better than to challenge Rider in his very own bar.

I stared straight ahead as I made my way across the bar to the back door, silently fuming. He'd warned me he was going to be an asshole. He wasn't kidding. I growled a curse as I saw the garage door. Good thing for Rider, I didn't know the code to open it. It would serve him right if

I jumped in his Ferrari and peeled out into the night, or what was left of it. But I didn't know the code, so I walked up the stairs and entered his private room. I always hesitated a little at his door since it had been magically spelled to only allow who Rider wanted inside. So far, I had yet to be locked out. Unfortunately, there was no way to lock him out. I missed the ability to do that at my apartment. Then again, I doubted simply locking a door would keep Rider out of anywhere he wanted to be.

Although my travel bag contained a nightgown Rider had bought me, it was way too sexy to don, given my mood, so I borrowed one of his dark T-shirts. I grabbed a pillow from his bed and tossed it onto the chaise before lying down on it. It wasn't nearly as comfortable as it looked, but I refused to sleep with him, so I let out a sigh and settled in as best I could. I thought about turning the TV back on, but I decided against it. If any screams, grunts, or crashes sounded from downstairs, I wanted to hear them so I could … hell; I didn't even know what I could do if Rider decided to kill Daniel. If I ran down there to defend him, I might make things worse for the poor guy. I stared at the ceiling and prayed Daniel wouldn't smart off to Rider. Doing so in Pigeon Forge was one thing. If he did it downstairs in front of Rider's men, the vampire would make an example of him.

I'd just started sensing the sun about to come up when Rider walked through the door, closing it behind him with his foot as he pulled his shirt off and tossed it to the floor. He stood hands on hips, and looked at me. "I said please."

"Mentally doesn't count."

His chest rose and fell as he took a deep breath. "Why are you on the chaise?"

"I'm not sleeping with you. Is Daniel alive?"

"Why the hell wouldn't he be? Damn, Danni, if you think I'm a bloodthirsty killer, why are you with me?"

"You mean I have a choice?" I shot back.

He sat at the foot of the bed to remove his shoes and

socks, and looked at me with a hardness that made me gulp. "If you don't want to be with me, then don't. I want to be with you, but if the feeling isn't mutual, I'm not going to force it. You ought to know that much by now." He dug in his pocket and withdrew his keys before tossing them so they landed on the floor beside me. "Take my damn car if being here is that awful. I asked you to stay because I sleep better with you next to me, where I'm not as worried about you, but you're not a prisoner."

"You didn't ask me. You ordered me." I sat up and looked at the keys. "You'd actually let me drive your Ferrari?"

"It's just a car. Are you staying here or not?"

"Gee, when you ask like that, I just get all tingly inside."

He sighed in exasperation. "You're a pain in the ass, you know that?"

"Then why do you want me here?"

"It hurts more when you're not with me," he said softly, and just like that, my traitorous heart did a little flip.

"That's not fair. You're not supposed to say sweet things like that when I'm mad at you."

"Tough shit. I don't play by the rules and I speak the truth." He stood from the bed and pulled his pants down.

"Hey!" I stood. "What are you doing?"

"I'm getting ready for bed," he answered, his brow wrinkled in confusion. "What's it look like I'm doing?"

"You're naked."

"Of course I'm naked. I sleep naked. You staying or not?"

I crossed my arms and gritted my teeth. It was almost sunup and honestly, I no longer felt like leaving, even if it meant I could drive his Ferrari. "I'll stay, but I'm not sleeping the entire day, and there will be no sex."

"Yeah, you didn't have to tell me that. Your face is screaming it at me."

I narrowed my eyes at him and fumed a moment more

before lowering myself back onto the chaise and turning my back to him. "Good ni—" I yelped in surprise as I was lifted into the air and a second later, bounced on the mattress. "I'm not sleeping with you!"

"Fine, but no woman of mine is sleeping on a chaise when there's a bed she can have." He lowered himself onto the chaise, and I tried not to laugh as his feet hung off the end. "Sweet dreams, mean-ass."

I let out a snort. "Yeah, I'm the mean one. What did you and Daniel talk about?"

He opened an eye and looked at me out the side of it as I settled under the covers. "Do I need to be worried about you and him?"

I froze and just stared at him for a moment, blinking. "Worried about what?"

He eyed me a little longer before shaking his head and settling in. "Nothing."

I rolled over, scooped my purse up from where I'd flung it to the floor earlier, found my cell phone, and set the alarm before connecting it to the charger Rider kept by his bed. I closed my eyes and waited for the sun I felt about to rise but kept getting annoyed by Rider's constant movements as he tried to find a comfortable position on the chaise. As hard as it was for me, I knew it was worse for him. He was too big for it. I sighed as he shifted again and I imagined his muscles rippling as he moved around, all naked perfection. "Good grief."

"Go to sleep," he muttered.

"I can't with all that dickstraction. Distraction!" I quickly said, realizing my flub, but it was too late. I sat up and looked over to see Rider sitting up, bent over at the waist, laughing hard enough to pull something. "Oh, shut up." I threw a pillow at him, which he caught effortlessly. "You know what I meant."

"Oh yeah, I know what you meant."

I rolled my eyes, suddenly very heavy. The sun had arrived. "Sleep in the bed or on the chaise. I don't care," I said as I turned on my side and closed my eyes.

"Why are you always trying to hit me with pillows?" he asked as he slid in behind me.

"No available anvils to drop on you," I muttered, sleep dragging me down as his laughter vibrated against my neck and something hard poked me from behind. "That better not be what I think it is."

"Shhh...," he whispered. "It's just a dickstraction."

SEVEN

I stood in a foyer constructed completely of marble, a large double door gilded in gold before me. I turned to see I had no other choice of escape from the room except to wake up. Sensing what lay beyond the double door was incentive to do just that, but I'd been here before. I knew that if I didn't hear what the monster wanted to tell me, I'd be here again. He would never leave me alone. If death hadn't stopped him, avoidance wouldn't work any better. Death had just been a short-term fix for evil as dark as him. I took a deep breath, squared my shoulders, and pushed through the door.

I was in the dining room where I'd last spoken with the handsome devil shortly before his physical death. Once again, he was dressed in white, his long blond hair down around his shoulders, his soul-sucking brown eyes gleaming with dark and twisted intentions as he sat at the head of the long dining table with a chalice of wine in his hand.

"Hello Danni."

"Hello Satan." I grasped the back of a chair, no intention of sitting.

His thin lips twisted into a grin. "Flattery will get you

nowhere."

"What will get you permanently out of my life?"

"Why ever would you want me gone? I created you."

"I'm pretty sure you were neither the sperm nor the egg that created me," I replied. "You're definitely not God. What you are is dead, Selander. I watched Rider rip your heart out of your chest and crush it. How are you still getting into my dreams?"

"I marked you," he answered. "You may have given your allegiance to Rider, breaking my control over you, but you can never completely remove my mark, not even with my death. You're still of my lineage."

I shook my head. "I'm not a hybrid any longer. I no longer have the succubus venom."

Selander Ryan just smiled. It couldn't have been any creepier if he was covered in clown makeup. For a moment I worried that Rider had lied to me about the venom to give me more confidence that he found me desirable without the added supernatural help, but I'd drank from Daniel too and he hadn't seemed the slightest bit turned on by it. He'd complimented me a few times, said I was cute, but that was nowhere near the reaction I got from men prior to Selander Ryan's death. Daniel was a shifter, I reminded myself. Maybe shifters were different? His blood had tasted different. Spicier. I shook my head. This was ridiculous.

"I saw you die. This isn't real. You're just a nightmare."

"If I'm just a nightmare, why did you spend so much of today fearing I would jump out and get you?"

"How could you possibly know that?"

"My physical body may not be in the same realm as you, thanks to my half-brother, but that doesn't mean I've left you. You are of my lineage. You carry me with you."

"No." I stepped away, hands clenched, nails digging into my palms. "You are no part of me. I'm not a succubus. I'm not anything like you."

"The last time we met here, I told you I would use you

to destroy Rider. I told you that even if I died, I would win. You may have lessened my physical hold over you and strengthened your bond with that blood-sucking bastard, but nothing you will ever do will change the fact that you have two sires. Nothing you will ever do will change the fact that I can and will use you to make Rider suffer. I waited too long for you to let something as small as death stop me from destroying him."

"You waited for me?"

He sipped from his chalice and set it on the table. "You know I didn't randomly choose you to be turned that night," he said as he ran his finger around the rim of the chalice.

"You had my co-worker send me to the bar and later that night you popped in, took me to the alley and attacked me. That's hardly a long wait."

He smiled that creepy smile again.

"What aren't you telling me?"

"Remember the last time we were here, when I told you part of the fun in playing the game is knowing more than your opponent, keeping them in the dark and watching them go mad trying to figure out your next move? I'm having a lot of fun now, Danni, and there's not much fun where I'm at, so I'm going to enjoy this. I'm going to savor every moment of you worrying about what I know that you don't, every moment of you living in fear of when I'm going to strike because I think you're starting to see that death is not the end for me. I'm going to watch your descent into madness with a smile on my face."

"Is that the way you think you'll win? Drive me mad? Make Rider watch me go nuts? You wish you had that much control over me. You're dead, Ryan. You're nothing."

His eyes darkened and all traces of his sinister smile left him. "Don't call me Ryan."

"Oh, does that bother you?" I asked, reading his eyes and realizing it did. After I'd first turned, I'd thought Ryan was just his last name, but later discovered it was his middle name, and what Rider, and I assume his mother, called him. Apparently, being called Ryan by anyone else struck a nerve. "You first introduced yourself to me as Ryan. Why does it bother you now? Did your step-mommy call you Ryan? You know, before Rider killed her?"

He stood from the table. "I can still kill you. You underestimate my power."

"Is that so, Ryan? I thought we were playing a game where you make Rider suffer forever. Do you really want to end it so quickly with my death? Go for it," I growled, anger overruling my brain, which was trying to tell me not to poke the bear. "Kill me. It still won't get you back to Mommy. I'm pretty sure the two of you are in separate locations and now that she's no longer one of your disgusting minions she couldn't be more glad to never see you ag—"

He appeared before me in a flash and wrapped his hand around my throat, squeezing until I saw stars dancing before my eyes. I tried to scream for Rider, but had no breath to make a sound.

"Danni! Baby, wake up now!"

I opened my eyes and sucked in air. Tears streamed down my face as Rider loomed over me, eyes wide, frantic. He'd lifted my upper body off the bed and now pulled me against his chest to hug me tight to his body, his cheek against mine.

"What the hell just happened?" he asked. "You were choking, and I sensed Ryan."

"Still think I'm just having nightmares?" I asked as I clung to him, my voice coming out hoarse. "I'm just asking because I'm pretty sure my nightmare just tried to kill me."

The alarm on my cell phone blared, making both of us jump. Rider muttered a curse and turned it off. "I killed that bastard," he said, but he didn't sound nearly as confident as he had telling me this after the first nightmare I'd had of Selander Ryan. "I crushed his heart. I crushed his fucking heart."

"Yeah, I know. I was there."

Rider rose from the bed and started pacing. "I don't understand this." He raked a hand through his hair, pulling some strands loose of the band at his nape. "It had to be a nightmare, but a nightmare can't kill you."

I rubbed my throat, still feeling the ghost of Selander Ryan's fingers pushing into it. "He came to me just like he did when he was alive. It felt exactly the same. He's dead, but he's not gone."

"Did he say anything to you or just try to kill you?" Rider asked, stopping to look at me as he awaited an answer. His hands were on his hips and his penis was hanging loose.

"Could you put some pants on?" I asked, unable to tear my eyes away from his genitalia. "You're dickstracting me again."

"It's just a body part," he muttered as he grabbed a pair of pants from his dresser and pulled them on.

Maybe it was just a body part on most men. On Rider, it was a magic wand with the ability to mesmerize, and that wasn't the only magic it could do, but the other tricks involved participation. I wasn't about to tell him that though, because I knew him well enough to know he'd tease me with my fascination. The fact he wasn't teasing me with it now clued me in to just how worried he was about Selander Ryan, which did nothing helpful for my own nerves.

"Well?" he asked, hands on hips again, having just zipped up his fly.

"We talked," I answered. "He was in a fancy dining room, the same place he was in when I last spoke with him before you killed him."

"What did he say?"

"He said he'd marked me and even death can't stop him. He still plans on making you suffer."

"How? By killing you while you sleep next to me? I felt you were in danger and it brought me right out of sleep. He can't win that way. As your sire, I can pull you out of sleep."

"Well, I don't think he actually planned on killing me. He kind of lost his temper after I started calling him Ryan, which clearly struck a nerve. I kind of dug in deeper by bringing up your mother." My face heated. "I didn't say anything derogatory about her, I promise. I just made a comment that killing me wouldn't bring her back to him and implied that wherever she was, she was most likely more than happy to be far from him."

"I know you wouldn't say anything bad about her," Rider told me, and smiled a little. "If he reacted that violently, that means he hasn't found her. She's not where he is. That means maybe she was forgiven for what she did under his control and maybe..." He looked down, worrying his lip with his teeth.

"Maybe she's in Heaven?"

He nodded. "I can't imagine many creatures like us getting into there, but if anyone could, it would be her."

"You're not a creature," I said. "You think I'm a creature?"

"No, not at all." He walked over to the bed and sat beside me, kissed my forehead. "But I don't have to worry about where you will go because I have no intention of ever allowing your death."

"Some things are out of our control." I looked into Rider's eyes, studied the hard set of his jaw, and knew he meant exactly what he'd just said. He would move heaven and earth to keep me safe. We'd known each other less than two months, but it felt like so much longer. Something about that seemed strange to me. "Selander keeps telling me he's using me to destroy you, and in this last visit he said something about having waited for me too long to allow death to stop him from carrying out whatever his sick plan is. What do you think that means?"

Rider frowned, his brow wrinkled in thought for a moment, before he shook his head and stood to resume pacing. "None of this makes sense." He raked both hands through his hair, yanking out the band at his nape when his fingers made contact. His dark hair tumbled loose around his shoulders.

"Holy cannoli," I said as I took him in.

He stopped pacing to look at me, confused. "What is it?"

"I've never seen you without your hair pulled back in a ponytail. You're like a sexy, dark archangel. I don't know whether to pray for forgiveness for my lusty thoughts right now or offer my body in sacrifice."

"An archangel, eh?" He grinned and waggled his eyebrows. "Are you regretting making me put away my flaming sword?"

"Ew." I scrunched my nose. "If it's flaming, you'd better apply some ointment before you even think of sheathing that thing in—"

He crossed over to me with the speed only a vampire could muster and cut me off with a deep kiss before pulling away just enough to chuckle against my lips. He rested his forehead against mine and intertwined our fingers. "I'm sorry I dismissed your earlier visit from him as just a nightmare. I have no idea how he's still able to contact you, but I believe you when you say he is. I'll find out how it's happening and kill him again if that's what it takes. In the meantime, you're going to be protected at all times, just like when he was alive."

"I thought you couldn't afford to do that anymore because your enemies will use your protectiveness of me against you."

"Yeah, there's that." He kissed my nose before standing again. He walked over to the bar and stood with his back to it, arms crossed. "I need to protect you from him without making you a target for anyone else. I can always sense your emotions, which is a pretty good way of knowing if you're in danger, but that doesn't do that much good if I can't get to you in the blink of an eye. I'll assign a team to you again anytime we're apart, not that we need to be apart for any real length of time. You don't have that stupid job anymore. You don't need to even be up in daylight for anything." He frowned. "You don't need to be up now."

"I've been out of town. I need to go home and check my mail, and I'm sure there are messages from my mother about my sister's wedding and who knows how many favors she will request, or rather, demand from me when I listen to those. And my job wasn't stupid."

Rider rolled his eyes. "You're a vampire now. You don't need to work for companies comprised entirely of humans and you definitely don't need to jump to your family's commands."

"They're my family."

"They're awful."

"You met them once," I snapped.

"And it was more than enough." He sighed. "Fine. I don't want you alone with them, an easy target for whomever may be watching you, so you're going to have to take someone with you when you're doing private things with your family. You can take Rome. He's human, so the threat of human law and going to jail puts more fear in his heart than the rest of us. That should keep him from strangling your mother and grandmother."

"Rome's human?"

"Yes. I thought you'd gotten better at determining between human and non?"

"Well, yeah, but…" I visualized Rome before me, with his cannonball sized muscles and ability to stand still for so long you'd start to question if he'd died and was just too sturdy to fall, and the unnerving way he projected strength without doing a damn thing. He was like a bulkier, darker version of Rider with less hair. "He seems more than human, and I wouldn't think you'd have a human as your bouncer."

"He's a very big human."

"He is that," I agreed. "You could go with me when I have to do things with my family."

"Babe, I'd definitely strangle your mother and grandmother. I don't even like your sister or that damn rat your grandmother carries in her purse."

"Terry's a dog."

"There's a fifty-pound weight requirement to be a dog. That thing's a rat."

I couldn't argue with that. I'd called the gassy thing a rat more than a few times myself, and I loved dogs. I just wasn't nuts about Terry. "I can't take Rome to private events with my family."

"Why not?"

"Because…" I felt heat climbing up my neck. "Besides being a very big man, he's also very black, and they would definitely make him feel very unwelcome."

"Oh, hell. They're racist too?" Rider threw his hands up in the air. "How did you turn out a decent human being after living with that?"

"My father's influence." The answer came to me immediately. I didn't even need to think about it.

"Thank God for him." Rider scratched his head. "I could send Tony. How are they with Asian people?"

"The same as they are with black and Latino. Don't even ask about Middle Eastern. Heck, I've heard them call Native Americans savages and my great-great-grandmother was Cherokee. Wait…" I remembered the tiger shifter bartending. The Asian tiger shifter. "Is Tony the tiger shifter who was bartending last night?"

"Yes. Why?"

"Tony… the Tiger?"

Rider rolled his eyes. "Yeah, yeah. Same as the cartoon tiger that sells the cereal. Trust me, he's heard it a billion times."

"I imagine so." I laughed at the coincidence before getting up and finding the jeans I'd discarded the night before. "If you want me to take someone with me when I do things with my family, why not a woman? You have women in your nest."

"I don't have any I trust enough to protect you, except Eliza and Nannette. Eliza isn't a fighter at all. She's the most docile vampire I've ever known, and as for Nannette…"

"She doesn't like me."

"Yeah." Rider grinned. "I'm working on that, but she's very loyal to me. She's also a no-nonsense, hard as nails fighting machine. She thinks you compromise me and after what happened with Marie and James, she's not entirely wrong. It's going to take a while for her to see you as something more than a dangerous risk. I think she'd be impressed by how you handled that wolf last night."

"Was that even me, though?" I asked, sitting on the foot of the bed to pull my jeans on.

"What do you mean?"

"I mean…" I struggled to put into words what had been niggling at me since the fight happened. "I've been in fights before. I can defend myself fairly decently when push comes to shove, or at least I've gotten lucky so far, but last night was different. There was this red hot anger burning through me and I didn't just want to defend myself. I wanted to end that woman. I may have been the person slamming that wolf into the ground, but it didn't feel like me. I thought maybe it had something to do with Daniel's blood in my system, but yours never turned me into a violent person. Then Selander Ryan came to me in my dream and said …"

"Said what?" Rider stood straighter, his hands fisted at his sides.

"He said I carry him with me. He even knew that I was afraid he was going to pop out and get me while we were out yesterday. How would he know that unless he really was with me?"

"He's a master manipulator," Rider said, as he kneeled on the floor between my knees and held my face so I would meet his eyes. "He's a con-man. Always was. The most dangerous thing you can do is let that devil get in your head."

"Too late. I'm pretty sure he's been in it since that first bite." I pushed Rider until he stood so I could stand and finish pulling my jeans on. I looked over at the bag of clothes Rider had bought for me for our trip and considered what to wear. I liked the shirt I already had on, although it was big. It was soft and warm and smelled like Rider. I tucked it into my jeans. "I'm keeping this shirt."

Rider shrugged. "Looks better on you than on me."

"That's debatable." I pulled on my shoes and finger-combed my hair. "I need to get home and check my mail, not to mention look for a new job. If I have to go somewhere with my family that's too private for the security team you put on me, they'll just have to wait outside."

"What do you mean, look for a new job?"

"I lost my job, Rider. Obviously, I need a new one."

He stood stone still in front of me, the only movement coming from the tick in his jaw as he stared me down with darkened eyes. "Do you have a death wish? My brother and all the evil crap that comes with him is still in play and you want to find a job? Let me guess, with humans? Working day shifts? Making sure you're weak all day long when you should be sleeping?"

"Bills don't magically pay themselves."

"Bring them to me and I'll pay them."

I blinked at him for a moment. He hadn't even hesitated or asked how many bills I had. "And my apartment?"

"You don't need it. You can stay with me."

I spread my arms out. "Thanks, but I wouldn't know

what to do with all this space."

"I told you I'll buy you a house."

Wow. I'd be a liar if I said it wasn't tempting to have someone pay my bills for me and buy me a house, but I didn't like what it would say of me if I accepted. More importantly, I didn't like the precedent it would set in our relationship. "You can't buy me, Rider."

"I'm not buying you. I'm offering to pay off your bills and give you a more secure home to share with me so you'll be safe."

"Unless that home comes with a wedding ring, I don't want it." His eyes grew wide and his skin paled. "Yeah, that's what I thought. I'm not shacking up with you and letting you pay my way in this world. If I need anything, I'll pay for it myself with my own money that I've earned from working hard. The only way I'll live with a man is if he's my husband and I'll still earn my own way. I'm not the women of my family. I will never be dependent on a man. Any man."

"Danni, you know that if I marry you, every enemy I have will be hunting you down before the honeymoon is over."

"I'm not asking you to marry me," I said, using every ounce of willpower to keep any trace of emotion out of my voice while also keeping my mind on lockdown so he couldn't creep in there and feel how painful it felt to confirm what I'd thought about him and marriage. "I'm explaining why I don't want you to buy me a love shack."

"A love shack?"

"I'm sorry, is sex cave more accurate? I'm going home now. My home. I don't think your evil half-brother can kill me unless I'm sleeping, so I'll just pretend I'm in a Freddy Krueger movie and stay awake."

"And if he sends someone still alive to do the job?"

"I'm not completely defenseless," I said with more confidence than I felt, "and you're paying a security team to keep me safe, right?"

"I'd feel better if you had someone close to you, not just watching from the shadows or outside buildings. If I stay glued to you, that could draw out yet another enemy and our focus needs to be on Ryan and whatever the hell he's planned."

I thought over the choices he'd given me. Tony was way too quiet. It was unnerving. Plus, I'd seen him eat someone and it didn't bother me. The fact that it didn't bother me bothered the hell out of me. Rome was just as unnerving, but mostly because of his size. I couldn't imagine the horror of either of them meeting my family. I'd die of embarrassment from the things my mother and grandmother would say. I didn't want any of Rider's security team interacting with them. If I had to have someone meet them I'd rather it be someone I felt comfortable with, someone I could see as a friend and not just one of Rider's security goons who were probably silently judging me and wondering why Rider was wasting his resources on me. Someone like…

"Daniel."

"What?" Rider folded his arms. "What about Daniel?"

"Give me Daniel."

"*Give you* Daniel?" Rider unfolded his arms and slid his hands inside his pants pockets. His jaw clenched. "As what?"

"As my guard. If you want someone to stay close to me and go with me inside places a regular part of the security detail can't go without being conspicuous, assign Daniel. I've actually spoken with him. I'll feel more comfortable with him than with Rome or Tony, or anyone else you might think of."

"How comfortable?"

I grinned. "Rider Knight, are you jealous?"

He didn't grin. His lips didn't even twitch. Nothing on him moved except the steam I imagined coming from his ears. "Do I need to be?"

I blinked at him, befuddled. I wasn't expecting that

response at all. "No," I finally said. "Daniel's the only person here newer than me. He's also the only person who doesn't watch me like a bug under a microscope. He's the only person who's been truly friendly to me since I turned except for Eliza, and you said yourself that she's not a fighter. The rest of your people that you trust? They're loyal to you, not me. I'd rather have someone protect me because they actually don't want to see me die than someone who's collecting a paycheck and wondering why they got stuck with the assignment."

Rider's jaw unclenched and his eyes softened as he ran his thumb over my cheek. "I've never heard you mention anyone other than your family and that coworker you had when you worked for that company. I gathered even she wasn't really a true friend. You don't really have anyone to talk to, do you?"

I looked away. "I kept busy at work. I had no time for frivolous friendships and the ones I have from earlier in my life are pretty much relegated to Facebook since everyone's married or moved away."

Rider grabbed a fresh shirt and slid his arms through the sleeves. "Okay. I'll call in the dragon. He'd better not make me regret it."

EIGHT

Rider's office had gray walls and a darker gray carpet. No windows. No paintings. Black bookcases lined the wall behind his desk and were filled with leather-bound books I assumed to be older than dirt. His black lacquer desk was massive and held a state-of-the-art computer. Two leather chairs sat in front of it and a black leather sofa sat in the corner of the room next to the door.

Rider sat in the leather ergonomic chair behind the desk with his fingers steepled before him, the sleeves of his crimson button-down shirt pushed up to reveal his forearms. His hair was back in its band, gathered at the nape of his neck. As I sat on the edge of the desk, my fingers itched to run through the black strands and release it from its imprisonment again.

"There are two chairs and a sofa you could sit on," Rider said, as we waited for Daniel to arrive.

"Am I bothering you?"

"You're asstracting me." He turned his gaze up to meet mine. "I'm imagining you on my desk in a very different way."

Heat flooded my body as I imagined what he was imagining. I started to lean toward him, but remembered we were waiting on Daniel, who would arrive any minute, and I was still perturbed with Rider. I was having a bit of trouble recalling why at the moment, but I was sure I was.

"Why don't you have any pictures on the wall?" I asked to change the subject.

"I don't see any need to make my business office personal. All anyone who comes into this office needs to know is that I'll kill them if they turn on me."

"Sheesh," I said. "That's kind of harsh."

"Better harsh than stabbed in the back… or heart, in our case."

"I guess." I remembered the painting of his mother that had been hanging on the wall of his room prior to the night he killed Selander Ryan. "I saw that you took down your mother's portrait after what happened with Selander. Why did you remove it?"

"I no longer need it there."

"You *needed* it there?"

Rider picked up a gold pen and fidgeted with it for a moment. "I've been alive a long time, and the human portion of my life was just a tiny sliver. I barely remember what it felt like to be human, but the majority of my mother's life was human. I remember how she was, and I remember what she was twisted into after Ryan worked his evil on her. He went dark fast, but he always had darkness in him. I've seen other vampires start out decent and slowly give in to the dark pull of power that comes with being a vampire. I've carried that portrait of my mother as a human with me everywhere I've ever laid my head so I could see her gentle eyes first thing upon awakening, so I could be reminded of the power I wield, and how this power could make me turn something innocent and beautiful into a monster if I let it rule me. I looked into those eyes and remembered them looking into mine as I ended her life to save her from what she'd become." He set the pen down. "Looking at her every day was the closest thing I had to someone keeping me in line, so yeah,

I needed that portrait."

"And having crushed Selander Ryan's heart fulfills all that now?"

"No."

"I don't understand," I said. "What else has changed?"

"I no longer need a guilt-inducing portrait of someone I loved and lost to keep me from going dark. You put your trust in me that night and I will fight the darkness every day of my life to keep your eyes as kind and gentle as they are now, and to stay worthy of your trust. I don't just sleep better with you at my side, Danni. I need you next to me when I wake to remind me of what I have and what I cannot lose or worse... destroy."

My mouth opened, but nothing came out. What could I say to something so sweet... and heavy? From the time I'd met Rider, he seemed to carry the weight of the world on his shoulders, and now he'd practically told me I'd become the weight. I'd always known he cared for me and would do everything in his power to keep me safe, but I hadn't known it was because he needed me as some sort of reminder of his humanity and why he couldn't give in too much to the lure of the dark side. What if I gave in to the darkness? I would destroy both of us. Selander Ryan's villainous grin filled my mind, and I wondered if that was his endgame.

There was a quick knock at the door and Daniel stepped in. His shaggy multi-colored hair appeared to be finger-combed, if that, his jeans were full of holes, and his black T-shirt said VAMPIRES SUCK... "Somebody order a dragon?"

"Are you trying to order an ass beating wearing that shirt in here?" Rider asked.

Daniel held up one finger and turned to reveal the back, which read ...BETTER THAN YOUR MOM. "It's a compliment, man. Chillax."

"I'm already reconsidering this arrangement," Rider told me. "Hell, he might get you targeted by more than just my enemies or Ryan's minions."

"Minions?" Daniel turned and looked between me and Rider. "Those creepy, yellow, one-eyed, talking Twinkies?"

Rider's brow furrowed, and I choked back a laugh, never having seen him so totally perplexed. "No, Daniel, those are fictional characters from a children's movie," I told him. "Rider's talking about actual minions. You know, people who follow a leader like obedient lapdogs or servants."

"Oh good. Those creepy yellow things scare the dragon drops out of me."

"Now *I'm* reconsidering whether he's the right person to guard me."

"Guard you?" Daniel's eyes brightened. "I thought I was just going to be on door duty here at the bar."

"It's still a possibility," Rider told him. "Danni needs protection. I'll have a team on her at all times, but she needs someone at her side when she goes inside places the regular team may not be able to go inconspicuously, like family events, shopping, things of that nature. This will be a full-time day and night job. Any time she is out of my presence, you will be the main person watching over her, if you can handle the assignment."

"I can handle it." Daniel squared his shoulders.

"Let me make sure you fully understand this assignment." Rider stood and rounded the desk to stand before Daniel. "You stick to her side like glue, no matter what. You don't eat, you don't drink, you don't take a piss unless she's one hundred percent safe in a secure location. You don't let her out of your sight. You don't let her sleep. You don't let her get too thirsty. You don't get to take any breaks away from her, not even when she's with her family of hell-bitches and you're desperate to escape. If she's shot at, you take the bullet. If anyone follows her, you break them. If anyone attempts to hurt her, you don't just stop them, you kill them." He stepped closer until he was in Daniel's face. "If *you* touch her, I kill you. Slow.

Understood?"

"All except one thing," Daniel said, holding Rider's lethal glare with surprising calm.

"What?"

"Why can't I let her sleep?"

Rider stepped back and sat on the edge of the desk, his hip touching mine. "Danni was attacked by an incubus named Selander Ryan shortly before being turned—"

"Yeah, she told me how she was attacked and you saved her by redirecting her change and then you killed that guy," Daniel said.

Rider turned his head and narrowed his eyes at me. *You told him?*

I told him about the night I was changed and my transition into being a vampire, and that you killed the guy who attacked me. I didn't tell him that Selander Ryan was your brother or anything personal about you.

You shouldn't have told him anything. You're still newly turned but you need to get used to not revealing your age or sire to anyone right now.

Everyone in this bar knows you're my sire and when you sired me.

Not everyone, just my nest. People I trust. Don't tell anyone else. Do you understand?

Yes, master, I snapped, and Rider's nostrils flared.

"Uh, guys," Daniel interrupted. "I know you're doing that vampire mind-talking thing, but from where I'm standing, it's awkward and kind of just plain rude. Just saying."

Rider muttered under his breath and turned his attention back to the dragon shifter. "So you know who Selander Ryan is, and what he is to her. You were also there when she had a nightmare at The Cloud Top. The nightmare was about him. She had another one this morning, and he was in it too. This time, he attempted to strangle her and what he did in the dream happened to her physical body. Had I not been lying right next to her, she could have been killed."

"Wait, wait, wait." Daniel was shaking his head, his hands held out before him. "Okay, first question: Can a vampire even die of strangulation?"

"No," Rider answered, "but it's damn painful, and I'm sure Ryan wouldn't have just strangled her. He would have taken her head off. That would have killed her."

Daniel stood there for a moment, blinking, then shook his head as if shaking himself out of the image Rider's answer had given him. "Okay, my second question is, didn't you kill Selander Ryan?"

"Yes, I did."

"You think you might need to kill him again? A little bit harder this time, so, ya know, it really takes?"

"The thought crossed my mind," Rider said dryly. "However, seeing as how I crushed his heart into nothing, I'm not sure how I could kill him any harder than I already did. Dark magic is at play here, so I'm going to need to converse with some witches and figure out what he's doing and how he's doing it. While I'm working on that, I need someone watching over Danni to ensure none of the evil bastards he controlled while physically alive are still under his power and after her, and that she doesn't sleep and fall prey to him. I'll be honest with you, Daniel. I'm asking if you're willing to give your life for hers, because if anything happens to her under your watch, you can believe me when I tell you death at the enemy's hands will be a lot more merciful than death at mine."

"I believe you," Daniel said without a trace of his usual wisecracking tone. "I know what she means to you and I understand, but you don't need to be concerned. She's a sweet girl. I'll protect her with my life because it's what I'd do anyway. I'm the man for the job."

Rider's eyes narrowed just a fraction as he held Daniel in his line of sight and seemed to look through him, right into his soul, as his fingers curled around the edge of the desk and his whole body tensed. I tried to push into his mind, but, as usual, it was locked up tighter than Fort Knox. He released his hold on the desk as his shoulders relaxed. Whatever he'd been thinking having run its course. "Fine," he said, nodding. "You'll need to communicate silently with the others on the team, and I'll need access to communicate with you at any given time. I'll need to bond with you."

"Whoa." Daniel backed up a step. "Is that like something I'll have to take my pants off for?"

I slapped a hand over my mouth to keep from laughing as Rider's face scrunched into a mask of grotesque horror.

"What?" he asked. "No. Just give me your wrist."

"Why? What are you going to do with—" Daniel's eyes grew wide as Rider appeared before him in a flash of movement, grabbed his wrist and took a bite. "Dude! Not cool!"

"Oh shut up, you're fine," Rider said after sealing the wound and stepping back, his lips puckered like he'd bitten into a lemon. "You weren't joking about his blood being spicy," he told me before turning back to Daniel. "Do you mainline hot sauce or something?"

"What? No," Daniel said as he marveled over the instantly healed flesh at his wrist. "What the hell was that for?"

"I have to taste your blood to be able to connect with you."

"That's like the worst pickup line ever."

"You sure this is the guy you want watching your back?" Rider asked. "I can't go five minutes without wanting to peel his wings off and drop him from the top of the building."

"Dude, you really have to work through those violent impulses," Daniel told him. "Have you tried journaling?"

"He's the one I want," I told Rider, smiling at the irritation etched into his face. "I trust he'll have my back, and he's got a good sense of humor that I think will help him survive meeting my family if he has to."

Rider's mouth slowly turned into a wide smile as he turned his attention back to Daniel.

"Oh, that's kinda creepy," Daniel said, noticing Rider's sudden delight. "I got used to the dark and stormy look. This tickled pink look is weirding me out. What's so wonderful?"

"You're going to love her mother," Rider told him, "and I'm going to love knowing all about it when you get to meet her." He sobered. "All right. Let's finish this bond. Come here."

Daniel hesitantly stepped forward, his brow heavily creased, and Rider touched his fingertips to the dragon shifter's temples. He held his gaze, and I noticed Daniel's shoulders relax as his eyes glazed over. They stood like that for about five minutes as I watched, fascinated, and felt the prickle of power around them. Rider removed his fingers from Daniel's temples and stepped back. Daniel swayed a little, but quickly regained his footing. "Man, I don't know what you did, but that was weird as—Whoa!" He grabbed his head. "You're in my head!"

Rider grinned and nodded. He recaptured Daniel's gaze, held it for a moment, and arched an eyebrow. Daniel nodded and Rider closed his eyes and pinched the bridge of his nose, a gesture I thought only I could make him do, and I deduced he'd asked Daniel to respond to him and Daniel had done so by nodding instead of speaking into Rider's mind. The annoyed look he gave Daniel next followed by the "Oh!" dawning of realization on Daniel's face confirmed my deduction a moment later. Rider tilted his head toward me, and a second later, I heard Daniel's voice in my mind.

Um… hey Danni.

Hey, Daniel.

"Holy crap," Daniel blurted out loud. "This is weird."

"You've never communicated telepathically with anyone else?" Rider asked.

"The wolves could all communicate this way with their

pack leaders and the pack leaders could communicate with all of them, but I was never an official member of any of the packs I was with."

"What about other dragon shifters?" Rider asked.

"Yeah, we weren't exactly chummy. If you recall, Imortian shifters were created as a form of punishment. There were a few groups of various shifters that banded together and I'd heard they could do this mind-talking thing, but I was never part of any group."

"Yeah, well, don't make me regret bringing you into this one," Rider warned him. "This bond was purely for necessity to allow more effective communication. I don't completely trust you yet, but I trust Danni and you're who she picked. I wouldn't suggest pissing her off either after what she did to the wolf last night, although I wouldn't mind seeing if she can Hulk out and slam a dragon around by its tail."

"That's what she reminded me of!" Daniel said, his eyes lighting up. "From the first *Avengers* movie! She totally Hulk-smashed her. I knew I'd seen that somewhere before."

"I know, right? Total Hulk versus Loki."

"Okay, boys," I interrupted. "You two have clearly bonded enough. I have things to do and Daniel has accepted the job, so I'm going to go now if you're done with your Marvel fanboying."

"What? I can't be proud of you?" Rider asked, grinning.

I rolled my eyes. "I really need to go so I can get some things done before my session with Eliza."

"She's working with you on strengthening your mental blocking?"

"Yes."

"Good." Rider reached out, dipped his fingers inside the front of my waistband, and pulled me over to him, not stopping until I was flush against his body. He moved his hand around my waist and let it rest just over the swell of my ass. "Do you need anything? Blood? Money?"

I hadn't fed since Daniel and would prefer Rider's blood to bagged, but I recognized the display of testosterone for what it was and didn't want any part of it. I certainly had never accepted money from Rider before. "Blood in my fridge and money in my bank account. I'm sure it won't be very long until I find a new job."

Rider's eyes narrowed. "We'll revisit the job thing," he said before lowering his head and capturing my mouth. He had my lips parted and his tongue deep inside before I knew what hit me. Heat pooled in my body as I grabbed a fistful of shirt and held on tight to the man making my legs two useless towers of pure gelatin. The knowledge that Daniel was in the room was the only thing that kept me from throwing myself on the desk and pulling Rider down on top of me, and I could feel the arrogant devil's satisfaction of knowing exactly what he was doing to me, and in front of a man he clearly felt the need to intimidate. I had no proof, but as he nipped my bottom lip and pulled back a fraction, I was pretty sure there'd been some vampire magic in that kiss.

"Be careful," he said, his voice low and irritatingly nowhere near as breathless as it should have been after the whammy he'd just put on me. "Only drink bagged blood and return to me at least an hour before sunrise," he added, louder and with more authority. "I have plans that require a good deal of energy."

I gritted my teeth together as he looked at Daniel with a sly grin, making sure the dragon shifter knew what he was hinting at. *I could always say no.*

Rider returned his gaze to me and the grin turned more wolfish. He knew damn well after that kiss there was no way I would say no to him. My heart was still trying to pound its way out of my chest and if he wasn't still holding me to him, I would have hit the floor the moment we came up for air. He handed me my purse from where it sat on his desk, playfully smacked me on the ass and gave me a gentle push toward the door. "Guard her with your life, dragon breath."

"That's my job," Daniel said, no emotion on his face as he stood there with his hands in his pockets and waited for me to exit the room before following me out the door.

"Oh, one more thing, Daniel."

We both turned to see Rider casually leaning back against the desk, his arms crossed, and a shit-eating grin on his face. His power pulsed, materializing as a golden glow around him. His eyes turned completely amber as the power filled the room, seeming to suck all the air out of it. He winked, and the door slammed shut.

I shook my head at the ridiculous display of power as Daniel stood there staring at the closed door. "I'm not sure how to respond to that," he finally said.

"You don't," I told him, grabbing his arm and prodding him along. "You just keep me safe and he won't unleash some of that on you."

"Correct me if I'm wrong, but was that kind of like the vampire equivalent of 'My dick is bigger than yours'?" Daniel asked as we passed the bar now being tended by a vampire I wasn't that familiar with.

"A little of that and a little of warning what he can do if he gets pissed," I advised as we passed the bouncer at the door, another bulky guy, but Latino and with a shifter vibe, and stepped out onto the street. I'd slathered the special sunscreen Rider kept me supplied with all over my skin so I wasn't burning, but I didn't exactly feel comfortable. "You have your truck? My car is at my apartment."

"In the main lot," Daniel said, turning left toward the parking lot the bar patrons used. He chuckled to himself. "That was pretty cute. I'll give him the power thing. The other part... Well, he can think whatever he wants to make himself feel more superior."

I looked at Daniel out the side of my eye and raised my eyebrow.

"Sweetheart, I'm a dragon," he said. "When I shift,

everything gets bigger."

Great. Now I was thinking about dragon dicks.

The parking space next to my car was empty, so Daniel slid right in. I immediately picked out one of Rider's shifters sitting on a bench with a magazine. He nodded at me as we got out of the truck, gave Daniel a curious once-over, and returned to pretending to read the magazine.

"This mental communication thing is so freaking weird, but in a totally cool way," Daniel commented as we passed the shifter and headed for the entrance to my building.

"Did you two just converse?" I asked, glancing back at the shifter.

"Yeah, I guess you didn't?"

"Nope. I really haven't used the telepathy with anyone but Rider and Eliza. She's a counselor for vampires, primarily helping the newbies understand the changes and all the ins and outs of the lifestyle." I grabbed my mail out of the box and we climbed the stairs to my floor. I immediately checked the corner at the end of the hall and sure enough, a vampire was there, hidden in shadow. I wouldn't have even noticed had I not already known that was the spot the same guy had previously guarded my apartment from. "Rider wasted no time assembling the team."

"He doesn't seem like the type to waste a lot of time."

"He has a lot of important matters on his plate," I said as I unlocked my door and stepped inside.

"Still, it's kind of weird that someone with so much time isn't more relaxed." Daniel closed and locked my door as I filtered through the mail I'd collected, sorting bills from the junk. "What is he, like a hun—"

"Hey!" I pointed my finger at him. "First rule of vampires. You don't talk about vampires' age. I thought you were told this already."

"Well, yeah, I was told not to ask a vampire his or her

age."

"Well, you don't ask a vampire another vampire's age either. You don't even think to ask a vampire another vampire's age. In fact, you don't even allow yourself the curiosity of wondering how old a vampire is in your own mind. That's the first thing Eliza drills in new vampires' heads. It's a very touchy subject."

"But why?" Daniel stood there, arms out, palms up, utter bafflement on his face.

I started to explain it the way it had been explained to me, but remembered how unhappy Rider was that I'd told Daniel about Selander Ryan. Even though he'd told him about him, I had apparently done so before he'd thought it wise. Rider had been alive as a vampire a heck of a long time, so I trusted he knew what he was talking about when he warned me about doing things. "Just don't do it, Daniel. Very bad things could happen. I requested for you to be my personal guard and I don't want you to get killed for something stupid, and then I have to have someone I'm not comfortable with breathing down my neck any time I'm away from Rider. As much as I enjoy being with Rider, I can't stay pent up in his lair day and night."

"Is it really a lair? Like, a coffin and everything?"

"No." I rolled my eyes. "It's not a real lair. It's just … Rider's place is very small. He's as efficient with his place as he is with his time."

"Efficient with his time, huh? So he lasts, like, what… five minutes?"

"What do you—" Realizing what Daniel was implying, I rolled my eyes. "What is it with you two? And for the record, that's one area where Rider Knight takes his time and makes sure the job gets done," I added.

"Yeah, yeah, yeah, I don't need to hear you wax poetic about how amazing he is. I was there when he melted your panties off in his office," Daniel said, plopping down onto my couch to pick up a *Cosmopolitan*. "As for what's going on between us, he started it. For a big-time master vampire who can slam doors and people with just his mind and is lord over a whole bunch of people too scared to even look at him the wrong way your boyfriend doesn't seem too secure in his ability to hold on to you. Very interesting."

I glanced at the red blinking light on the phone that sat on my end table and decided I needed my strength up before I listened to the messages it held. "I don't know what you're talking about," I said as I tossed my mail onto the coffee table and walked over to my kitchen area to open the fridge and grab a bag of blood.

"He's jealous," Daniel said. "I had a good talk with him in the bar last night. He didn't say it, but he wasn't happy you and I seem to get along so well. Hell, I thought I might never see you again with the way he was looking at me, yet here I am assigned as your personal guard because it's what you requested. I just find it curious he would allow it. He didn't seem to really like the idea."

"He doesn't seem to really like *you*," I pointed out as I dumped the blood into my Dollywood mug and put it in the microwave to warm up. "Rider isn't my prison warden. He's protective of me, but not possessive. He doesn't control me."

"Could he if he wanted to?"

"He could make me do anything he wanted if he desired. Fortunately for me, he's a better guy than that."

"So, why did you request me?"

The microwave beeped, and I took out the mug of disgusting blood and stirred it around with a spoon, regretting my decision to skip drinking from Rider before I'd left. His blood was thinner, yummier, always clot-free, and the fact I couldn't actually see it as I swallowed it down was the cherry on top. "I wasn't comfortable with Rider's suggestions."

"That's it? The whole answer?" Daniel asked as I sat next to him on the end of the couch closest to the phone. "You haven't even seen me fight."

"You breathe fire."

"When I'm a dragon."

"Grey told Rider enough about you for him to know what he was getting into with you. If you couldn't hold your own in a fight, he would have never agreed to have you as my personal guard." I advised. "Besides, there's a whole team watching me and I'm not entirely useless. Rider's connected with me and will feel it if I'm in danger. I picked you because you're new to Rider's group, and I really am too. I feel comfortable with him and I get along well enough with Eliza, but everyone else watches me like they're waiting to see what I do or what chaos my existence creates. Two of his people were already killed for betraying him because of me, there are women who want me dead just for sharing his bed and he's lost men to Selander Ryan and his minions because they were the ones chosen to protect me and they were fatally wounded in the process. I don't feel very welcome by most of his people, but they are loyal to him, so they do as he tells them. I'd just rather not have any of them close to me. I'd rather my personal guard be someone I can talk to, and last night in the bar was the first time in a long while that I've really talked to someone as a friend."

"It was for me too," he said. "You don't have to worry, Danni. I meant what I said in Rider's office. I know I'm a wise-ass, but I'm serious about you being safe. You're a sweet girl, and I really like you, even though you're drinking blood out of a mug with Dolly Parton on it, and that's about the wrongest thing I've seen in my whole damn life."

I snorted and nearly choked on the swig of blood I'd just swallowed.

"Don't laugh while you're drinking," he said. "If that stuff comes out your nose, I'm going to throw up and die. I can fight, maim, and kill your enemies all day long, but seeing other people's blood shoot out your nose is where I draw the line."

"Stop!" I swatted him on the arm. "I already feel

ghastly enough doing this."

"You feel ghastly? Imagine poor Dolly. That poor woman had no idea what that mug was going to be used for."

I set the mug on the coffee table and wiped my eyes. "I know, it's horrible. I need to get mugs without people or cartoon characters on them."

"I'm just playing with you," Daniel said, smiling. "It's good to hear you laugh. You seemed really upset about the whole Selander Ryan nightmare thing and if Rider's agreed to have me be your personal guard, he's got to be worried too, and that makes me wonder if I should be worried. The two of you are pretty sure he can only get to you in your sleep?"

"I don't know," I said, sobering. "Do you think people can crawl up out of Hell once they've been cast there?"

"Depending where they were in hell and how they arrived there, I know they can."

"What do you mean?" I asked, my blood chilling in my veins, "and how could you know that?"

"Easy," he answered. "I escaped from Hell to get here."

NINE

"Danni." Daniel waved his hand in front of my face. "Did you have an aneurysm or something? Snap out of it."

I blinked out of the stupor I'd fallen under and shook my head. "You wanna run that escaped from Hell bit by me again?"

"Sure," he said, eying me cautiously. "You promise to hear me out? You look like you're about to run for your life, and I know vampires are pretty fast. I'd hate to lose you my first day on the job."

I looked down at myself and realized I was gripping the edge of the couch, my knees together, my body turned away from Daniel. I was ready to spring from my seat and flee, and I hadn't even known I was getting myself into position. I forced myself to relax. Rider wouldn't have set me up with a personal bodyguard he had serious doubts about. "Rider knows about your time in Hell?"

"He had a whole file on me before you two even arrived in Pigeon Forge. It was in the file. To be completely accurate, I was in Hades, which is part of Hell."

"I thought Hell and Hades were the same thing."

"Eh…" He shrugged his shoulders. "Kind of. Hell is its own realm, and there are several layers to it. If you're a truly evil person or you've made a pact with the devil, your soul goes to the fire pits when you die. Hades is another area you can be thrown in, body and all."

"So you were actually alive while you were there?"

"Very alive," he answered. "Selander Ryan was killed so he wouldn't be in Hades. He'd be in one of the even worse layers. The only known way of escaping is to get through the Hades layer and find a portal. There are hellhounds and demons blocking every exit. I can't imagine fighting a way through them without a corporeal body."

"Without a corporeal body, couldn't you pass right through them?"

"No. Souls have mass there, but without a corporeal body, there's not much power to them. There's no way they could fight their way through what's down there keeping all the bad shit in. If Selander Ryan is in Hell and reaching out to you from there, he's doing it through some serious black magic."

"If he's in Hell? Where else do you think he could be?"

"There's always Purgatory," Daniel suggested. "Sort of an in-between realm when you haven't done enough evil to get into Hell, but you haven't done enough good deeds to get into Heaven. From what you've told me about him, he doesn't seem like the type of guy to have done any good deeds, so I wouldn't bet on him being there. I know you said Rider crushed his heart. What happened to the rest of his body?"

I thought back to that night and shrugged. "Everything happened so fast. One moment he was about to snap my neck, the next moment his heart was in Rider's hand, and then it was dust on the ground. My focus was on Rider after that. I didn't pay any attention to what happened to Selander Ryan's body. Is that important?"

Daniel's brow creased as he watched me and I realized he'd think it weird I was focused on Rider when it had been me under attack and Rider had just defeated the enemy. It wouldn't be a time to worry about him. Not knowing Selander had been Rider's brother, Daniel wouldn't understand that. I focused on the wall in my mind, careful to keep any random thoughts Daniel shouldn't know from leaking out. I didn't think Rider had given him enough ability to actually read thoughts not directed toward him, but I wasn't taking chances. It was bad enough having Rider dipping into my mind whenever he wanted. I didn't need two men in there.

"It's definitely important," Daniel finally said. "If someone preserved his body and was skilled enough in black magic, they might be able to use his body as a way to get him out of Hell, or at least provide a way for him to communicate with those outside Hell, like you."

"Well, that's just great," I said, making a mental note to ask Rider what had happened to Selander's body. "So... you were there, and you found a portal to here?"

"I was with a small group. We'd already been cursed with the ability to shift, but in Hades you can't shift. You're on your own. We looked all over for a way out, but Hades is huge, dark, and deadly. It's the universe's most horrific prison. There is no day or night, just endless time spent running, fighting, or hiding. That's if you're lucky. You don't want to know what happens to the unlucky there. If you can find a portal and fight your way through it, you can escape because you aren't dead and don't really belong there, but if you don't find it in time, eventually you lose yourself and become part of Hades itself."

"But you escaped. You found a portal."

"I told you about Fairuza, the queen of Imortia. After she was defeated, Zaira and Addix formed a search party and, using some sort of blood magic, came back for those of us who Fairuza had imprisoned. Addix had been imprisoned the same way, but he had been cursed to hold the spirit of a unicorn which backfired on Fairuza. He could null the magic that kept the rest of us from shifting and he could find portals. He was the one who originally led a team out to get Zaira and retake Imortia to begin with. Unfortunately, I wasn't with him on that mission and a lot of the people who were imprisoned when I was didn't make it out. We might have been alive when we were cast into Hades, but if you die there, you stay dead."

"That sounds awful," I said, knowing it was a dumb statement. Of course it sounded awful. He was talking about Hell. I couldn't think of anything else to say though.

"Sometimes I thought dying there was the best thing you could do. I'm not sure if those who died went to another level of Hell or maybe they went somewhere else entirely. Honestly, they weren't bad people."

"Why were you cast into Hades?" I picked up my mug and stirred the blood before it could cool and congeal.

"Fairuza was a tyrant. If you committed what she considered to be a minor crime, she'd strip you of your immortality and leave you caged near her palace as a public display that no one was above her rule. Casting prisoners into Hades started off as a punishment for only the most cruel of villains. Murderers went there. Baby snatchers. Unicorn abusers. One day she just snapped and started cursing people she couldn't make bow to her with the spirits of animals. If you still didn't bow, off you went to Hades."

I sipped the warm blood and waited for Daniel to tell me his story, but he didn't. I drained the mug and set it on the table before turning to face him fully and rested my hand on his forearm. "Why did she cast *you* into Hades? What was your crime?"

Daniel looked down at my hand for a moment before standing and walking over to the window. "Fairuza killed the woman I loved right in front of me," he said, shoving his hands into his pockets as he stared out the window, "so I grabbed a sword from the guard closest to me and attempted to cut her down just as swiftly, but I wasn't quick enough. I'd never fought before, had never even held a sword before that moment. She imprisoned me in her dungeon, subjected me to a mixture of daily beatings and training. She thought the best punishment for trying to kill her was to force me to protect her. The beatings were to break me. The training was to make me into a fighter fit to protect her royal ass. The training turned me into a fighter, but she didn't break me. They couldn't beat the image of the love of my life being killed out of me. They couldn't beat out my desire to make Fairuza pay."

"Why did she kill her?" I asked.

"She was too beautiful. Fairuza had a lot of consorts and she didn't like for them to pay special attention to other women. One of her consorts was an artist. He saw Salia walking through the village and, inspired by her beauty, he sketched her. Fairuza found the portrait and the next night she personally came to Salia's home and knocked on the door. Salia opened the door and Fairuza ran her sword straight through her heart. She died instantly, not even ten minutes after she'd accepted my marriage proposal."

My mouth fell open as tears streamed down my face. "Daniel, I'm so sorry. I can't imagine what that must have felt like."

"The last I saw her, she was lying in a puddle of her own blood. I wasn't at her burial. I was in the dungeon. I was there for a year before Fairuza cursed me with the dragon spirit and brought me up to the upper levels of the palace to be her new guard. She'd done the same thing to others and, with their spirits completely broken, they served her. It didn't work on me."

"You turned on her."

"I tried to roast the bitch, but she had magic on her side. She'd created some sort of shield to protect her from flames, so all I did was piss her off. She cast me into Hades with a group of other so-called criminals who had defied her. At first, I didn't even care. I'd not only lost Salia, I'd failed her twice. I did nothing to protect her from Fairuza. The sword was sticking out her back before I even knew what had happened. I should have killed Fairuza then, but

I couldn't get past her guards. I took all that abuse from her guards for an entire year so I could finally make her pay for what she did to Salia, and I failed again. I was ready to die when I entered Hades."

"I'm glad you didn't," I said. "I understand it has to be hard to live with what happened, but you didn't fail her. From what you told me last night, there had to be a revolution. If you had killed Fairuza, then it would have thrown Imortia into chaos. She was defeated when she was supposed to be. I'm sure that wherever Salia is, she doesn't blame you for what happened."

"She wouldn't," Daniel said. "She was too kind for that, but I know I was weak then. I wasn't a fighter. I am now."

"I believe you. I may not know the details of what Hades is like, but I know surviving it couldn't be done by the weak."

Daniel looked at me, not a single trace of humor on his normally jovial face. "You remind me of Salia. There's something in your eyes, a vulnerability, that's achingly familiar. The thought of those eyes glazed over in death scares the hell out of me. I'll never let that happen. You don't have to be afraid of me because I've been to Hades, Danni. It made me a better fighter. It made me a man who will take out anyone or anything who dares try to hurt you. If this Selander Ryan guy found a way to escape Hell, he'll still fry. I'll burn him until there's nothing left to send back there."

I just sat there, staring at Daniel. He was a wise-cracking goofball with rainbow colored hair and a penchant for annoying the hell out of people. I didn't completely recognize the man standing in my apartment telling me Selander Ryan wouldn't get to me through him, but I believed him.

"I know, I know," he said, scratching the back of his head. "I just got real serious. I've seen and experienced some seriously bad shit, so I try to find humor in everything to keep from losing my damn mind. Hades stays with you. I screw around as much as I can to even out everything in my head. When it comes down to life or death matters, though, I don't play around."

"Well, as far as traits go in bodyguards, that's a pretty good one," I said, feeling better about my decision to have Daniel in place as my personal guard.

The phone rang, and we both looked at it. Unease slithered through my stomach as I listened to the ringing and watched the red light flash, indicating messages I still hadn't scrounged up enough fortitude to check.

"You gonna get that?" Daniel asked.

"Letting it go to voicemail so I can listen to all the angry messages from my mother in the order in which they were received," I answered. "I never checked in while out of town. I wanted to actually enjoy the time away." I waited until the phone stopped ringing and the little number next to the red flashing light changed, indicating another message had been left.

"Here goes," I said, bracing myself for emotional and psychological impact as I pressed the button to listen to the messages.

Danni, this is your mother, came the first message left shortly after I'd last left my apartment. *I just saw an infomercial on the television about breast enhancement pills. It says you can go up two full cup sizes just by taking the pills. It won't happen as quick as the surgery, but since you can't have the surgery, these pills are the next best thing. I'm going to email you the information.*

I looked over to see Daniel frowning. "Since you can't get the surgery? You were going to get a boob job?"

I groaned and waited for the next message, which turned out to be my mother exactly one hour later. *Danni, this is your mother again. They have a tea too. It speeds up the process. I've been looking at their website. If you start taking the pills right now, along with the tea and the special massage oil, you might see results by the time your sister's wedding rolls around.*

"Massage oil?" Daniel grinned like an evil imp. "You need any help with application?"

"Do you want Rider to kill you?" I asked, shooting him a glare.

"You have a point," he said, "but there are worse ways a guy could go out."

You can get a monthly subscription for just under fifty dollars a month, my mother's voice continued. *It says there might be a slight maple scent due to the amount of fenugreek in the mixture, but I don't think a man would mind that if it meant you had breasts.*

"I think I'd prefer a more tropical or maybe some kind of flowery scent," Daniel said, dropping onto the other end of the couch and settling back. "I'm a bit confused though. You have breasts. I haven't stuck my head in there and given them a good sniff, but I'm sure they smell just fine. What's with the maple-scented pills?"

I rolled my eyes and skipped to the next message, simultaneously wishing the floor would open up and swallow me whole. I skipped through three more messages touting the benefits of the breast enhancement pills and a fourth message in which my mother announced she'd ordered me a kit and it was on its way. The next message in line came from my grandmother. *Danni, this is your grandmother,* she announced as I heard her tiny rat dog yipping in the background. *Have you seen this infomercial about this breast enhancement machine? It's called the Jug-Jolter 2000. Just a few zaps each day and it'll plump your little stubs into actual breasts. It's on sale for under two hundred dollars if you act now.*

"Holy shit," Daniel exclaimed. "You're not gonna electrocute your tits, are you? What's wrong with your family?"

I sighed and skipped to the next message. *Danni! Why aren't you picking up? The price is only good if you act now. They're throwing in a massage cream to round out your breasts and make them nice and supple. Don't you want nice, supple breasts?* I felt a vibration and looked over at Daniel to see his entire body shaking with laughter as his face turned red with the effort to hold it in. I skipped to the next message. *I bought the Jug-Jolter before the deal ran out. I upgraded the shipping, so you'll have it in three to five days at the latest. You owe me two hundred and thirty dollars to cover it, plus the tax and shipping, unless you want this to be your next Christmas present. You'll need money for good bras once you have something to put in them!* I skipped through two messages of my mother asking where I was and why I wasn't returning her calls before reaching a message from my sister. *Hey Danni, my maid of honor and her husband decided they couldn't be considerate enough to wait until after my wedding to start their family so she's pregnant and eating everything in sight. She looks like an absolute whale in the dress. I'm just going to make you my maid of honor, which really works out better anyway because now your dress doesn't have to match the others exactly and we can work with your flaws. Meet me at the dress shop Wednesday at four. Oh, have you seen those TV ads for those breast enhancement pills? I ordered you some since you can't have the surgery. Start taking them as soon as you get them and maybe you can snag a husband for yourself at my wedding if things don't work out with your boss or that Rider guy! Please don't get knocked up before my wedding. Seriously, people can be so selfish. Toodles!* The last message was from my mother asking why I hadn't returned her calls and why didn't I have a cell phone like a normal person of this decade.

"I have some questions."

I turned toward Daniel and sighed. "What?"

"Are all the women in your family nuts?"

"Pretty much," I answered.

"Second question. What's with their breast obsession? I don't know men *that* obsessed with breast size and we're generally the ones who like to do stuff with them."

That was a question I'd wondered my whole life. I was pretty obsessed with my lack of breasts myself, but I thought maybe I wouldn't be if I hadn't been reminded of my flat-chested state on a regular basis. "Every woman in my family is pretty well endowed," I advised. "No one knows what happened to me and they just want to fix the problem, I guess."

"What problem? I know I'm from another realm, but I'm pretty sure it's a universal fact that breasts come in all different shapes and sizes. There's nothing abnormal about the way you're built. From where I'm sitting, there's nothing wrong at all."

I opened my mouth to respond, but couldn't think of anything to say. Embarrassed by the topic of conversation, I crossed my arms over my meager chest and looked at the phone, actually hoping it would ring and give me something to do instead of trying to scramble up a response.

"I've made you uncomfortable," Daniel said. "Sorry. I just have one more question. Why do they think you don't have a cell phone?"

I arched my eyebrow at him. "If those people were your family, would you give them a way to reach you at any given time?"

Daniel laughed, shaking his head. "No, no, I don't think I would. They have to know you have a cell phone though. Who doesn't have a cell phone? Even I have a cellphone and I'm from a realm that never heard of them before some of us jumped through a portal to get here."

"I told them my cellphone is a work phone and I'm not allowed to use it for personal calls. They think I'm living on poverty level and can't afford a personal cell phone and I just let them think that. Whatever buys me a small amount of peace."

He nodded. "I have another question."

"I thought your last question was the last one you had."

"Questions are like bunnies. They multiply."

I groaned. "What?"

"They kept saying you couldn't have the surgery. What surgery?"

"I was going to get a boob job!" I snapped, feeling his judgment. "I was attacked right before the scheduled date and when my family asked why I didn't have it I had to tell them the doctor said it was too risky due to an issue with my blood type, which really was kind of the truth since vampires bleed out so easily and any kind of surgery is a major risk."

"Well, I'm glad you didn't get the surgery," he said. "I don't think you'd look good with big ol' jugs on your small frame. Big breasts really aren't everything."

"Says the guy who was just recently bragging about how when he shifts into a dragon, everything gets bigger."

"That's a whole different matter," he said. "Interesting you remember that factoid."

"It was like five minutes ago that you said it," I reminded him, earning a laugh in response. It was actually a bit of a relief to see Daniel back to his teasing self. The seriousness he'd displayed a moment ago while talking about Salia and his time in Hades had left me feeling uneasy. I had one dramatic, overpowering force of nature in my life. Two would probably suffocate me.

"So they don't know you're a vampire?"

"Of course not. I can't just go around telling people."

He nodded his understanding. "Guess your sister doesn't have to worry about you rudely getting pregnant and ruining her wedding."

"Yeah, she's a bit on the conceited side," I said, understanding where he was going.

"A bit?"

"My mother and grandmother spoiled her. She was the perfect, beautiful one, and it's all she knows."

"If that's all she knows, sounds like she's pretty ignorant."

"You're talking about my family," I said, allowing my irritation to slip into my tone. "They're not perfect, but they're my blood."

He held his hands up. "Understood. Don't slam me around by my tail."

"As tempting as that is…" I stood and walked over to the kitchen sink with my mug. "I need to update my resume and send it out to some prospects before my appointment with Eliza. Make yourself comfortable. I know you couldn't have gotten much sleep since you were in a meeting with Rider right before sunrise and then got called in today, so feel free to take a nap. Rider will have the perimeter pretty covered."

"If I sleep, you might sleep, and that can't happen. Do what you need to do. I didn't take this job thinking it'd be easy or comfortable."

I finished cleaning out the mug and dried my hands on my pants as I crossed the room into my bedroom and sat down at my desk to boot up my laptop. I deleted a ton of emails my mother had sent me about the breast enhancement pills, paid bills, checked my bank balance, and pulled up my resume to update before uploading it to a job search site.

"Hey, Daniel," I yelled out into the living area where I'd left him on the couch. "Can you change your shirt before my session with Eliza? I know it's a joke, but it can offend some vamps."

He walked into the room. "I don't have anything with me. You have anything manly I can borrow? I don't want the other guys on security detail trying to kick my ass if I walk out of here in glitter and lace."

"Lucky for you, I have a ton of T-shirts in the closet."

"Awesome," Daniel said, rifling through my T-shirt collection. "You have some cool bands in here. This realm's music is great."

"Can't go wrong with classic rock," I said, glancing at the Guns N Roses T-shirt he'd pulled free of its hanger. My glance stuck as he pulled his T-shirt over his head, revealing a six-pack and pecs that looked hard enough to deflect bullets. Although lean, his arms were corded muscle and there was a treasure trail leading from his naval down to somewhere I had no business thinking about.

"Something wrong?" he asked, pausing with the old shirt on the floor and the one pilfered from my closet halfway over his forearms.

I shook my head, unable to find my voice as I wondered how I'd thought of him as just an average young guy and cursed the universe for once again planting me with two very attractive alpha male types. The last time that had happened, very bad things occurred and frankly, I'd had my fill of attractive hunks who turned out to be psychotic.

TEN

"Everything all right?" Daniel asked as he took a left and we headed toward Eliza's office.

"Yes," I answered as I continued to stare out the window. "Everything's fine."

"Are you thinking about dealing with your sister at the dress shop tomorrow?"

"No, I purposely avoid thinking of my family as much as possible."

"Did you get your resume sent out everywhere you wanted to?"

"I sent it out for every position I was qualified to do." I heard chuckling and glanced over at Daniel to see a huge smile on his face. "What?"

"Nothing." He shrugged, the wattage on the smile growing even brighter. "Are you, uh, qualified for a lot of positions?"

"I'm not talking about those kind of positions." I smacked his arm, earning more laughter for my effort. "Act like a professional."

"Hey, I'm just doing research," he said. "If I'm supposed to be guarding your body, I should know what it's capable of doing."

"You're so immature," I said, cutting a sideways glance at him. Since he'd changed his shirt in my room, I couldn't really look at him long without seeming to develop x-ray vision and see all those hard muscles I knew were hiding under the black fabric. "How old are you anyway?"

"Twenty-seven," he answered. "You?"

"Twenty-eight." I'd been hoping he was even younger. I'd never really been into younger guys and I didn't like how I couldn't look at him now without thinking of that treasure trail. "I'm older than you. You're only twenty-seven. You're a younger guy."

"Yes, that is how age works." His brow creased as he studied me for a moment. "Are you sure you're all right? You've been acting kind of weird since we left your apartment."

"Weird how?"

"I don't know." He frowned. "You're squirmy."

"I am not squirmy."

"Yeah, you're pretty squirmy." He put his attention back on the road. "Do you have enough of that sunscreen on? Rider will skin my scales off if you start sizzling under my watch."

Ah, Rider. Hot Rider. Sexy Rider. *My Rider.* Why was I even thinking about Daniel's treasure trail when I'd already had the pleasure of finding the treasure at the end of Rider's? I was content with what Rider had. Hell, I was more than content. A woman couldn't ask for anything more, and I wasn't. I looked over at Daniel with his rainbow-colored hair and silver nose ring and shook my head. Okay, so the guy had a nice body, and it had taken me by surprise. I was feeling guilty for my very brief moment of ogling. That was all.

"What is it?" he asked, shooting me a curious sideways glance.

"Your hair is ridiculous."

"Gee, thanks. You look nice today too."

"Sorry," I mumbled. "I just mean... You're my

bodyguard now. It's not a professional color, or colors, to be exact. Are you going to dye it back to its original color?"

"I never dyed it these colors," he said. "I'm Imortian. Multi-colored hair isn't all that strange there."

My mouth dropped open as I gawked. "That's natural?"

"Yep."

My gaze fell to his crotch and my cheeks filled with heat as I struggled to keep from asking a question I had no business asking. The treasure trail had been a dark honey color, as were his eyebrows.

"Geez, Danni." He overcorrected his steering. "Keep staring at my goods and I'm gonna run off the road."

"I wasn't—"

"Yeah, you were." He laughed. "The rainbow's only up here if you must know. Down there's where I keep the pot of gold."

"Oh, ugh." I crossed my arms and went back to staring out the window, my cheeks aflame. "I couldn't care less about all that."

"Whatever you say," he said, voice full of amusement as he pulled up to the curb in front of Eliza's small house and parked. "I won't tell Rider you were curious if you won't."

"I won't tell him you're being inappropriate if you want to stay alive," I shot back before exiting the truck and making my way toward Eliza's front door.

"You're adorable when you're all miffed and flustered," he called after me, quickly catching up to my stride.

I rang the doorbell and ignored him, choosing not to dignify his comment with a reply. That, and I couldn't trust myself not to dig myself down into an even deeper hole of embarrassment. I should have just let the guy wear the VAMPIRES SUCK T-shirt and I'd never known what he was hiding under his clothes.

Eliza's office was inside her house, which was a small

gray brick house in a very quiet subdivision. It had white shutters, white lace curtains, and an array of yellow, pink, and white flower bushes lining the front of the house. I wasn't much of a gardening type, so I had no clue what kind of flower bushes they were, but they were pretty and smelled nice. From the few times I'd seen her neighbors out and about, they seemed to all be human and I wondered how terrified they would be to find out the nice lady with the pretty flower bushes and the butterfly welcome mat was a vampire, not that she was a particularly frightening one at all.

Eliza answered the door, carrying a Grateful Dead mug that smelled of microwaved blood. She wore a loose, flowing, sleeveless cotton dress with a floral design, no shoes, and about five different crystals hung around her neck. Her long blonde hair flowed loosely and even without a drop of makeup, she looked like she could take home the crown in any small town beauty pageant. Kindness radiated from her, which might have been why the mouse sitting on her shoulder seemed perfectly content in its location.

"Welcome!" she greeted us, her pale cornflower blue eyes glowing with genuine happiness to see us at her doorstep. "Come in. I see you've brought someone new."

We stepped inside and Daniel leaned into me to whisper, "Is that a pet on her shoulder or a snack?"

"I heard that," she said, still smiling, but some of the shine had left her eyes. "I would never harm any creature and would not allow anyone in my home to harm any of my animal friends either." She narrowed her eyes at Daniel. It wasn't that scary, but we knew she meant business.

"Oh, I wasn't insinuating I wanted to eat the mouse," Daniel quickly explained. "I was concerned for its safety."

Eliza blinked, seeming to have trouble deciding if she was offended or relieved. "You love the animals?"

"Animals are awesome."

"I agree." She gave him a thorough once-over. "You are a shifter, but I don't recognize exactly what kind."

"Daniel's a dragon shifter," I advised, "and he's my new personal guard. He'll be out here standing guard while we're in session in your office."

"No, I'll be in whatever room you'll be in," he told me.

"You're not going into my session with me."

"Is this like a psychiatric thing?" He looked from me to Eliza, back to me again. "I know your family is kind of screwy with all the breastomania, but what's your issue? I thought this was just new vampire counseling stuff. It can't be that top secret. We're all some kind of special freak."

"You're not a vampire."

"I'm still special." He winked at Eliza, charming his way into her good graces, which I didn't imagine was a very hard thing to do. The woman loved stray animals and I couldn't think of a better way to describe Daniel. "Tell her it's no big deal."

"Well, I want Danni to be comfortable speaking openly with me," Eliza told him.

"And I want to stay alive." Daniel directed his attention back to me. "Look, I got pretty clear instructions from Rider. I have to have you in my sights at all times. This isn't your apartment. There's not a vampire guard right outside your front door, and this is a house. There's more entry points. You chose me as your bodyguard, so let me guard your body so your cranky sire doesn't rip mine apart."

I chewed the inside of my jaw as I fixed Daniel with a hard look. I had no doubt Rider could effortlessly kill him, and was sure Daniel was fully aware of that fact too, but I wasn't buying his concern for bodily harm. Daniel wasn't an idiot, but he wasn't very fearful either. "You just want to meddle."

"We're supposed to work on your ability to lockdown your mind today anyway," Eliza said. "We could use his help. I assume Rider bonded with him so the three of you could contact each other telepathically?"

I nodded, my jaw dropping open as I remembered Daniel and I had been able to talk to each other in our minds earlier in the day and I'd been thinking some excruciatingly embarrassing thoughts about him as he'd changed shirts. "Have you been reading my mind today?"

"What? No." He looked genuinely confused. "Can I do that?"

"Can he do that?" I asked Eliza.

"Highly doubtful," Eliza answered. "He's not a vampire, so although he can speak with you telepathically through the bond, he wouldn't have the actual ability to read any thoughts not directed straight at him. However, as a vampire bonded to him, you may be able to read his mind eventually, provided you ingest enough of his blood and grow in your mental abilities."

I'd just drank from Daniel the day before. I looked at his head and focused, as if by boring a hole through his skull with my gaze I might be able to hear what was happening in there.

"Hey! Quit trying to read my brain!" he said.

"I'm not," I quickly fibbed.

"Yeah, then why are you scrunching all hard like you're about to crap your pants?"

"I don't know, I must have drunk bad Mexican."

The corners of Daniel's mouth twitched as he shook his head. "Whatever. Stay out of my head and get used to me standing right next to you, because that's my job."

"This way, please." Eliza ushered us past her living room and into her office. The walls were soft yellow and covered with large prints of hummingbirds. The carpet was light beige and stain-free. She didn't have a desk and usually sat in a tan recliner during our sessions while I sat on the blue and beige floral sofa. Sometimes we sat in the beanbag chairs she had strewn about the room. For this session, we chose the recliner and sofa while Daniel plopped down into a beanbag and wiggled his bottom, amazed by the cushy piece of furniture.

"All right," Eliza said, scooping the mouse off her shoulder and setting it free on the carpet. It looked from me to Daniel and scurried off, disappearing behind a bookshelf. She grabbed a tablet from the end table next to her chair and handed it to me. "For this exercise, I want you to scroll through the web and find something to focus on. It can be a news story, an article from a magazine, a blog, anything. Nod once you've found it. I want you to focus on whatever it is while I try to read your mind. While I'm trying to read your mind, Daniel will be speaking to you telepathically, trying to distract you. Okay?"

Daniel and I both nodded, and I set off on an internet journey to find something to focus on. The news was depressing, so I avoided it. Facebook and pretty much all social media sites were full of stupid people, so I avoided those too. I looked up Hades and found various sites. I pulled one up and nodded as I simultaneously focused on blocking Eliza out of my mind and doing actual research. About a minute into my research Daniel started popping random words and thoughts into my head like monkey balls, tater tits, ass boils, how long did it take Rider to give me an orgasm, was Eliza an actual hippie, why did this realm have so many old people and why did they all smell like mold and depression, and what the hell was a labradoodle anyway? I lasted all of five minutes before Daniel telepathically whispered *Danni Keller wants to see a dragon dick* and I lost my mental hold on the wall I'd set up, Eliza slid right in to my mind, and gasped at the violent thoughts she found there a moment before I slugged Daniel in the shoulder.

"Danni, stop!" Eliza dove in to help Daniel as he struggled to grab my arms while laughing so hard at me as I continued to deliver jabs.

"You're such a child!"

"I think I need a bodyguard to protect me from the body I'm guarding," he replied, still laughing. "Geez, as riled up as you are, you'd think what I said was true. Interesting."

"Oh, shut up," I snapped, settling back onto the couch. "I need to talk to you about something else today anyway, Eliza."

The willowy blonde took her seat in the recliner and took a calming breath, no doubt annoyed by the juvenile antics from the two of us supposed adults making a mockery of the professionalism she expected in her office. "What's on your mind?"

"You're kind of knowledgeable about a lot of different supernatural stuff. I've recently had two nightmares about Selander Ryan and this morning he choked me in one, and it really happened. Rider sensed him as if he were really there. Is it possible that he's back?"

Eliza's naturally pale skin grew deathly white, and I was actually a little glad I still couldn't eat cupcakes because if I had, they'd be all over her clean carpet.

"Well, that's not a good look," Daniel said, all humor lost.

"Did it feel like a dream or did it feel like he was really with you?" Eliza asked.

"It felt real," I answered, my hand going to my neck. "He was really choking me. It was exactly like when he would come to me in a dream before Rider crushed his heart."

"Selander Ryan is a very evil, twisted man," Eliza said. "These are not words I use lightly. I have belief that many can be redeemed, but there are a few I believe have no prayer of redemption. They've done too much evil, enjoyed it too much to ever fully cleanse themselves of it. Selander Ryan was known to associate with many masters of the dark arts, many vile creatures. It would not surprise me if he found a way to remain after death."

"Can he hurt me? He said he's going to make Rider suffer through me."

Eliza flicked a glance at Daniel before telepathically

asking me, *Do you trust the dragon enough that we can speak openly?*

I looked at Daniel, studied him. He was a jokester, and he liked to toy with Rider in his own way, but I'd seen a different side of him when he'd spoken of his lost love. He knew what it was like to love someone enough to do anything for them, and he respected it. "I trust him," I said, not bothering to respond telepathically. This earned raised eyebrows from Daniel, catching on that Eliza had asked me about him.

"I assumed you would, and I highly doubted Rider would give you a personal bodyguard he didn't trust to keep his mouth shut," Eliza said. "Still, I thought it best to check. I believe Selander Ryan has many tricks up his sleeve."

"I notice you are referring to him in the present tense."

"If he's choking you in your dreams, he isn't gone." She folded her hands in her lap. "There are many ways one can still exact revenge after their body has departed this world. Heaven is the only realm no dark magic can find entrance to. Hell, Purgatory, and other realms souls go to after dying here are a different matter."

"So you're saying there's no way to truly defeat an evil person, even if you kill them?"

"No, that's not exactly right." She shook her head. "Anyone can be killed, but if desperate enough, someone can devise a way to remain in some capacity. Selander Ryan's heart was crushed, which should have silenced him forever. He must have bound himself somehow, so his spirit could still reach out." She studied me, her mouth in a grim line.

"What is it?" I asked, my stomach suddenly feeling very hollow.

"He came to you. He and Rider bit you the same night, and Rider redirected your change to keep you from turning into a succubus, but you weren't a full vampire. You were as much Selander Ryan's fledgling as you were Rider's.

Selander Ryan lost control over you when you gave yourself to Rider, but he clearly still has a connection. You could be what he bonded to."

I swallowed. Hard. "You both told me that if I gave myself to Rider, he would be my master."

"Hybrids aren't very common," Eliza said. "If Rider and Selander Ryan hadn't been about the same age, the same power level, Rider may have not been able to stop you from turning full succubus at all. We thought that by giving him your loyalty, accepting him as your true master, it would wipe out Selander Ryan's mark altogether. Maybe we were wrong. It did lessen it. I sense the vampire in you is much stronger now. I don't pick up the succubus vibe from you, but I do feel something … different about you, so I know it's there."

"I don't have the venom anymore. At least Rider said I didn't." I looked over at Daniel, who was hanging on our every word, fully engrossed. "How did you feel when I drank from you?"

"Honestly?" He grinned. "A little scared, but mostly curious."

"It didn't give you any kind of sexual feeling?" Eliza asked.

"Uh… no," he answered. "I don't have any kinky blood fetishes. That's kind of weird."

"If you still had the venom and drank from this man, he would have been affected by it," Eliza said. "Your vampire abilities grew stronger after you accepted Rider and after Selander Ryan died. It is possible you lost some of your succubus abilities, but kept enough of some others to still keep a connection with Selander Ryan."

I thought about how I'd changed since that night. I no longer had the venom. I no longer had a strong aversion to women. I still had moments of lust, but I couldn't pin that on being a succubus. Rider could make a nun lustful. "I always leaned more toward the vampire side than succubus. Other than the venom and the way I got so cold around women, I can't really recall anything else that was an actual succubus trait, but I know I feel something there, something ...off. I don't know what it is, but I feel like there's something different about me. I thought I was just still a newbie, and that's why I felt different from other vampires."

"Always trust your instincts," Eliza advised. "They are your greatest weapon and a natural defense system."

My instincts were telling me I was still Selander Ryan's plaything. "Selander told me he was going to destroy Rider through me. If I'm his link, what's keeping him connected to this realm or whatever? Would Rider have to kill me to truly end Selander Ryan's existence?"

Eliza studied me for a moment. "That would definitely destroy Rider."

"Shit."

"That man isn't going to kill you," Daniel said.

"What if it's the only way to destroy Selander Ryan?"

"He'll find another way, or just live with the villain," Daniel answered.

"How can you be so sure? Maybe Selander Ryan's whole plan was for Rider to kill him so that he'd eventually have to kill me to truly wipe him off the face of the earth?"

"I don't know much at all about this Selander Ryan guy, but I've seen the way Rider looks at you. You could torture him every day for the next five centuries and he wouldn't kill you."

"Or..." I swallowed, my mouth dry. "Could Selander Ryan still have enough power over me to make me do something to Rider? Would Rider allow me to kill him if Ryan somehow forced me to do it?"

"That, I could actually see happening," Daniel said.

Eliza leaned forward and placed her hand over mine. "Don't lose hope, Danni. I'll go through all my books and see what I can find. Rider is still just as much your sire, and very powerful. He's not an easy man to go against and although Selander Ryan has masters of dark magic in his corner, Rider has his own army. Light magic is a force to be reckoned with. Selander Ryan will not win this battle."

"Maybe I should stay away from Rider to be safe."

"I don't think that idea would go over very well with him," Daniel said.

"Rider can control you," Eliza reminded me. "If you were attempting to physically harm him, he could stop you with a single thought. If Selander Ryan wants to use you to physically assault him, it will only be to frustrate him. He knows he can't win that way. We'll figure out his game, and we'll beat him at it."

"You're sure of that?"

She smiled. "Rider has been playing this game with Selander Ryan for a long time, and he has yet to lose."

Yeah, I thought, but he had yet to truly win it either.

ELEVEN

"Everything's going to be all right," Daniel reassured me as we left his truck in the parking lot and walked toward the bar. It was just a little after six in the evening, but I'd updated my resume, applied to every online listing that seemed decent, paid my bills and gotten through the session with Eliza. I'd suffered through watching Daniel eat a delicious, greasy cheeseburger and fries and slurp down a chocolate milkshake, but although I could get him to feed himself while on duty, I couldn't get him to sleep and I knew the poor guy had to be tired so I thought it best to allow him to dump me off on Rider so he could finally get a good night's rest.

"I don't know. The situation seems pretty bleak."

"Well, the situation didn't seem so great when I was in Hades getting chased down by hellhounds with fiery, snapping jaws dripping acidic drool, but I got through that. You'll get through this."

"Okay, you win," I said, earning a laugh as he held the door open for me and we entered the bar.

Rome was on duty, standing near the door with his meaty arms crossed, dressed in his usual all-black ensemble of T-shirt and pants. He gave a quick nod of his head in our direction, which I took to be his way of saying hello before he returned his attention to scanning the room, searching for any signs of trouble. It took me under a second to find trouble in the form of Rider sitting in a dark booth in the corner... across from a woman. He looked across the room, caught my eye, and in the dark, I could just make out a barely perceptible grimace. *Come sit. Both of you.*

"Damn, woman," Daniel whispered, grabbing my arm before I could storm over to the booth. "Even I can feel the anger coming out of you. Calm down. They're fully clothed, in a crowded bar, and he's sitting *across* from her. Geez."

I looked down at where Daniel's hand had locked on my arm and noticed my clenched fist, and the heat flooding my body. Maybe he had a point. "I'm cool now. I just had a moment."

"If that was a moment, I'd hate to see you have a while."

He let go of my arm, and we walked over to the booth. As we neared, I saw that the woman with Rider was Rihanna, the witch who had helped clean up the mess left after I'd killed my former boss in self-defense. Her hair hung in long dark ringlets, a few locks dyed purple to match the slinky dress she wore. She wore glittery purple eyeshadow which was fabulous against her brown skin, a more natural color on her lips, and large silver moons hung from her earlobes. Rider stood as we reached the table, pulled me flush against his body, and kissed me like he'd just got out of a long stretch in prison. Once I was left sufficiently lightheaded, he waited for me to slide into the booth and then he took a seat next to me so that I was safely settled against the wall, out of immediate danger if anything should happen. Rihanna sat across from me, having scooted over for Daniel to sit next to her.

"Hey girlfriend," she greeted me. "You kill any deserving bastards lately?"

"No," I answered as Rider slung his arm around my shoulders and pulled me snug against his side.

"She beat the shit out of a werewolf," Daniel said, sharing a grin with Rider. "It was all good today. Kept my head on a swivel and didn't see anyone lurking, nothing out of the ordinary."

"Good," Rider said. "You meet any of her family?"

"Not until tomorrow."

Rider's grin spread into a full smile as he pushed a basket of fries toward Daniel. "Can't wait to hear the details."

"And what flavor are you, sugar?" Rihanna asked, studying Daniel closely as he took a fry. Her eyes narrowed, then widened as her mouth dropped open. "You're one of those Imortians."

"Guilty," Daniel said.

Rihanna rolled her gaze up and down his body. "You're something real big and powerful."

"Dragon."

"Ooh lord." She fanned herself, causing Daniel to grin impishly. Rider shook his head. I just stared at the fries and tried not to cry.

"You'll be able to eat without getting sick eventually," Rider said softly, picking up on my desperation. "Hang in there."

"Oh you poor thing, you're still that new," Rihanna said, wrestling her attention away from Daniel long enough to look at me. "That's some straight bullshit that newly turned vampires can't eat. This won't last long, but here." She flicked her wrists and mumbled something in what I assumed was Latin. "You can eat whatever you want for about an hour and it won't bother you. After that hour's up, I wouldn't try it."

"I can eat anything at all?"

"Anything, girl."

I looked at Daniel. He was looking at his watch, laughing. "The bakery down the street should be open another fifteen minutes. Chocolate?"

"Hell yes," I answered, and he winked before taking off.

"What was that about?" Rider asked, as he watched Daniel zip out of the bar.

"I want a cupcake bad," I answered. "Daniel said he'd get me one the moment I could eat."

"How nice of him." Rider stiffened, glaring at the last spot he'd seen Daniel.

"Tell me about this dragon," Rihanna said.

"He's a pain in the ass," Rider said, extra grumpy.

I elbowed him in the side light enough that no one would notice but him. "He's a nice guy."

"He got a girlfriend?"

"I don't think so," I answered.

"Well, if you don't mind, I think I'll be on my way. I'll check in with some witches and see what I can find out, Rider, sugar." She adjusted her boobs so they nearly spilled over her neckline and slid out of the booth. "I suddenly feel like grabbing some goodies at the bakery."

"Seriously?" Rider asked, his expression half amusement, half disbelief. "That guy?"

"Shoo, honey, *he can get it.*" With that statement, Rihanna sashayed out of the bar, leaving Rider and me laughing.

"Poor bastard," Rider said, shaking his head. "I can barely stand him half the time and even I wouldn't wish Rihanna on him."

"I thought you liked her."

"I do, but I've never been intimately involved with her. She once dated a guy who made the mistake of calling her by another woman's name. He woke up the next morning thinking he'd lost a very important part of his body. Turned out she'd just shrank him so much he couldn't find it without a magnifying glass."

I sat there blinking at him for a minute or two. "How important of a part?"

Rider winced. "Well, I'm very fond of my own, and if Daniel values his, he better treat her right or find a way to avoid her altogether."

"Yikes."

"Yeah. Rihanna takes revenge seriously."

"Is that what the two of you were discussing?"

Rider turned toward me and grinned before pulling me in for another toe-curling kiss. "We were discussing Selander Ryan," he said when he came up for air. "There was no reason for you to feel so much rage when you saw me talking to her."

"I thought you couldn't kiss me in public," I said, finding a spot on the wood tabletop to focus on to avoid his gaze.

"Nice change of subject. I never said I couldn't kiss you in public. I said people couldn't know I'm in love with you. It doesn't matter how many know I'm in lust with you." He kissed me again and continued until someone cleared their throat across from us.

Daniel sat across from us holding a chocolate cupcake topped with a mound of chocolate buttercream. My mouth watered and I may have let out a small cry as I snatched it from his hand and took a big bite. "Ohmygawd it's so gooooooooooood," I practically moaned as my eyes rolled into the back of my head and I savored the rich chocolate flavor exploding on my tongue.

"Daaaaaamn," they both said. I ignored them and took another bite, moaning in appreciation before I licked a dollop of the sweet buttercream off the top.

"Dude, I think that cupcake is ruining her for men," Daniel said. "You might have to dip your dick in chocolate to satisfy her."

"Hell, you might be right," Rider surprised me by agreeing.

I paused in my annihilation of the cupcake to see them both completely transfixed. "Why are you staring at me?"

"Can't look away," Rider said. "It's like porn."

I shot them both a dirty look and pushed at Rider. "Let me out. I'm going upstairs to finish my cupcake alone."

Rider slid out. "I'll be up in a few," he said. "Save some of that enthusiasm for me."

"Yeah," Daniel said. "Let him enjoy your breasts before you shock them off your chest."

"What the hell is he talking about?" Rider asked, helping me up from the booth as Daniel sat there laughing.

"My mother and grandmother called. My grandmother bought me a Jug-Jolter 2000."

"I probably don't even want to know what that is," he said, stopping me from going any further, "but if anyone does anything to your breasts, they're going to have to deal with me and I'm not going to be happy. That goes for you too."

"Yes, sir."

"Damn straight." He kissed me and led me toward the back door. "Go on up. I'll be there in just a moment and we can discuss why Daniel is wearing your T-shirt."

The cupcake was gone before I reached the door to Rider's inner sanctum, and I was depressed. I should have told Daniel to get me a dozen. I'd grabbed some toiletries from my apartment which were in the purse slung over my shoulder, but Daniel had carried in my laptop and it was still downstairs with him. I sent Rider a mental message to bring it up with him and I went to grab the nightgown Rider had bought me from my travel bag, but the bag wasn't on the floor where I'd left it.

I checked the closet and found the bag at the bottom, empty. Rider had hung my clothes next to his. The slinky gown wasn't there, so I checked the dresser and found that Rider had cleared a drawer for me. I removed the gown and a tiny pair of panties, grabbed the necessary toiletries from my purse, and made my way to the bathroom. I'd never been in it before and I regretted that the moment I saw it. It was bigger than I'd expected and everything was black marble. I had my choice of using the rain shower or soaking in the clawfoot tub, which was big enough for two people. Considering the possibility of never wanting to leave the giant tub if I got in it, I opted for the rain shower, using Rider's shower gel to make me silky-soft and after towel-drying with one of his luxurious, ultra-thick towels, slid into the panties and body-hugging black lace nightgown. I brushed my teeth, finger-combed my damp hair, and stepped out to find Rider lying in his bed, the silk sheet covering him from the waist down. His hands were clasped behind his head and I had no doubt he was naked.

"Even sexier than I thought it'd be," he said, his gaze rolling down my body. "Peel it off and get over here."

"I thought you wanted to talk about why Daniel was wearing my shirt," I said, suddenly nervous.

"That was before I saw you in that gown. Now I want you to take it off and do to me what you did to that cupcake."

Oh boy.

"Wow," I said an hour later. "That was... Wow."

"Yeah, you must have been pretending I was the cupcake." Rider brushed a lock of hair away from my brow and kissed my forehead, a far gentler kiss than the passion-fueled ones he'd been planting on me since I'd walked into the bar. "I missed you."

"I thought I drove you crazy."

"You do. You're a pain in the ass."

"I thought I was a mean ass."

"That too, and a wiseass. You're all kinds of ass. Fortunately for me, I like ass." He grinned and traced my lips with his finger. "You're a little pale. That cupcake wasn't all you had today, was it?"

"I had a mug of refrigerated blood."

"Just one?"

"It's not exactly fine cuisine."

He made a rough, frustrated sound in his throat,

something between a sigh and a growl. "You're too new to allow yourself to get that low. Come on."

He sat up and pulled me onto his lap so I straddled him, and tipped his head to the side, allowing full access to his neck. My fangs descended, and I sank them into his skin. His thin but powerful blood spilled out, and I lapped it up greedily. The cupcake tasted better, but my body knew it needed the blood more, and it came with a powerful hit, strength flowing through me with every swallow. I drank my fill, sealed the small wounds with a swipe of my tongue and pulled back. Maybe it was the hour of sex we'd just had, but it was the first time I'd drank from Rider and hadn't grown all lusty.

"Think any harder and you're going to sprain something," he said, running a finger over the curve of my ear. "What's rolling around in that head?"

"You're not going to just delve right in there and check for yourself?"

"Just because I can do something doesn't mean I should. You may not believe this, but I do try to not piss you off."

I smiled at that. "Me too."

"Yeah, I'm not buying it. You live to drive me crazy."

"I do not." I rolled off of him and sat with my back against the headboard, the sheet covering my chest and my arms folded. "Just because I happen to do something easily doesn't mean it's intentional."

This got a chuckle. "Fine. It's just a natural talent. Now, what are you thinking about?"

"You're positive there isn't any trace of succubus venom left in me?"

"I'm positive. Your bite is just a normal vampire bite. I wouldn't have allowed you to drink from Daniel otherwise."

"When I left with him earlier, you told me to only drink bagged blood."

"That didn't have anything to do with venom," he said.

"If you don't know what you're doing and you drink repeatedly from the same source, you can create a bond, especially now that your sire has created a telepathic bond for communication."

"And a bond with Daniel would be bad?"

"Why was he wearing your shirt?"

"I thought it best he not continue to walk around wearing a shirt that said VAMPIRES SUCK," I answered as I held Rider's gaze. His eyes revealed nothing, but the hard set of his jaw told me he wasn't happy I'd loaned the shirt to Daniel. "It's a shirt. What's the big deal, and how did you even know it was mine? You've never seen me in it."

"I've seen it in your closet, and the big deal is how would you feel if I loaned one of my shirts to another woman?"

My jaw dropped. "You're actually jealous."

"I'm territorial, and I don't trust him."

"You wouldn't assign a bodyguard to me if you didn't trust him to protect me."

"Oh, I trust him to protect you from harm," Rider said. "I don't trust him not to fall in love with you and make me have to rearrange his organs."

"Why do you even think he'd fall in love with me?"

"I can't imagine any man with an ounce of taste being around you for an extended length of time and not falling in love with you," Rider said. "Plus, I've seen the way he looks at you, and I don't like it."

"That's absurd. How does he look at me?"

"Like I should punch him in the face, and why did he know you wanted a cupcake? I didn't know you wanted a cupcake. He shouldn't know things about you that I don't know."

"It was just a cupcake."

"It's not about the fucking cupcake."

"Then what is it about?" I threw my hands up. "You're being ridiculous."

"You talk to him in a way you don't talk to me," Rider said, nostrils flaring. "The guy has a reputation for being a complete jerk, interested in nothing but pushing people's buttons, slacking off and being a general ass boil, but he's gung-ho to go to work guarding you and when the two of you talk to each other, it's not like when you and I talk to each other. It's like…"

"It's like I'm talking to a friend?"

Rider nodded. "Yeah, it's like that."

"And that's bad, how? I haven't had a real friend in a long time. I need one."

Rider's gaze rolled over me, assessing. "I don't like that he can be something for you that I can't be or know things about you that I don't. I don't like that there's a void because I'm not filling it."

"I need a friend," I said, laying my hand on Rider's arm, "but I need what you give me too. It's just that what you and I have is so … intense. Sometimes it's nice having someone I can just joke around with or talk about non-important things without all the emotional stuff. He knew I wanted a cupcake. He doesn't know my life story, and he doesn't have the connection I have with you."

"I should have known you wanted a cupcake," Rider said softly, intertwining his fingers with mine. He stared off into space, deep in thought. "I don't know how to explain what this is that we have. I've existed for so long and I've never fallen so fast and hard for anyone. In my mind, I know I just met you a little over six weeks ago, but in my heart, it feels like I've known you so much longer than that, like I've known you forever. Hell, Danni, it feels like I've been waiting for you and I have no explanation for that, but when I realized Daniel knew something about you that I didn't it really threw me. It just didn't seem right."

A cold chill skittered up my spine as Selander Ryan's words came back to haunt me. "You feel like you were waiting for me?"

He nodded, slowly. "I know it sounds crazy."

"No." I shook my head. "I've also thought it weird how I keep forgetting I just met you. Mostly because it doesn't feel that way. The truly weird thing is that Selander Ryan said he'd waited so long for me and now you're saying you feel like you were waiting for me."

Rider looked over at me and we shared a look that did nothing favorable for my belly before he swung his legs off the side of the bed and started pulling out clothes. "I take it from the gown you were planning on staying in for the night, but there's someone we both need to see. Get dressed."

Twenty minutes later, we were in an alley behind a row of dilapidated houses in the West End. The West End of Louisville didn't get the most favorable news coverage in the area. It was a predominately low income black neighborhood known for drug deals and drive-bys. I'd gone to a high school in the area where I was one of three to four white kids per each classroom of thirty students. The West End didn't bother me so much. I grew up with a lot of the kids who lived there, and had never felt threatened driving through. However, there were specific streets in the West End I wouldn't dare drive through and we were currently standing in the alley behind one. At night. At least we were dressed in dark, non-gang colors.

"You know where we are, right?" I asked Rider as I stepped out of his SUV.

He grinned down at me as he closed the door. "You know we're vampires, right?"

"Does that even matter on this block?"

This earned me a small laugh. Rome, Tony, and Daniel got out of another SUV and walked over to where we stood. Rome nodded toward Rider as they shared some silent communication and tipped his head in the direction of where the alley ended. Rider placed his hand along the small of my back and we followed Rome. Tony and Daniel stayed back to guard the vehicles.

"I was hoping Daniel could get some rest tonight. He's going to go with me to another fitting tomorrow, unless you want to go with me."

"Hell no, I don't want to go with you," Rider said, voice low, as we crept through the alley. "My brother is an evil bastard, but even he's less irritating than your family. It's not even late. Daniel will get plenty of rest. This is his job now anyway. He has to be on call, just like anyone else in my employ."

Rome stopped behind a small shotgun house. The back windows were lit and two beefy men stood on the steps outside the back door. Rome approached them, exchanged a few low words and did some complicated handshake thing before motioning us over. The men stepped aside but watched us with predatory eyes as we entered the house and Rome guided us through a door hiding a staircase to the basement.

The basement smelled of mold and laundry detergent. Paint chipped off the walls, and the floor appeared to be poured concrete. A small round table had been placed in the middle of the room and covered with a white tablecloth. A single candle burned in the center of the table and four chairs rested around it. A dark-skinned woman with thin arms and wise eyes occupied one of the chairs. She looked to be in her seventies, small, but fierce. Her cornrowed hair was gray, with several threads of white woven throughout. She smiled lovingly as Rome bent down to kiss her head.

"My sweet boy, you seem bigger every time I see you," she said, patting his cheek.

"Rome's great-aunt," Rider whispered to me.

Suddenly, the woman smacked Rome upside his head. "I see you with a slut from Indiana and a slut from the bar. Why don't I see you with a nice girl from church?"

"Auntie Mo, you don't know what you're talking about," Rome said, holding the ear she'd just hit.

"Are you saying I don't have the gift? Are you calling me a liar?"

"No, ma'am," he said. Next to me, I felt Rider vibrating with silent laughter, but I couldn't take my eyes off the scene before me. Rome's great-aunt grabbed his other ear and pulled him down to her eye level, which would have been low even if she'd been standing. "You think because you work for a vampire, you don't have to worry about your soul?"

"No, ma'am."

She pushed him away. "Shoo! Next time I have a vision of you with a girl, it better be a nice church girl. I'll see your friends now."

Rome averted his gaze as he walked past us, rubbing his ears, looking like a gigantic child who'd just been spanked in front of his playmates. "Auntie Mo will see you now."

"You two!" Auntie Mo pointed at us, snapped her fingers, and pointed to the chairs on either side of her. "Sit down."

We walked to the table, Rider still vibrating as poor Rome took the stairs up behind us. I elbowed him as we took our seats.

"Well, well, well, Danni and Rider," Auntie Mo said, looking between us. "You've finally found your way to each other once again."

TWELVE

"Again?" Rider and I both asked.

"You were together your very first life. It is quite rare to find your soulmate in your very first lifetime, but you did. It created a powerful bond," she continued, holding her fingertips to her temples. Her eyes were squeezed shut and her lips pursed for a moment. "A love that strong becomes a form of magic. Throughout your lives, you will always be drawn to one another."

"Lives?" Rider shook his head. "I've been on this same life for a long, long time. How many could I have possibly had?"

"You are on your second life. Danni has had many." She gave me a pitying look. "You have always had a tendency to die young. Even now, you have already escaped one death, only to be hunted for a second."

"Hunted by who?" Rider asked as I just sat there, suddenly queasy. "My brother? If you knew I was going to meet my soulmate again, why didn't you tell me?"

"I did not know of Danni until ten minutes before you arrived." Auntie Mo took each of our hands in her own and closed her eyes. She took a deep breath and released it slowly before reopening them. "Your half-brother is no

147

longer in this physical world, but he can still move about it through others. He worked some powerful dark magic to ensure he could continue his torture of you here. He is dead, but not gone."

"Can you give me more detail than that?" Rider asked. I could tell by the tight set of his mouth he was clearly frustrated.

"I see what I see and in whatever way it chooses to be shown," she answered. "I know he is still a threat to both of you, and he is connected to you." She narrowed her eyes at me, studying. "He has planted a seed inside you that blooms in cycles. He is always there, watching, waiting... He is most powerful during the Bloom."

I had no clue what the woman was talking about, but I had goosebumps. I looked at Rider and could tell he wasn't happy, but I couldn't tell if he was baffled and nervous like me. He had his blank mask face on and had locked down his emotions. I got zilch off of him.

"You already know I'm a vampire," Rider said. "Do you know what Danni is?"

"She is your fledgling," Auntie Mo answered. "You are her master, but not her only sire. She was marked by you and by your brother. His mark is still there, but not as strong as yours. She is still a creature of different worlds, and many want to spill her blood. Those who have died trying to kill her left behind others to try to finish the job. It has always been her destiny to die young. It was her destiny to die young in this reincarnation. You changed her destiny, but fate does not give up so easily."

Rider reached across the table and grabbed my hand. "What do I have to do to keep her alive?"

"Keep destroying what wishes to destroy her. Don't focus so much on the obvious enemy that you miss the other snakes in the grass. Be careful during the Bloom."

"What is the Bloom?" I asked.

"The cycle in which your non-dominant sire is at his strongest and you exhibit the traits you received from him."

"I'm still a succubus?"

"Yes." Auntie Mo nodded. "You gave your loyalty to your vampire sire, making him your master. He will always have control over you, but during the Bloom, that control will be harder to maintain."

I gulped. "How long is this Bloom?"

"I do not know, but it will not last. It is a cycle. That means it will come and it will go, and it will come back again." Auntie Mo's eyes rolled into the back of her head and she fell forward, cradling her head. "I must rest."

"Thank you, Auntie Mo." Rider patted her shoulder. "I appreciate your help."

Auntie Mo looked up at him. "I see you are a good man, despite the cloak of darkness around you. That is why I sent my great-nephew to work for you and stay safe from these streets. I did not send him to work for you just so he could get swallowed up by other bad things. He's a good boy, but he likes women too much. Keep him away from the sluts."

The corners of Rider's mouth twitched as he fought against a smile. "Yes, ma'am."

"I expect to see him in church on Sunday. It wouldn't hurt you to go either."

Rider stood from his chair and took my hand, pulling me up from mine. "I'll see what I can do."

Rome was talking to the two men guarding the back door when we stepped out of the small house. He did another of those complicated handshakes with each of them and caught up to us.

"Your great-aunt told me to keep you away from the sluts," Rider advised him, grinning from ear to ear.

"Aww, man. I love her, but she's crazy, man." Rome shook his head and I could almost feel the heat of embarrassment steaming out of his pores.

"She's a nice lady. Go to church Sunday morning. It will make her happy."

Rome looked over at Rider and smiled. "Did she tell you that you needed to go too?"

"She did."

"Will you be there?"

Rider grinned, Rome laughed out loud, and we trekked down the alley toward the waiting SUVs.

"So Auntie Mo is a psychic?" I asked once I was buckled back into Rider's SUV.

"She has visions of the past and future that come to her at whim," Rider answered as he drove toward the mouth of the alley, the men he'd brought for security all in the vehicle behind his. "She can't predict lottery numbers or see everything that will ever happen in the future, and don't believe any psychic who tells you they can. Rome had some trouble with a local gang when he was a teenager. He was always a really big guy, and they wanted him. He didn't want that life, and that just pissed them off. Auntie Mo had a dream about me and knew I could offer a level of protection he wouldn't find on the street, and I could give him a job better than what he'd find there too. She sent him to find me while he was still in his teens and he's been working for me ever since."

"Why does his great-aunt still live in this area? I assumed your staff was well paid."

"They are. Auntie Mo is a tough lady who refuses to leave the neighborhood. She's well respected and everyone in the area knows she's under protection. They just don't know by who."

"She's protected by you?"

"We make it look like Rome is in charge of her security detail, but yeah. She's under my protection. She refuses to take money, and she refuses to leave the area." Rider shrugged. "What can I do?"

"I assume the gang eventually left Rome alone?"

"It took a bit of persuasion, but yeah. They don't give

him any trouble now."

I looked out the window and watched the buildings progressively get better looking as we left the West End and traveled toward The Midnight Rider. I replayed the information Auntie Mo had given us through my mind, trying to make sense of it, but I didn't understand it any better. I did, however, understand why it felt like I'd known Rider way longer than the short time we'd been together, as mind-boggling as the reason was.

"I can feel you thinking over there."

"Can you hear me thinking?" I asked.

"I'm trying to stay out of your mind. I know you don't like it when I hear what goes through it, and fortunately you've gotten better about projecting, so it's easier to ignore."

"Thanks." Honestly, if I had the skill to easily slip into someone else's mind, I don't know if I could keep myself from doing it. I gave Rider hell for doing it, but I could understand the temptation. "She said we were soulmates and would always be drawn to each other."

"Explains the instant, overwhelming need I had to protect you when I first saw you in my bar."

"It doesn't explain how I've died over and over again while you've been stuck on your second life and we never met despite having this bond." My belly did a nauseated flip. "I should have asked how I died. Was it natural each time, or have I always attracted psychopaths?"

Rider reached over for my hand, brought it to his mouth, and kissed it. "I don't know the answer to that, and she might not even know. Her visions don't always give a clear picture of everything. As for how we never met a second time before now, maybe you were born in a different country than I was in each life and our paths didn't cross until this one."

"I was supposed to die that night."

"You didn't."

"Your brother said he was waiting for me. How did he

know about me? About us?"

"I don't know." Rider's hands tightened around the steering wheel. "He associated with some very dark witches. Maybe one of them had a vision long before Auntie Mo did."

I shook my head. "I don't know if I buy all this. The only reason I'm even considering believing in this reincarnation stuff is because I do feel like I've known you a lot longer than I have, but... do people reincarnate and fall in love with the same people over and over again? How does that even work? Are we exactly the same in each life? Does everyone reincarnate? Explain ghosts then, because I think ghosts are real, and your brother clearly isn't reincarnating. Are there requirements?"

"I don't know, babe, but we'll keep looking for answers until we find out. The important thing is we've found each other in this life and you didn't die that night. We just have to keep you safe."

"What about this blooming stuff?"

"Sounds like a bitch, but we'll get through it. Don't drink from anyone other than me though. Sounds like the venom might come back."

"Shit."

"Yeah."

Daniel and the guys used the main parking lot next to the bar, but Rider used the attached garage for his personal vehicles. He pulled the SUV into the garage and parked it alongside his black Ferrari and black Harley-Davidson.

"The night's still young," he said, helping me out of the SUV. "I have some work to do in the office, but if you'd like to do anything, I can squeeze some time in for you."

"Oh gee. I feel so spoiled."

"I meant that better than it sounded."

"I'm sure you did. I know it's nighttime and we're full of energy, but I think I'm just going to watch TV upstairs or do some internet surfing. Remember what Auntie Mo said. Keep Rome away from the sluts."

Rider barked out a laugh. "Hey, I can make sure the guy has Sunday morning off for church, but there's nothing I can do about sluts."

Rider and I split apart at the stairs behind the door at the back of the bar. He gave me a kiss and went through the bar door to get to his office, and I took the stairs up to his tiny apartment. I took off my pants and shoes and climbed into the bed with my laptop. It was time to research.

I googled REINCARNATION and received 22,300,000 results back. I surfed through the abundance of information, clicking on any links that looked promising, and avoiding anything having to do with celebrities. Most of what I found hinted that reincarnation was a popular Buddhist or Hindu belief so I did a silent plea for forgiveness if I was being un-Christian in searching for the information and possibly believing in it, and did another couple of silent pleas for forgiveness for being a vampire, fornicating with a vampire, and killing a couple of guys even though the second one really deserved it and I doubted the first one had been missed by anyone. I did another plea for forgiveness for justifying the two murders I'd committed and then I just cringed, reminded that I'd murdered two men. The reminder that I was essentially a killer led me to search for information on Hell just in case I ended up finding my way there. My search branched out to levels of Hell, including purgatory, and that's when I started getting several hits for *Supernatural* and got distracted. Yes, learning all this information might help me figure out what Selander Ryan was up to and what danger Rider and I were in, but helloooo... Dean Winchester.

I was ogling a screen capture of Jensen Ackles as Dean Winchester, all shirtless and muscly, when Rider walked in and kicked his shoes off. "What are you up to?"

"I was researching reincarnation, but then I started

getting results back for *Supernatural,* and now I'm virtually cheating on you with Dean Winchester."

"As long as you don't ask him to slay me."

I glanced up from my screen to see him undressing. "You're not jealous that I'm virtually cheating on you with Dean Winchester?"

"Dean Winchester isn't real."

"Jensen Ackles is real. Are you jealous of Jensen Ackles?"

"Do I need to be?" He dropped the last of his clothes to the floor and slid into the bed, next to me.

"I would be jealous if you were ogling an actress."

"Babe, you'd be jealous if I said hello to the eighty-nine-year-old greeter at Wal-Mart, and we both know if you ever met Jensen Ackles you'd probably piss your pants and die of mortification immediately after."

I let out an indignant huff. "How are you so confident all the time?"

"I know what I'm working with and it's all good," he answered and kissed me on the temple before taking the laptop away. He glanced at the images on the screen and powered the laptop down. "Maybe I'd be a little jealous if you ever actually met the bastard. I'm not convinced he's human. No human man looks that perfect."

My mouth dropped open and was still hanging that way after Rider placed the laptop on the floor and turned toward me. "What?" he asked. "I'm a heterosexual male, but I'm not blind. I can see when I have competition."

I grinned. "You are jealous."

"Not really. Jensen Ackles can't do this." He reached for me and about five minutes later I didn't even remember who the hell Jensen Ackles was.

I woke up tangled in Rider's arms and legs, the alarm on my cellphone blaring.

"Kill the damn thing," Rider grumbled, running a hand

down his face.

"Sorry." I sat up and grabbed the phone from the bedside table. One press of my thumb and the alarm died.

"When I was a newly turned vampire, I never even saw daylight for at least ten years. Why can't you be a normal, newly turned vampire?"

"Because I'm a hybrid."

"I guess that could do it." Rider sat up. "At least you slept through the morning. When's the fitting?"

"It's scheduled at four, so I have thirty minutes to shower and get ready, which will leave me just enough time to get to the shop."

"I'll call Daniel and make sure he's downstairs waiting for you."

"You could just come with me."

Rider narrowed his eyes at me. "Do you really want to punish me that badly?"

I gave him a quick kiss, pulled his discarded shirt from the night before over my head, and headed for the bathroom.

"You know you're going to have to say goodbye to your family eventually," he said as I entered the bathroom, pretending I didn't hear him.

"So what exactly am I in for here?" Daniel asked as he parked his truck along the curb across the street from the dress shop. He'd gone with a white button-down shirt, cuffs rolled and pushed up to beneath his elbows and three buttons undone to show his throat and a hint of chest. His jeans fit well and were without holes. A small silver hoop plugged up the extra hole in his nose. "Rider seemed tickled to death about me meeting your family. I can't imagine him being excited about anything that great happening to me, so I'm assuming they're rabid."

"They take some getting used to," I said. I had chosen to wear one of the new pairs of Ralph Lauren jeans Rider had bought for me and a white cotton top that fell off one shoulder. It required more sunscreen but was pretty enough for me to take the risk.

"Rider told Grey your sister was a hell-beast."

"Seeing as how you've actually seen hell-beasts, I'm sure you'll survive her. Besides, my family will be too busy ripping me to shreds to bother you much." I opened my door and stepped out of the truck. Somewhere on the street, Rider would have more security, but Daniel was my personal guard and the only one I could see at the moment.

"I think that would bother me," Daniel said as we crossed the street together. He held the door open to the dress shop, and we stepped inside. I felt instant relief once I stepped out of the sun. The sunscreen kept me from burning alive, but it was a bright, sunny day and the sun's warmth did not feel pleasant on my exposed skin.

"Danni! It's about time you arrived," my mother's shrill voice carried out to me and just like that, my instant relief was gone. My mother came out from behind a dress rack and stopped in her tracks, gaping at Daniel. "Is this ... gentleman... with you?"

Normally my mother would be overcome with joy to see me with a man, but between the rainbow-hued hair and the silver hoop piercing his nose, Daniel was not what my mother would consider quality man material. "This is my friend, Daniel. Daniel, this is my mother, Margaret Keller."

"Nice to meet you, Mrs. Keller." Daniel offered his hand and my mother took it gingerly, her eyes darting between the two of us. I could almost hear her screaming on the inside, envisioning a horde of rainbow-haired children she couldn't show in public.

"Friends?" Her voice was nearly a squeak.

"Friends," I said again.

"What's taking so long?" Shana asked, coming out of the dressing area. She saw Daniel standing next to me and stopped. Her gaze took him in from head to toe, and she started twirling a piece of her blonde hair. "Who's your friend, Danni?"

"Daniel, this is my sister Shana, the bride-to-be." I put extra emphasis on the bride-to-be part in an effort to remind Shana her days of flirting with every good-looking man she came across were over. She hadn't seemed to have gotten the memo yet. "Is Grandma here?" I asked, praying she wasn't. My grandmother had the personality of a cactus and I was pretty sure loved no one but Terry the Tiny Terror, the little dog she carried around in her purse everywhere she went despite its habit of releasing farts strong enough to kill nearby foliage. I was relieved to not see her.

Daniel nodded in my sister's direction. "I hope you don't mind me tagging along. Danni and I were hanging out today."

"The more the merrier," Shana said, her white-toothed smile beaming a million watts as she grabbed my hand and pulled me over to the dressing area. "Who is he?" she whispered. "He's adorable. He's not like a gay friend, is he?"

"No," I answered. "What does it matter? You're engaged, remember?"

"I'm engaged, not dead." Shana rolled her eyes and took a light pink gown from a dress rack that had been placed outside the dressing rooms. There were at least twenty dresses on the rack, all a pale shade of pink, and I knew I was going to have to try them all on before I would be allowed to escape. "What happened with your boss? And that hot guy from the restaurant? Rider?"

"My boss disappeared weeks ago and is thought to be dead or living under another identity in another country," I told her, omitting the fact that I'd actually killed the slime ball. "Rider is still around."

"Are you dating?"

"We're in a relationship," I said, hoping she wouldn't

question me further. I didn't know how to classify my relationship with Rider, and I'd been warned that his enemies would go after anyone they felt he cared strongly about. I doubted my family conversed with many vampires or other paranormal entities, but I'd worked with a woman who had been unknowingly ensnared by an incubus and had been set up by her to be attacked. I supposed anything was possible.

My mother entered the sitting area outside the dressing rooms and directed Daniel to one of the many ottomans that had been pushed together in the middle of the room for seating. "What kind of job do you have, Daniel?" she asked, her gaze still going back and forth between his hair and nose ring.

I mouthed a *sorry* and took the first dress into one of the try-on rooms to begin the torture. I tried on one pink dress after another, receiving critiques on each one in-between. I could tell Daniel was steadily growing more irritated with each dress change but whether it was from having to hang around with a woman trying on a dress, enduring how close my sister sat next to him which may or may not have been a hardship for him, or dodge the multitude of questions he kept receiving from my mother, I wasn't sure.

It took about an hour for me to get to the last dress. It had a shiny bodice that fit like a second skin and thin spaghetti straps which would have never supported a larger woman's breasts, but mine seemed fine since there wasn't as much weight to them. It molded to my body from chest to hip before it flared out into a slight ruffled design that fell to my ankles. A huge, wide slit down the front that stopped about three inches below my unmentionables showed plenty of leg. I stared at my reflection in the mirror and gulped.

"Does it fit?" My mother asked. "Do you need to go up a size bigger to fit your rear end in?"

I gritted my teeth and walked out, ready for the

massacre. Whereas my mother and sister's eyes narrowed as they prepared to pick me apart, Daniel's eyes widened. His mouth dropped open just a little, and he smiled. *If Rider is reading my mind right now, I'm a dead man because dayyyyyum,* he projected into my mind.

Don't even joke about that, I projected back to him. It was the first time we'd actually chosen to converse in that way since Rider had created the bond, with the exception of Daniel projecting random annoying thoughts into my head as part of Eliza's exercise. It felt a little strange.

"I suppose that one wouldn't look so bad if she could lose a couple pounds off her rear by the wedding and take the enhancement pills I ordered for her," my mother said. "What do you think, Shana?"

Shana scrunched her nose and shook her head. "It's too Jessica Rabbit for her. Danni is more of a loose sheath kind of girl. Plus, she'll be next to me, which will make her look even flatter in front."

"No offense, ladies," Daniel cut in, "but I don't know what the hell you're looking at. All I see in front of me is *hot damn*. She looks great in all of the dresses and there's no flatness anywhere in this one. Hell, if she wears this dress, no one's going to be looking at the bride. Danni's going to steal the whole show."

"I've never seen my sister turn that red before," I told Daniel fifteen awkward minutes later as we left the dress shop. "You didn't have to say all that stuff. That's the way they are. They're very critical."

"That wasn't just being critical. That was being a pair of straight-up bitches," Daniel said. "I meant every word I said. You looked great in all those dresses and men would have been swallowing their tongues if you'd gone with the last one. Your sister knows it too. That's why she selected one of the dresses that didn't cling to your curves."

"Curves?" I rolled my eyes. "My sister isn't worried about me upstaging her. She is far curvier than me."

"Your sister has a big chest and a flat ass. Give her

enough time and her nipples will be hanging out with her bellybutton just like your mother's."

I burst out laughing and gave Daniel a playful shot to the arm. "That's awful."

"What's awful was sitting between the two of them for an hour. They asked if I had any other piercings and I'm willing to bet that if I said yes, your mother would have made the sign of the cross and your sister would have asked for a closer look."

"Do you have any other piercings?" I asked.

We were on the sidewalk across the street, next to the truck. Daniel paused with his hand on the handle of my door. He looked down at me and smiled. "Wanna take a look?"

His eyes suddenly lost their playfulness, and he pushed me to the ground as something whizzed over my head where I had just been standing. It was déjà vu except I wasn't in Rider's garage, bullets had whizzed over my head instead of an arrow, and my protector was Daniel, a dragon-shifter currently shielding me with his body.

The truck blocked my view of the street, but I heard multiple vehicles screech to a stop and doors slam, and I knew we were in trouble. Daniel lifted me off the ground and shoved me toward a narrow gap between two commercial buildings. "Go! Go! Go!"

I ran as fast as I could, which was surprisingly fast. I knew I had vampiric speed, but I really didn't use it much. It was nice to have when enemies were shooting at me. The narrow space opened up to a parallel street, and I ran right out to it and found myself surrounded by a circle of pissed off men with guns trained on me.

A heartbeat later, I was airborne, looking down at the men as they looked up at me, jaws dropped. I looked up and realized Daniel had shifted into dragon form and was now flying high in the sky with me in his enormous dragon claws. I looked down again at the tiny buildings beneath us and started screaming.

THIRTEEN

Are you all right? Rider asked through our mental link.

Hell no I'm not all right! I'm five hundred bajillion feet in the air in a dragon's claws!

Five hundred bajillion? I could sense him laughing.

I'm HIGH! You'd better not be laughing like this shit is funny!

I'm just relieved, babe. I thought you might have been hit. I'll see you in a few.

What was probably only a few minutes later but felt like hours due to the fear I could fall to my death at any moment, Daniel dove alarmingly fast toward The Midnight Rider and released me the instant my feet hit the roof. I turned in time to see him shift from ginormous dragon to normal sized man within a myriad of sparkling colors. If I'd blinked, I would have missed it.

"Boy, can you scream," he said.

"I was afraid you'd drop me."

"Never in a million years, sweetheart."

A door opened and Rider rushed out, followed by Rome and Tony, both of whom had guns pointed toward the sky as they scanned for an aerial threat. Rider pulled me to him and kissed my temple. "Good work, Daniel," he said before ushering us toward the door. "Let's get inside."

The staircase led down two floors before we came to a door, but we passed that door and kept going down to what I assumed was one level under the bar. Rider placed his hand on a panel next to a heavy metal door, and I heard it unlock. The door slid open, and we entered what appeared to be what I could only describe as some sort of mission control room. A long black table occupied the center of the room and supported the weight of ten computers, five on each side. A mix of ten men and women, none of whom I'd ever seen before, manned those computers. It was hard to tell who was who with so many people in close proximity to one another, but I sensed vampire, shifter, and human in the room. While that group of people tapped their fingers over keyboards at warp speed, men and women in dark clothing stood at attention behind them, watching a large plasma screen taking up the wall before them. Some wore gun belts, and some had knives strapped to their arms. A few had nothing at all. I assumed those were the ones with claws. A door on the other side of the room opened, and a man walked out with a gun. I looked beyond him and saw the room was used to store a weapons cache.

"I've got it," a petite, dark-haired woman working at one of the computers said, raising her gaze to the plasma. "There was a jewelry store across the street with a feed."

"I have the bank on the parallel street," a wiry redheaded guy said, pointing to the plasma.

"I got a boutique on the parallel street," another said as two more chimed in with various businesses.

I stood between Rider and Daniel and watched the plasma as multiple security camera feeds appeared on it. I watched black and white video of Daniel and I leaving the dress shop. We walked across the street, chatting along the way. We rounded the truck and Daniel paused at my door. The camera angle changed as Daniel pushed me down and shielded me with his body. The footage was stopped and the computer team hacked away at their keyboards, playing with various angles from the footage they had.

"Can't get a clear image of the shooter or the vehicle," the brunette said, "but we may have better luck on the parallel street."

I heard them clicking away and then the footage continued. I watched Daniel push me toward the gap between buildings and then another set of camera angles popped onto the screen. I watched myself run out of the gap and Daniel emerged behind me, quickly shifted into dragon form, grabbed me in his talons, and up we went.

More furious clicking took place, and I was looking at closer shots of the men who'd been training guns on me when I'd run out of the narrow gap.

"Those are from the Black Skull Brotherhood," Rome said, pointing out three young men in baggy jeans and wife-beaters. One black, one Latino, and one white.

"Those are Quimbys." Rider nodded his head toward a trio of white men in the center of the group. "Anyone recognize the remaining shooters on the right?"

Everyone in the room studied the images, but no one recognized anyone else.

"It must have got back to Barnaby Quimby's family that he was killed and they've figured out it was by my hand," Rider said. "It's no surprise they'd be here to avenge him. I would assume the others are hunters as well, or more gang members the Quimbys are getting help from. There hasn't been any buzz on the street about hunters?"

"I haven't heard anything at all," Rome said, "but I'll

dig around and see if anyone knows what the Brotherhood has been up to. I doubt they know who Danni really is. None of the local gangs have dared cross you in years."

"Keep working on this," Rider told the group on the computers. To the team waiting behind them, he ordered, "Go." They immediately departed.

Rider closed his eyes, and I felt the power rolling off of him, filling the room. Suddenly my head was filled with images of the people who'd attacked me and Rider's voice warning the nest and all his employ that we were under high alert. The power snapped back into him and he opened his eyes. He blinked slowly until his eyes no longer shone with the golden glow of his power and turned toward Daniel. "Take a gun and a blade, and take her to my room. Under no circumstance is she to leave."

I opened my mouth to object and Rider sent me a withering glare that caused my voice to promptly disappear before he turned and started barking out commands at the remaining staff in the room.

Daniel dipped into the weapons room and came out with a gun in his right hand. "Let's go," he said, taking me by my elbow and leading me out the door.

"What is that place?" I asked as we took the stairs up.

"The Bat Cave."

"I'm being serious."

"So am I," he answered. "They call it The Bat Cave. Your boyfriend doesn't really keep you in the loop on things, does he?"

"I guess not."

"I was shown The Bat Cave the first night I was here." We reached the door we'd passed earlier on our way down and Daniel placed his hand on the panel next to it, waited for the click, and pulled me through. It opened behind the stairs that led to Rider's apartment. I'd seen it before and had assumed it was some sort of utility closet. "It's the main security hub. Those computer geeks can hack into security cameras and databases, track suspicious activities, monitor the security teams, and who knows what else. There's a weapons room loaded with all kinds of shit. Silver bullets, hawthorn bullets, flamethrowers, holy water grenades. He's got some seriously badass stuff."

We'd climbed the stairs and reached Rider's door. I stepped through and held my breath as Daniel walked in. I knew the door was spelled to only allow those Rider wanted inside and was a little surprised Daniel was on the list. I had no clue what happened to those not allowed and was glad Daniel didn't burst into flame.

"There's no lock on the door?" Daniel asked.

"It's spelled to only allow those Rider approves inside," I explained. "According to Rider, this is the safest place for me to be."

Daniel looked around the room and laughed. "He thought you were safe with me in his bedroom? Nice."

"Am I not safe with you in his bedroom?"

"You're safe with me anywhere," he answered, moving over to the bathroom and looking in. "Your boyfriend has a tendency to look at me like I'm the enemy sometimes though. It's kind of amusing. Is this it? Just a bedroom and a bathroom? I thought this was his home."

"It's where he sleeps," I said, sitting on the edge of the bed.

Daniel had grabbed a utility belt from the weapons room and he slid his gun into it. He stood in the center of the room, hands on hips, and looked around. "What the hell do you do in here once you're awake and the sex is over?"

I grabbed the remote and pushed the button to make the TV rise out of the bar. "Anything in particular you want to watch?"

"I'm here to watch you," Daniel answered. "As long as you stay in this room, I don't care what you watch."

"What are you going to do if I decide I want to leave?" I asked, looking at the gun.

"Stop you," he answered, not a trace of amusement in his tone. His eyes were hard, his mouth a firm line.

"I don't think I've ever seen you so serious."

"I don't like people hunting you. I've heard of the Quimbys. I was under the impression there was some deal between them and Rider that they wouldn't hunt him or anyone under his protection. Why were three of them in that group after you?"

"Barnaby Quimby broke the pact last month when he tried to shoot me in Rider's garage with an arrow dipped in hawthorn oil. Rider killed him. I guess when he fell off the face of the earth, his hunter buddies and family put two and two together."

"Why did he break the pact?"

"Apparently incubi and succubi were never under the umbrella of protection. Quimby knew I was a hybrid and refused to allow my existence. He was actually stalking me the night Selander Ryan attacked me, using me as bait to capture the bigger prize. Rider knew what he was doing though, and had taken him aside for a little *discussion*. That was when Selander Ryan slipped into the bar, conned me into leaving with him, and attacked me."

"How were you bait? You should have just been human then. What was so special about you?"

"My blood. It's all kind of nuts, but supposedly there are different blood types and mine has a sweetness that attracts incubi. They can't turn every human into an incubus or succubus, but those with my blood type can be turned. Sweet blood draws them so Quimby thought he

166

could follow me until I lured the incubus he knew was in the area. Maybe it's not so weird," I said, looking at Daniel. "You have spicy blood. I suppose if there's such a thing as spicy blood, there's such a thing as sweet blood. How did you know I was about to be shot at? You were looking right at me, talking. I didn't sense anything."

"You weren't focused," he answered. "Even while interacting with you, I was on the job. You need to work on compartmentalizing. You can go about your day, doing whatever you want to do, but you need to keep part of yourself on high alert. Also, dragons have an incredible ability to track movement and sense danger. That's why dragons are used as guardians. Your fairytales here aren't all fiction."

I thought about that. "You don't lay eggs, do you?"

"Lord, I hope not," he answered before smiling wide. "You know that whether I'm in dragon form or my regular self, I'm always a dude, right?"

"Oh, yeah." I flipped through channels on the TV. "I wasn't sure if dragons were one of those species where the males can have the babies too."

"To my knowledge, I don't think so."

"Can you have sex in dragon form? And then does the female dragon lay an egg? Would a baby dragon hatch out of it or a baby person? How do dragons—"

"You ask a lot of weird shit," Daniel cut me off. He sat next to me on the bed and took the remote from my hand. "Even when I'm a dragon, I'm still me. Even if the hottest woman in the world was a dragon shifter, I don't think I'd want to do her as a dragon. There's certain lady parts I like to work with that dragons don't have, and the whole idea is creepy. Here, weirdo. There's a *Supernatural* marathon on. I haven't met a single woman in this realm who doesn't love those guys. Watch this."

"Okay." My eyes were on the screen, but my mind was still on dragons. "Do dragons have balls? Are they all hard and scaly too?"

"Dear Lord. Where's Rider at?"

"Finally," Daniel said when Rider walked into the room shortly after midnight. "Your woman keeps asking me about my genitals and mating habits."

"Dragon genitals and mating habits, not his," I clarified, noting the dark look in Rider's eyes and the way his body had instantly coiled, ready to pounce.

"Why are you asking him about dragon genitals and mating habits?" Rider asked me.

"Why wouldn't I be?" I answered. "Don't you want to know about dragon genitals and how they procreate?"

Rider stood still except for his eyes, which slowly blinked while he looked at me, thinking. "I love you, but you're fucking weird."

"Of course I'm weird. I'm a vampire-slash-succubus, and whose fault is that?"

He stood hands on hips, and just looked at me for a moment before heaving out a resigned sigh. "You're done for the night," Rider told Daniel. "I need to talk with you downstairs for a moment and then you can go home."

"Sure." Daniel stood and walked toward the door, turning his face away from Rider to covertly wink at me before walking through it.

"If you kill him, I'll be grumpy," I warned Rider.

"Good to know." He turned and left the room, and I went back to watching the Winchester brothers eat diner food, bicker at each other, and kill monsters.

"Are you thirsty?" Rider asked an hour later as he stepped back into the room.

"I'm good," I answered, my eyes glued to the TV as I watched Dean Winchester raise his gun and kill the demon who'd killed his mother. I'd seen that particular scene a million times, but it remained one of my all-time favorites. "How's Daniel?"

"He'll live to fly another day."

I raised an eyebrow. "Did he get scolded or something?"

"No. He did a good job today. Why don't you come down to the office with me? We're on high alert, so I can't even think about resting until sundown. I didn't want to keep Daniel here all night, but I don't want to leave you alone either, not even up here with the warding."

I looked up at him. "It seems like you're asking me to go to your office, but I get the feeling it's not really a choice."

"You're very perceptive." He grinned.

"You're bossy."

"Trust me, I have worse qualities than that. Come on."

I gathered up my laptop and followed Rider down to his office on the first floor. "I thought maybe you had another office in the level below us," I said as he closed the door and took a seat at his desk. I plopped down onto the couch and booted up the laptop. "I'm surprised your apartment isn't down there instead of on the second floor. It seems like it would be more secure down there."

"I've spent a lot of time underground or in caves, especially toward the beginning of my life after being turned," Rider said as he tapped various keys on his keyboard, his eyes focused on his monitor. "I wouldn't go so far as to say I developed a phobia of being underground, but I definitely don't care for it. Running the control room out of the lower level is one thing. I'm not going to sleep there."

"Daniel said it was called The Bat Cave."

"Yeah."

"You really do like the whole vampire shtick, don't you?"

"Are you judging me?" He cut a look my way. "It doesn't seem like a woman interested in dragon gonads should be judging me."

"Oh, come on. You've never wondered what dragon balls look like?"

"I don't spend a lot of time thinking about balls that aren't attached to myself, babe."

I didn't really know how to respond to that, so I checked my email and found two replies from applications I'd submitted on a job search website. Each provided a link to answer pre-interview questions and set up an in-person interview. "I already got some responses back from a couple of applications I put in yesterday and I need to schedule the in-person interviews. I assume you want Daniel taking me to the interviews. Do I need to schedule around his availability or is he, like, on call or something?"

I waited for a response as I reviewed the set of pre-interview questions for the first job, didn't hear one, and looked over at Rider to see him staring at me with hard, dark eyes and an indentation in his jaw from how tightly clamped his mouth was. "What?"

"Are you shitting me right now?" he asked, voice low.

"I told you I was looking for another job."

"I told you that you didn't need one."

"I have my own place to pay for, Rider."

"You don't need that either."

There was a rap on the door and Rome stepped in. He saw me on the couch and paused, his eyes wary. I imagined

170

I didn't look very friendly, what with the steam I felt coming out of my ears and the way my fists clinched. I knew Rider didn't look friendly. "I just got back from collecting intel, but if I'm interrupting something important, I can just wait out here until you call me in."

"I don't have time to wait," Rider said, tone sharp. "What did you find out?"

Rome closed the door behind him and approached the desk. "Word on the street is that the Brotherhood was approached by a group with access to a lot of guns. They're willing to trade guns and even offered up some serious cash for help taking down their target. You already know who the target is. The Brotherhood doesn't know what it's gotten itself into. They were told the target has an allergy to hawthorn, so they're using hawthorn bullets provided by the group that contacted them. Their instructions were to shoot to maim and while she's weakened by the allergy they're supposed to…" Rome looked at me, a mixture of fury and concern in his dark brown eyes. "They're supposed to pass her around before handing her over to be slaughtered."

It felt like the bottom of my stomach dropped out and my skin grew cold and clammy. Stars burst before my eyes as my head swam. When my vision cleared, I saw Rider looking at me. Everything about him was cold, hard, and terrifying. He looked back at Rome. "Who is the Brotherhood's biggest enemy lately?"

"The South Side Scorpions."

"Make them an offer. Let these bastards take each other out of the equation. You've already put out word that Danni is under our protection?"

"Of course. I have some trusted men spreading the word as we speak."

"Good. Stay on this. You're on permanent Danni detail

171

until this threat is over. If you need to jump out to deal with the gangs, tap in Carlos."

"Yes, sir." Rome nodded, looked at me, and left the office, closing the door behind him.

Rider sat rigid in his chair, his gaze on his computer screen as he tapped his fingers on the desk. I didn't need the power to read minds to know he was barely containing his anger. "Did you hear what he said?" he finally asked.

"Yeah." My voice came out timid, like a mouse. If he wasn't a vampire, he probably wouldn't have known I'd spoken.

"Do you understand what he meant when he said they were told to pass you around?"

I swallowed. Hard. "Yes."

Rider looked at me. "Now, do you understand how fucking stupid it would be to get a job and go out there every day unprotected?"

"So, am I to just stay locked in here for the rest of my life?"

"If I had my way, yes, but you choose to be difficult."

"Wanting to earn a living is being difficult?"

"All you need to survive is blood and protection, two things I can provide for you."

"I don't want you to provide everything for me. I don't want to be indebted to you."

"You won't be," he said. "I would never ask for anything from you in return. You're not a slave here, Danni. I just want you to be safe."

"So you don't care whether or not I'm actually happy?"

"Of course I want you to be happy."

"I can't be happy just surviving," I explained. "I didn't bother going to college just to sleep all day and then sit in a room all night watching TV. I've been a vampire-succubus-whatever for less than two months. I still have

172

human needs. I need a job, I need purpose. What about my sister's wedding? Are you going to ban me from that too?"

"You can't hold on to your family forever," he said. "You're going to have to cut them out of your life eventually."

"Good grief, Rider, I was just turned. I have years before anyone would notice that I've quit aging. I'm not going to just cut them out of my life right before my sister's wedding. I'm the maid of honor. I have to go. You'll be there to make sure I'm safe."

"I won't be there," he said. "It's one thing to be seen with you in the bar, but going to a wedding with you is something I wouldn't do with a woman I was just casually sleeping with. I can't put an even bigger target on you than the one you already bear."

My eyes burned with unshed tears. "I'm not missing my sister's wedding. You're really not going to go with me? You know they think I can't keep a man and you're going to make me go alone to a function one would typically bring a date to?"

"You need to get over giving a damn what your family thinks about you. You won't be going alone anyway. I don't want you to go at all, but I understand you still have an attachment to your human life, so I'll make sure security is in place. Daniel will be your escort. Being seen around with him might actually even work to throw my enemies off your scent."

"How is that?"

"They wouldn't expect me to send the woman I love off with another man. If you're seen with him enough, my enemies might think you're his."

"Well then, maybe I should slide my tongue down his throat and see if that does the trick," I said, still feeling the anger of him refusing to go to the wedding with me. "You wouldn't need to worry about me at all anymore."

I thought I'd seen Rider angry before, but there weren't words to explain how frighteningly hard his eyes became as he pinned me to the couch with his dark glare. He sat still as a stone, not drawing a single breath. I felt his fury roiling inside him and imagined if he unleashed it, being slammed into a wall as I'd seen him to do to others would be the least of my worries. "I wouldn't do that if I were you. Unless, of course, you want Daniel to die."

I swallowed. "If I kissed him, you would kill him?"

"Yes."

"Why wouldn't you just kill me?"

"I could never bring myself to kill you." He shook his head. "You still don't grasp how much I care about you. I'm not keeping you here or telling you to forget the job search just to be an ass, Danni. I'm sorry you can't just come and go as you please, and you can't put your college education to use right now. You went to try on dresses today and you were surrounded by a group of men with weapons right after. We never even saw that coming. If you hadn't been with Daniel, you might have died. You were surrounded. His ability to shift and fly was the only thing that saved your life today. You have hunters and a gang after you. There are men searching for you right now so they can gang-rape you and then pass you off to be killed. What kind of man would I be if I didn't keep you here where you're safe? I certainly wouldn't be a man who loves you."

As much as I hated to admit it, he had a very valid point. I deleted the emails and set my laptop aside. "I'm sorry. I'm really not trying to be difficult and I do appreciate you protecting me. I just feel completely useless here, like my whole purpose here is sex."

"I could get that from anybody, and I damn sure wouldn't put a whole security detail on them afterward. You know you're more to me than that."

"I don't do anything else here."

"You give me joy," Rider told me. "At least, when you're not being a giant pain in the ass."

He stood from his desk and collected an assortment of books from his shelves. "Here, if you really want a job..." He stacked the books next to me. "Go through these and see what all you can find out about reincarnation, succubi, and soulmates. Try to see if there's any kind of dark spell that can bring a soulmate back to someone or just anything funky that seems like something my dickwad half-brother would be using to his advantage. We can't forget about him just because there are now hunters and a gang after you. I was going to do this myself, but I'm dealing with other problems." He moved back to his seat and muttered a curse as he read something on his monitor. "Daniel did a great job saving your life, but he was seen landing on the roof. People have been tweeting and posting on the bar's Facebook page. I have to shut all this down before it spreads. I've got my tech team scouring security camera feeds, searching for where your assailants are at now and we still haven't identified who actually shot at you. I have teams on the ground working in rotation and just gave Rome the go-ahead to turn a rival gang after the gang going after you and hope they wipe each other out. I'm a little too busy for that much research right now."

I picked up one of the thick, heavy books and flipped through its many pages. It looked like it could have been written when my ancestors came off the Mayflower. "I can't do this research on the internet?"

"The last time you attempted research on the internet you got distracted by pictures of Dean Winchester. You won't have that problem with the books, plus they contain information you're not going to find online. It could be worse. I'm having to read comments from conspiracy theory morons claiming everything from aliens to lab-created pterodactyls have invaded downtown Louisville."

I sighed and flipped back to the first page of the book I'd picked up. I had no idea what exactly I was looking for or where to start, so I just started from the first page. The pages were thin and yellowed, and the words were handwritten in black ink. I assumed a quill had been used, which was undeniably cool, but the words were hard to read in places, making deciphering the pages tedious.

"Shit," Rider snapped a while later.

"What is it?" I asked, looking up to see him shaking his head in disgust.

"For a second there, I had a fleeting thought about dragon balls. I'm going to make you pay for that."

I grinned and went back to my research, pretty sure I was already paying by slogging through the pages of the ancient book.

FOURTEEN

Almost six hours later, I'd skimmed through three of the books and listened in on countless updates as various members of Rider's security team entered the office to advise of the latest developments, not that any of the developments were that spectacular. They still hadn't identified the asshole who'd shot at me or located the men they actually had identified. The bastards had gone underground like the rats they were. A lot of the updates had to do with actions being taken to ensure the police didn't get involved. The security camera footage had all been wiped clean before local law enforcement had a chance to view it in order to keep Daniel and me off their radar and Rider was deflecting reports of a large monster landing on top of the roof as fast as they came in.

Rider shut down his computer, leaned back, and stretched. "I hate this type of crap," he complained. "I'd rather be out there rooting out those bastards."

"Your tech team couldn't handle responding to the monster rumors?"

"They could, but I'd rather have them focused on more important issues. Besides, if I was out there, I'd be worried about you here. Dealing with the rumors is simple enough to do while overseeing everything else going on."

"What happens when you sleep? Are you leaving someone else in charge?"

"Tony will take over overseeing the operation. He'll wake me if something major happens. I'm going to feed you before sunrise, and I want you to sleep until nightfall. I also want you trained to fight, so trust me, you're going to want a full day's rest."

"I'm going to want a full day's rest after going through these books," I said. "These are so old. Where did you get them?"

"I've collected them from various places throughout the years. I had to kill for some of them."

My mouth dropped open. "You killed people for books?"

"No. I killed horrible monsters for knowledge," he corrected me. "Not to mention, those books are extremely dangerous in the wrong hands."

"Yeah, I've stumbled along some pretty terrible spells," I said. "The spells are real?"

"Yes."

"One of them required the heart of a newborn child."

"Yeah, I killed the previous owner of that book. Unfortunately, I only learned of her after she'd worked a spell requiring the eyes of twenty holy men. Still want to look at me like I went too far to get that book away from her before she started slicing up infants?"

I shook my head. "No. It's hard to believe people can reach that degree of evil."

"Power and money have always had a way of corrupting people."

"How have you managed not to give in to the lure of it in all this time? I know you said looking at your mother's portrait helped, but there has to be more to it than that."

Rider stared at his hands for a moment before standing up and taking the books from me to replace on the shelves. "The more you kill, the easier it becomes. If you keep killing innocent people, the guilt loses its power. Vampires, by nature, are monsters. I feed the monster in me without completely losing the good man inside by killing other monsters."

"You've never killed a human?"

"I've killed several. You saw me kill Quimby. I've also killed rapists and child abusers. Monsters come in a lot of varieties."

"Would you really kill Daniel if I kissed him?"

"Do you want to kiss the guy?" Rider asked, tone sharp.

My mouth dropped open, and I sputtered a moment before I could form words. "Of course not. Why would you even ask me that?"

"I don't know, maybe because you've mentioned it twice now? I left you alone with him for five minutes earlier and you were asking about his balls."

"It was a lot longer than five minutes and I was asking about dragon balls!" I stood up and fisted my hands on my hips. "I wasn't asking about *his* balls."

"Who the hell else do you know with dragon balls?"

"No one. Why else do you think I was asking him?"

Rider stared at me for a moment before putting his fingers to his eyes and growling. "How can I love you so much when you drive me so crazy?"

"Welcome to the club," I snapped, walking over to his bookshelves to check out the inventory. "Maybe there's a spell in one of these to help you stop since I'm so much trouble."

"Oh, spare me the overdramatic tantrum."

"Spare me the brooding vampire act," I shot back, looking through his books. "Robert Pattinson already took that gig."

"Who the hell is Robert Pattinson?"

"From *Twilight*. Duh."

"You're comparing me to that douchebag now?"

I rolled my eyes and continued looking through his

books, stumbling on a collection of rabbit-eared paperbacks that looked like they'd been read at least a thousand times. I pulled one off the shelf and opened it to see notes written in the margins in large, messy script. It and the books I'd found lumped with it were various religious books and two were about karate. "These are dangerous?"

"I never said every book in here was dangerous. Be careful with those. A good friend gave them to me."

I flipped through the well-read pages. "Seeking enlightenment?"

"Elvis was. He was a very spiritual person, and he didn't just read books, he absorbed them."

"Oh." I shrugged and put the book back on the shelf, then froze as the name sank in. "Elvis? Like... *Elvis* Elvis? The King of Rock and Roll, Elvis the Pelvis?"

"He hated being called both of those names."

I just stood there, gaping. "You knew Elvis?"

"Yes."

"How did you know him?"

"I owned a bar in Memphis. He was a night owl, so he'd come in a little before closing when it was almost empty and not that many people were left to recognize him. I'd let him stay after I closed and we'd talk."

"Wow. What was he like?"

Rider folded his arms and leaned back against the bookshelf behind him. "Sometimes his presence filled the whole building. His smile could light up a room. He gave off energy unlike any human I've ever known. Other times, he was the saddest, loneliest person you could ever meet. He was smart, kind, and generous. He was always searching for something. I think he would have been a lot happier in life had he never become famous."

"Wow. I can't believe you actually knew him."

"Yeah, I was lucky. Has our stupid argument ended now?"

I rolled my eyes. "Yes."

"Good ol' Elvis. Still winning over the ladies. It's time for you to feed and go to bed."

"Yes, Master."

Rider took a deep, controlled breath. "Danni, please don't start another argument with me. I know you're upset with everything, but I'm doing the best I can. I really don't need the attitude right now, and all you're doing is making yourself even more unhappy. I hate seeing you unhappy, especially if I have anything to do with it."

Boom. Direct hit to the guilt zone. I sighed and crossed the room, raised up on my tiptoes and brushed a light kiss on his lips. "I'm sorry. I feel cooped up, and it's making me snarly. I appreciate everything you do for me, and I swear you're the only man I want to kiss. I wouldn't even take Dean Winchester over you."

"That's a wise decision," he said, grinning. "Because you're a vampire and he'd kill you."

I playfully punched his shoulder. "Fine. I'd take you over Jensen Ackles. Better?"

"Better." He kissed my nose. "Not that long until sunrise. Let's go upstairs."

I followed him up the stairs and grabbed one of his big T-shirts before going into the bathroom to get ready for bed. When I came back out, Rider was already in bed, his nudity from the waist down covered by the sheet.

"I don't know why, but seeing you in nothing but one of my shirts is sexier than any lingerie could ever be," he said. "You should feed before sleeping so you don't wake up ravenous. You want my wrist or throat?"

I pulled the sheet back and straddled his lap. "I'll start with the throat," I said. "Then we'll see what happens next."

Oh, hell. I was in the foyer again, standing in front of the gilded doors. I knew a snake waited for me on the other side, coiled and ready to spring. I could stay in the foyer out of his reach, but I wasn't confident the marbled room was a safe space. I was pretty sure Selander Ryan had created this place and could change it with a mere thought. I'd found information about incubi in the books Rider had given me to search through. Incubi could invade dreams and take control, changing everything to fit their needs. Succubi, of course, could do the same, which made me wonder if I could alter the world Selander Ryan had created for our meeting place. I looked at the walls and tried to conjure up a different door. The walls blurred, but the only thing that appeared was a deep chuckle from beyond the gilded door. The bastard was amused.

The gilded door swung open to reveal the dining room, Selander Ryan once again sitting at the head of the long dining table, dressed all in white. He grinned wickedly, an evil gleam in his dark eyes as he crooked his finger, beckoning me closer to him. "You don't want me to come get you," he warned.

"You can't kill me," I told him, standing straight, faking bravery. I knew Rider wouldn't let me die, but whatever part of my body produced fear didn't care. Ryan could still hurt me before Rider yanked me awake.

"I can still enjoy my time with you," Ryan said, "in ways you wouldn't very much enjoy." He let his gaze travel the length of my body, which was encased in a slinky champagne-colored gown and stilettos.

"Rider wouldn't allow you to harm me," I told him. "The moment I feel pain or real fear, he'll pull me right out of here, so what can you really do in such a short timeframe?"

Ryan's grin stretched wider. "Do you truly want to find out?"

I'm here, Rider's voice whispered in my mind. *I'm awake watching over you. I sense him in there. Be careful, but try to get answers from him. If he tries to hurt you, I've got you.*

Can you hear me?

Now, when you speak directly to me. I can't hear what's

happening in there, but I can feel you.

Ryan's eyes narrowed, so I looked him in the eye and folded my arms before he could figure out that Rider was already tapped in. "Is that what you brought me here for? You went to all this trouble for a minute of amusement? Go for it."

"So bold," he said. "I wonder how bold you will be once that gang catches up to you and starts passing you around for endless sloppy seconds."

I tried to hide my surprise, but my eyes instantly widened. "You sent the gang after me?"

"No." He shook his head. "I would never work with the Quimbys and they certainly wouldn't work with me, but just because I'm removed from your realm doesn't mean I'm unaware of what's going on there or that I can't get to you."

Interesting. "You have spies."

"I have a loyal family. You could have had a loyal family, but you chose to honor that murderer."

"I have loyalty from someone I can trust," I told him. "I never had anything from you except constant threats, and you have nerve calling anyone a murderer with all the blood on your hands."

"I never killed anyone I claimed to love. I wonder, will Rider do to you as he did to my beloved? He claimed to love her too."

"He loved her enough to put her out of the misery of being the vulgar creature you turned her into when you, in fact, killed her."

Ryan's nostrils flared as his eyes burned with anger. "I gave her eternal life."

"Clearly you didn't or Rider wouldn't have been able to end her. Of course, he only killed the abomination she'd become. You were the one who killed the person she really was."

"You don't know anything about her."

"The moment Rider crushed your heart, I saw

everything. I saw Rider kill her so clearly I could have been standing there next to him. I saw the relief in her eyes. The love Rider had for her was the pure love of a son. What you felt was perverse and twisted, sickening."

"Watch your tongue lest you lose it," Ryan warned, voice low.

What's happening? Rider asked. *Where are you? What's it look like?*

It's the same dining room he always brings me to, I responded before telling Ryan, "I'm really not that afraid."

Ryan stood and approached. My body stiffened in response, and I forced myself to release my breath and calm down. I didn't want Rider yanking me out of the dream until I'd learned something more useful than just the fact Ryan knew what was happening in the real world. He circled me, a predator circling its prey.

There's a foyer with a gilded door and no other way out, I told Rider while Ryan circled, either trying to intimidate me or looking for an attack point. *Once I go through the gilded doors, I'm in the dining room. Ryan is always sitting at a long table with a chalice in or near his hand. He is always in all white. A crystal chandelier hangs above the table. Everything looks expensive. Lots of crystal, lots of fruit and wine. There are some paintings on the wall and there's a door in the back of the room.*

Can you change the room?

I tried to form a new door and couldn't. The walls blurred, but that was it.

What do the paintings look like? See if you can focus on them and send me the images.

Do what now?

Focus on them, absorb every detail and send the images to me just like you send your thoughts to me. It sounds more complicated than it is.

Yeah, sure. I looked at the paintings. One was a pale-skinned woman in a black hooded robe. She looked down at a skull in her hands. I really couldn't see her eyes, but her lips were slightly turned upward as if her image had been captured just before she smiled. I focused intensely on the painting and imagined I was taking a picture. I closed my eyes, retaining the image in my mind, and sent it to Rider as I sent him my thoughts.

"What are you up to?" Ryan asked, stopping before me. He looked over at the portrait.

"Viewing the artwork," I said. I moved across the room and stopped in front of another painting.

Did you get that image? I asked Rider.

Yes. Good job.

"So since I'm sleeping, I assume this is actually my dream," I said to Ryan as I studied the painting in front of me. It looked like a cavern, with flames climbing the walls to lick the ceiling. Men and women twisted in various directions, their mouths open in silent screams as they stretched their arms out, seeming to try to reach out of the portrait. They were unclothed, covered only in ash. "This doesn't look like anything I would dream about. I'd prefer something with prettier colors, and maybe some unicorns. I wouldn't have a bunch of fruit and wine in here either," I said, and sent an image of the painting to Rider before moving back to the table. I picked up a grape and squeezed it. It felt real. I moved toward the head of the table where Selander Ryan always sat and looked beyond to the archway at the back of the room. I saw shadows moving along the wall and the flicker of flames. "What's back there?"

"Your business is here." Ryan stepped in front of me, blocking my path.

"Why build this place for me if you didn't want me to see it?"

Ryan glared at me before he pulled out a chair and shoved me down onto it. He reclaimed his seat and lifted his chalice to his mouth, watching me over the rim with hard, assessing eyes as he drank the dark liquid.

"You are putting on an air of bravery, but I know better," Ryan said, as he lowered the chalice to the table.

"You can only keep up the façade for so long, Danni."

"I think what you're sensing is an air of annoyance. You're interrupting my sleep, and for what? Why am I here? You scared me the first time, I'll give you that, but the more you bring me here, the less I'm afraid. Rider won't let you kill me here, so I have nothing to be scared about. Oh, and I know about the whole soulmate thing, so I doubt you can even bother me with all your vague commentary. I get it now. You waited for me to be reborn and find Rider."

Ryan smiled. "You didn't find him. I led you to him."

"Yeah, and you tried to kill me but didn't succeed. In fact, you got your own ass killed. Why are you still playing this game? You already lost."

"My death was not the end. I don't know how many different ways I can tell you this before you understand that."

I'm not getting much out of him, I told Rider.

You need to take away his control. See if you can rile him up enough to loosen his tongue. I'll snatch you right out of there if he tries anything.

I wasn't sure how to rile him up in a way that would get information and not just send him lunging straight for my throat, but I squared my shoulders and winged it. "So to recap, you know I'm Rider's soulmate so you led me to him, failed to kill me, died yourself after I chose him as my master instead of you, you can't kill me before Rider pulls me out of here and you can't get out of whatever the hell this place is to do any damage to me in the real world so what's the deal? What's the great big revenge on Rider? Seems to me all you can do is hear from your people on the outside about what's happening out there. You're just sitting in here all dead and useless, hoping someone out there will do what you want to do, but can't. You know what I think? I think you're just toying with me. You said you wanted to drive me mad so you keep bringing me here, acting all elusive and shit trying to drive me crazy but the truth is you have no power over me and you're just not all that mysterious anymore. I'm losing curiosity, so good luck driving me mad."

He studied me for a moment, so straight-faced I knew he was putting effort into appearing expressionless. "You are very different than you were at our last meeting. You're acting skills have improved. I can almost believe you aren't shaking beneath your skin."

"Maybe you're just not that scary anymore," I told him as I grabbed a cluster of grapes. "Face it, Selander, if you really had some big master plan, you couldn't hold it inside. You're an arrogant villain and arrogant villains love to hear themselves talk, love to brag. Sadly for you, you have nothing to brag about, so you just make empty threats of some mysterious way you're going to finally destroy Rider. So far, a gang has come closer to harming us than you have. A gang. Humans. That's got to burn."

Ryan grinned. "It's killing you inside, not knowing when, where or how I'm going to strike. I'm not going to deny myself the fun of making you and Rider live in fear of—"

"Fear this." I threw a grape at him. It hit right between his eyes with a satisfying plop, leaving him bug-eyed and gape-mouthed with shock.

Get ready. I might need a quick exit, I warned Rider as Ryan's skin infused with red.

"Tell me something useful or don't waste my time," I said. "Go pop a villain impotence pill if you can't get your diabolical plot up. Do something."

"Gladly," he said, and snapped his fingers. His gaze dropped to my chest and his mouth spread in a wicked grin.

I looked down and realized I was buck-ass naked, sitting in the chair with nothing but my heels left on. "You sonofabitch!" I yelled as I crossed my arms over my breasts.

"Bored now? You're about to drop the brave act." He

lunged forward.

NOW! I mind-screamed to Rider as I raised my leg just in time to connect my stiletto heel with Ryan's throat.

FIFTEEN

I came awake with a rush of adrenaline, sitting straight up in the bed. I was still naked, but I'd fallen asleep that way.

"Are you all right?" Rider asked. He sat next to me with a pad of paper and a pencil in his hand. Unlike me, he was dressed for the day in black pants and a sapphire blue dress shirt, sleeves rolled to his elbows. "What happened?"

"I'm fine." I pulled the sheet up far enough to cover myself and settled back against the pillows. "I wasn't getting anything out of him except more of the 'you'll never see me coming, but when I strike it's going to be soooo terrifying' threats, so I hit him in the face with a grape. He snapped his fingers and presto, I was naked. I raised my leg when he moved to attack me and shoved the heel of my stiletto into his throat just as you pulled me out."

"You were naked?" Rider's eyes narrowed.

"Only for about five seconds," I told him. "Five seconds I'll have nightmares of for years to come. That bastard knows I hate being naked. The whole rile him up to get info thing didn't really work. I got nothing from that guy. I was acting like I thought he was full of crap and didn't really have a big, evil master plan but now I'm thinking maybe his master plan is that he really doesn't have a master plan and he's just getting his jollies by driving me screwy."

"Screwy?"

"I'm starting to feel a little screwy."

Rider nodded his head. The corners of his mouth twitched, showing I'd amused him. "You really threw a grape in his face?"

"I should have sent you an image of his reaction. It was pretty funny."

"I bet it was. I'm bummed I missed it."

"So… My heel was in his throat and blood was spurting out when you woke me up. Do you think that did any lasting damage or will he instantly heal? Can he actually be injured in reality?"

"I'm not sure what reality is for him anymore," Rider answered, "so I wouldn't get my hopes up that he's been permanently maimed. I know if he were alive, he could heal from that type of wound with enough time and magical aid. Also, your visit wasn't as fruitless as you think it was."

"I got nothing."

"I got something." He turned the pad of paper toward me, and I saw it was an artist's sketchpad. "I noticed a common factor in the two paintings you showed me."

"You drew that?" I asked, studying the symbol that had been etched onto the pad in charcoal. At first glance, it resembled a cross, but the ends were curved. The bottom point looked like a fish hook and the top point curved slightly less in the opposite direction. The left point dipped down and the right side dipped up. A scroll shape ran diagonally through the middle.

"Yes."

"I didn't notice that in the paintings."

"It was hidden, and you wouldn't see it unless you knew to look for it. The first painting was of a cloaked woman holding a skull. The symbol was disguised as a crack in the skull. The second painting was harder. Most people would look at it and just see the people, not paying any attention to the way they were arranged."

"The way they were arranged?" I tried to remember the paintings. I did remember there being cracks in the skull, but I hadn't paid that much attention because a crack in a skull wasn't odd. The second painting just looked like a bunch of naked people covered in ash to me. "You're saying the people in the painting were forming the symbol themselves?"

"Yes."

I looked at the symbol. It didn't ring any bells for me. "So what is it?"

"No idea."

"Then how did you know to look for it?"

"I knew to look for something," He clarified. "A lot of symbols are used in magic. If he's bringing you to the same place every time he appears in your sleep, there has to be something special about that place. If it's not a familiar place for you, then it's his creation. When you said there were paintings, I had a hunch there had to be something special about them. Also, you said he was always with or near a chalice?"

"Yes. He sips from it sometimes while talking to me. It looks like a dark wine."

"Could it be blood? Did you smell it?"

"I guess it could be. I didn't smell it. Now that I think about it, I don't think I could smell anything there, not even the bounty of fruit on the dining table. I could see shadows from flames beyond the archway at the back of the room, but I didn't smell anything burning."

"Interesting."

"What does it mean?"

"No idea."

"Well, what do you know?" I asked.

"I know you're cute when you're exasperated." He

leaned over and kissed my nose. "I also know that if you stay there like that much longer and I'm going to get naked and do things to you. The sun's almost down. Go on and get dressed. I've arranged for you to have a fighting lesson tonight, and then you can do more research."

"Oh boy. I can hardly contain my excitement." I took in his attire and noted how perfectly coifed his hair was. "Why are you already up and dressed?"

"I slept as much as necessary to properly fuel mind and body. I've been up for hours."

I frowned. "You're always next to me when I wake up. I thought you slept as long as me when we're together."

"I usually do, seeing as how you have a tendency to set that damn alarm on your cell before you go to sleep, and it wakes me up with you. My inner alarm buzzed early today. There's too much going on for me to just sleep the day away. We're still looking for the group who attacked you on the street, and now I have this symbol to look into. I'm going to see if Rihanna knows anything about it."

"Oh, I forgot about her." I scooped Rider's T-shirt off the floor and pulled it over my head. "Didn't she run after Daniel the night he got me the cupcake? I saw that cupcake and completely forgot to ask what happened." I looked at Rider, awaiting a response. He was grinning. "What?"

"Why do you put a shirt on just to get out of the bed and change into something else?"

"Why shouldn't I?" I shrugged. "Not everyone likes to just let everything hang out all over."

"You know I have every inch of your body memorized, right?"

I shuddered, drawing a laugh. "Don't tell me that."

"You're ridiculous, and I love you for it." He pulled me in for a kiss that started light and built to smoldering. "Damn," he whispered against my lips and drew back. "Seriously, now. Go shower and get dressed before I forget everything going on and lock us both in this room for the night."

"I'm going, I'm going." I gathered leggings and a T-shirt since he'd said I was getting a fighting lesson, and collected underwear. "You didn't answer about Rihanna. What happened with her and Daniel?"

"You're the one who talks to the guy, babe. I have no clue."

I started to ask what Daniel had done all day since he hadn't been needed to guard me, but decided against it. Rider had been pretty surly about Daniel the night before, and I didn't want to start anything with him again.

"Okay," I said, and entered the bathroom to get ready.

Rider took me downstairs to The Bat Cave again. The tech team barely glanced up as we walked past them, focused on the information on their screens. I saw several lines of code on the plasma but didn't bother asking what it was for, figuring I wouldn't understand it. Working my iPhone and running simple searches on Google were the extent of my technological expertise.

We passed the armory and went through another door that led to a hallway. "The locker rooms are there," Rider said, nodding his head toward the doors with male and female symbols on them. "I prefer you use my bathroom. Those are really for staff."

That was fine with me. I never had been able to shower in public. It would take more than a shower curtain for me to strip down in a room full of people. I'd rather drive home from the gym covered in sweat than take the chance of someone seeing me in my birthday suit.

Glass ran the upper half of the left wall, allowing us to see in to the gym where large men and extremely toned women were working out with weights or running the treadmill. "Were all of them so muscular before turning into vamps and shifters, or did they have to work for all that?"

"Shifters are naturally strong and they gain muscle mass over time. Some work out with the weights to gain it faster and they use the treadmills to burn off excess energy. My human staff uses the gym a lot, and as you know, we gain in strength the longer we live and we automatically tone up once we turn, but a puny runt of a man won't automatically bulk up like a football player just by turning. He'd have to work for that muscle, and a heavy vampire would lose some weight, but it won't *all* fall right off. He'd have to burn the excess weight off."

I looked down at my body. "I didn't change when I turned."

"Yeah, you did. It's not as noticeable with some. If you're already in good shape, you'll only experience minor changes. Your skin was paler before you turned. Your eyes are brighter now, your muscle more toned, hair smoother."

"Really?" I didn't know if I was more surprised about the changes, or the fact he'd noticed. He'd just met me as a human right before the attack that led to my change. I hadn't even noticed these changes until he'd mentioned them. "It's weird that our bodies can change, yet we don't age."

"You eventually get used to the weird and just accept it without question." He pushed a door open after we'd passed the long window and gestured for me to enter. "You're working in here today."

I stepped inside a brightly lit room with gymnasium flooring, a mat running along the far wall, a couple of boxing dummies, and a mirrored wall in back. Rome was sitting in a chair in the corner, tightening his laces. He wore sweatpants and a Louisville Cardinals T-shirt with the sleeves cut off to accommodate his massive biceps.

"Rome is going to train with you tonight. He'll teach you some techniques and spar with you, and—"

"Spar with me? Are you nuts?" I exclaimed. "He could punch a hole through steel!"

"You'll be fine," Rider assured me, grinning as a

chuckling Rome stood and moved toward us, flexing. He was clearly amused by my reaction. "Think of it this way. The more time you train, the less time you'll have to do research."

"Isn't the research important?"

"Yes, but so is the ability to defend yourself properly. You beat the hell out of that wolf, but she wasn't a trained assassin, and you didn't view her as anything other than an average woman. Rome's a human and you're intimidated by him because of his size. Most of the bastards sent to kill you will be men, and most will be big. You can't be intimidated by size or gender and although rage has worked well for you so far, I'd rather you not have to depend on that kicking in to save you."

The door opened behind us and Daniel stepped in, also wearing sweatpants and athletic shoes. He topped off his look with a white muscle shirt. I noticed again how toned his arms were.

"Daniel's going to observe and make sure you don't Hulk out on Rome and start a real fight. I don't want either of you hurt." He looked at Rome pointedly when he said this. "Call me if there are any issues."

"We got this, man," Rome assured him. "I'll have her ready to take out Ronda Rousey in no time."

"She can already do that," Daniel said, taking a seat in the chair Rome had vacated. "She needs to be able to take out Blade."

"What he said," Rider said, and turned to leave. "I'll be back in about an hour or two. Don't break each other or I'll be pissed."

"Is he physically incapable of leaving people without threatening them?" Daniel asked.

"Watch yourself, new guy," Rome answered. "His threats aren't empty."

Daniel's reply was an exaggerated salute.

"I'm gonna laugh my ass off when the boss knocks that attitude out of him," Rome said with a smile, shaking his head as he turned toward me and raised his hand, palm out. "Show me what I'm working with. Punch me right here."

I looked at his palm. "Now?"

He nodded. "Give me a good solid punch."

I took the stance Rider had shown me during our one fighting lesson in my apartment shortly after I'd been turned and punched Rome's hand.

Rome looked at his hand, a mix of confusion, laughter and maybe a bit of irritation in his eyes. "What the hell was that? You hit me like a girl."

"I am a girl," I reminded him.

"You're a vampire. You have to hit harder than that. Now hit me like you mean it." He raised his hand again. "You see my muscles, baby. I won't break. Really go for it."

I rolled my eyes at his cockiness and took my stance again. I balled up my fist, drew back... and dropped it. "This is stupid. I don't want to hit your hand."

"Why not?"

"It's dumb. I already know how to throw a punch."

"I haven't seen that yet. That wasn't a punch I just felt a moment ago. That was your knuckles gently kissing my palm, all sensitive and shit. Now punch me like a man."

I narrowed my eyes. "I don't want to. Show me something else that isn't dumb."

"Dumb?" He laughed. "What's dumb is some little piss-ant vampire telling me to show her something else when she can't even throw a single decent punch. I thought you said she was tough, Daniel? She's a marshmallow."

"I know what you're doing," Daniel said, glancing up from the cell phone he'd been texting on. "I wouldn't rile her up too much. When she gets pissed, she gets mean as hell."

"This cupcake?" Rome looked me over and shook his head in disgust. "I've never heard of a vampire that can't throw a decent punch. That's just sad, man. It's a disgrace to your kind. Man, my granny could throw a better punch than that."

My body started warming as Rome continued griping. A whirring sound started in my ears, and I grit my teeth together. My hands curled into fists.

"Come on, baby. Show me something. I can train you to kick ass, but you have to throw a decent punch first. Just throw one good—"

I released my growing irritation with a quick jab to the groin that sent the large man crashing to his knees. His eyes rolled up in his head as he doubled over on a cry far too high-pitched for his massive frame.

"NUT-PUNCH!!!" Daniel jumped from his seat, laughing and pointing. "I told you not to piss her off, dude. Hey … you all right, bro?"

"Are my balls hanging out my ass now?" Rome asked, still bent over on the floor, clutching his junk. His voice was still a higher pitch than his normally deep voice, strained with pain. "I feel like my balls are hanging out my ass now."

"Well, I'm certainly not going to check," Daniel answered.

"Are you all right?" I asked the big guy, guilt setting in. I hadn't meant to hurt him.

"No, I'm not all right, devil woman! What the hell's wrong with you?"

"You told me to hit you."

"I told you to hit my hand!"

"Why would I ever hit anyone's hand?" I asked. "I'm a woman. When I hit a man, I go for the balls or the face."

"Why didn't you go for my face, then?"

"I couldn't reach it as easy."

Rome glared at me like he was considering punting me across the room, then slowly got back to his feet and took a deep breath.

"All better now?"

"Still waiting for my balls to drop back down. Just so you know, men tend to look out for cheap shots like that when in combat with a woman. Don't count on nut-punches to save you if you find yourself in a real fight. It's an extremely predictable move, so you'll almost always get blocked."

"Why didn't you block me?"

"I wasn't in a fight with you. I told you to hit my palm and expected that. I never suspected you'd do something so brutal to me when I had no intention of hurting you."

Now I felt really bad. "Sorry. It was a reflex."

Rome grunted in response and ambled over to where Daniel sat. "Grab me an ice pack and take over."

Daniel smiled at me as Rome took his seat back, slouching with his legs spread wide apart. "Practice with the dummies," he said as he passed me to leave the room and fetch an icepack.

I looked at the dummies, which were basically punching bags shaped like men's torsos. "What am I supposed to do with these?"

"Hit them," Rome answered. "They don't have nuts, so you'll have to actually hit them in the chest or face like you have some integrity."

I shot him a dirty look, but he didn't seem affected by it. Punch a guy in the balls and you were pretty much on his shit list. "Anything I can do to make this up to you?"

He looked at me for a moment and a grin slowly spread across his face. "Nut-punch Daniel."

"I'm not going to intentionally hurt him. He'd have to piss me off first."

Rome muttered something that didn't sound very friendly under his breath and gestured toward the dummies. "Start jabbing. We're on the clock. Rider will expect for you to have learned something."

I walked over to one of the dummies and started punching it. The dummy was an inanimate object and I couldn't summon anger out of thin air, so I hit it similarly to how I'd hit Rome's hand. It swayed back and then lurched forward, springing back to its original location. I hit it harder, making it go back even farther before springing back. I switched hands, noting the dummy moved considerably less when I struck it with my left hand, which was my non-dominant hand.

Daniel reentered the room after I'd gotten a decent amount of punches in, tossed a couple of icepacks to Rome and moved next to me to observe. "You're right-handed?"

"Yeah." I switched back to my right hand, showing how I did more damage to the dummy with it.

"You'll want to practice on the dummy with your left more so you can build up your strength in that arm and compensate for the difference. A smart opponent will study you, figure out your dominant hand, and use that information to his advantage. Now hit that thing like you mean it."

I stood hands on hips, and sighed. "I have to be angry, otherwise I feel stupid."

"Then get angry."

"I can't just get angry at a dummy."

"You did ten minutes ago. Nut-punched him too."

"I heard that, Puff," Rome said. "Don't think just because I'm human, I can't hold my own with all you members of the animal kingdom up in here."

"Puff?"

"As in Puff the Magic Dragon," Daniel explained. "Okay. Hit it again."

I rolled my eyes, unsure why Rider would arrange for this lame training that really wasn't teaching me anything. I half suspected he just wanted to get me out of his hair without having me leave the safety of his building. "This is so lame."

I threw some punches at the dummy while Daniel and Rome watched and glanced at the clock, hoping to see time had raced by and my boring lesson was almost over, but sadly, that wasn't the case. Just as I was about to drop my hands and tell the guys I was done, whether Rider liked it or not, Daniel stepped behind me and straightened my shoulders.

"Shoulders back like this," he said softly, enveloping me as he reached around to grab each of my wrists. "You want your throwing arm back like this and your other one needs to be raised so you can block your face when your opponent tries to hit you." He moved behind the dummy. "Now try it again, but keep your stance."

I punched the dummy and Daniel reached around it and smacked me in the side of my head.

"Hey!"

"Wasn't me," he said, grinning. "It was the dummy. I put your fist up for a reason. You have to block. Try again."

I positioned myself as he'd instructed and tried again, jabbing the dummy and blocking the swipes Daniel delivered from behind it. Every once in a while he'd succeed in connecting with the side of my head and I'd feel myself growing hotter with anger. My punches became faster and harder as I connected with the dummy instead of the dragon shifter getting on my nerves. I delivered a solid punch to the center of the dummy, had my other hand up, ready to block Daniel when he swiped at my head, but he swiped lower, catching me in my side. "What the hell, Daniel?"

"Your opponent isn't always going to go for the head, Danni. There are no rules when the shit gets real. You have to be ready for anything. Again."

I took a deep breath, rolled my shoulders, and started punching the dummy again. Daniel took his swipes, and I deflected them. This went on for about five or ten minutes, then he started swiping at me faster. He connected with my head twice, not hard enough to hurt me, but the fact he connected pissed me off. Every time he got past me to connect with my head or side, it felt like a fail. I didn't like failing. My eyes started burning, my stomach rumbled with hunger, and Daniel's heartbeat thumped like a bass beat in my ears. I was staring at the pulse point in his throat when his arm came around the side of the dummy to connect with my rib. Acting on pure reflex, I shoved the dummy aside with a growl and aimed my fist at Daniel's face.

"There she is!" Daniel exclaimed, laughing as he ducked my punch and came back up to block another. "Don't forget to block."

Daniel blocked my blows and delivered his own. Completely focused on him instead of splitting my focus between the dummy's torso and his arms, I found a rhythm much easier, but he still managed to get a few swipes in at me.

"Be careful, Puff," I heard Rome warn from behind me. "She's starting to throw like she's aiming to break shit."

"I noticed," Daniel said from behind clenched teeth as he blocked a fast jab. "Calm down, Danni. This is just sparring, sweetheart."

"Spar this!" I said, sending my fist careening toward his chin.

Daniel's hand came up and clamped over mine. He spun me around as he pulled me against his body. "Cool down, Danni."

In the zone now, I elbowed him in the face, causing him to release me, which allowed me the chance to spin around and grab his shirt. I fell onto my back, raised my legs up and used the leverage to catapult him through the air. He landed on his back with a sharp exhale six feet from where I stood.

"Enough!"

I turned my head to see Rider standing just inside the door, hands on hips, surveying the room.

"Daniel, are you all right?"

"Living the dream." Daniel gave a thumbs up but

didn't try to stand.

"He's all right," Rome said, laughing. "Dragons are supposed to fly."

"At least I lasted more than a minute with her," Daniel shot back, sounding breathless as he slowly sat up and rubbed the back of his head.

"Are those ice packs?" Rider asked, noticing the square bags on Rome's crotch before directing his attention to me. "You neutered my human."

"He started it," I said, but my gaze was on Daniel. I was still frustrated and thirsty, but guilt was a powerful extinguisher. I'd gone too far and could have seriously hurt someone I cared about.

"Look at me," Rider said, approaching. He wrapped his hand around the back of my neck and studied me. "You need blood. Lesson's done for the day. Looks like you beat the shit out of your trainer anyway and were going for a second victory."

"She snuck in a punch to my balls," Rome explained, standing. "I'll watch for that from now on."

"Are you going to be all right to go out tonight?" Rider asked him.

"I'll be all right. I think my boys finally dropped back down out of my stomach."

"How about you?" he asked Daniel.

"I'm good," Daniel said, standing. He rolled his neck. "She just knocked the wind out of me."

"All right. Come on, Danni." Rider took my hand and led me out the door. "We really need to do something about this obsession you have with balls. If you're not wondering what someone's look like, you're trying to destroy someone else's."

Rider fed me in his room, then joined me in the shower, where we got very dirty before getting clean. By the time we were dressed, the anger that had been burning inside me had dissipated. "Did I hurt them bad?"

"Rome's built like a tank, but he's still a man. Any time you hit a guy in the balls, it's going to hurt bad, especially if that man is just a human and you're a vampire. As for Daniel, he's an Imortian. He's built tough. Had you pulled that elbow move with Rome, you would have most likely broken his nose."

"Are you mad at me?" I asked as Rider placed his hand at the small of my back and led me out of his room.

"No, but I am concerned. You've had quite a few violent outbursts since being turned."

"Is that abnormal or something?"

He shot me a side glance as we walked to his office, but didn't say anything. He'd already grabbed some books and placed them on the couch for me to look through.

"Rider?"

"I wouldn't say it's abnormal," he finally answered as he closed the office door and took his seat at the desk. He read something on his computer screen and tapped a few keys before looking back at me. "It can be dangerous. Not everyone can succeed as a functioning vampire."

"Succeed as a functioning vampire?" I sank down onto the couch, my stomach sinking too. "You're saying vampires can fail as vampires? Can I? What's that even mean?"

He sat back in his chair and stared at me for a moment while he chose his words. "It's not so much that they fail as a vampire, more that they struggle to rein in the power that comes with the turn. Vampirism strengthens certain characteristics. Some vampires naturally have more physical strength than others. If a person possessed any amount of psychic power as a human, it increases greatly as a vampire. Gluttonous people become very bloodthirsty vampires. Any darkness that resides in a person, or any type of special gift they possess, has the ability to intensify during the change. Depending on the characteristic and how greatly it intensifies after turning, some vampires have to be put down before they can do grave danger to humanity."

I felt my mouth drop open as I looked at Rider, measuring his words.

"I would never allow anyone to put you down," he said, reading my mind. "Of course I wouldn't do it myself either. A temper isn't necessarily a bad thing, but you need to work on controlling yourself. Daniel is your friend and you let your temper get the best of you. You could have hurt him if he wasn't a trained fighter. People will notice these outbursts if you keep having them and they will feel threatened by you. With Ryan and the Quimbys already after you, we can't afford for you to attract any more enemies right now. It's bad enough anyone wanting to usurp my power could jump into the mix at any moment."

"Does being a hybrid have anything to do with my temper?"

"It's hard to say." He sighed. "Hybrids are rare. I've only known one other, and she is certainly a violent creature, but that may just be her nature." He smiled as if remembering this person, and I felt a little twinge of jealousy.

"You know another vampire-succubus?"

"No. You are the only vampire-succubus I have ever heard of. The other hybrid I know is a vampire-witch. She is extremely powerful and has the traits of both species. Of course, witches are born witches, so I can't compare her turning to yours. You kind of had two turnings, whereas she had one. Your temper flares might sort themselves out with a little time. In the meantime, try to be aware. Come to me before lashing out if you can."

"You have a temper yourself," I pointed out.

"Yes, but I'm in control of mine. When I hurt people, I mean to." He nodded toward the stack of books next to me. "Get to work on that. Maybe you'll find some answers."

"Do you really think I'll find any useful information in

these books?" I asked. "Or are you just trying to keep me busy so I don't fuss about being locked down in here?"

He grinned. "Maybe both. Look for that symbol too. Rihanna wasn't familiar with it, but despite the sassy attitude and penchant for shrinking genitalia, she doesn't really dabble in the dark stuff."

"On it," I said and opened one of the books. The mention of Rihanna reminded me of Daniel. "You asked if Rome and Daniel were going to be able to go out tonight?"

"Yeah, we got a lead on the gang members at the scene of the attack. Rome and Daniel are going out with a group to retrieve them."

SIXTEEN

After midnight, I was worried about Daniel and Rome and sick of looking through Rider's books. I'd found information about various realms in one which had been interesting, but the print was small and the pages were bountiful. I'd set it aside when the words started running together and grabbed another book about magic. It had a lot of pictures and drawings in it to break up the monotony of endless words, but I had trouble focusing. "Have you heard anything yet?"

"You've been right here with me all night," Rider answered, not bothering to look up from his computer. "If I'd heard anything from them yet, you would have too."

"I thought they might contact you telepathically."

"I would tell you immediately if they did. Rome doesn't really communicate with me that way unless necessary. I created a link with him, but he's human. His preferred method of communication is texting. Daniel is new to the ability. It's probably second nature for him to use a phone as well."

"How do you call him in to work?"

"Phone. I don't see any use wasting mental energy when it isn't necessary. It takes more energy to communicate with him that way than it does with you. You're my fledgling. Communication between us takes no effort."

"How much energy did it take to fill the room with power and slam the door in his face?"

Rider grinned. "That wasn't a waste."

"Sure." I flipped through more pages in the book I was currently looking through. "What are you doing over there anyway?"

"I was doing some business-related work earlier. Right now, I'm doing research. Daniel told me about Hades, so I'm researching the layers of Hell."

"Seriously? You've got me going through these old tedious books, but you get to research on the computer?"

"My research is no less tedious and unlike you, I don't get distracted when *Supernatural* references and Jensen Ackles pictures pop up in my search results. Happens a lot, by the way."

"Poor thing."

"Trust me, I'd much rather be out there hunting whoever the hell is hunting you."

In a way, so would I, even though the thought of actively seeking someone who wished me harm, or death to be more exact, seemed insane. At least I would be with the people searching instead of being in Rider's office, worried about those people. Rather than obsessing about Rome and Daniel, and whether they were just acting tough when they said they were fine earlier, I returned to the book in my lap. Each page featured a drawing or picture and information on it. I seemed to be in a section devoted to different spell ingredients, most of which were plants or odd things like raven claws, toad eyes, and demon blood. The pages were handwritten, leading me to believe it was a journal some witch or person otherwise involved with magic had put together. I flipped the pages quicker until I came to a section of spells, most written in Latin and some in other languages I couldn't determine. I looked closer and realized they were different languages because they weren't original to the book. They'd been collected separately and affixed to the pages.

"I can't even read most of this one," I told Rider. "It's in different languages." I flipped a bunch more pages, then flipped back when something caught my eye.

"Holy crap!" I ran over to the desk and set the book in front of Rider, opened to the page featuring a hand-drawn symbol identical to the one Rider had discovered in Ryan's paintings. "It's the symbol, but I can't read whatever this says on these two pages. It's some weird language."

"It's Hungarian," Rider said, studying the pages. "Good job, Danni."

"It's not that helpful unless you can read Hungarian. Can you read Hungarian?"

"I *am* Hungarian."

"Oh." I studied his dark hair and blue eyes. "I didn't know that."

"It's not common knowledge and I haven't been in Hungary in ages. I don't even think I could fake the accent, I lost it so long ago."

I looked down at the book. "Can you still speak and read the language?"

"Among others," he answered. "This is a symbol used in dark magic spells. It says that if a person carves this symbol into his bone, he can travel to other locations marked with this symbol when drawn with his blood."

"Are you telling me that the place I see Ryan at in my dreams is an actual physical location?"

Rider shook his head and continued reading. "It doesn't say anything specifying that it has to be a physical location, and it isn't a physical location for you because while there you're actually here."

"But he can touch me. I can feel him."

"But you can't smell anything?"

"Right."

Rider tapped his fingers on the open book, studying it.

"I just left his body there that night. We'd been battling each other for so long I didn't care if he had a proper burial, and I didn't think he'd be a threat without his heart. I should have burned the damn thing. If he has a dark witch working with him, she's probably guarding his body now in some hidden location and with this symbol carved into his bones, his soul can travel."

"Can it travel here?" I asked.

"According to this, it can travel to anywhere this symbol has been written in his blood."

"He's dead. Wouldn't his blood be dried up?"

"You are my blood, Danni. You are his blood too, and so are the other succubi he created over his lifetime. Magic isn't always literal."

Fantastic. He'd marked himself with a magic key that let him run amuck and left an unlimited supply of blood to keep him in action. A chilling thought entered my head, causing my hands to tremble. "Can his soul go into his body since the symbol has been carved into his bone? Could he be here in this world now?"

Rider took my hand and kissed my knuckles. "This symbol is called a soul stitch. I'm going to have to look into it further. My gut is telling me that if he could be here in his physical body right now, he would be. He's too arrogant not to use that trick if he has it up his sleeve. My gut is also telling me that just because he isn't here now, it doesn't mean he can't be later. He's visiting with you for a reason, and it has to be for a bigger reason than just screwing with us for kicks." He looked at me with worry in his eyes. "My main concern is the fact that you are his blood and he pulls you into this place he's created using that symbol. Once there, you can't leave unless I draw you out or he releases you."

My blood grew cold. "What are you saying?"

"You tried to create a door last time and couldn't?"

I shook my head. "The walls just blurred."

Rider picked up his desk phone and dialed a number.

"Hey, can you get a full body scan done on Danni? As soon as possible. All right. We'll be there."

"What was that about?" I asked as he hung up.

"We're going to the hospital so Nannette can do a body scan."

"Why?"

"Because… I think when that bastard marked you, he may have really marked you… with that damn symbol."

My hand automatically went to my throat. "He could do that with just a bite?"

"Yeah, a bite and a hefty dose of dark magic, and that wasn't just a bite. He mauled you like a rabid dog. I should have crushed his heart right then." Rider stood and took my hand. "Let's go get this scan done so we can see if my suspicions are correct."

I felt Rider's power as we left the office and knew he was communicating telepathically with members of his staff. "Calling in the troops?"

"The Quimbys and whoever they're working with are still out there. I wouldn't even risk taking you out of here if this wasn't important. If we're going to travel, we're going to travel in a pack."

The garage was empty when we entered, but I still checked all the dark places in search of a boogeyman. The garage was where Barnaby Quimby had attempted to kill me roughly six weeks ago, so despite the security Rider had in place, I was a bit nervous stepping back into the garage, knowing that other members of the Quimby family were currently hunting me.

"Quimby got in here last time because of James and Marie. I don't think anyone else on my staff would be stupid enough to cross me like that. You can relax."

I didn't think anyone else on his staff would be so stupid either, considering he'd put James's head on display after killing him as a warning what happened to those who betrayed him, but fear isn't always rational. "Am I projecting my thoughts again?"

"No, but you're biting your lip and trembling a little." He pulled me to him as we reached the Ferrari and enveloped me in his arms. "You're going to be all right. I won't let anything happen to you. Ever."

"I know."

He stared down into my eyes for a moment before kissing me on the forehead and opening my door. He knew I was full of it, but wasn't going to call me out on it. "The team's in place. It's time to roll out."

Tony and another man were in a car just outside the garage at one end of the alley, and an SUV filled with more of Rider's security team sat at the other. They sandwiched us as we pulled out of the garage and stayed with us to the hospital. All three vehicles pulled into the hospital's attached garage and found parking spots together near the elevator.

"Hank and Juan, stay with the vehicles," Rider instructed two of the men as the rest of us entered the elevator. Rider pushed the button for the basement level three times in quick succession, which was the secret way paranormals got to what we called the underworld ward. I'd never been, but Eliza had told me about it.

The elevator descended past the basement level containing the morgue and opened up to the underworld ward. The lights were dim, but other than that, I didn't notice anything else strange about the hospital as Rider, Tony, and the three other members of Rider's security team stepped out onto the floor. It smelled of antiseptic, just like every other floor in the building.

Rider gave his team directions to guard all the possible entry points and walked over to the sign-in desk. A thin redhead with a pert little nose looked up and paled. "Mr. Knight. You don't need to sign in. We're ready for you."

"Quick service," I commented as we followed the small woman down the hall. Tony, the only member of the security team still with us, followed behind.

"I'm on the board of directors," Rider replied. "Plus, I

called ahead so Nannette would be expecting us. As part of my nest, she received the alert on the Quimbys and their gang buddies and knows I need to get you in and out as quickly and safely as possible."

"The board of directors?"

"Not of the whole hospital, just the ward that services the paranormal community, and no, I don't have a medical degree or any real medical expertise. It's just a title given to those of us who back the ward financially and oversee operations."

The little redhead took us through a door marked radiology and directed us into an empty room dominated by a massive white machine that resembled a CT scan machine on steroids. "Nannette will be right with you just as soon as she finishes up with the patient she's working on," the woman said, smiling as she turned to leave. On her way out, she nodded and giggled flirtatiously at Tony, who remained just outside to stand guard.

"What was she?" I asked, unable to detect any vampire or shifter vibes.

"She's human. Some work here in the underworld ward, but they have special abilities. I'm not familiar with her, so I don't know what hers is."

"Humans are safe here?" I asked.

"The security is very good here. In fact, security here is from my own employee pool. There is zero tolerance for violence, so the odds of anything happening to a human in this ward are very low. Ryan and predators like him wouldn't even try to enter. They know this ward is under my protection."

"So you own the bar and you're on the board of directors here. Any other businesses?"

"I'm the owner and chief operator of MidKnight Enterprises. I own multiple businesses, but MidKnight is primarily a security company. Currently, I personally manage the security company here in Kentucky, but I have them in Maryland, Tennessee, Ohio, and Virginia as well. I service and employ the paranormal community, but take on some human accounts as well if the money is high enough."

I stared at him as I contemplated this information. "You own a company large enough to function in multiple states with, I assume, full staffs, yet you live in what is essentially a bedroom with attached bath over your bar?"

He shrugged, grinning. "My office is at the bar. My Louisville base is under the bar. Short commute."

"It's just a bedroom and bath. You could afford so much more. Doesn't it drive you crazy being in such a little space?"

"Danni, before you came along, I spent every waking minute working, and not at my desk. I worked right alongside my security teams on patrols. On slow nights, I monitored the bar for trouble. I've worked here on the hospital security team, and there's always some evil bastard out there that needs to be taken out. I do that for free. All I ever needed was a place to sleep and shower."

"You spent *all* your time working?" I raised my eyebrow.

"There were women, yes, but I never brought anyone home with me, so again, I didn't need anything fancy. I never even fed in my room until the first night I brought you there, and that was just because I didn't want to leave you alone."

"You've had to have had real relationships. You've been alive too long not to."

"Yes." He nodded. "Mostly with other vampires. I learned the hard way that getting attached to humans is only asking for a lot of emotional suffering later. I move around between states and even countries. Wherever I've been, I've enjoyed female companionship, but never serious enough to share a home with anyone. It took me a long time to even consider myself worthy of such a thing, being what I am, and once I did, I'd known and mourned too many good people to risk the pain of losing someone I care about. I would only allow myself relationships with women who understood what we had would never evolve to spending eternity together, even if they too were vampires. Honestly, I didn't even choose to be with you. There was no choice, no decision to make. The moment you stepped into my bar, I had to be with you."

"Is that a bad thing?" I asked, unsure if his revelation was a compliment or a complaint.

"Only because it puts a target on you. The truth is, I should stay far away from you, but I'm too selfish. Being with you makes me feel things I haven't felt in … ever. Plus, you make me want something more than just doing this job I've been doing forever. You make me more man, less killing machine."

"You've had to kill since meeting me, even because of me."

"Yes, but the hunting isn't what fuels me now. I spent so many years searching for the next biggest predator. That's not necessarily a bad thing, as I've taken out quite a few, but it seems like every time I destroy one enemy, another emerges. It's a never-ending cycle which I've accepted, but the need to find and kill the next Big Bad isn't what drives me so much anymore. Your protection drives me. Being with you drives me. I have something to enjoy other than the thrill of the hunt."

The door swung open and Nannette entered dressed in navy blue scrubs that showed off the rich hue of her chocolate skin and coffee brown eyes. She eyed us curiously. "Interrupting anything?"

"No," Rider answered. "We were just waiting for you."

"Sorry about that. I had a new vampire with severe sunburn."

Rider's eyes darkened. "Someone here created and abandoned a fledgling?"

"No, her dumbass boyfriend turned her and got himself killed the next night where they were living in Ohio. She traveled here to be with her family and didn't take proper precautions. I'll send her to Eliza when she's released." Nannette walked over to a small desk and started tapping away at the keyboard while looking at the monitor. "What are we looking for?"

"Have you heard of a soul stitch?"

"Sounds like the name of some long-haired white guy band performing out of the same garage they sell weed in. I'm guessing that's not it?"

"It's a symbol. Selander Ryan has been visiting Danni in her sleep, and I found the symbol in the room he uses for their meetings. It's how he's able to visit her. I need to see if he somehow carved that symbol into Danni's bone."

Nannette glanced up at me, assessing, before returning to whatever she was doing at the computer. I straightened my shoulders, refusing to wither under her gaze. Nannette tended to look at me like I was a bug on her windshield that Rider wouldn't let her squash, so she just kept watching it, waiting for the day it would blow away on its own and get splattered across someone else's windshield.

"Remove your jewelry and any other metal or magic items you have on you," Nannette ordered.

I removed the small hoop earrings adorning my ears and handed them to Rider. They were the only metal I had on me and, to my knowledge, I didn't own anything magical.

"Lie down and keep still," Nannette instructed, walking over to the machine.

"I don't need to change into a hospital gown?" I asked as I lay down.

"No. Just stay still. You're not claustrophobic, are you?"

"No."

"You'll feel yourself moving and you will enter the chamber. It's just like stopping inside a tunnel. This won't take very long at all."

I relaxed my body and closed my eyes as I started to slide into the chamber. I could hear a soft whir and some clicks, the hum of voices outside the chamber, and then I was sliding out. Rider helped me up and handed me back my earrings. His eyes told me they'd found something. "He marked me with the soul stitch, didn't he?"

"He marked you with something," Rider said, his voice vibrating with anger as he led me to where Nannette stood tapping away at the computer. She turned the monitor toward us and I saw an image of my skeleton with something red glowing on my chest.

"What is that?"

Nannette fiddled with the computer and blew the image up, zeroing in on the red object. She did something to remove the color, and it was like I was looking right at my bone. The image was very clear and showed a symbol similar to the soul stitch had been carved into my sternum. "Something is different about it."

"The line in the center." Rider pointed to the middle of the symbol. On the symbol in Selander Ryan's paintings, there was a scroll shaped line diagonally across the center. The symbol that had been carved into my bone didn't have the scroll shape. It looked more like a squishy infinity sign. "It's close enough to be related."

"But different enough to mean something else?"

"We need to look into soul stitches more. There may be variations." He looked at Nannette. "Have you seen anything like this?"

"It's not the first time I've seen something magically carved into flesh or bone," she answered, "but I can't say I've ever seen this symbol. I can email copies of the scan to some colleagues and see if anyone has come across it. I'll be discreet, of course."

Rider nodded. "Do that. Email me copies of her scans too. Make sure her name doesn't appear anywhere."

"I didn't even enter her name into the system. As far as anyone is concerned, she's Jane Doe."

"Good. Now, you were there the night I killed Ryan. Did you notice what happened to his body?"

"I was busy tending to the wounded on our side. Many bodies were brought here to the morgue, and I'd assumed his had been, but I never saw it."

My heart sank. "Not all his people were killed. Someone could have taken his body while your people were trying to save the injured."

"Our people," Rider corrected me. "It's possible. Damn it, I should have burned his body right then."

"You weren't thinking clearly," Nannette said, cutting me a cold look. "A lot was going on. I've sent over these images to you and now I'm sending to some colleagues. I'll erase everything from the system once done. Is there anything else you need tonight?"

"Yeah, do you know anything about something called the Bloom?"

"Yeah, that's the cycle sirens and other sex demons go through where they basically feast on sex with anyone and anything they can corner. Some cat-shifters go through it too, but they just refer to it as being in heat."

"Succubi go through it?" Rider asked.

"I believe so," Nannette answered, then looked at me suspiciously. "Why?"

"Shit," Rider and I said in unison as we looked at each other.

"I'm a sex demon."

"Nannette did not call you a sex demon," Rider said as he navigated the Ferrari away from the hospital parking lot and toward the bar.

"She lumped me in the same skanky category!" Fresh tears spilled from my eyes. "I'm going to go into heat and you heard what she said. I'm going to be like a super-hussy, boinking anybody I can get my legs around."

Rider cringed. "Please don't say that again." He looked over at me. "And please stop crying. It's not that bad. You'll just stay close to me and if you go into heat, you'll just have a lot of sex with me."

"What if you're not around? She said I'd do it with anyone I could catch!"

"She was probably exaggerating. You're only half succubus and it's not like you're an animal."

"No, I'm a sex demon. Auntie Mo said that Ryan would have more control over me during the Bloom. Maybe this is his plan. He's going to turn me into a whore and make me screw everything in sight. You won't even want me after that."

"That's not going to happen." Rider grabbed my hand and kissed it. "Now that we know what it is, we can watch for it. If you start having any unusual feelings or desires, let me know. During the cycle, we'll keep you away from other men."

I studied him as he drove. He was focused on the road and his breathing was even. "How are you so calm about this? You got mad when I loaned Daniel my shirt. According to Nannette, I'm going to want to loan a lot of men something a lot more personal than that."

"Geez, Danni. Quit talking like that!" Rider flashed me an annoyed look. "I'm not happy, but I'm not going to sit here and imagine the worst possible thing. You had active succubus traits when you first turned, and you survived that without wanting to do every man you came across. Maybe it will be worse during this Bloom thing, maybe it won't. It will not do us any good to obsess about it. We'll handle it when it happens."

"And what if I can't control myself and I sleep with some random guy? What then?"

"I'll kill the bastard."

"Will you kill me?"

"Of course not." He looked over at me, surprised. "You think I'd kill you for that?"

"If I jump some random guy, it won't be his fault. It will be mine."

"It'll be Ryan's," Rider growled, tightening his grip on

the steering wheel. "I love you, Danni. Nothing is going to change that, not even this Bloom crap. It's just something we'll have to deal with."

"I'd rather you killed me than let me become something like that." I took a deep breath and stared out the window, unable to look at Rider without erupting into tears. "I don't want to be a whore."

"Babe…" He looked at me but didn't say anything. We arrived at the garage attached to the bar and pulled inside, parking between his Harley and his SUV. Rider got out and walked around to open my door. "Come here."

I dissolved into a mess of tears as he pulled me from the car and wrapped his arms around me. He rested his cheek along the top of my head and made soothing noises as I continued to bawl, knowing in my heart it would ruin what we had forever if I gave in to the Bloom and allowed it to turn me into a sex-craved monster.

The door leading to the hallway opened and Daniel stuck his head in. He instantly stiffened, and his eyes warmed with concern as he took in my state. "What happened?"

"Got some rough news," Rider said, rubbing my back. "Did you and Rome find the bastards?"

"We got one downstairs in a cell. The other two didn't make it."

Rider thumbed away the tears dribbling down my cheeks and kissed my forehead. "I know you're upset, Danni. Can you pull it together enough for me to interrogate this asshole? The Bloom isn't your worst threat right now. We'll get through that when it hits, but we have to keep you alive long enough to deal with that."

I took a deep breath and nodded. "Yeah, I'm better now."

"You sure?"

I wiped at the wetness on my face. "Yeah. How do you interrogate someone?"

"Ask a bunch of questions and beat the shit out of

them if you don't like the answers."

"That sounds like fun."

"That's my girl."

SEVENTEEN

We went upstairs so I could wash my face and calm my emotions. Rider and Rome would be doing the talking, but just in case I decided to give interrogation a try we thought it best I not show up with tear tracks staining my face. I couldn't appear weak.

Daniel eyed me curiously when Rider and I descended the stairs, meeting him at the basement level. "Everything all right?"

"I'm fine," I told him. "It's a story I don't really feel like going into right now."

Daniel looked at Rider over my head and for a moment I was afraid he'd accuse him of having done something to cause my earlier emotional breakdown, but either he thought better of it or decided he didn't have enough information to make assumptions.

"The white one was already dead when we found the other two," he said, turning to lead us to the cell they'd placed the remaining gangbanger in. "He was a victim of the Scorpions. They got him in a drive-by earlier this afternoon. His name was Joey Foote. Trey Carter and Jorge Fernandez are the other two. Trey tried to be a hero and shoot me while we were apprehending them."

"He shot you?" My voice rose several octaves as my heartbeat increased.

"He shot *at* me," Daniel clarified. "We fought. His neck snapped. We managed to get Fernandez here in one piece. He's black and blue, but he's alive and capable of speaking."

"Did you reveal what we are?" Rider asked as we reached the room. Rome stood outside, waiting.

"Nope. No one on the team shifted or used any special abilities other than our strength to grab this sonofabitch."

"Good." Rider looked at me. "Have you ever dealt with a gang member before?"

I shook my head. "There were rough guys in high school who bragged about being in gangs, but I'm pretty sure that was all bullshit."

"This guy took a deal to help capture you. He and his friends had every intention of gang-raping you and then passing you over to the Quimbys to be murdered. A bastard like that generally isn't very cooperative and even when he knows he's lost, he'll try to play tough. Part of that involves saying disgusting things to and about you. Do you want to go in there with me and slap him around a bit, or do you want to just watch from the observation room?"

I stared at the steel door, picturing the beast on the other side, the devil who'd chosen to defile me for money or street cred or whatever else he'd been offered. Anger simmered inside me, but didn't boil over. There were too many emotions battling it out inside me and anger wasn't in the lead. "I don't want to go in there. I'm not sure that my presence would help."

"Will you be all right in the observation room, or do you want to stay in my bedroom? The spell will keep you secure there. I'm probably going to lose my shit after a while of talking to this punk and it might not be something you want to see."

"I'd rather stay close to you," I said. *I don't want to be away from you if and when the Bloom strikes.*

222

Rider nodded his understanding. "I'll make an effort to not lose it, but any man who thinks of hurting you brings the darkness out in me."

Daniel opened the door to the observation room and guided me in. It was a small room with dark gray walls and tile flooring. The light was off, which I knew was because of the one-way mirror hanging on the wall that separated us from the brightly lit interrogation room.

Can we be heard in here? I mentally asked Daniel.

"Soundproof walls," he answered. "You're fine as long as you don't yell." He pulled out one of the chairs in front of the mirror and motioned for me to sit with him. "You sure everything's all right?"

I gave him as reassuring of a little smile as I could muster. "No imminent danger, and nothing you can do anything about." I looked through the mirror at the man sitting in the interrogation room. He was in a chair at a table. It was like a scene out of *NCIS* but there were no video cameras and this wasn't some random actor. The Latino guy with the two teardrop tattoos under his eye was a very real bad guy who had been pointing a gun at me, ready to sexually assault and then kill me. The black and blue bruises all over him weren't makeup either. He'd clearly put up a fight.

The door to the interrogation room opened and Rome and Rider walked in, both moving in like angels of death.

"We didn't know she belonged to you," Fernandez said. He spoke to Rome, but kept a wary eye on Rider as he leaned against the wall and folded his arms. It appeared casual and relaxed, but the dark look in Rider's eyes was anything but relaxed.

"Give me a reason not to break you in half," Rome said, sitting on the opposite side of the table, his back to us.

Fernandez trembled under Rider's murderous glare, licked his lips, and leaned toward Rome. "We ain't out for her no more," he said. "These white dudes just rolled up to us talking about this bitch they needed taken care of, said this dude killed they dude and so they was gonna do his bitch and put two in her skull. They needed us to track her down and have some fun with her before handing her off to let them kill her. We didn't know she was your bitch. Everybody in the hood knows you don't mess with Rome's bitches. We stopped the minute we heard."

"I don't have bitches," Rome said. "I have women, and this one isn't mine. She's his, and he's far worse than I am. I'm only here to get information before he loses his temper and rips out your spine."

Fernandez looked over at Rider. "He's the real boss man, ain't he?"

"Keep calling his woman a bitch and find out."

"I told you what I know," Fernandez said. "We didn't know who she was or who those white dudes was after."

"That makes it right?" Rome asked. "You were going to rape an innocent woman and deliver her to be killed. You know we don't allow that shit."

Fernandez shrugged. "You ain't the only one gotta make it, bro. We stay clear of your family and we give you respect, but you can't claim everybody without notice. We gotta do what we gotta do to feed our own. You turned the Scorpions on us and now I gotta bury twelve of my brothers. Where's my sympathy?"

Rome stood, yanking Fernandez out of his seat, and threw the man into the wall to his left. "You're rapists and murderers! You don't get sympathy."

Fernandez's body slid to the floor, and he sat there for a moment, dazed, before speaking. "You would been out there with us if this dude didn't find you. You got nice wheels, a nice job. Easy to forget where you came from."

"I know exactly where I came from," Rome said.

"Then you know you'd been out there with us hunting the bitch too."

"No, I'd be dead because you'd have killed me before I'd ever do the shit you pieces of shit do. Who else is involved in this?"

Fernandez glared at Rome. "I told you we out of it. That's all you get. I ain't no snitch."

Rider's body tensed, and his eyes started to glow as his power seeped out, filling the room.

"What the fuck is that?" Fernandez asked, eyes all boggled. "Who the hell you workin' with? We saw one dude turn into a big ass monster and fly off with that bitch. What the fuck is you motherfuckers?"

"Who shot at her?" Rome asked, standing over Fernandez, his meaty fists clenched.

"Fuck you," Fernandez said. "We ain't after the bitch no more. We already losing money and guns, you gonna get us all killed too."

"You're gonna get killed right here if you don't tell us who shot at her."

"Those motherfuckers got weapons I ain't never seen before. I ain't telling you shit. We left the bitch alone. Drop this shit and find the dudes yourself."

Rider crossed the room in three quick strides, hauled Fernandez up from the floor, slammed him onto the table, and sank his teeth into his neck. The man screamed like a terrified woman as he fought to escape, but couldn't move Rider at all. Drinking to punish, not to fulfill his nutritional requirements, Rider had torn into him savagely and blood pooled on the table beneath him. When Rider pulled up, his chin dripped with the red liquid.

"Shit," Daniel said next to me.

"That's nothing," I told him. "He hasn't even lost his temper yet."

"Devil!" Fernandez screamed, pointing at Rider. "You're the fucking devil!"

"No, but I'll drag you down to Hell to meet him," Rider said. "Who shot at her?!" He waited a moment and when Fernandez didn't answer, he snarled, showing his blood-dripping fangs.

"Fuck!" Fernandez bellowed. "It was Little Peanut!

Little Peanut pulled the trigger!"

"Little Peanut?" all four of us said at the same time.

"I was almost shot by someone named Little Peanut?" I asked as Daniel bit his lip to keep from laughing. "That's just embarrassing. I'm seriously offended. Who the hell was going to rape me, Little Twatnugget?"

"What the fuck is a Little Peanut?" Rider asked. "What's his real name?"

"Julio Delgado!" Fernandez yelled. "Julio and Big Mike were in the car and Julio pulled the trigger."

"Who's involved other than your boys and the Quimbys?"

Rome pulled up an image on his phone and put it in Fernandez's face. "Who are these assholes?"

"I don't know them. They were with the Quimby dudes. I heard one of them called Torch. Other than them, it was all us. That's all I know. They had weapons, but they needed more manpower."

"You got a number for them?" Rome asked.

"No, they said they was going underground after that monster grabbed the girl and we was supposed to stay looking for her. They were going to contact us."

"How were you going to get Danni to them if you'd caught her?" Rider asked.

"We were supposed to snatch her and just keep her entertained until they came back to this abandoned building we been hanging at."

"Entertained?" Rider asked, his voice a growl.

"We didn't know she was your bitch," Fernandez said. "She was just random puss—"

Rider and Rome both punched Fernandez. Rider's fist smashed his nose while Rome's more than likely cracked a rib, causing an ungodly scream to come out of the man.

"Fuck," Daniel said in awe. "That was awesome."

"What building?" Rider asked. "WHAT BUILDING?" he repeated after not getting a response.

Fernandez rambled off two street names and coughed

up blood. "I... need... hospital."

"No, you were going to rape my woman," Rider reminded him. "You're not going to the hospital. You're going to Hell." The pale golden color of his power glowed around him as he reached into the man's throat, right through the flesh, gripped his spine and ripped it out of his body. Rider dropped the spine and everything that had come out with it onto the table. "Take that to the Brotherhood and let them know that's what happens to rapists in my city," he said before he moved toward the door. "Make sure this gets cleaned up."

Rome nodded once, then bent over and hurled. Daniel, who had gone stone still next to me the moment he saw bone, followed suit, barely making it to the wastebasket in the corner of the room. I just sat there, amazed. I'd heard Rider threaten to rip out a man's spine before, Rome had actually told Fernandez he was there to get information before Rider ripped his spine out, but despite seeing him rip out a man's heart I never actually thought it possible to rip out a whole spine.

"Did I just see what I think I just saw?" Daniel asked, wiping his mouth with the back of his hand, still on his knees by the wastebasket.

"Yup."

"You're not bothered by that?" Daniel asked, looking at me incredulously.

"He said he was going to do it. Honestly, the only thing getting to me is the smell of vomit. I gotta go before I start puking too."

"I like you, but you're kind of scary sometimes," Daniel yelled after me as I exited the room in time to see Rider coming out of a bathroom. His chin was blood-free, but some still stained his shirt.

"Hey," he said. "Sorry about that. He brought the rage out in me."

I rose on my tip-toes and kissed him.

"I take it you're not too upset about what just

happened?"

I shook my head. "Rome and Daniel threw up."

Rider grinned.

The interrogation door opened behind us and Rome stepped out. "Man, when I said you were gonna rip his spine out, it was just a figure of speech," he said, one hand covering his belly as he passed us. "Somebody's gonna come down and get that cleaned up. I'll take Fernandez's spine to his crew after I get a bag for it."

"Am I going along for that ride?" Daniel asked, stepping out of the observation room.

"No, you're off the clock now," Rider told him, grinning. "You're looking a little green."

"Must be a dragon thing," Daniel said. "That or a byproduct of the fact you're just nasty as hell. Once my stomach settles, I'll probably think that was pretty awesome though."

"Get some rest," Rider said, laughing softly as Daniel left us. He looked down at me. "You sure you're all right with what happened?"

"He got what he deserved."

Rider frowned.

"You're worried about me."

"As relieved as I am that you aren't completely disgusted by my actions, it's a little disconcerting that you aren't even a little upset about it."

"You're afraid I'm losing control of my humanity?"

Rider didn't say anything, but his eyes told me I was on the money.

"That man was going to rape me and pass me around to his friends to do the same thing over and over again before handing me over to hunters. It's not vampirism or some darkness inside me making me not care what you just did to him. I'm a woman. Women can't ever walk down a street at night without fearing that sort of thing. I was almost raped by my freaking boss, and that was before I bit him and injected the venom into his blood system.

Selander Ryan attacked me and turned me into this sex-starved creature and I now have to live in fear of going into this bloom thing and doing things I would never do if I had control over my own body. I'm not going dark-side, Rider, I'm just pissed the hell off. If you can kill even one man who wants to sexually assault me, I don't care how you do it. It's one less man I'll have to worry about when Ryan takes control of my body and tries to put it through hell."

Rider pulled me into his arms and kissed my forehead. "I'm so sorry this happened to you. I promise I'll do everything in my power to keep you protected from danger, even the danger of whatever is inside you."

"Just stay with me and don't let me do anything I'll hate myself for."

"You don't even have to ask that. We're going to kill these bastards hunting you, and we're going to destroy Ryan and whatever curse he's put on you."

"Will destroying him destroy this thing he carved into me?"

"Hopefully. If not, we'll find another way." Rider released me and turned away. "We have a few hours until sunrise. Let's see what all we can find out about soul stitches and the variation you have."

I closed the book I'd been looking through as the impending sunrise tugged at me, causing my eyelids to grow very heavy. "I think it's a bust."

Rider cut his eyes to me. "No, I just got an email from one of Nannette's colleagues. It's not the greatest news, but it tells us what we're dealing with."

I stood from the sofa and walked over to Rider's desk. I stood behind him and looked over his shoulder at the monitor. "The thing he carved into my bone is a soul stitch attachment."

"It's pretty much what it sounds like. He's bound you

to him. The mark strengthens the mark he left on you when he sired you, so even though I am your true master because of your allegiance to me, he still has some control. If you were pure succubus, he'd make a puppet of you with this thing. This mark is why he can still call you to him when you're asleep and your defenses are less secure. Incubi have long hunted victims through dreams. It makes sense he'd have more power over you in yours."

"Is the mark why I can't just wake myself up?"

Rider nodded. "Most likely. Once he has you in there, you need him to release you, or me to pull you out. You're never sleeping unguarded again."

"For the rest of my life?"

"Until we figure out how to break this damn attachment."

"He carved the symbol into me with magic. Can it be removed with magic?"

"Depends on the magic." Rider forwarded the email he'd received to someone named Seta along with a message that a member of his nest had been attached to an incubus with the mark and he needed to know if it could be removed.

"Who's Seta?"

"An old friend," he answered, booting down the computer. "It's time to get some blood into you and get some sleep. Hopefully, there will be a response from her by the time we wake. My tech team identified the other hunters who attempted to capture you. Fernandez said one of them was named Torch. I've heard of a hunter with that name and he routinely works with the same crew, so once we got his street name, it wasn't that hard to figure out who the others were. My day staff can handle hunters and gangbangers so I can stick with you and guard you from any more attempts from Ryan. I already sent out a team to the property Fernandez told us about. I got the notification about ten minutes ago that they cleared it of the gang members holed up there. Now they'll sit and wait for the Quimbys to show up, expecting the gang members to be there waiting for further instruction."

"How friendly of a friend?" I asked, completely ignoring the way more important information he'd just given me. Sure, he was talking about taking out the hunters who intended to wipe me off the face of the earth, but all I could think about at the moment was that he'd emailed some woman I didn't know and the term *old friend* had a bitter taste to it. And how old of a friend could she be if he had her email?

Rider looked down at me, his blue eyes assessing, but didn't say a word.

"Why can't you answer?"

"I can answer. At the moment, I'm a little busy worrying if these surges of rabid jealousy you keep emitting are stemming from your vampire side or your succubus side, and just how big of a problem they're going to be."

"I'm a problem now?" I felt myself grow hot, as if my very blood boiled. "Like you've never been jealous, and I'm not jealous. I just want to know who this woman you're conversing with is!"

"I have a grip on my jealousy," Rider said, his voice completely even. "You don't have a grip on yours. Your rage practically leaks out of your pores when you see me with another woman, even a woman you know, and right now all I did was send an email to a woman, an email I sent in order to help you by the way, and look at you. You've got steam coming out of your ears."

"Who is Seta? Why are you being evasive?"

Rider watched me for a moment, his nostrils flaring. Finally, he gave his head a slight shake and sighed. "Seta is a vampire-witch, an extremely powerful vampire-witch who might actually know what to do about the soul stitch."

"The hybrid you told me about before. The one you smiled about while taking a walk down memory lane in your head."

Rider smiled slightly now, but there was no amusement in it. "Seta isn't anyone you have to worry about losing me to. We have a history, but I haven't actually seen her since the late sixties and even then she wasn't sleeping with me. She was sleeping with Elvis."

I blinked. "Elvis slept with a vampire-witch?"

"Elvis slept with everything. Women melted in his presence."

"Those rumors about him being alive aren't true, are they? He's not a vampire now, is he?"

Rider shook his head. "Not that many high-profile people get turned. It's not wise to have super famous vampires. Makes it harder for us to stay in the shadows."

I narrowed my eyes. "But there are some?"

"I have my suspicions about a few."

"Jensen Ackles?"

"I was joking about him."

"Then who do you suspect?"

"Pharrell, and Lenny Kravitz for sure."

"Lenny Kravitz is hot."

Rider tilted his head sideways and just looked at me.

"Well, he is. You're all powerful and stuff. Can't you just find him and see for yourself if he's a vampire?"

"I'm powerful, babe, but I'm not private access to Lenny Kravitz powerful," Rider said, pulling me against his side as my eyelids grew heavier.

"But you knew Elvis."

"Different time. I don't rub elbows with celebrities much these days."

"What a shame," I said, feeling my eyes go glossy as I recalled Lenny Kravitz's *Again* video. "I can see him as a vampire. That man is so hot."

"All right. You'll notice my head isn't steaming. My eyes aren't filled with bloodlust. I'm reacting normally to your attraction to another man. Can you see the difference between my reaction and the reaction you get any time I mention or even appear near another woman?"

Now it was my turn to sigh. "It's not like I can help it. Since turning, I just have all these really strong emotions."

"I know. That's what concerns me. You need to get your emotions under control before you do something dangerous."

"Such as?"

"Such as snap and kill someone you don't want to kill or make the community view you as a loose cannon. Loose cannons get dealt with... permanently. I'm already protecting you from Ryan, the Quimbys, Torch and his crew, and at least one gang. Help me out here and don't do anything to attract the hostility of the whole damn paranormal community, and I beg you that if by some chance you ever meet Seta, do not piss that woman off."

The heat of jealousy crept through my blood again. "Why? Are you afraid of offending her?"

"I'm afraid of the both of us getting killed by her."

I stood frozen in surprise for a moment. "You're afraid of a woman?"

"Seta's not just any woman. She's a vampire and a witch, and she's been around a very long time. Rumor has it she once took out an entire army all by herself. If there is any woman on this earth who might beat my ass in a fight, it's her." He held my gaze a moment to make sure his warning sank in. "Enough of this. It's time for bed. Let's go on up."

I followed him up to his bedroom, processing what I'd learned. My emotions were a little crazy, and he'd done nothing to earn the rage I felt any time I saw him with a woman or thought of him just communicating with another. The Bloom popped into my head and I grimaced, remembering how much I craved Rider when I was going through the turn and how much I hated Nannette and Eliza when they'd entered my room during the change to help him out. I hoped my jealous episodes weren't an indication the Bloom was near and I was closer to going super-succubus.

I drank from Rider's throat, sealed the wound, and snuggled under the sheets, a little relieved the act didn't get me all hot and bothered like it usually did. Maybe the Bloom wasn't so near after all. Maybe I was safe for a while. Maybe.

Hopefully.

EIGHTEEN

I was in the marbled foyer again. Armed with a little knowledge of what Selander Ryan had done to me, I wasn't so much afraid this time as I was pissed. I threw open the double doors and entered the dining room. He sat at the head of the table, as expected, dressed all in white and sipping from that damn chalice. I peered at it closer, noting the soul stitch engraved into it this time. I scanned the room, noting the symbol was hidden in every part, even the tiles. I looked down at the long, flowing white dress I wore and saw the soul stitch was in the actual stitching of the dress.

"I don't think they sell the soul stitch collection at IKEA," I said. "Did you create all this out of your head?"

Ryan grinned over the rim of his chalice. "Someone's been researching."

"I found the attachment too."

He set the chalice on the table but kept the smug grin. "No matter. You can't get rid of it, unless, of course, you set yourself on fire. That wouldn't work out very well for you though, but who am I to tell you not to?"

"I'm not going to make things that easy for you," I told him. "You'll have to think up a better way to get revenge on Rider than by killing me. He's not going to let you kill me and I'm not going to take my own life, not even to get rid of this thing you've branded into my bone."

Ryan just smiled his lecherous smile as he looked me up and down. "I could have had a lot of fun with you, Danni. I still could."

"I said I wouldn't kill myself. I never said I wouldn't kill you."

"Do you really think you can kill me? I'm already dead, remember? Killing me didn't seem to do much good, now did it?"

Well, he had me there. "Why haven't you just come back? You carved the soul stitch into your own bone. That's what's making these meetings possible. Why haven't you left this place and come for me if you want to torment me so bad?"

"Is that an invitation?"

"No. I want you to go to the bottom of the deepest, hottest fire pit in Hell and burn until nothing remains."

"Ouch." He placed his hand where his heart used to be. "That's harsh. Did I really do anything to earn such disdain? I could have killed you, but I didn't. I allowed you to live. Already you have lived longer than many of your other lives."

I narrowed my eyes. "How do you know about my other lives?"

"My brother is not the only one with gifted friends. My friends found you sooner, and more often. I've known many variations of you, Danni. Tragically, I've never known you well. You always had a tendency to die so young." His mouth spread in a wicked grin. "You always died shortly after we'd meet."

My blood chilled. "You sonofabitch. You're the reason I died young in my other lives. Why? Rider didn't even know about me. How was killing me over and over again hurting him if he didn't even know me?"

"You were his soul mate, no matter who you were,

whether you were blonde or brunette, Asian, African, or Caucasian. You were his soul mate, and you kept coming back. It wasn't fair. I didn't kill you all those times so he would suffer your loss. I killed you so he would never have you again."

"Why? He might not have even found me."

"As long as you were alive, there was the possibility he could. I couldn't allow it, not when he killed my soul mate."

It was starting to make sense. "How many times did you kill me?"

"I lost count. You were constantly coming back. I'd kill you on Monday and you'd be forming in another woman's womb by Thursday. I once killed you in the damn womb. You just kept coming back. Sometimes I found you quickly. Other times it took a decade or two."

"You killed me when I was just a child?"

"A child can be just as dangerous as anyone else," he replied without a trace of guilt. It unnerved me, but I had an inkling of why he'd been so hell-bent on keeping me dead, and I chose to stay focused.

"How many times has Rider's mother come back?"

"Katalinka! Her name is Katalinka."

"How many times has Katalinka come back?"

Ryan grabbed the chalice and drained the contents before slamming it down on the table.

"She hasn't come back. You're angry because I keep coming back and she hasn't come back once."

Ryan turned dark eyes to me. "He took her from me and he has kept her away from me ever since."

"I'm pretty sure he doesn't have that power. Rider would love to see his mother again. He loved her. He still loves her."

"I love her!" Ryan yelled, standing from the table. "I've searched for her for centuries!"

"You turned her into something she hated," I reminded him. "That's not love."

237

"You know nothing of our love, or of her!" He reached for me and I quickly moved to the other side of the table. I felt Rider in my head, knew he was there, waiting for me to give him the signal to pull me out. I forced myself to bottle my fear so he wouldn't act on his own and pull me out before I was ready. I needed more answers.

"Why didn't you kill me this time? Why did you lead me to Rider and then attack me instead?"

Ryan laughed. "Killing you didn't work. It was just an endless cycle. You kept coming back to him while my love was stuck wherever she went to. I started thinking, why was she different? Then it hit me. You were always just a human when you died. She wasn't. You wouldn't go to the same place."

"And?"

"And killing you didn't stop you from coming back for him. Killing you kept him from finding his soulmate again, but as you yourself said, it didn't really hurt him. He never knew what he'd lost over and over again. He'd only met you in his first life. He made it fifty years into his second life, twenty of those as a vampire, before you were reincarnated the first time. I'd already had a witch seeking the best way to avenge my love. She tracked you down, and I killed you shortly after your twentieth birthday as you got off a boat that brought you to the same country Rider was in. It didn't bring me the satisfaction I thought it would. I knew I'd killed his soulmate, but he didn't. Each time I killed you, the thrill became less and less. Finally, it clicked. He had to meet you, fall in love with you again, and then I would kill you. But first I had to turn you into a succubus so that when I killed you, you couldn't come back again. It took so damn long, but finally you came back with sweet blood so I could turn you and make him truly suffer."

"You didn't get to kill me though. He killed you first."

"I'm still here," Ryan said, holding his arms out as he laughed. "I planned ahead, and honestly, he did me a favor. Now I can move around the underworld searching for my Katalinka while he falls more and more in love with you. His every living moment is spent watching over you, waiting for me to strike. He is suffering, living in fear of losing you to me, and now that you know about the soul stitch, he knows death isn't the only way he can lose you. The Bloom is coming, Danni, and when it hits you, both of you are going to suffer."

My legs shook, but I buckled my knees together and forced myself to remain standing. I wrapped my fingers along the back of a chair, gripping it for support and maintained eye contact with the devil before me until light caught my eye from my left. I turned to look at the arched door at the end of the room. I saw the shadows of flames licking up the walls and realized why it was there. The soul stitch allowed him to move to different spaces, to create this room, but he didn't want to be far from where he thought Katalinka was. He'd created this room just outside a doorway to Hell. Maybe he could use the soul stitch to reenter his own body, but he hadn't yet. He wanted to reunite with the woman he thought to be his soulmate.

"You're suffering too," I told him. "You went through all this, waited this long to be reunited with Katalinka and now you've died and gone to the place incubi and succubi go, but you still haven't found her."

His eyes narrowed. "The underworld is vast."

"I imagine so. It has to be hard finding someone, especially if they have no interest in being found. Did anyone tell you Katalinka was your soulmate, or did you just decide she was?"

He moved toward me but had to stop when his legs hit the dining table between us, knocking over bowls of fruit. His chalice tipped over, two tiny spots of liquid spilling out and staining the white tablecloth. Blood.

"She's not your soulmate."

"She is. The same witch that found you for me confirmed it."

"Was she the first witch you asked or the one smart enough to give you the answer you wanted?" I asked the question, already knowing the answer. Katalinka was Rider's mother, and Ryan's stepmother. There was no way she was the sick bastard's soulmate. I saw Ryan's mouth move, could tell he was chewing on the inside of his lip, biting down to keep from losing himself to the rage. He knew I knew the truth and wanted to kill me for it, but killing me now didn't fit his big plan.

"That's what I thought, Ryan. I don't know what was available as far as psychiatry went back when you were an actual human, but you clearly needed help. You were a sick bastard then and you've grown sicker with time. That woman was a mother to you. A *mother*! What you turned her into, what you made her do, was disgusting and pure evil. She's not your soulmate and she will never be with you in that way again."

"Shut your lying mouth!"

"If I was telling lies, you'd be in a much better mood. The truth hurts, doesn't it?"

His eyes burned with anger as his mouth twisted into a gruesome mockery of a smile. "Act tough with me now, bitch. That's going to change when the Bloom hits and I turn you into a sniveling sack of tortured waste. I'm going to run men through you like you're the finish line of a marathon and there's not a damn thing you're going to be able to do to stop it, and that's only the beginning of what I'm going to do to you. And all the while that I'm torturing you, Rider is going to watch and suffer even more, knowing he can't save you."

I felt the pressure of tears building, knew that if I blinked they would spill over, so I used every ounce of willpower I had in my body to hold Selander Ryan's evil glare, refusing to give him the satisfaction of my fear. Maybe as one of my sires he could feel it, but I damn sure wasn't going to show it. "Taunt me. Torture me. Turn me into a demonic whore. You can do these things, you can even kill me, but it won't change the fact that Katalinka was never your soulmate, will never be your soulmate, and you will never be loved the way Rider has been loved because you are not worth the emotion. You are evil and disgusting, and a complete waste. You won't find Katalinka because she doesn't want to be found. She's free of you because of Rider. He gave her that gift. All you gave her was shame and degradation, and she hates you for it. She hates you!"

Ryan let loose an animalistic growl of rage and leaped across the table as I screamed Rider's name.

I sat straight up and gasped, my heart pounding furiously.

"Are you all right?" Rider asked, his voice full of concern as he checked me over. He was already dressed for the day in a black button-down shirt and pants. "What happened?"

"I just *really* pissed your half-brother off."

Rider studied me for a moment. "He brought you back to the same place?"

"Yes. This time I noticed the soul stitch. It was embedded in pretty much everything, even the dress I wore. It was on his chalice, and the chalice was full of blood."

"I figured. Blood is usually needed for dark magic."

"Where would he get blood in Hell?"

"Everywhere, I imagine. From what I hear, there's a lot of torturing in Hell. That usually produces a lot of blood."

I shivered. "I always imagined Hell as a horrible place your spirit went to, but I didn't think there could be actual blood there."

"I've been studying it. There are a lot of levels and even though it is filled with spirits, they feel pain. They suffer. And they bleed."

"There's a doorway to Hell off the dining room he

241

brings me to. I can't hear anything coming from it. I can't smell anything, but I can see the shadows of the flames."

"The meeting place he created is just outside Hell? Did you find out anything about his plan? Why hasn't he used the soul stitch to reenter his own body?"

"He's happy to be in Hell right now. He's searching the underworld for your mother." Rider's nostrils flared as his hands instinctively curled into fists. I reached over and held one of his hands in mine. "I don't think he'll find her there. She may not even be there. She may have reincarnated. It turns out Ryan has been the reason I've died young in my previous lives. Well, I'm not sure about my first life, the one where we were together, but lives two through however many I had before this one were all ended by him."

"He's been killing you repeatedly for centuries?"

I nodded. "Some dark witch or psychic or something could see I was your soulmate and tracked me through my many lives. Every time I showed up on the radar, he went out and killed me before we had a chance to reunite."

"That doesn't even make sense. I didn't know about you during any of that time. How was that hurting me?"

"In his head, keeping you from meeting your soulmate was payback because he was upset his never returned to him."

Rider's eyes darkened to the color of ink. "Who did he think his soulmate was?"

"Katalinka. Your mother."

"She wasn't!"

"I know." I squeezed his hand. "I know. I did enough questioning and reading between the lines to gather he'd killed the first witch or psychic or whoever who'd told him this so when he asked the one who'd led him to me if your mother was his soulmate she said she was, if only to ensure her own safety. This same person he used to locate me could find me over and over again, but could never locate your mother. It was as if she vanished from existence when she died."

"How many times have you reincarnated?"

"No telling. Your ass-wad brother said he lost count because I kept coming back no matter how many times he killed me. He even killed me in the womb once. Sometimes I lived a decade or two before he found me. I imagine if I kept coming back over and over again and only living a maximum of twenty years or less each time, it added up to a lot."

"But my mother has never returned."

"Maybe. Maybe the person working with him lied because she knew your mother wasn't his soulmate and was afraid he'd find out somehow that she'd lied. Maybe she's reincarnated a dozen or more times by now, but can't be tracked because she isn't his soulmate? Maybe she went to Heaven and once you go there, you don't come back? Maybe you only come back if you have unfinished business."

Rider leaned back against the headrest and released a deep breath, mulling this concept over. "Maybe. Maybe she's somewhere where she's being tortured for what he turned her into, for the things he made her do."

"He was thinking along the same lines after I kept coming back and he could never find her. That's why he didn't kill me this time. He thought maybe I was coming back because I was human when I died and she wasn't. He waited until I was born with sweet blood and then he led me to your bar and attacked me, but left me alive so you would have a chance to find me and fall in love with me. He decided that instead of just taking away your chance at having a soulmate, he would allow you to meet me, then use me to torture you. He's not even upset that you killed him before he could kill me. He seems very excited about the Bloom. He said he'd planned ahead, and I'm afraid to even think what that means. He was way too happy about the Bloom." A cold chill crept up my spine, and I wrapped my arms around myself.

Rider pulled me over so that I was snug against his side, his arm draped around me, and kissed my temple. "We'll beat this, Danni. I have some pretty badass witches in my corner too, and vampires, shifters, you name it. Even my humans kick ass."

"In all fairness, I brought your biggest human down with a punch to the testicles."

Rider chuckled. "Yeah, but if it had been any other human but Rome that got nut-punched by a pissed-off vampire, he wouldn't have survived the pain to tell the story."

"Rome is telling the story?"

"Hell no, and he's threatened to put dragon meat on the bar menu if Daniel blabs, but he's alive and he's walking. He's as tough as humans come."

"Do you plan on turning him into a vampire eventually?"

"That's up to him. I think he'd make a good one, but it's his choice whether he wants a crack at immortality or if he wants to live out his human life and die naturally. He's only in his twenties, so he's got plenty of time to decide."

"Unless he gets hurt bad enough or develops a disease."

"Then he'll have to decide sooner." Rider stood from the bed and pulled me to my feet. "Get dressed. It's a half hour from sundown so you'll be wide awake soon enough. I sent a team out to capture the punk who shot at you. They should be back soon enough, and that bastard will be providing your blood this evening. I thought it only fair."

"Sounds pretty damn fair to me."

I dressed in a stretchy red T-shirt, black leggings, and black running shoes, and followed Rider down to his office. He immediately went to his computer and checked his email. "Seta wrote back."

I walked behind him and read the email over his

shoulder:

What the hell have you gotten yourself into? The soul stitch attachment is a bitch of a curse and an even bigger bitch to get rid of. Witch's fire can do it, but it's dangerous and you need a powerful and highly skilled witch to do it or else your cursed vampire is as good as dead. Also, it can't just be burned off. The attachment has to go to someone else. Think about it. If the cursed one is willing to take the risk, contact me. You'll owe me. I don't come cheap.

"Do any witches come cheap?" I asked after reading the email. I let out a soft breath of relief that she hadn't addressed him with any flirtatious nicknames. I knew I was being incredibly insecure, but I'd been insecure for twenty-eight years and it was a hard habit to break.

"Not the really good ones. Unlike Rihanna, Seta doesn't deal in money though. She deals in power. I'll owe her a favor and that favor could be anything from taking out an enemy to joining her in battle. From what I've heard, she's been in some pretty epic battles the last few years. I'm not worried about that though. I'm worried about this risk she speaks of. Witch's fire is magic, but it's still fire. The mark is on your bone, inside you. She could kill you trying to remove it."

My hand automatically rose and rested over the bone the mark had been branded into. "My other option would be to stay stuck with this thing?"

He nodded. "I'm afraid so. I can pull you out any time he brings you to that meeting place and we can keep you locked in my room during the Bloom."

"Forever? Rider, what if it happens while you're busy fighting another enemy? You have so many people you're responsible for. You said yourself that you protect this whole city, even the humans who don't know you exist. You can't do all that if you're spending all your time watching over me. Selander Ryan is a snake, and not a stupid one. He has people watching. He's waiting for his moment. He'll attack when your guard is down and it isn't like he can't wait forever. He's freaking dead." I looked at the email, rereading the message. "You said she was really powerful."

"She is."

"You don't think she could successfully burn this thing off me without killing me?"

"She could, but there's a chance she could fail. If there's even a one percent chance she could kill you, I don't want to take it. We don't even know how bad the Bloom is going to be or how long it will last. If I keep you locked in with me, it might just be a really great weekend for me and on Monday morning you're walking a little funny, but hey, no big deal."

"Or Ryan could use the attachment to control me, make me hurt or even kill you, and I can escape your room and go on a sex spree, making it a very good weekend, week, month, or longer for every man I come across, except for the ones I kill in the process, and wake up from it overcome by the urge to kill myself to escape my guilt and shame. You said if I was pure succubus this thing would make me his puppet. Auntie Mo said he will have more control over me during the Bloom. What if that's enough to make me his puppet during the Bloom? It's bad enough he will have more control over me then anyway. With this thing branded on me, it'll be fueling him, strengthening his hold over me. Can you guarantee you can even keep me locked in your room when there's a symbol on me that physically connects me to another man? He could force me to the other side of the damn world if he wants to." I clutched the fabric of my shirt over the place the symbol taunted me. "I want this thing off of me."

Rider had turned his chair toward me and sat patiently, watching me in silence until I wound down. He stood and wrapped his hand around the back of my head, pulled me close and kissed my crown. "I know this is very scary for you. It is for me too, but I don't want fear to cause us to make a rash decision that may not be a *good* decision. Let's just process this a bit. If the Bloom hits while we're still processing and it's as bad as you fear it will be, I can get Seta here in a flash. She can teleport."

I thought about that a moment as I calmed down. "All your friends are weird."

This drew a small laugh. "Yeah, well, so are we. We drink blood."

"We're disgusting."

"Yeah. I like us anyway."

The door opened and Daniel leaned in. "We got Little Walnut and Big Mike downstairs."

"I thought it was Little Peanut," I said.

"Little Peanut, Walnut, My Left Nut. Whatever the dumbass goes by, we got him." Daniel stepped back out, closing the door behind him.

I rolled my eyes as Rider silently laughed and shook his head. "You like him."

"He has his moments," he said. "I hope you're thirsty. I intend to turn that interrogation room into an all you can drink buffet."

I walked into the interrogation room with Rider at my side and immediately could tell which of the two men was Little Peanut and which was Big Mike. Big Mike was more like Massive Mike, with his chocolate-colored girth wrapped tight in a blue T-shirt and sweatpants stretched to capacity. Four inches of ass hung off each side of the chair he sat in, and his stomach nearly reached his knees. I assumed he had a neck somewhere, but it was lost in an avalanche of cascading chins. His face was round and almost child-like, completely smooth. Little Peanut was much shorter, much thinner, lighter-skinned and had a lot more facial hair. His attire consisted of a T-shirt with a graphic too vulgar to describe, baggy jeans, and LeBrons. He looked more like an ass-nugget than a peanut to me, but maybe that was because he'd shot at me and I tend to carry grudges. Both men were watching Daniel as he leaned back in a chair in the corner, arms crossed, but completely relaxed. Rome leaned with his back against the wall next to him. He was a much more physically intimidating presence, but the men paid him no attention.

"I guess they're not even going to acknowledge us," I said to Rider as we stood inside the room, looking at the two men.

"The big badasses are afraid of me," Daniel explained.

"What did you do to them?" Rider asked.

"Nothing. Hell, they didn't even run when we barged into the house they were at. They just stuck their hands up in the air and started shaking."

"The big one cried a little," Rome said. "He might have pissed himself too, unless he just always smells like that."

"Man, we ain't no weak-ass bitches," Little Peanut said, still not taking his eyes off Daniel. "That dude's a flying demon. Snatched that bitch we was after off the ground and took off with her."

"Snatched that what?" I asked, stepping in front of Daniel so Little Peanut had no choice but to acknowledge me.

"Oh, shit!" His eyes widened. "You're the bitch we was supposed to tranq out. I thought he dragged you to Hell."

"He flew up with me. Hell's in the other direction, dumbass." I looked at Rider. "Did you need something from them, or can I drain him now?"

Rider shrugged. "They're just dinner. I was going to let you get your fill first, then call in the others for whatever's left."

"Hold up," Daniel said. I turned to see him holding his finger up for me to wait. "You don't have a peanut allergy, do you?"

"Shut up, Daniel."

He grinned and relaxed in the chair. "Bone appletits."

"It's bon appétit," Rome corrected him.

"That doesn't sound nearly as fun."

I shook my head and turned my attention back to the man who'd tried to shoot me. "You tried to shoot me. You helped a group of men who were trying to kill me. You have to pay for that."

He stared at me for a moment and smiled. It was a nervous smile, but still a smile. It suggested I wasn't nearly as scary as Daniel. A whirring noise started in my ears. My blood heated. "Shame your demon boy over there made me miss my shot. We was gonna have some real fun with you. We still can," he said, elbowing Big Mike as he laughed. "Why don't you bring your skank-ass over here and suck my—"

I moved in like a streak of lightning, grabbed a handful of his hair and yanked his head back, exposing the full length of his throat. Before he could register what I'd done, my fangs were in his neck, ripping out flesh. I'd hit the jugular and Little Peanut's warm blood gushed out like water out of a fire hydrant. He never had time to scream. His buddy, however, screamed at a pitch dogs could hear the next county over. I glanced over, my fangs still deep in Little Peanut's throat, and saw Big Mike on the floor flapping his arms and legs, trying to get to the door.

Rome squatted down in front of him. "What the hell are you doing, man? There's no water. Why are you swimming?"

"Oh lawd, oh lawd!" the big man screamed. "Help me! Help me! The devil is gonna drink me! I'm in Hell! Oh, lawd!" He let loose another high-pitched scream that caused Rome to scrunch his whole face up as he turned his head away, covering his ears.

"Shut this dude up!" He pleaded and Rider stepped over, effortlessly picked Big Mike up by one of his neck folds, set him back on his chair, yanked his head back and sank his fangs into his throat, cutting off the screaming.

"Damn," I heard Daniel say. "If this was Vampire 7-Eleven, he'd be a Double Gulp. If you drink all the blood in him in under a minute, do you get your picture on the wall or something?"

Rider lifted his head after a few big gulps and gave Daniel an annoyed look before I felt his power filling the room. I sensed him calling in the other vampires on his staff, advertising fresh blood on tap in the interrogation room, and I closed my eyes, focused on draining every drop of blood I could get out of the bastard who'd tried to shoot me. Blood dripped down my chin and coated strands of my hair that had fallen forward, but I didn't care. I drank until the blood slowed and my stomach was so full one more gulp would make me hurl, and only then did I step back.

Rome handed me a towel he'd had hanging out of his back pocket and I used it to wipe the blood coating my chin, dripping onto my chest. I looked over at Rider and found him flawless, not a drop of blood on him. He'd been less savage than me when he'd fed. He'd simply did what was necessary to shut the man up and took a few gulps of nourishing blood in the process. I'd drained my victim, reveling in the slowing of his heartbeat as each swallow brought the bastard who'd shot at me closer to death. I drank his blood but fed on the power of knowing I was ending the man who'd tried to end me. I looked down at the dead body that used to be a pathetic gangster named Little Peanut, and I didn't feel the slightest bit of remorse. I looked back up at Rider, met his gaze, and knew he knew what I felt, and he wasn't happy about it.

"Rome, you know what to do with the bodies after they're drained," he said as other vampires started filing in to the room, accepting their invitation to the blood buffet. "Show Daniel." To me, he jerked his head toward the door and left the room, knowing I'd follow his command and follow.

"You told me to get my fill," I said as we walked down

the hall toward the stairs.

"I did."

"You're mad."

"No, Danni, I'm not mad."

I grabbed his arm and forced him to stop and look at me. "Then what is it?"

He looked at me with some emotion in his eyes I couldn't put a name to, but it gave me a hollow feeling in my chest. "I'm worried." He wiped blood from the corner of my mouth with his thumb and looked at it in a way I wouldn't expect a vampire to look at blood. "I'm really worried."

NINETEEN

I let out a heavy sigh and closed the book I'd been looking through. I added it to the stack I'd already finished, lifted them from the sofa, and walked behind Rider's desk to replace them on his bookshelves.

"Bored?" he asked, not looking up from whatever he was doing on his computer.

"Very."

"I feel your pain."

It was the most we'd spoken to one another since I'd gotten out of the shower after feeding from Little Peanut. He'd told me he was worried, and that was it. Not one more word on the subject. He said he wasn't mad at me, but I could tell he wasn't happy with me. He barely looked at me, which was unusual. I couldn't help but feel that I'd disappointed him somehow, and that made me feel like crap.

"What are you working on?" I asked as I put the last book back in its place, trying again for conversation, anything to break the uncomfortable silence.

"Not much." He stretched and rolled his neck. "I finished up some business stuff, and I'm monitoring the reports I'm getting in from the tech team. The Quimbys still haven't dropped in on the site my guys took over from the gang so they're out there in the wind. Torch and his buddies are still underground as well. We're checking whatever security cams we can hack into and reaching out to anyone who might know something. I can't do a whole lot stuck in here."

"Stuck in here watching over me," I clarified.

"I didn't mean it like that." He reached behind him, snagged my wrist, and pulled me down onto his lap. "It's never a hardship to watch over you. I just wish I was out there actually hunting those bastards down. I don't like it when you have predators on the loose and I feel like I'm not doing enough sitting in here at a computer monitoring what everyone else is doing. It's a weird feeling for me, just supervising."

"And you can't leave me here in case the Bloom hits."

He nodded his head and tapped a button on his keyboard, bringing up a report from his tech team. I gave it a cursory read, saw something about coordinates, and lost interest.

"Maybe we should go out together. They came out of nowhere when I was at the dress shop. I can draw them out again."

"You're suggesting I use you as bait. I'm not comfortable with that."

"Clearly, they know better than to enter your property. Sitting in here is just dragging this on longer. I know you want to get out of here for a while as bad as I do, and if we're together, you can hunt for them and monitor me for the Bloom at the same time."

He tapped his fingers on his desk, thinking it over. "It might do you some good to spend some time with other humans outside of here."

"You're afraid I'm losing my humanity."

He studied me for a moment and tucked a stray strand of hair behind my ear. "I think you've faced more than a normal amount of danger in the first two months of being turned than any other vampire I've known, and it has had an effect on you. There's the jealousy thing. Jealousy itself isn't abnormal, but the intensity of yours is extreme. I looked into your eyes when you walked into the bar and saw me sitting in that booth with Rihanna and I saw pure murderous intent there. There was the fight with the werewolf at the Cloud Top. By all means, you should have kicked her ass, and you did, but you kept going after you had her beat. Then there was earlier tonight."

"He shot at me."

"I know. That's why I thought it right for you to feed from him. He wasn't going to leave here alive anyway. No one leaves my interrogation room alive. Still…"

"What?"

"You enjoyed his death too much. I had a lot of kills under my belt before I ever felt close to what you felt tonight. I don't think you even saw that man as human."

"He tried to tranquilize me so he could take me back to his disgusting friends and rape me. Of course I didn't see him as human. Why are you giving me crap about this?"

"I know he was a filthy waste of flesh, Danni. He needed to die. I brought him here to kill him. I figured I might as well not waste the blood, and you needed to feed, so why not from him? Karma and all that. I knew there was a chance you might drink him dead, but I didn't think you'd enjoy it so much."

Was he serious right now? I'd watched him do way worse in that same room. "You ripped a man's spine out."

"I know."

"How was what I did half as bad as that?"

"It took me years to drink a man to death and not care that I had, and I went through men far worse than gangbangers. It took a lot longer than that to get to the point I could snap those men in half. The more my power grows, the harder it is to resist its pull, but I do because I don't want to give in to it and become a monster. I fight against it. Ripping that man's spine out last night wasn't as bad as what I really wanted to do. I fought against what I really wanted to do, even though I was enraged. You've been a vampire just under two months. You shouldn't be so comfortable killing. I have to wonder if it's my mark or Ryan's mark making killing so easy for you. You scare me sometimes, Danni."

"I scare you?" I stood and paced the room, my hands clenched. "You brought the guy for me to feed on. I fed on him. You had Rome give me a fighting lesson. You want me to fight, you want me to feed, and then when I do, I'm wrong for doing it?"

"I want you to protect yourself," Rider said, leaning forward, elbows on his desk. "But I don't want you to lose yourself when you do. You can't lose yourself. You're the light in my world. If you go dark... I don't even want to think of what I will become."

I stopped pacing and stared at him, gobsmacked. He'd told me this before, that he needed me with him to retain his own humanity. I never thought I might do something to make him lose it. "I don't know how to stop being jealous. It's always there. I want the people who tried to hurt me to suffer. I don't know how to stop feeling that way either."

He nodded. "I know. It's not your fault. You're a hybrid and that makes you a little unpredictable. I have to remember you may not be blatantly exhibiting succubus characteristics, but you still have them, even if they're buried deep under the surface. I want you back on bagged blood and I'm sorry for that. I know you think it's disgusting. I want you to spend more time with females. You've been spending most of your time with me, Daniel, and Rome. It has to be strengthening your succubus side."

I took a deep breath, already hating this. Just the bagged blood alone was a drag, not to mention I felt like a chastised child. "Anything else?"

"You need to be around humans more. I hate to say it, but maybe you should spend some time with your family."

"Shit." I thunked my head with my hand, realizing I'd completely forgotten about Shana's wedding with all that had happened within just the last twenty-four hours. "I haven't even checked messages since the attack outside the dress shop. Shana's wedding is right around the corner and she's probably been calling me like crazy with things for me to do. I'm the maid of honor now, or at least I was. Maybe she's given that job to someone else now."

"She'd give it away that quick? You only got the dress picked out two days ago."

I just looked at him. "You met her, remember?"

He grinned. "Yeah, but I thought I wasn't allowed to speak ill of your family. You make this really mean face when I do."

I narrowed my eyes at him. His grin widened, and I was pretty sure I was making the mean face. "Whatever," I said, not wanting to argue about something else. I didn't want to feel any worse than I already did and now I had to check my messages and suffer through who knew how many ranting voicemails my family had left.

I walked over to his desk and used his office phone to remotely dial in to my answering service. I went through the prompts, perched on the edge of the desk and gritted my teeth. As suspected, I already had a plethora of messages from not only my family, but from the dress shop. I suffered through a call from my mother making sure I wasn't in a romantic relationship with the rainbow-haired guy who'd escorted me to the dress shop and a series of questions about the good-looking rich guy who'd danced with me at the restaurant the last time she'd seen me, an inquiry from my grandmother about the Jug-Jolter 2000 she'd paid extra for the faster shipping on, another call from my mother asking why I was never home when she called and she hoped it was because I was with the rich guy with the long black hair and not the rainbow-haired freak, and at least twenty calls from Shana about her bachelorette party and the dress I needed to pick up. The final call was from Shana and she bitched me out for not returning the previous calls, stated her original maid of honor would be performing all the maid of honor duties since I was too busy with my new stud, but I was still wearing the dress and acting as maid of honor at the wedding because the original maid of honor couldn't stop cramming cheese puffs into her pregnant face and she didn't want a fat maid of honor in her pictures. She gave me the information for the bachelorette party and demanded I be there *or else*, and disconnected.

"That sounded cheerful," Rider commented, watching me as I returned the handset to its cradle.

"Shana's bachelorette party is tomorrow night," I told him. "I think she intends to murder me or at least beat me severely if I don't attend."

"I think you can take her."

"No doubt. I could before I was turned. She just screeches, scratches, and pulls hair." I sighed. "You said I need to hang around more humans and more women. A bachelorette party covers both bases."

"Where is it going to be at?"

"The Pussycat Playhouse," I mumbled.

Rider closed his eyes, dropped his head, and gave it a slight shake. "Any chance it could be moved to my bar?"

"Doubtful," I said. "You have alcohol here, but I'm pretty sure they chose Pussycat Playhouse for dancing and, more than likely, male strippers." I shuddered.

"What was that?"

"What was what?"

He smiled. "Did you just shudder?"

"Oily men in thongs give me the creeps. Sue me."

This got a laugh. "At least I don't have to worry about any *Girls Gone Wild* moments from you, but Pussycat Playhouse is harder to secure. It's larger, louder, and depending on the night's activities, easy for hunters to get in unnoticed and snatch you while everyone is too focused on greased up bodies or drowning themselves in alcoholic beverages."

"It could draw the Quimbys out, and that Torch guy. Honestly, it's not like they could kill me inside the club. You can have your team on the doors."

Rider's eyes narrowed in thought as he tipped his head to the side and studied me. "That's not a bad idea, but an even better idea is to have my team inside the club, and two on you."

"It's a bachelorette party and I'm pretty sure all the female members of your nest hate me," I reminded him. "Besides, the club has their own employees."

There was a light knock on the door and Daniel stepped in. "Hey, we uh… *discarded the mess* after that little buffet downstairs. Rome's back out on patrol, and I realized I have nothing to do. Need anything?"

Rider looked at me, taking in my attire of black joggers and a dark fitted T-shirt. "You're dressed for a workout. Why not take in a training session with Daniel while I work on getting you to that bachelorette party?"

"You're going to let me go?" I asked, instantly hating the fact I did. I knew he only wanted to keep me safe, but there was something about having to get his permission that really grated me.

"If all the stars align and I can get sufficient security in place, yes. Go on with Daniel. I'll be right here in the office if you should need me," he said, dipping his voice a little. I knew he was thinking of the Bloom. "You need to work on technique, but more than that, I want you to work on controlling your temper. Daniel is not your enemy. There's absolutely no reason I should go down there and find his bones broken or his testicles in his throat. Understood?"

I felt the heat of anger rise in me, yet the backs of my eyes burned with unshed tears. My emotions battled it out inside me where I fought to keep them as I snapped a terse, "Understood," and left the room. I kept my hands tightly fisted, the urge to slam Rider's office door shut behind me too great.

"Remember, no hitting below the belt," Daniel said as we entered the room I'd trained in previously with Rome.

"Yeah, yeah, I got it."

"Are you all right?"

I glanced over at Daniel and just as quickly glanced away. I suspected if I opened my mouth to answer, way too much information would come tumbling out. I had a lot on my mind, and a lot aching in my chest. Rider was the only person who knew the full extent of what a colossal clusterfuck the impending Bloom could be, but I couldn't really talk to him about it while he sat there worrying I was losing myself to all the dark bits that came with being a vampire-succubus. I needed reassurance from him, not more crap to feel awful about.

"Okay, I guess we can start with the dummies," Daniel said, accepting I wasn't going to answer. "Do you want gloves?"

"No." I moved to the dummy and started jabbing at it while Daniel observed my form.

"Shoulders back a little," he suggested as he stood to the left of me with his arms crossed. He was in jeans and a Foo Fighters T-shirt, not his workout clothes, so I didn't know if he intended to spar or just watch me smack the dummy around, and I didn't care. I was starting to get into the exercise.

I hadn't been able to muster a lot of enthusiasm the last time I'd worked with the dummy, but I found it much easier during this session. Maybe because my anger was directed at Selander Ryan last time and I couldn't put his face on the dummy. I wanted him in front of me, getting pummeled. Now my anger was directed inward to the symbol burned into my bone, and to the craving I had for blood and justice. I wanted to beat everything dark out of me. My hunger, my rage, my jealousy, my insecurity, my fear. What I wanted to destroy had no face, so I didn't struggle to visualize a person before me as I hit the dummy. The dummy itself became the visualization for every horrible part of me, for every bad thing that had happened to me since turning. It represented the monster Rider was afraid I was becoming.

I hit it harder and harder, my knuckles burning from the friction as my vampiric speed took over. Daniel faded away, staying quiet. Soon, hitting the damn thing wasn't enough. With tears leaking out of my eyes I gave it one last solid punch, delivered a roundhouse kick to the torso of the thing, and still not satisfied, I picked the heavy piece of equipment up and flung it across the room with a roar that shook the walls. It hit the wall across from us and the base exploded in a cloud of sand, and all I could think was great, something else to disappoint Rider. I stormed over to the mirrored wall behind us and sank down on the floor, pulled my knees to my chin, lowered my head and, ugly-cried.

Daniel slid down next to me a moment later, his shoulder touching mine, spreading his warmth to me. "Want to talk about it?"

I willed myself to stop crying, took a deep, calming breath, and raised my head to see a towel dangling in front of me. "Thanks."

"No problem," Daniel said as he watched me wipe my wet face. "Now tell me what's wrong. Clearly, something is eating you up inside."

"I'm eating me up inside."

He was silent for a moment. "Elaborate, so I have some idea of what that means."

"I drank that man to death."

"That's what has you so upset? Danni, he was never leaving that room alive. Also, he shot at you and you know what he planned on doing with you if he hadn't missed."

"But I enjoyed it." I lowered my eyes, stared at my hands as I twiddled my fingers. "I didn't care if he had children, or parents, brothers, sisters. I still don't. I don't feel any remorse at all that I took his life, but I know I should. I know killing is wrong. I know he's someone's son, someone's family. I know this, but I don't *care*."

"I don't care either. He and his gang members were going to rape you. I don't care if Mother Teresa gave birth to him and he left behind three sets of twin toddlers. He was going to do a lot worse to you than you did to him. It's not like you just grabbed some innocent guy off the street and murdered him for shits and giggles."

I leaned my head back against the mirror behind us and composed myself before I gave in to another urge to cry. "I hadn't even been turned for a full week before I killed a man. I was walking at night and I was hungry. I could hear every person who crossed my path's heartbeat, and I wanted blood so badly. This disgusting drunk came spilling out of a bar and the second he made a vulgar suggestion to me, I tore into his throat. Rider arrived and pulled me off of him, but it was too late. I drank him to death. That's what I do. I'm a killer."

"How did you feel?"

"I felt nothing, just hunger."

"After," Daniel said. "How did you feel after, after your hunger was sated and you realized you'd taken the man's life?"

"I felt like a murderer." Fresh tears slipped from my eyes. "Like a monster. I vowed to never get that hungry again."

"That doesn't sound like a monster or bloodthirsty killer to me. You can't blame yourself for something you did right after turning into a vampire. I imagine it can't be an easy transition."

"I am a monster," I said, the words coming out in a whisper. "I'm going to become an even more vile one any day now."

"That sounds scarily definite. Something going to happen that I don't know about?"

I looked over at Daniel, found him watching me intently, genuine concern in his gray eyes. For the first time, I noticed the ring of brown around his pupil. He had nice eyes. Honest eyes. Trustworthy. "I'm a hybrid."

"Yeah, a vampire-succubus."

"Do you know anything about succubi?"

"Not much, but I've heard some things." He studied me. "They weren't very flattering things, but Rider killed the incubus who sired you. I know he's somehow haunting your dreams, but from what I can tell, he doesn't have much power over you. Rider is your master. You're mostly vampire, right?"

"I wish that were true." I looked down again, not wanting to see judgement in Daniel's eyes when I told him the horrible truth. "When Rider ripped out Selander Ryan's heart, I felt stronger, more connected to Rider. I felt more like a vampire. I'm more tired in the daytime now, and although the sunlight was never pleasant, it's harder to bear now. Being around women doesn't make me as uncomfortable as it did before or turn me ice cold. When Rider confirmed I didn't have any venom in my bite, I really thought I'd managed to escape the curse of what Selander Ryan had done to me. I thought his mark might have died with him, but when we spoke with Auntie Mo, she gave us some pretty bad news."

"The mark is still there?"

I nodded. "My succubus side isn't gone. It's in some sort of hibernation. There are cycles I'll go through and during this cycle called the Bloom, Ryan's mark will be stronger. He will have more control over me, maybe even more than Rider. I will more than likely have the venom and all the other succubus traits that come with being this demonic thing. During the Bloom, I'll be in heat."

Daniel's mouth twitched a little. "This is where the dumbass guy part of me wants to make a joke, but I'm guessing being in heat is worse than I'm thinking."

"From what I've learned, when sex demons and certain

shifters go into heat, they aren't picky. I'm basically going to be a whore on steroids." Silent tears slipped from my eyes. "Rider thinks it might not be so bad and that as long as I stay close to him, he'll be my only *victim*, which I can live with, but what if he's wrong? And what if the Bloom takes over hard and fast, like what if it happened right now and I attacked you before he could make it down here? What if it hits in the club at the bachelorette party? Ugh, I can't go. I'll have to cancel. It's too much of a risk."

"What bachelorette party?"

"My sister's bachelorette party is going to be tomorrow night at Pussycat Playhouse. Rider wants me to hang around more humans, especially females, because he's afraid I'm losing myself to all the darkness that comes with being a vampire, and I guess the succubus side of me isn't helping with that either. I suggested drawing out the remaining hunters after me by leaving the bar. He's checking into arranging security at the club and if he can manage it in time, he was going to let me go. But how can I? I'll be inside a club full of people, many of them men. If the Bloom hits while I'm there, I'm afraid of what I might do, especially since Selander Ryan branded me with a symbol, something called a soul stitch attachment. It binds me to him and increases his power over me, which will also be increased by the Bloom. There's no telling what I will do when the Bloom hits."

"I'm your personal bodyguard, remember?" He bumped me gently with his shoulder. "I got you covered, hon."

I looked him in the eyes. "I could attack you, bite you, inject my venom into your system and make you my sex slave."

He grinned. "As awesome as that sounds to me, I know you would hate yourself forever, so as your bodyguard, and more importantly, as your friend, I guarantee you I will not let that happen."

"You can't stop it."

"Danni, you'd have to catch me first." He disappeared in a shower of sparkling colors. I blinked, watched the space he'd been sitting for a large dragon to appear, but it didn't.

"Hey."

I turned my head toward his voice and saw him standing across the room, arms folded, and smiling ear to ear. "How did you do that?"

He disappeared again and reappeared sitting next to me. "When I shift from human to dragon, there is a stage where all my ... particles? Molecules? I don't know the science of it, but I become mist. It only lasts a second during a shift, but I've learned how to hold on to that stage and move during it, then go back to human. You can't sink your teeth into me and inject your succubus venom if I'm not solid. If you go to the bachelorette party, I'm going with you, and if you get too friendly, I'll use my abilities to make sure nothing happens. I won't let you attack me, and once I get you outside, I'll shift to dragon form if needed and fly you back here, or wherever you and Rider have arranged for you to be during the Bloom. You can't mate with a dragon."

I thought about this. "I could still bite you in dragon form. If I injected my venom into you as a dragon, you could just shift back to human under the influence."

"I'll be covered in scales, sweetheart. You'd break your fangs or at the very least, just get really pissed off."

"Dragons can be killed, so you can't be armored everywhere. What about your... soft parts?"

Daniel stilled for a moment and burst out laughing. He ruffled my hair, stood, and offered me a hand up. "Time to spar, Rocky. I'll demonstrate how good I am at protecting my soft parts."

We were still sparring when Rider walked through the door a couple hours later, his eyes immediately zeroing in on the busted punching dummy on the far side of the room. Daniel caught my fist in his hand, signaling we were done.

"Hey, at least she took her anger out on the dummy and not on me," he told Rider. "That's progress." To me, he said, "by the way, just the base of that thing was like two hundred and seventy pounds. Impressive."

I stared at the demolished dummy, surprised. The most I'd been able to lift before turning into a vampire was probably about forty pounds and involved a lot of grunting. I couldn't even do a single pull-up.

Rider didn't seem impressed, but he'd been a vampire longer than me and all the tricks and abilities that came with the condition had probably lost their thrill ages ago. He walked over to us. "We have a lead on the Quimbys and their hired goons. I've assigned a team to watch them and wait for the opportunity to strike. I also made arrangements for MidKnight to provide security for Pussycat Playhouse tomorrow night. You're going to the bachelorette party. You're being hunted because of me, so it's safest I don't go with you. We don't want to confirm the theory that you're extremely important to me. I'll have two female members of my security staff stay close to you."

"Not the best idea," Daniel said. "I've heard enough talk from the females in your nest to know they don't care for Danni too much. I'll protect her better."

Rider's eyes displayed his annoyance. "I know I assigned you as her personal bodyguard, but the situation has changed. She needs female guards."

"I know about the Bloom. She will be safe with me. I'll protect her from your enemies, and from herself."

Rider looked between the two of us and I didn't have to read his mind to know he wasn't pleased I'd shared the information about the Bloom. "So you found out Danni will be going into heat, losing control over her ability to control her sexual urges, and you want to be close to her, just in case? Explain to me why I shouldn't kill you right now."

"It's not like that," Daniel said, standing tall under Rider's withering glare. "A beautiful, majestic creature was killed so that I could shift into its form and use its abilities to make me a better fighter. That was not my choice. I come from a realm that embraces and loves magic, but I had the misfortune of living during the reign of an evil woman who twisted magic into something dark and hideous. I know what it's like to have dark magic forced on you, to become something you're not with no control whatsoever. I abhor it, and this Bloom thing sounds a hell of a lot like dark magic to me. The symbol Danni was branded with? Definite dark magic. Trust me when I tell you there is no one on your staff better to protect her than me, except you, but you can't be at her side and risk alerting more enemies to the fact she's your weak spot."

Rider stared him down, considering. "That sounds good, but all she has to do is bite you once and you're useless to her."

Daniel disappeared, reappeared across the room by the dummy, disappeared, reappeared behind Rider, disappeared, reappeared behind me, disappeared, appeared by the door, and continued to zap himself around the room, leaving only a quick flash of rainbow colored sparkles in his wake. Rider followed him, eyes wide in surprise, until he reappeared at my side, grinning with arrogance. "Dude… She won't get a chance to bite me."

"I didn't know you could do that."

"There's a lot you don't know about me, like I would never take advantage of Danni's weaknesses. Ever."

Rider narrowed his eyes as the two men appeared to hold a staring contest. Finally, Rider turned his attention to me. "Do you trust him?"

"Yeah." I nodded. "I do. And I'm more comfortable with him watching my back than I am with any of your female staff. I'd rather have you at my side, obviously, but if you're not willing to go with me, I'd feel safest with

Daniel."

"We've had this discussion." His tone indicated his irritation. "I will not lead any more of my enemies to you."

"Then stop trying to assign the women in your nest to guard me. Those bitches hate me."

"Women," he muttered, extracting a syringe out of his pocket. He handed it over to Daniel. "Keep this with you at all times. If the Bloom hits, use it. It's low dose hawthorn oil and some other stuff that won't hurt her, but will knock her out so she can't attack. If you have to use it, get her to my room immediately. The effect won't last long."

"Wait a damn minute! You've been walking around with a tranquilizer in your pocket... that you planned to use on me?!"

Rider sighed. "We don't know how strong Ryan's hold over you during the Bloom is yet. If it hits while we're in a room with someone else, would you rather I let you have your way with me in front of an audience or knock you out and take you to the privacy of my room?"

My cheeks heated, and I kept my eyes on Rider, not wanting to see Daniel's face as he stood at my side, listening to this conversation. "I thought you would do that mind-control thing."

"I hope and pray I can do that mind-control thing, but I don't *know* that I can. All I know is I need to protect you from harming anyone, including yourself, and I know one of the worst ways you could harm yourself would be to do something you feel is immoral and humiliating while Ryan controls you. I know you well enough to know you won't easily recover from that. If I have to tranq you to protect you from that, I will tranq you."

"I hate everything!" I yelled as I marched toward the door, clenching my teeth and my fists, using every bit of willpower I had not to scream.

"Dude," I heard Daniel say as I left the room. "You might wanna guard your nuts until she calms down."

"I'm pretty sure she's going to cut them off eventually anyway," Rider said.

I flipped them the bird, although they couldn't see it and felt a tiny bit better.

TWENTY

Vampires can't drown. I learned this by sinking underneath the waterline in the big clawfoot tub in Rider's bathroom and staying there. At first, I struggled for air, just as I had when Selander Ryan had strangled me, but I remembered what I was. I calmed and I let the human fear of death by drowning leave me before it could escalate to the point Rider would sense it and crash through the door to save me. My lungs burned for a moment, but quickly passed and all I felt was a gentle calm. I was wrapped in a cocoon of warm water, snugger than if I had been wrapped in a blanket. I stayed there enveloped in the water, in a little wet world all by myself, until I felt the sun preparing to rise. I imagined I could sleep there, but was afraid the water would wrinkle my skin while I slept and I'd wake up looking like a giant prune, so I broke the surface, climbed out and toweled off.

My reflection in the mirror was flawless, not even my fingers were wrinkled. It was as if my skin were impenetrable to water. Some would consider this to be a benefit of being a vampire. I viewed it as more evidence I was a freak. I dressed for bed in one of Rider's T-shirts and emerged from the bathroom, still towel-drying my hair.

Rider was already in the bed, sheets to his waist, bare chested, his hands clasped under his head. "I was starting to think you slipped down the drain."

"I slid under the water and I liked it there, so I stayed."

"You weren't trying to drown yourself, were you?"

"If only it were that easy to escape the Bloom."

"That's not funny," he snapped harsh enough to make me jump. "Don't ever joke about taking your life."

"Geez, I wasn't serious." I looked over at his closet and saw a short dress hanging on the doorknob. It was black, a little sparkly, and had a deep V-neck. A pair of black stiletto heels rested on the floor beneath it. "What is that?"

"I figured none of the clothes you have here were suitable for a bachelorette party at Pussycat Playhouse, so I sent someone to your apartment to pick something out of what you already have."

"And they picked that dress? That thing was in the very back of my closet and for good reason."

Rider looked at the dress. "Looks good to me. What's the problem?"

"The problem is, I had to cancel my breast augmentation after you turned me into a vampire and gave me this frigging thin blood. I don't have the boobs for that dress."

Rider rolled his eyes. "What you have is fine. Wear the damn dress."

"No. I'll go to my apartment and get another when I wake up."

"My staff will be stretched to the limits as it is tomorrow night. The day shift is busy tracking the men hunting you. I sent Ginger to your apartment so we wouldn't have to arrange a full security detail to get you there just for a dress. Wear the damn thing. You'll look fine in it."

"Who the hell is Ginger?" I asked, standing hands on hips as I glared down at him. "You sent one of your women to pick out a dress for me? One of the jealous women who hate me for sleeping up here with you? Oh, I'm sure she deliberately picked that dress knowing I can't pull it off!"

"First of all," Rider said, sitting up, "don't say 'one of your women.' I don't care for the way that sounds. I sent a female member of my nest, yes. Secondly, Ginger is a lesbian and doesn't give a damn who I'm sleeping with. If she picked that dress out for you, she probably thought you'd look hot in it so enough with the tantrum. It's time for bed."

I folded my arms. "I'm a grown woman," I shot back. "You can't tell me when it's time for bed." My eyelids drooped heavily, the sun almost fully up.

"Suit yourself," Rider said, smirking. He knew the pull of sleep as the sun rose had become incredibly stronger after he'd killed Ryan, and my vampire traits had strengthened. He slid back under the covers and closed his eyes.

"Jerk," I muttered as I stepped over to the bed and pulled the sheet back to slide underneath. "Why are you always naked? How can you sleep that way? What if there was a fire and we had to get out quick?"

"For one, I'm a vampire so I have this thing called vampiric speed that makes it easy for me to get dressed quickly. Also, I have this entire building warded against fire. If I didn't my enemies would have burned me out a long time ago."

"You have wards to keep people out of here and wards to protect from fire. Why didn't you have something in place to keep your brother from walking in here and leaving with me that night?"

"The type of warding required to keep him out of the bar would take a ton of blood magic and the type of witch who could work that spell isn't the type I'm on good terms with. The magic that keeps people out of my personal area up here was ridiculously expensive. I'd go broke using such magic on all my properties. Warding against fire is cheaper. I have staff in place to handle any other threats that enter my property."

"I still don't see why you can't wear pajama pants to bed. Boxers, at least," I grumbled as he wrapped his arms around me, cuddling close.

"It's a habit and not one I particularly care to break, considering I've been sleeping like this since…"

"Since before the automobile was invented?"

"Yes."

"Geez, you're *old.*"

He laughed. "I thought that had been established."

"Yeah, but I didn't really think about it. You're super old. *Old,* like *ancient. Prehistoric.*" I shuddered and made a little *ugh* noise.

He opened his eyes and narrowed them at me. "I haven't physically aged in centuries. Physically, I am within your physical age range and I am not prehistoric. I already told you I wasn't around with the dinosaurs. You're being incredibly childish right now."

"I'm not—"

"You're angry at me because I gave Daniel that tranq and you're insecure about wearing that dress around your sister and her friends tomorrow because you care too much what other people think about you, and instead of manning up and overcoming your insecurities you're taking this shit out on me. You're being petty and honestly, you're being insulting, trying to make yourself feel better by picking apart someone else like a bully, like what your family does to you. What's worse is you're doing it to me, the man you know damn well loves you more than anything. I don't know why you're trying to pick a fight with me, but it's not happening."

My eyes filled with tears as I realized he was right. I was being horrible, and I didn't even know why. Rider had done nothing but build up my confidence, and I was being a complete bitch to him. "Rider, I—"

"Go to sleep, Danni."

I woke to see Rider buttoning himself into a fresh black shirt, his wet hair perfectly coifed, pulled back into the low ponytail without a strand out of place. My internal clock told me the sun had gone down again, and I'd slept through the entire day, although it felt like Rider had just snapped at me to go to sleep a second before.

"You put me to sleep."

"You were almost out anyway," he said, keeping his eye on the holes he threaded buttons through as he finished dressing.

"You used your control over me to put me to sleep."

"You were being obnoxious." He glanced at me as he rolled up his sleeves. "You actually slept peacefully and under my sleep command, Ryan didn't break through. You're welcome."

"You know I don't like it when you use your power over me."

"I don't like it when you try to pick fights with me. There's blood on the bar. Drink it before it gets cold and then get ready. We were able to take out one of the Quimbys and the two hunters working directly with Torch. Torch got his street name because he's a pyro nut. Got some of my shifters with a flamethrower. No one died, but they probably wish they did. They're at the hospital until they fully recuperate."

I sat in the bed for a moment, processing. "When did all this happen?"

"Tony woke me around noon. Two of the Quimbys showed up at the building they'd prearranged to meet the Brotherhood members at around eleven. There was a fight and one Quimby was killed on scene. The other got away and was followed back to where the remaining Quimby, Torch, and the two hunters with him were holed up. I went in with Rome and a group of shifters. We took out two of them. Torch and two of the Quimbys are left. They had some gang guys guarding their spot, but we took them out of the equation. Torch had a lot of explosives he used to make their escape."

"You left me alone?"

"You were under my command to sleep and under the command, your mind was pretty much on lockdown. The only way you were getting out of it was if you went into the Bloom and Ryan gained control, which I would have immediately felt. Even under his control, you couldn't get out of this room unless I allowed it. No one could get inside to reach you. You were safe."

"I was safe if he tried to kill me in my sleep?"

"You were under my sleep command. All you could do was sleep. Dreamlessly. Even with that thing burned into you, he couldn't bring your mind to him if I had it closed down. Hell, I should put you under the sleep command every day to keep him out, but you don't like for me to use my power, so I don't."

"But you did."

"Like I said, you were being obnoxious. I didn't want to fight with you last night, Danni. I don't want to fight with you now. There are still three hunters out there after you. Please, just drink your blood and get ready for the party."

I kicked off the bedsheet and walked over to the bar. The bagged blood had been poured into a black mug and heated. I stirred the spoon inside and wrinkled my nose. "I hate this stuff."

"Danni, please."

"I know, I know." I downed the contents as quickly as I could, grimacing as a lump of something nasty went down my throat. I started to make a disgusted sound, but controlled myself. Some of Rider's shifters were in the hospital, burned because they were protecting me. The least I could do was drink the blood without griping like a spoiled brat. "I'm sorry people were hurt. I feel horrible about it."

"It's not your fault."

"Those hunters are after me. They were burned because of me."

"They were burned because Torch tried to fry my ass. They took the bullet, or flame, for me. They're kind of like my secret service. The hunters want to make me pay for killing Barnaby. All this shit happening is because of me, Danni, not you. This is my guilt to feel. You're another innocent bystander caught up in it. This is why I can't go to the party or the wedding with you. Take the guilt you feel about those shifters in the hospital and multiply it by a billion. That's what I'd feel if you were hurt because of me, only worse. I can't actually put into words what I would feel if you were hurt because of me."

"Even after last night?" I looked at the floor, unable to maintain eye contact as my cheeks warmed. "I'm sorry. I don't know why I was trying to start something."

"It's fine. I know you didn't mean anything. I just wish you could get your family's voices out of your head. You are so beautiful, Danni. I wish you could see that."

I looked at the dress and sighed. My self-esteem had gotten better since my relationship with Rider began. Around him, I did feel beautiful, more beautiful than I ever thought I could feel, but with just the thought of wearing that tiny dress around my sister and her uppity friends, I felt sick to my stomach, imagining their judging eyes on me. Worse, Daniel would be there listening to it all.

"Put the dress on, Danni. I promise you're going to look great in it."

I took the dress and my purse into the bathroom. The dress was snug, but not too tight. The hem rested a few inches below my bottom and overall, it didn't look too horrible. It was sleeveless and the deep V in front that stopped just below the sternum was supposed to show a lot of cleavage, but the dress had been an impulse buy when I'd first started considering getting the boob job. I'd been turned into a vampire the week before my scheduled surgery and couldn't go through with it because I would have bled out under the knife. I had no real cleavage to display in the dress, so I fluffed the chiffon panels in front, stretching the material as much as I could to try to provide more coverage. I brushed out my hair and used gel to give it a sleeker appearance. It had grown to just below my shoulders since the turning. I applied a coat of wine-colored lipstick and swiped on a neutral eyeshadow. I rooted around through my purse and came up with dangly diamond earrings. I didn't have a necklace on hand and wouldn't have worn one if I did. I was hoping the makeup and earrings would draw attention up, away from the plunging neckline.

"This is as good as it's going to get," I whispered to my reflection before opening the door and emerging from the bathroom.

Rider had waited in the room for me and was sitting at the bar. His eyes warmed as I approached. "Damn. Daniel's going to have to guard you from hunters and from every man with a pulse."

"Yeah, right," I said, slipping into the heels.

"Those don't help make his job easier."

I rolled my eyes. "Do you have a jacket I can wear with this?"

"You're welcome to anything I own, but it's awfully warm for a jacket. You'd draw attention wearing one, and if you're asking because you don't think you look good, you're crazy." To emphasize his point, he moved over to me, grabbed me around the waist and pulled me in close for a deep kiss that left my legs wobbling. "How important is this bachelorette party? I feel a private party coming on right here."

"My sister would never forgive me for missing it," I said, somehow managing to form words despite the sensation of his mouth gliding down my neck.

"You don't even like her." He kissed my shoulder.

"She's my sister. I love her."

"Yeah, but you don't *like* her." His hands slid down to the hem of my dress and his fingers slid underneath. "She'll be so busy being the belle of the ball she won't notice you're gone, and even if she does, I promise I'll make skipping out worth it."

"I'm doing this to draw out the remaining hunters, remember? And you want me around humans more."

"Damn it." Rider groaned, adjusted my dress, and kissed my forehead before stepping away. "I can't believe we let those bastards get away. We had them, all of them. They were right there, and they slipped right through my damn fingers."

"You had injured people to care for. You got three of them, plus the gang members they recruited."

"That's not good enough. I want this over with. I want you safe. It's bad enough worrying about Ryan and whatever his plan is without these assholes hunting you down and distracting us from whatever he's planning." He looked at the bed, then at me. "Speaking of distracted, I can't look at you dressed like that while you're in my bedroom and concentrate. Let's go downstairs. Daniel should be waiting already."

I followed Rider down the stairs, adjusting the neckline of my dress. I should have grabbed a jacket. Hell, I should have gone in jeans and a T-shirt and told anyone who didn't like it to go jump. It was a nightclub. There would be people dressed down. Of course, those people wouldn't be part of Shana's bachelorette party and wouldn't be expected to dress up or else get an earful. Looking down at my meager chest, I imagined I was going to be criticized either way.

Daniel was sitting on the couch when we entered Rider's office. He looked me up and down. "Shit. I'm going to have to protect her from the hunters and every dude with a pulse."

"I told you," Rider said, sitting on his desk and patting

the spot next to him. I slid up on the desk and the hem of my dress inched up my thighs. "Maybe you shouldn't sit at the club."

"Maybe I should just wear jeans and one of your silk shirts," I suggested.

"If I have to wear this, you're not wearing jeans," Daniel said, sweeping his hand out over his attire. He was wearing black slacks, dress shoes, and a black dress shirt with a black tie with a colorful dragon design. With the messy rainbow hair, he was looking very Punk GQ.

"Nice tie."

He grinned. "It seemed to suit me."

There was a knock on the door and an auburn-haired woman in black leather pants and a black T-shirt with a giant skull created from rhinestones stepped inside. Her black leather boots went up to her knees and her pretty face was accentuated by thick black eyeliner and blood red lip gloss. Her eyes were hazel, more brown than green, and they were giving me a long once-over. "So you're not even a little gay?" she asked me.

"Uh... no," I answered.

"Curious?"

I shook my head.

"Bummer." She plopped down on the couch and looked over at Daniel. "What up, Puff?"

Daniel just smiled at her.

"Danni, this is Ginger," Rider introduced us. "Ginger and Daniel will be at your side inside the club and, of course, traveling with you to and from it. Rome and a full team from my security pool will be working the club as well. I will be going out with another team, tracking the remaining hunters from the point where we lost them. They attacked you first, but they really want me dead. Hopefully, they'll come after me tonight, but if they do go after you, you're well-guarded."

Only Daniel knows about the Bloom and he has a tranquilizer just in case. Being female, you won't attack Ginger if the Bloom takes over and you have no worry about her being jealous of our relationship. If she's jealous of either of us, it's me, he added with a mental laugh. *She likes to joke, as you can tell, and she doesn't know how strongly I feel about you due to overall safety reasons, but she knows you're my property, so she won't try anything with you. She will protect you with everything she has, which is a lot. She's a damn good fighter. She just got back from assignment out of state or I would have put her with you sooner.*

"Why can't I dress like her?" I asked.

"You didn't have anything like this in your closet," Ginger answered. "Besides, I have to be dressed to kick ass. You just have to play the party girl role and attract the bad guys."

"I'm not much of a party girl."

"Samesies," Ginger said, batting her eyelashes.

I looked over at Rider, and he just grinned. *She's just playing with you. I'm pretty sure.* "Ginger, can you go check in with Carlos and the others? Make sure everyone's ready to roll out?"

"Sure thing." Ginger left the room, closing the door behind her.

"I think the redhead has a thing for your girl," Daniel said, grinning. "No promises to rip out her entrails?"

"Yeah, well, my girl's half succubus, so I'm not worried about her leaving me for a woman," Rider replied. "I am worried about her getting hurt. You heard what Torch did?"

"Yeah, he likes fire," Daniel said, standing. "I've got a whole lot of fire for him if he finds us and tries that shit tonight."

"You can't shift shape in a club full of humans," Rider warned him, "but by all means, if you can find a dark alley big enough, light him up. Just be careful you don't hit any of my people, especially the vampires. The young ones are highly flammable."

"Understood."

"You're armed just in case?"

Daniel lifted his pant leg, showing a gun holstered at his ankle.

"Ginger doesn't know about the Bloom. I don't want to announce it to everyone in case there's a chance we can keep it private. The less who know, the less we have to worry about that information falling into the wrong hands. Use the tranquilizer if you have to. We'll worry about explanations later. Just get her under control and get her back here as soon as possible. Rome doesn't know the full details, but he knows you have a tranquilizer and that you've been given the authority to use it. He has one on him as well, in case you need help. He'll be keeping close watch on the two of you."

"And if Ginger sees me use the tranquilizer and goes all pissed off vampire on me?"

"Try not to get your ass kicked. She's pretty damn good. Rome will be there to assist." Rider glanced at the clock and sighed. "I really hate doing this."

"There's only three of them now," I reminded him.

"One of them has a flamethrower and two of them come from a long line of really good hunters and they're pissed because I killed one of their family members and now my men have killed another." Rider stood and helped me up, smiling softly as I tugged down the bottom of my dress. "Maybe they'll be too mesmerized by that hemline to do much damage."

"It's a definite possibility," Daniel said, earning a dark look from Rider. His mouth twitched in response, clearly amused.

Rider pulled me against him and gave me a long, lingering kiss. "Be careful, babe. Don't feel like you have to hang out at the club all night, baiting these bastards. Go to your sister's party. Stay however long is required not to get bitched at by your family, and if you want to come back early, go for it. And if you feel weird at all, tell Daniel and get back here immediately."

"I will," I promised, wishing I'd never suggested going

to the party to begin with. I had a bad feeling in my gut about it, and the bad feeling didn't even have anything to do with the hunters.

Daniel guided me out of the office. We were leaving out of the front of the bar, where a small convoy of SUVs waited. Rider and his team were leaving through the back. I looked over at Daniel as we moved toward the front of the bar and found him grinning. "What is it?"

Daniel shrugged. "It's kind of funny. Ginger flirts it up big time with you and Rider is amused. I say the least little thing and I get death glares and threats. When I say something about it, he says he's not worried because you wouldn't leave him for a woman."

"And?"

"And… using that reasoning, it sounds like I get the glares and threats because he's a little worried you could actually leave him for me."

I rolled my eyes. "He's not worried I'll leave him for you, and he has no reason to be."

Daniel just kept grinning.

Rome and several of Rider's security staff were already in the club when we arrived. I didn't know the others in the SUV with Ginger, Daniel, and me, but they got out with us and walked inside, walking right past the bouncer at the door, who I recognized as one of Rider's guys. Rome was standing just inside the door as we entered. He nodded his head at Daniel, sharing some silent communication and guided us through a crush of gyrating bodies on the dancefloor as loud music pumped through the air. His back was ramrod straight, his shoulders back as he scanned the crowd on high alert. Ginger and Daniel stayed with me, but the others who'd arrived with us peeled off from our group and spread out.

Rome guided us to a room at the back of the club. There was no door, but a red velvet rope sealed the area off from the rest of the club. The large man standing before the room exchanged nods with Rome and unhooked the rope, allowing us inside.

"Can't wait for you to eat a chunk of that cake," Rome said to Daniel as we entered. I looked back to see him standing beyond the velvet rope, a huge smile stretched across his face.

"What was that about?" I asked.

"I'm afraid to find out," Daniel answered.

Two full walls were lined with the longest L-shaped sectional I'd ever seen, providing plenty of comfortable seating. A table near the back held a large cake box and a bucket of champagne bottles. My sister and her friends were in front of it, pouring drinks, all decked out in short, tight dresses, even the original maid of honor who I easily picked out by the fact her pregnancy was starting to show, particularly in the tight white dress she'd worn. I winced, knowing it was a dumb thought, but still couldn't help thinking the poor baby was getting smooshed.

"Danni!" Shana said, turning to see me arrive. "You showed up... and you brought friends." She eyed Ginger quizzically, then turned her attention to Daniel, smiling friendlier than I thought an engaged woman should. "Daniel, right? Did you come to watch the entertainment... or participate?"

"I'm just here making sure Danni stays out of trouble," he said, scanning the area.

"Oh, like Danni could ever get in trouble," Shana said, laughing. "She's as goody two shoes as they come."

"Ooh, is this one of the dancers?" A tall, thin woman with strawberry blonde hair asked, eying Daniel like a snack as she came up next to Shana. I knew I'd met her before, but couldn't remember her name. I'd never gotten along particularly well with Shana's friends.

"No, this is Danni's friend, Daniel."

"Oh, Danni and Daniel," the woman said, clapping her hands. "How cute. Your celebrity couple name could be

… Danniel with two N's… or Danny Squared."

I get the feeling I'm going to lose brain cells hanging out with this group, Ginger said telepathically, *and none of them are hot enough to lose brain cells for.*

Really? I responded once I got over the shock of the mind intrusion. I still wasn't used to communicating telepathically with other vampires in Rider's nest. Other than Eliza, they didn't really talk to me at all. *Not even my sister? Everybody thinks my sister is hot.*

She looks like someone that everyone would say was hot. Kind of fake. Not my type.

"Oh, they're not a couple," Shana said. "Right, Danni?"

"Right," I said, pushing my answer through gritted teeth. Her snide tone wasn't lost on me.

"I love your dress," her friend said. "I can never wear dresses with that kind of neckline without looking cheap. I pop right out of those necklines."

"Yes, Danni's lucky that she doesn't ever have that problem," Shana said. "Speaking of dresses, I really need you to pick up yours at the shop, Danni. They keep calling. You're my maid of honor. I need to be sure you're going to be there at the wedding on time, in the dress, smiling, thin, and perfect."

I glanced over at the original maid of honor, who was rubbing her swollen belly and eying me with a mix of disdain and sadness. "I'll be there, but I haven't had time to pick up the dress. Can you just pick it up and bring it to the church? I can get dressed there before the ceremony. You'll probably want to make sure my hair and makeup are perfect anyway, right?"

"You have a point," she said, taking in my light makeup. "Just don't be late. We have pictures scheduled prior to the ceremony."

"What in the fresh hell is this?" Daniel asked. He'd moved over to the table and was staring down into the cake box with a mix of horror and revulsion on his face.

The women closest to him laughed. "Isn't it adorable?"

a brunette in a hot pink halter-style dress asked. "There's little candy fish inside the balls. Get it? Little swimmers!"

Ginger and I exchanged a look and walked over to check out the cake. I gawked, taking in the gigantic fondant covered penis, complete with testicles and a smattering of buttercream short and curlies piped strategically at the base.

"That's a big ol' dick," Ginger said.

"What's coming out of it?" Daniel asked, his nose wrinkled.

"Buttercream, I hope," I answered, taking in the white stuff designed to look as if it were shooting out of the tip.

"That's just nasty," Ginger said.

"That woman said there's candy fish in the testicles," Daniel said. "Please tell me these women know sperm doesn't look like fish."

"Please quit saying sperm while talking about cake," I requested, my stomach turning. My bad feeling about the party was growing steadily worse. I looked over to where we'd left Rome standing and saw him watching us, laughing. "Rome is laughing."

"Of course the jackass is laughing," Daniel said. "He wants me to eat a piece of this so he can tell Rider I ate a big chunk of dick."

"Are you going to eat a piece?" I asked.

"Hell no," he answered, still staring at the cake like it was a car crash he couldn't tear his disgusted eyes away from. "Not even for a million dollars. Are you?"

"Nope." Even if my newly turned vampire stomach could handle cake, I would not be touching one shaped like a penis and filled with white cream. I shook my head and looked at Ginger.

"Don't even ask me," she said. "I don't like real ones, much less ones covered in nasty fondant. I can't imagine which would taste worse."

A group of men entered the roped off area, varying in height and skin tone, but all twelve were young and muscular. "Ladies! Are you ready to party?" a golden-skinned Latino man asked, drawing a cacophony of squeals from Shana and her friends. A pair of less impressive looking men quickly set up chairs in the middle of the room, before the sectional, and left.

"Oh shit," I said, looking around for a way to extract myself from the nightmare about to unfold.

"Danni, come on!" Shana grabbed me and attempted to shove me onto one of the chairs. I broke away and scampered to the sectional lining the wall directly behind the chairs, but in front of the men who were now standing in two lines, heads down and hands clasped behind them. Daniel and Ginger sandwiched me on the couch and shared a look of discomfort.

"Is this what I think it is?" Daniel asked.

One of the men hit a button on the wall and curtains were drawn around the area, sealing our group off from the rest of the club. The curtains closing caused the area we were in to darken, but the club's music was still loud and clear. The current song ended, and I heard the familiar beat of Ginuwine's *Pony* blast out of the speakers as the men in front of us started rotating their hips.

It was a succubus's dream and one of my biggest nightmares.

TWENTY-ONE

"I didn't sign up for this," Daniel said, starting to lift himself up from the sectional. I grabbed his arm and yanked him back down.

"If I have to see men shaking ass, you have to see men shaking ass," Ginger said.

"You're my bodyguards for the evening," I reminded both of them. "Guard me from shaking ass. Don't let it near my lap."

The gyrating quickly became more forceful and shirts were tossed through the air with perfect synchronization, eliciting squeals of excitement from Shana and her party. Shana sat dead center in the chair placed in front and the rest of her party sat behind or next to her, careful to leave space for personal attention, which they clearly wanted, judging by the way they all bobbed up and down.

"I'm so sorry," I whispered to my guards.

"I'd rather have gone up against Torch," Daniel complained. "Appreciate me. Appreciate the hell out of me... and never speak of this again." He looked at the curtain that had been drawn where we'd left Rome and I knew he was dreading the ribbing he knew was coming.

"At least Rome can't see what's happening," I told him.

"Yeah, but he knows what's happening, and he's probably going to embellish when he tells everyone later."

One of the dancers tipped Shana's chin up with his finger, winked at her, backed up into formation with the rest of the men, and then BAM! The pants came off and before the fabric hit the floor, all twelve men turned around, bent over and jiggled everything hanging out of their thongs.

"Yikes!" I turned toward Daniel in an attempt to hide, acting on pure reflex, and saw he'd covered his eyes with his hands and was muttering to himself. I couldn't hear what he was saying over the other women's screams.

"This is what straight women like?" Ginger asked, her head angled sideways, taking in the view. "I don't get it."

Two of the women turned to shush her. "Shush and enjoy!" one said.

"I do not enjoy this," I said as the men straightened up, maintaining their jigglage. It looked like someone had rammed a quarter up their asses and set them on vibrate.

"Kill it!" Daniel said. "Kill it with fire! Kill *me*. Just make it stop."

The men slapped their asses and turned around, dipped down and started thrusting their barely covered genitals toward the screaming women. Then they started moving forward and lowering themselves onto laps. My stomach turned. Here's the thing. Every man before me was actually very attractive, but the minute their clothes came off and I saw body oil and various colored strands of floss up their asses, I could no longer view them as even remotely desirable. There was just something about a man jiggling around in a thong that shut my libido down immediately. I'd find an average-looking man in boxers sexier than the assorted beefcake before me. Not even Rider could don a thong and turn me on, and Rider was pretty damn perfect.

My sister and her friends, however, ate it up. They giggled, squealed, screamed, begged for more, slipped dollars waaaay down the front of thongs and holy crap… the pregnant one licked the guy grinding his unmentionables against her.

"That's it," I said. "I came, I saw, I want the hell out. There has to be a billiards room in here somewhere."

"Yes!" Ginger said. "Those are some balls I can play with."

We moved to stand and a buff, blond guy with washboard abs locked eyes with me and smiled. "Oh, shit."

Daniel opened his eyes. Refusing to look at anything happening in front of him, he hadn't been aware we'd started to get up. "What?"

"Hey, sweetheart," the blond said, moving toward me. "Whatcha doin' hiding back here?"

"Hiding," I told him. "Move along to someone else, please. I don't want the personal service."

"Yeah, keep that devil snake back," Ginger warned him, but he kept coming. I could see it in his eyes. He was arrogant and used to the adoration of women at these types of parties, and I had just made myself a challenge.

"Girl, you're gonna fall in love in a minute," he said, dangerously close to my lap.

Suddenly, Daniel had a gun pointed in the dancer's face. "Back the hell up, Thrustin' Bieber. The lady said she's not interested."

"Whoa!" The guy jumped back, hands raised. "What the hell, man?"

Daniel stood, gun hand steady. "When a woman says move along, you move along."

One of the other dancers noticed the commotion in back, looked up from grinding in one of the women's laps and yelled, "Gun!" He jumped back, knocking into the dancer behind him and then it was chaos. Half-naked men knocked each other down like dominoes, piling on top of each other as horny women reached out to grab hold of whatever they could get their claws into, upset the dancing had stopped. Shana glared at me and started yelling at us for ruining her party. That's when the blond narrowed his eyes, had the worst idea in his life, and lunged for the gun.

Daniel sidestepped, effortlessly picked the dancer up by the skin of his neck since the only clothing the man had on was an article Daniel wasn't touching with a ten-foot pole, and flung him across the room just as the pile of beefcake had gotten up. The blond hit the other dancers and down they went, half landing inside and half landing outside the curtain.

"I think you got a strike," Ginger said, shaking her head. "I'm kind of enjoying the party now."

"What the hell is all over my hand?" Daniel asked, grimacing as he looked at the shiny oil while the dancers struggled to their feet and started to scatter.

The curtain was yanked all the way open and Rome stepped inside. Two men also dressed in matching black T-shirts that read SECURITY in bright yellow flanked him. His mouth curved as he fought back a smile. "Problem in here? I just saw a bunch of men in panties running out, looking pretty frazzled."

"He pulled a gun on me!" the blond dancer said, marching up to Rome. Still in a thong despite the curtain being open and his bare ass displayed to the entire club, he didn't seem to care as he clasped Rome's biceps and pointed at Daniel. "Do something about it!"

"I'm going to do something about you if you don't get your half-naked ass at least four feet away from me," Rome said, looking down at the dancer, "and get your hand off me, boy, before my foot is up in your ass deeper than that piece of ya mama's lingerie."

The dancer dropped his hand and stepped back, looking between the two men. He opened his mouth to protest, thought better of it, and stormed off.

Rome looked at us and laughed. "You pulled a gun on him?"

"I told him to leave me alone and he wouldn't," I said.

"Daniel stopped him before he could rub all that nastiness in my lap."

"What the hell, Danni?" Shana was marching round, waving her arms, flapping them all around like a demented chicken. "Don't you know how to have fun? You should be happy a hot guy pays you attention. You're supposed to enjoy it, not threaten him!"

"Are you going to be our entertainment now?" The pregnant friend asked Rome, squeezing his muscles.

"Do I look like the type of guy that shakes his bare ass for dollars?" Rome asked before moving her aside. "Hands off the merchandise, ma'am."

"We paid for strippers!" Shana's brunette friend yelled. "We demand our money's worth!"

"Everybody shut up!" Rome yelled, then turned to one of the men who'd entered the area with him. "Go gather up the strippers and get them back here."

"What if they don't want to perform?" the man asked.

"Persuade them," Rome said. "Tell them the security threat has been handled."

"You better not screw this up again," Shana snapped at me. "Just relax and try to be a normal person."

"Clearly this isn't my thing," I shot back at her, "so I'll leave."

"You can't leave!" She crossed her arms and stomped her foot. "How can my own sister leave my bachelorette party? What kind of statement does that make?"

"Well, I'm not staying here and going through another horrorfest of ass-jiggling and pelvic thrusting," I told her. I looked at Rome. "Is there a billiards room?"

He jerked his head to the left. "Toward the back of the club, just past the bathrooms."

"We'll be there," I told Shana. "We're not leaving your party, we're just skipping the strippers."

"Make sure you come back for cake," Rome said, eying the undisturbed dessert.

"I'm not touching that cake," Daniel told him. "Sorry,

bro, but you don't get to tell everyone I ate dick."

Rome barked out a laugh. "That's fine. I can still tell them you got to enjoy the strippers."

"Go for it," Daniel said. "And I'll tell everyone you told that guy you were going to go deep in his ass."

"I didn't——" Rome's mouth closed in a tight line as he recalled the words he'd used to threaten the dancer. "I hate you, Puff."

We found the billiards tables before the dancers could return to the party and managed to somewhat enjoy ourselves despite the fact none of us really wanted to be there. I wasn't very good at billiards, but I'd play all night long if it meant I didn't have to deal with my sister.

"The hot blonde is checking you out again," Ginger advised Daniel as she took her shot, just barely missing getting her ball in the pocket.

"What can I say? The ladies love me." Daniel rubbed chalk on the tip of his cue stick as he scanned the area for trouble. He didn't give the hot blonde a moment's attention, which I found surprising. Ginger wasn't lying. The woman ogling him from across the room was a knockout. She made my perfect sister look plain.

"You must really be focused on the job," I said.

"Of course. The job is keeping you safe." He studied the remaining billiard balls on the table and lined up his shot. He tapped the cue ball with the stick and performed a tricky shot that sent two balls into the pockets.

"Showoff," Ginger said, rolling her eyes.

I saw the hot blonde sigh and turn toward a man who'd approached her, giving up on Daniel looking her way. "Hey, so what happened with Rihanna?"

Daniel frowned. "Rihanna?"

"Yeah, when you went to the bakery to get me a cupcake, she left right after. She kind of gave the impression she was going after you. She was very interested in you."

"Oh." He studied the billiard balls. "Yeah, she caught up with me and flirted some, but I didn't talk much with her. She's not my type."

I looked at the hot blonde again while he lined up his next shot. "The hot blonde can't get your attention. You passed on Rihanna. Gorgeous women aren't your type?"

Daniel hit the cue ball and watched the aftermath, cursing softly under his breath when he failed to get any balls in the pocket. "I'm on duty tonight and can't get distracted by hot blondes. As for Rihanna, yes, she is a very attractive woman, but I've been on the bad end of magic. I'm not going to date a witch, even if she's supposed to be a good witch. Once bitten, twice shy, that kind of deal."

I nodded my understanding and moved forward to take my shot. I bent over the table and Daniel sucked in air.

"Don't lean over any more, Danni, or you're going to make a lot of guys in here very happy."

"Don't listen to him," Ginger said, stretching her neck for a better view.

I laughed and straightened up, pulling the bottom of my dress down. I'd learned Ginger liked to joke flirtatiously, but as Rider had said, she wouldn't encroach on his territory. She teased me similarly to the way Daniel did, and I didn't find it offensive from either. I made my shot as well as I could, considering I couldn't really lean forward much without revealing too much of myself to the room behind me. "We should have chosen a table by the wall."

"We should have chosen a game you can actually play," Daniel said, winking at me.

Ginger glanced at the clock over the bar. "How much longer do you have to stay? So far, it doesn't seem like anyone's tracking you. I keep checking in with security and it's crickets on the hunter front."

I'd reached out to Rider a few times through our link

just to make sure he was safe, and it seemed as if his night was just as uneventful. "We can go check in with my sister. Surely I've been here long enough to represent the family or whatever it is I'm supposed to be doing. I really don't know why she cares so much about having me here. I'm not into the strippers and penis cake, so there's no point in me being part of the party."

"Sounds good to me." Daniel collected our cue sticks and put them away as Ginger racked the billiard balls for the next people to use the table.

Rome was standing guard at the archway that separated the billiards area from the dancefloor. Daniel caught his eye, and he shook his head, indicating there'd been no trouble so far. "Have the dancers evacuated the bachelorette party?" Daniel asked.

"According to the man I have on them, all but the one Danni's sister was making out with left after one more striptease. She took that one in the bathroom for a while, but she's out now. They all ate cake and have been drinking and dancing. They're all around in here now."

"I'm sorry." I looked up at the big man, unsure I'd heard him correctly. "Did you say my sister made out with one of the strippers and took him into the bathroom?"

"Yeah." Rome looked down at the floor for a moment before returning eye contact. "She's the one getting married, right?"

"Yeah, clearly not to the love of her life." I shook my head in disgust and marched forward, cutting through the crowd of bodies writhing to music, making a straight line for the area I'd left my sister at, Daniel and Ginger close on my tail. Rome walked a couple feet behind us.

I entered the party area to see it had been vacated by everyone except the pregnant former maid of honor, who was busy shoveling penis cake into her mouth. "It's really good," she said, glancing up. "There's some left if you want any."

I looked in the box and saw the testicles were all that

remained. "No thanks. Where is my sister?"

"Off sowing her wild oats. If you want to leave now, she won't notice. She's hooked up with like two guys already and has had way too much champagne."

I looked over at Rome for help.

"I'll assign a guard to her to make sure she gets home safe. Are you leaving now?"

I nodded. "It's nowhere near dawn and I'm already exhausted."

"Torch and the Quimbys must be regrouping after what went down earlier," he said. "Tonight's a bust. Give me a few minutes to assign someone to your sister and get transportation in order."

A few minutes turned into fifteen as Rome organized our departure plan, and then he was guiding us to a side door with a sign that said to only use in emergencies. "A fire alarm won't sound?" I asked.

"Deactivated it," Rome explained. He opened the door and stepped out. The SUV we'd be traveling back to Midnight Rider in was parked right in front of the door, but Rome still scanned the narrow alley for signs of trouble before giving us the all clear to exit the building.

I stepped out, sandwiched between Daniel and Ginger, and felt odd. I looked around, sure I was being watched, but other than us and the three SUVS which all belonged to our convoy, the alley was empty. We piled into the vehicle, Ginger up front with the driver, and me in the backseat between Daniel and Rome.

"Roll out," Rome ordered and settled in. He chuckled, shaking his head. "I was really hoping to see you eat that cake, Puff."

"Sorry to disappoint." Daniel loosened his tie. "So Rider's providing security to the club for the whole night?"

"That was the deal. He wanted to make sure the club was full of his people while Danni was in it. We left enough behind to keep things running smoothly until they close up. Tomorrow night, it'll be business as usual with the regular staff."

"How'd he manage to swing such a deal? The club owner had to think it was weird."

"MidKnight has contracted out security for the club before, when they draw in big names for their live music nights. The owner is familiar with his work, and Rider told him he had a VIP client attending and he wanted his own security in place. Didn't take a lot more than that. Rider's good at this business stuff."

The men continued talking and joking with each other as we headed toward the bar. I listened for a little bit, but my head started swimming. My body grew cold as a breeze wafted past me. I looked at the windows, trying to find the source of the brisk wind, but they were all up. I thought it must be the air conditioning but didn't ask to turn it down. I figured the others would if they were cold. Rider's staff had already had to provide protection for me all night, potentially risking their lives. The least I could do was let them be comfortable.

"Danni. Danni?"

I looked over at Daniel. "What?"

"Are you all right?"

"Yes, why?"

He studied me. "You were kind of spaced out."

"Oh." My stomach tightened painfully, and I reflexively put my hand over it. "I think I'm just thirsty. I only had bagged blood tonight. It's not as quenching as the fresh stuff."

"Rider said you can't have any blood fresh from the source," Rome said. I turned toward him and watched his throat as he spoke. "We're close to the bar. You'll have blood there, so you don't have long to wait."

I nodded my head but said nothing, transfixed by all the smooth chocolate skin covering Rome's throat as he continued talking to Daniel. It reminded me of the chocolate buttercream on the cupcake Daniel had given me when Rihanna worked the spell to allow me to eat without getting sick. I wondered if Rome's skin tasted as good as that buttercream, if it was as soft. I knew it wouldn't make me sick. In fact, I was thinking it and what it covered would make me feel real good. I let my gaze roam over the T-shirt stretched over impressive muscles and licked my lips as my gaze settled on equally muscular thighs. Warmth flowed from his body, calling me toward him. In the back of my mind, I knew something was wrong and started to reach out to Rider.

Uh-uh, a familiar voice said from inside me. *It's my turn now. You're free, Danni, free to take what you want. Take it!*

My fangs elongated as I pounced on Rome, straddling his lap as my open, drooling mouth went for his throat and my hands yanked down on his zipper.

"What the hell?" I heard him bellow as he shoved me away and I registered a sharp stab of pain in my neck and multiple voices cussing and shouting before my eyelids, suddenly heavy, snapped closed and I fell down a black hole.

"Shit, she's coming to. Where's Rider?"

"On his way. Maybe you should leave, Rome. If she has venom in her fangs and I'm betting she does, one bite and you're going to be a major problem. You already came too close in the car."

"What about you? She's supposed to go after everything male."

"She can't catch me."

I opened my eyes and stared up at the ceiling above me as I waited for the room to stop pulsating. Everything was red. I blinked, clearing my vision until the redness went away and the pulsating stopped.

I was in Rider's room, on his bed. Daniel and Rome stood over me, watching me warily. Cold crept into my body and I realized it was because a woman was holding me. I looked behind me to see I was resting against

Ginger's chest.

"Hey there, sweetie," she said.

Something inside me growled. It was angry and cold, but mostly, it was hungry. I dug my fingers into Ginger's hands and tried to force her off of me as I lunged toward Daniel and Rome, the heat of their testosterone promising me the warmth that Ginger's estrogen-filled body was draining out of me.

"Get out now," Daniel ordered Rome as he crossed to the bar and picked up a glass of dark red liquid.

"Good luck," Rome said, and he exited the room in three quick strides.

"Danni, you need to drink this," Daniel told me, bringing the glass to me. He stepped back when I tried to jump at him and waited until Ginger had me secured. "Please, Danni. Drink."

Ginger's arms were wrapped around me tight from behind, binding my arms to my sides, her legs wrapped around mine, pinning me in place as best she could. Daniel pushed my head back, his palm pressing on my forehead so that my head rested in the hollow between Ginger's neck and shoulder. If she'd been male, I'd have made a slight turn and attacked, but she was full of estrogen, the hormone that made the succubus in me writhe as the chill of it attacked my body. I didn't want to be near her. Just being close to her, I felt my strength being zapped away. I felt the coldness creeping out of her and into me, shutting me down. I heard an unhuman sound come out of me as I strained against her hold, trying to free myself, and then Daniel placed the glass to my mouth and poured the warm liquid down my throat.

The blood coated my tongue and ran down my throat as I gulped greedily. It was good, but it wasn't enough. I stared at Daniel's throat longingly. I heard his heartbeat beckoning me closer. I imagined how fast the flow of blood would be once he was naked underneath me, how the harder I rode him, the sweeter his blood would taste, how filling his very essence would be as I drained him of everything he needed to live and absorbed it into me where his warmth would chase away the bitter cold clinging to my bones. I drained the contents of the glass and rammed the back of my head into Ginger's face. I heard her nose shatter, felt the moment her arms loosened around me, and surged forward, grabbing Daniel's shoulders. He disappeared the second the tips of my fangs touched his skin and I tumbled off the bed onto the floor.

"You all right, Ginger?" he asked, appearing by the door.

"She broke my fucking nose," she answered, her voice funny as she ran to the bathroom, her hand covering her nose. Blood seeped through her fingers.

"Shit," Daniel said as I stalked him. He stayed close to the wall as he moved around, never taking his eyes off of me. My head was lowered, my gaze locked on to the pulse point in his throat. "Danni, you don't want to do this. I know you're going through this thing and your body's telling you one thing, but listen to your heart. You love Rider. You only want to do this with him."

"I want to do this with Rider," I said, nodding my head in agreement. "First, I want to do this with you."

"I'm flattered, but I'm going to have to pass." He'd reached the bar and inched down the length of it, headed in the bed's direction. If I could get him close enough to it, it'd be a simple tackle. His eyes cut over to the bed, then back to me, reading my mind. He stood still. "Hang in there, Danni. Rider's on his way."

I felt cold creeping in behind me and turned to see Ginger had returned with cotton balls shoved into her nose and she didn't look happy. "You have another one of those tranquilizers?" she asked.

"Oh, sure, now you want to use one," Daniel said. "You were about to rip me apart in the car after I hit her with the first one."

"I didn't know what it was or why you used it," she

said. "I understand now, and I'm cool with it. She's kind of freaking me out and I'm afraid I'm going to have to seriously damage her and piss Rider off."

"I'm out. Rome had the other one, and he took it with him. Just grab her and keep her restrained."

Ginger stepped toward me and I made my move toward Daniel, using my vampiric speed to cross the room in a flash and grab him. Once again, he disappeared the moment my fangs touched him. I let out a rage-filled scream which was cut off as I found myself slammed to the floor, Ginger straddling me.

"Chill the hell out!" Ginger snapped, using both hands to pin my shoulders to the floor as I bucked and strained, trying to get out of her hold. I raised my hands, grabbed two fistfuls of hair and rolled her over so I was on top. I slammed her head into the floor and opened my mouth, determined to rip her throat out, but before I could make contact, I was yanked off of her and tossed onto the bed.

"Stop it, Danni!" Daniel loomed over me. "Fight this!"

"Don't wanna," I said, leaping for him, but he vanished and I stumbled forward, crashing into the wall. "Stop doing that!"

I turned to see the two of them standing in the middle of the room. The door was to their left and beyond that door was a staircase that would take me down one floor to a bar filled with people, many of them men filled with what I desperately craved. Men who couldn't disappear before I got my fangs into them and made them beg for me to take all I needed from them. I ran for the door, wrapped my hand around the knob and pulled, but nothing happened. I growled, yanking harder on the knob, but somewhere in the haze of my sex-craved mind, I recalled Rider telling me the room was spelled. No one could get in or out unless he wanted them to, and apparently he wanted me to stay in.

"Sonofabitch!" I screamed, punching the door, but it did nothing to release my ire. I turned toward my captors and attacked. Daniel did his disappearing trick, so I focused my energy on Ginger, knocking her back with a hard jab to her already broken nose.

"That's it!" She delivered a solid punch of her own, knocking me on my ass, but I didn't stay down. Fueled by rage and desperation, I jumped back onto the balls of my feet, hunkered down and charged her like a bull. My head connected with her midsection and I rammed her into the wall.

The air pressure in the room dropped, the door opened, and Rider stepped inside. He lifted his hand, and I flew back onto the bed. I struggled to get up, but an invisible weight held me down. Rider's eyes bore the strain of using his power to hold me in place. His mouth set in a straight line. The indentation in his jaw showed his teeth were clamped tight together. I smelled blood on his clothes and the thirst inside me intensified. I dug my nails into the mattress and pushed with all I had, managing to raise my shoulders off the bed.

"Get out," he said from behind gritted teeth. "Ginger, get to the hospital before you lose too much blood. Daniel, get Rihanna. Tell her I need a gallon of fresh blood witch-delivered up here every hour. Tony and Rome are in charge of operations until this is over."

Ginger quickly left through the door that wouldn't open for me. Daniel followed her, looking back at me with sympathy before leaving. "What's going to happen? Is she going to be all right?"

"She's going to try to screw me to death, which isn't nearly as fun as it sounds," Rider answered. "As long as I keep enough blood in me to fuel my power and keep her locked in here away from anyone else, she should come out of this fine. Go about business as normal. Go now. I can't hold her like this for very long. That bastard's control over her is pushing against mine."

"Good luck, man. Don't die," Daniel added as he slipped out the door, closing it behind him.

I could sit up all the way now. I leaned toward Rider as far as his hold would allow and licked my lips, already salivating. He kicked off his shoes and removed his shirt, causing my heart to race as I looked at his chest and thought, *so much flesh to bite into, so much blood to taste.* I struggled against his hold as he eyed me warily and managed to get to my knees.

"All right, Danni." He unbuttoned his pants. "Try to take it easy."

He released his hold on me, and I was on him before his pants hit the floor.

TWENTY-TWO

Everything came to me in flashes. Rider underneath me. Rider on top of me. In the bed. On the floor. Rider pushing me away. Rider feeding me from his wrist, from a glass. Gulping blood from his throat. Rider holding me down, pleading with me to be patient as he drank blood, guzzling it out of a gallon jug. Rider's eyes full of power. Rider's eyes drained, tired. Under water in the big bathtub, the warm liquid chasing away the cold. Kissing Rider. Biting Rider. Tearing at Rider with my fingernails. Flames engulfing me, reaching out to lick my skin. Selander Ryan grinning, waiting. Sun rising, pulling me down into the abyss. Sun descending, giving me energy for another go-round on Rider. Rider telling me he loved me, telling me it was going to be OK. Crying. Growling. Screaming. Rider telling me he was sorry. Rider telling me to fight. Rider catching his breath next to me as I stared at his throat and imagined ripping out his jugular and bathing in the blood, imagined the power I could drain out of him. Selander Ryan laughing louder. The soul stitch on my breastbone burning. Rider looking at me with eyes full of fear, seeing something in me I was thankful I could not see myself. Red. So much red.

Fire everywhere.

I stood in the dining room, naked as the day I was born, but I didn't care. The monster that had come to life inside me had no virtue, no modesty. It only had a thirst that could never be quenched. Selander Ryan watched me from where he sat at the table, sipping from his chalice, eyes alight with something close to joy, but far too dark. Flames licked up the walls, eating the walls around us, but neither of us feared its heat.

"Are you having fun, my pet?"

"I'm thirsty."

He smiled, his teeth as dazzling white as his suit. His fangs descended, curving over his bottom lip. The suit bled with color, changing from white to crimson. The flames grew closer. "You won't get what you need from his blood. You have to take everything."

"He's too strong."

Ryan set the chalice down and stood. "You are in Bloom, my pet. You have the power."

I shook my head. I longed to devour Rider, to drain every last drop of blood from him, to ride his body until it broke, to completely possess every ounce of his power, but he was protected. The closer I got to draining him, the tighter my heart constricted. Pain filled me, stabbing right down into my soul. If he died, he would drag me into the grave with him.

"You are afraid. You have no need to be scared. You are mine." Ryan wrapped his hand around my neck, ran his thumb across my jawline. "You have my protection. Drain his power and together we will rule. Would you like that?"

Tears escaped my eyes, sizzling from the heat of the flames burning around us. The ache was back in my chest, but my stomach cramped with hunger. "I'm so thirsty."

"I know. Allow me inside, Danni, and you will never be thirsty again." He pulled me against him and covered my mouth with his own. His tongue slithered against mine and I choked. Ryan was gone and in his place black smoke poured into my mouth, forcing its way down my throat, filling my body. The flames were upon me.

"Danni!"

I saw Rider through a red haze, his eyes wide. Hands were wrapped around his throat, digging into his skin. He pried them off, shoved the owner away. The hands tore at him and all I could see was red. I tasted blood, heard growling. Suddenly, I looked up into Rider's eyes as if he were above me, but I couldn't move. His neck had been mauled, ripped savagely. Blood oozed from the wound and from the many claw marks on his chest and arms. "Fight him, Danni! Fight him!"

I screamed his name, but no sound came out. I tried to run to him, but I couldn't move. I reached for him, but had no arms. Cold realization washed over me. I was trapped inside my own body, and my body had been taken over by Selander Ryan. I tried to claw at the soul stitch attachment, but I couldn't operate my own hands. I could only watch through a red haze as Selander Ryan forced my body to knock Rider to the floor and gulp blood from the large gash in his neck. I tasted the blood and silently screamed, knowing I would stop at nothing to completely drain him as long as Ryan operated my body.

Suddenly, I was high above Rider, looking down as he lay naked on the floor, his neck bleeding profusely. Blood oozed from his many cuts. Empty gallon jugs that had been filled with blood littered the room, there were holes in the walls and furniture had been toppled. A woman stepped into view. She was petite but curvy, with long dark hair and dark eyes. It was hard to see exact shades of color with everything I saw tinted red, but her features hinted of Latina or Native American ancestry. She wore dark jeans and a dark long-sleeved shirt that fit her like a second skin, the deep neckline revealing an abundance of cleavage. Her arm was raised above her as she stared at me, and I realized she was holding my body, pinning it to the ceiling.

Another woman, this one with darker skin I imagined

to be a light brown and medium length hair pulled back into a large afro puff, dressed in jeans and a dark T-shirt, kneeled by Rider and ran her hands over the wound in his neck. Light formed beneath her palms and his skin mended. She moved her hands, healing the rest of his injuries.

"About fucking time," I heard Rider say, his voice strained. "What took so long?"

"I was in the middle of something, and you should have called for help sooner," the woman pinning my body to the ceiling said. "Put some pants on and quit complaining."

My body was rolled around so that I stared at the ceiling, then dropped onto the bed. The women stood over me, one on each side of the bed.

"Possession?" The black woman asked.

The other woman nodded. "She is your fledgling?"

"Yes." Rider came into view, standing next to the petite woman as he fastened his pants. "Ryan attacked her, and I tried to change the direction of her turning so she'd be a vampire instead of a succubus."

"You created a hybrid." The woman's eyebrows rose. "Interesting combination."

"Yeah, real interesting. I especially like the part where my brother just possessed her. That was real fucking great."

"It's the soul stitch attachment. It must be reassigned if he can possess her. There's no other option to stop him from doing this to her again."

"Seta... Can you do it without killing her?"

She looked at the woman across from her. "Malaika will use healing power while I reassign the attachment. I assume you want me to reassign the attachment to you?"

Laughter filled the room and as three sets of eyes bore down on me, I realized it was coming from me, although it sounded nothing like my laugh.

"Why is that bastard laughing?" Rider asked.

The woman I now knew to be Seta sat on the bed next to my body, her palms out, still using her magic to keep Ryan from moving me. She rested one hand over my breastbone where the symbol had been burned into me and placed her other hand at my temple. "It's a strong attachment," she finally said. "Maybe he thinks I'm not powerful enough to reassign it, but he doesn't know who he's dealing with. I'm going to have to burn a soul stitch into you first and then reassign her attachment to that. I see you've had blood delivered. You both need to drink as much as possible. You'll both need your strength. This is going to be painful and all around horrible."

I could feel Selander Ryan's rage as he fought against Seta's hold, but he was no match for her. The two women dressed me in a button-down shirt and underwear, and the one named Malaika fed me a gallon of blood before positioning my body so that I again lay supine. I still couldn't feel my own body, much less move it, but neither could Ryan. I wasn't sure how they got the blood down my throat unless my body drank it by reflex, or it had something to do with their magical abilities.

"You look better now," Seta said as Rider reappeared next to her. He was still shirtless and his hair was nowhere near as tightly combed-back as it usually was, but it hadn't escaped the elastic band gathering it at his nape. "Lie down next to her and brace yourself. Malaika will do all she can to quickly heal the burning, but it's going to be rough."

"I can take the pain," he said, lying next to my body. "Just save her."

I tried to turn my head toward him but couldn't. Seta moved closer to him and a moment later, I heard a horrible sound. It was a cross between a scream and a guttural cry. It seemed to last forever, but I knew it was only a few minutes before Rider gasped.

"You're done," Seta said. "Let us just stop the internal bleeding, get more blood into you, and I'll reassign your fledgling's attachment."

"She's going to feel this pain?" Rider asked. He sounded completely spent.

"Right now I don't think she can feel anything, but once I start reassigning the attachment, it'll push Ryan back wherever the hell he crept out of and yes, she will feel the pain. It's the only way, Rider. I can't hold the incubus back, create the symbols, reassign the attachment, *and* ease the pain all at once. Malaika can heal, but easing this type of pain is too advanced for her to do. It takes a lot to heal burning, especially on our kind, so she has to focus all her power on that. I'm sorry."

"I understand. I appreciate this."

"Oh, it's not like I won't cash in on the favor later," she said. "There. Now drink. I'm not starting on her until you're in better condition."

I stared at the red-tinted ceiling, wishing I could look at Rider just to see that he was doing well. I'd tried to kill him. Yeah, it was Ryan, but it was because of me. My fangs had tried to rip out his jugular. I tried to fight against Ryan, to move my body, but I couldn't even blink my eyes. I couldn't feel anything physical, just the emotional ache of knowing what I'd tried to do to the man I loved, and the pressure of Ryan pushing against Seta's power, trying desperately to break free and destroy Rider before his window of opportunity closed.

Seta and Malaika came into view over me, and the pressure inside my body intensified. The two women exchanged a look and held their hands in the air above me. Light grew from Malaika's hands. Seta's produced fire. The red tinting everything I saw receded and my body was flooded with pain. My back arched off the bed as my breastbone burned. Something clawed at my insides, trying to break free of my skin. Tears spilled over my cheeks and I regained my ability to move just in time to grab the bedsheets, throw my head back and scream.

"No!" I heard Seta cry.

"What's happening?" Rider asked.

"I can't reassign the attachment to you. Damn it, he added in a fail-safe. It can't be reattached to a vampire!"

"Then stop!"

"If I stop now, he'll completely take her over and you'll never get her back!"

Flames stung my flesh, leaving hot red marks on my skin. The entire room was engulfed. Ryan stood before me in his crimson suit, smiling as the dancing flames reflected in his black eyes.

"You sonofabitch," I growled. "This was your plan. You toyed with me for kicks, just waiting for the Bloom to hit so you could take me over and use me to kill Rider!"

He spread his arms out and shrugged. "Did you expect anything less wicked of me? I am an incubus and an incubus is, after all, a demon. As are succubi. You should have known you'd be his downfall, Danni."

"He has friends. They saved him."

"They tried. They're still trying, but they will fail. I know my brother, Danni. I know he has friends with powers. I knew there was a chance at least one of them might know about the soul stitch attachment and how to reassign it, but I also knew Rider would only allow it to be reassigned to him. It was so very tedious having to wait for the Bloom to hit for me to be able to use the special gift I branded you with, but if making it resistant to vampires kept my brother from shutting it down, I was willing to endure that wait."

"So they won't reassign it. The Bloom won't last forever. Seta can hold you back until the cycle ends."

Ryan laughed. "And when the next cycle occurs? You will go into heat, sate yourself with sex and blood, but you won't get the power you really crave because it's my craving you feel through the attachment, and my craving is Rider's life. I'll keep possessing you until either I win or he kills you to save himself. And if he does, I'll still win because the besotted fool will be torn apart if he has to kill his soulmate."

"No." I shook my head, ignoring the flames writhing around me. "He can just lock me away until I cycle through."

"Danni, Danni, Danni... as long as you bear that attachment, I can bring you anywhere I am. My bones weren't burned. I have friends too, keeping my bones and the soul stitch safe. The only reason I didn't go into my old body and bring you to it was because you were right where I needed you to be. If locking you away and waiting it out becomes his plan, I'll alter mine as well and steal you right out from under him." He chuckled. "Of course, none of these scenarios will happen because Rider's witch altered the attachment before realizing it couldn't be assigned to him. If she just stops, I'll have complete control of your body forever. If she attempts to burn it away, you'll die. The game has ended for you, Danni."

"No!" I screamed at him as the flames died down, revealing the dining room he'd created for our meetings, everything in it now charred.

"It's not so bad, Danni. You'll be here with me soon. At least you'll have a familiar face to guide you around." He stepped toward the archway I'd seen on previous visits, where shadows of flames still danced on the walls and gestured for me to follow.

I followed out of morbid curiosity and stopped when we reached the archway. I looked in, biting back a scream as I saw endless caverns of fire, a massive pit of bubbling red lava sucking the flesh off of writhing bodies, and tortured souls bound in chains.

"You'll be here with me soon, Danni. Once you're fully here, you'll be able to smell the sulfur, blood, and rot, and you'll feel the burn. I'll even be nice enough to give you the full tour before I use the soul stitch to go back into my body and continue torturing my brother, if he survives the loss."

"No! It's not over!" I turned and ran, but I had nowhere to run to. I could either remain in the burned dining room or I could step through the doorway to Hell.

"You're mine, Danni. You always were."

"No! I belong to Rider!" I pointed at him. "He beats you every time and he'll beat you now!"

"The only way he can save your life now is to assign the attachment to someone who isn't a vampire. He's not going to entrust someone else to have that much control over you, especially not after all of your going on and on about not wanting anyone to control you." Ryan laughed. "Your own words have sealed your fate."

Tears poured down my face as I recalled all the times I'd complained about being controlled. Rider had still used his control on me when it was absolutely necessary. I closed my eyes and prayed he'd do the same now. I wasn't ready to leave him, and I couldn't let Ryan beat him. I had to live for Rider.

I gasped, so much pain filling my body, attacking every nerve ending, I couldn't produce any sound. I could see Seta and Malaika over me, and I saw Rider. I reached for him and he grabbed my hand.

"Do it!" he commanded.

"Are you sure?" Seta asked.

"Yes, just do it! Do it now! Save her, damn it!"

Pure white light filled the room. I heard a deafening crack of thunder, and realized it was my chest splitting open as I found my voice and released a scream I was sure would burst my larynx. I could still hear the ungodly sound as I sank into blackness.

TWENTY-THREE

I smelled blood, but I didn't lunge for it. I moved toward the scent of rain, turning toward Rider. He smiled down at me, propped on his elbow next to me on the bed. "Hey. How do you feel?"

I covered my sternum with my hand, expecting to find a hole, but my fingers connected with the white silk of one of Rider's button-down shirts. "What happened? I was ripped apart."

He kissed my temple. "No, you weren't, but I know it felt that way. I'm so sorry you had to go through that, Danni. If there was any other way to save you—"

"You're apologizing to me?" I sat up, taking in the state of the room. It was miraculously neat, as it had been prior to the Bloom striking. I couldn't even see where the holes in the walls had been. The source of the blood I smelled came from a glass on the nightstand. "Wait. Did I dream everything? This room was destroyed."

"Magic," Rider explained. "Seta couldn't stand the mess so she did her witch thing and cleaned it up, and repaired the walls."

"What happened to the walls? I saw holes."

"You slammed me into them on multiple occasions."

I sighed. "And yet, you're apologizing to me? I destroyed this room. I tried to destroy *you*."

"That wasn't you. That was Ryan."

"It was me, Rider. I remember staring at your throat, wanting to rip out your jugular. I wanted your power." Tears spilled from my eyes. "I allowed Ryan to take total control of me and use my body to try to kill you."

"Don't blame yourself for that." Rider wiped away my tears. "You couldn't help any of that. It was the Bloom. It brought out the succubus part of you, and he had more power over you than I did. He spent every moment chipping away at what power I did have until he broke through. Fortunately, Seta and Malaika arrived just in time. I couldn't bring myself to kill you, and he was determined to use that to his advantage."

"I remember them." I rested my hand over my breastbone again. "I don't know everything that happened. Everything was in flashes. I remember a lot of sex and drinking blood. I remember being in the bathtub, soaking in the warmth, and I remember Ryan. It was like I was in two different places. I have flashes from here, and I have flashes of being in that dining room with Ryan, and then it was burning. We were in Hell."

"You were in Hell?"

I nodded, trying to remember everything. "He possessed me. I couldn't move or speak. I could only see, but everything was tinted red. The witches tried to help, but something went wrong when they tried to reassign the soul stitch. I was screaming and everything was burning. It felt like he or something inside me was clawing its way out. Then I was with him again. The dining room was on fire, but we stood there talking. He told me I lost. He'd had the attachment designed so it couldn't be reassigned to a vampire. He told me his bones were with a friend, being protected and he could go back into his body. He could have made me go to his body too if he'd wanted, but I was where he wanted me to be. He wanted me here so I could kill you. It was his plan all along. He had to wait until the Bloom struck because he'd made the soul stitch attachment resistant to vampires. He could only meet with me in dreams before the Bloom. He couldn't possess me or make me go to wherever his bones are being kept because the vampire part of me affected the magic in the attachment symbol he branded me with."

"And once the Bloom hit, he could jump right into your body. Except, I fought him tooth and nail with what power I had over you. The more you fed on sex and blood, the stronger you became while I struggled not to let my power drain dangerously. Speaking of blood, you need to drink." He reached across me and picked up the glass from the nightstand. "It's warm. I'm pretty sure the Bloom is all gone for now and there's no venom left in your bite, but I still want you drinking bagged for a while."

I held the glass but didn't raise it to my mouth. I thought back to the beginning of the Bloom. I remembered leaving Shana's party and everything becoming chaotic after that. I vaguely remembered launching myself into Rome's lap and I knew Daniel was there too, and in the room. "Who all did I inject with venom?"

"Just me. You went for Rome in the SUV after the bachelorette party, but Daniel acted fast with the tranquilizer. They got you up here where Daniel and Ginger stayed with you until I could get here. We'd just located the Quimbys and were taking fire when Ginger reached out to me. You tried to bite Daniel, but he used his ability to evade you. You only bit me. You only slept with me."

I choked on a sob, half overwhelmed with joy that I hadn't succeeded in attacking any other men, and half upset Rider had gone through so much. "Succubi don't stop at sex. They go for the kill. How did I not kill you despite injecting all that venom into you? I know you're powerful, but after so much of it, how did you not lose yourself to it and let me finish you off?"

"I'm not sure. I avoided getting bit as much as possible, but you still succeeded often enough to make resisting you a struggle. Honestly, I think you somehow managed to hold yourself back from really going in for the kill. You cried sometimes, and you screamed and growled. It was like you were fighting with yourself to maintain control."

"I remember crying. I remember you telling me everything would be all right, but I also remember you looking so drained sometimes. I was afraid I was destroying you."

"Yeah, a sex-fiend girlfriend isn't the ultimate fantasy every man thinks it would be. Don't get me wrong, sex is great, but when it goes on and on and on, it can get exhausting." He grinned. "I had to put you in the bathtub sometimes and do that boiling hot water trick I used during your turning to keep you from craving my body heat long enough for me to recover. I had blood witch-delivered every hour to keep my strength up—"

"What's witch-delivered mean?"

"Do you remember when I called in Rihanna to clean up that mess with your former boss and she just zapped herself to the room?"

I nodded.

"Witch-delivery is when a witch delivers something the same way. From the time the Bloom hit you were insatiable for sex. I know how modest you are, so I didn't want anyone entering the room while we were... indisposed, so I had her witch-deliver a gallon of blood every hour."

My face filled with heat as I looked at the glass of blood in my hand. I set it back on the nightstand, my stomach too queasy to attempt drinking it. "So even Rihanna knew we were up here having a sexfest? It's bad enough I don't know how I'm ever going to look at Rome or Daniel again, and Ginger! I broke her nose! How is she?"

"Vampires heal fast. You know this. Once she got the bleeding stopped, it was no big deal. One day of sleep and she was like brand new. I'm sure she hasn't even thought about it since."

"Since? It wasn't that long—" I remembered feeling the sun rise and descend multiple times. "Rider, how long did the Bloom last?"

"About two weeks."

"Two weeks?!" I grabbed my cellphone off the nightstand and looked at the date. "I've been dead to the world for two weeks? My sister's wedding is in two days!"

"You were far from dead to the world during those two weeks. You may have left my junk dead to the world after all that—"

"Rider!" I lowered my head into my hands and forced myself to take deep breaths. "My sister is probably going ape shit, and I don't even want to know what my mother is doing."

"They'll get over it. You had bigger things going on than your sister's wedding. You almost died."

I raised my head and looked at him. "That's right. Seta started to transfer the attachment but couldn't. I was in that place with Ryan and it was all burned up. He showed me what was behind that arch I told you about, the one I saw flames through. It was Hell, complete with a molten lake and souls in chains. He said I'd be joining him because she couldn't reassign the attachment to you, so either he'd permanently control me or I would die, depending on whether she stopped the reassignment process or tried to burn the branding off of me."

"There was another option." Rider took my hand in his. "I hope you can forgive me for the choice I made. I couldn't lose you, Danni. I just couldn't do it."

"What choice?" Fear slithered through my chest, wrapped around my heart. "What did you do?"

"I had Seta reassign the attachment to someone else who could accept it."

My stomach sank, but I remembered hoping he would save me that very way. "Who did you reassign the attachment to?"

He watched me for a moment and sighed softly before giving my hand a squeeze and saying in a near-whisper, "Daniel."

An hour later, I was dressed, fed, and mostly calm. I was wearing jeans and a pink Pigeon Forge T-shirt I'd gotten when Rider had taken me there. As I descended to the basement level of Midnight Rider, I wished I was still there, or anywhere else for that matter. I imagined everyone I passed knew how I'd spent the past two weeks and were judging me, but when I looked at them, they didn't appear to be staring. I hoped it was because they somehow had missed the club gossip and not just because they were afraid Rider would hurt them.

I made my way to the training room, took a deep breath, and opened the door. All the air I'd just taken in left me in a whoosh. I'd known Daniel was in the room, had specifically made the trip downstairs to see him, but I hadn't known he was sparring with Rome.

"Hey!" Rome said, stopping the session as he spotted me. "Welcome back."

Welcome back? I stared at him, blinking a few times as I tried to process his reaction. I'd jumped in the man's lap and tried to sink my fangs into his neck. Daniel just watched me, offering no help with the awkward situation.

"You okay?" Rome asked, noticing my silence.

"Yeah, yeah, I'm doing pretty good." I stared at the floor for a moment while I gathered my courage to address the incident in the SUV. "I, uh, came to talk to Daniel about something. I didn't know you were here. I can come back."

"Nah, I'll clear out and let y'all have the room." He took his gloves off and tossed them in a corner as Daniel did the same. He smiled as he neared me and flexed his muscles. "Don't even worry about what happened, girl. The ladies are always throwing themselves at Big Rome, what with all this sexiness. It's no big deal. That wasn't even the craziest thing that's happened to me after a night at a club." He winked at me as he passed and held up two fingers in a peace sign as he left the room.

"Imagine if he had confidence," Daniel joked, smiling. He sat with his back against the mirror lining the wall and patted the floor next to him. "Have a seat," he said, taking a sip from a water bottle in his hand. He was wearing gray drawstring sweatpants and a matching shirt with the sleeves cut off. The shirt was soaked with sweat. "I just took about five jabs to the kidneys from that big muscle-bound turd. I'm a little winded. Don't tell him I said this, but he's unnaturally strong for a human. It's downright freaky."

"I didn't know he'd be here."

"Nobody's judging you for what happened, Danni. Honestly, it wasn't that bad." He squeezed my hand. "We're just glad you're all right."

"Everyone knows about the possession?"

He shook his head. "Not everyone. Rider told me, Tony, and Rome, and we had to clue Ginger in on the whole Bloom thing because she was there to witness when it hit, but that's all she knows. She seems pretty cool, not much of a gossiper."

"She must hate me."

"No." Daniel laughed. "She's pretty kick-ass. I have a feeling a broken nose is the most minor injury she's ever received in a fight, and she doesn't hold you accountable for what you did under the influence of the Bloom. No one does. I promise."

I sighed. "I hear I'm attached to you."

"Yeah. There's a whole lot to this personal guard job that wasn't in the description." He nudged me with his shoulder. "Stop with the frown lines. It's not that big of a deal."

"Yes, it is. I know Seta had to burn a soul stitch into your bone in order to reassign my attachment to you. I was out of it or something when she did it because I don't even recall you being in the room, but I know it hurt like hell. I heard when she did it to Rider, and I thought I was splitting open when she was reassigning my attachment."

"Man, that was horrible to watch. You screamed so loud and everything was so chaotic by that point."

I winced, remembering the pain. I had no idea what had been happening around me though. "Rider told me Seta reassigned my attachment to you but didn't give much detail. Seta and Malaika were both gone when I woke up. Apparently, they had somewhere else to be. I remember when she burned a soul stitch into Rider and then she tried to reassign my attachment to him and … I don't know what happened after that."

"Rider used his mind-thing to call me to the room, and I thought you were dead when I first walked in. You were so pale and you were just out of it, staring up at the ceiling like a corpse. Both of the witches were hovering over you, using light and fire to keep you alive. They told me that Ryan had designed the attachment so it couldn't be reassigned to a vampire, but they'd already started the process. If they stopped, you could be permanently possessed by Selander Ryan. If she tried to get rid of the thing, you would most likely die. The vampire-witch told me she could burn a soul stitch into my bone and reassign your attachment to it."

"And you did it."

"Hell yeah, I did it. I wasn't going to let you die."

I shook my head, amazed. "Weren't you scared? And I know you're not a fan of dark magic. I was under the understanding the soul stitch was dark magic."

"The way it was used on you by Ryan was dark magic. What Seta was doing was correcting a wrong." He laughed a little. "And honestly, I was scared to death. Rider was lying next to you on the bed when I first walked in and he looked so rough. You looked even worse. Still, I couldn't let you die or allow that bastard to stay in control of your body, so I gritted my teeth, and somehow managed not to piss my pants while Seta did what needed to be done. It hurt getting that thing burned into me, but it wasn't anywhere near as bad as hearing you scream when she did the reassignment. By the time she added another attachment symbol to your bone, you were out cold. I think the pain knocked you out."

"What?" I touched my chest where the symbol rested under my skin. "She added another attachment symbol to me?"

"Yeah, she reassigned Ryan's to me and added a new one to attach to the one she'd burned into Rider."

"Why?" My eyes narrowed. "He didn't tell me that."

"Before you get all mad at him, he did it as an added layer of protection. Like I said, it was chaotic, especially since Seta had to burn a soul stitch into me while you were already in the reassignment process and both witches were doing everything they could to keep you alive, so they weren't taking their sweet time with lengthy explanations, but from what I gathered, having two attachments will keep you from being possessed. If Rider or I die, we can bring you to us and communicate with you from wherever it is that we'll go in the afterlife, but neither of us can actually possess you. If you had only the one attachment, I could possess you. Not that I would," he quickly added, "but I can understand why Rider didn't want to risk it. The important thing is, you're alive and Selander Ryan can no longer possess you."

"But I'm still half succubus," I reminded him. "The Bloom will come back, and so will Ryan, eventually. The soul stitch attachment was reassigned, but he told me his bones are still here somewhere, being guarded. He can reenter his body if he wants to."

"We'll deal with all that when and if we need to, and

the Bloom might not be so bad the next time around. I know some good people from Imortia who might be able to help with that. Don't get your hopes up just yet, but … don't worry too hard either. I'm never going to let anything bad happen to you."

I studied Daniel and couldn't help smiling as I noted the intensity in his eyes as he looked back at me. "You care about me."

He kissed my cheek. "Look who's catching on. So… your sister's wedding is in two days and there's still one Quimby and Torch out there. How excited are you?"

I rolled my eyes and thunked my head against the mirrored wall, earning a chuckle. I removed my cell phone from my back pocket and sighed. "I was going to remote in to my voicemail and see how many times my sister called me to leave shrieking messages."

"Oh, good." Daniel rubbed his hands. "Let's do this. Those messages are hilarious, especially when they talk about zapping your boobs."

"I now pronounce you husband and wife. You may kiss the bride."

The guests applauded, Shana kissed her new husband, and I used every ounce of willpower in my body not to roll my eyes, remembering she'd hooked up with at least two other men during her bachelorette party. I caught my mother's eye, and she gestured for me to stand up straighter and smile. Beside her, my grandmother pet the tiny dog she kept in her purse and glared disapprovingly at my dress.

"You looked completely uncomfortable up there," Daniel said as I joined him outside the church a few minutes later, "but beautiful."

"I don't like being in front of a bunch of people, especially when two of them are nit-picking family members."

"If you'd looked at me, I would have made silly faces to cheer you up."

"That's exactly why I avoided looking your way," I told him, laughing, as he guided me to the waiting SUV and off we went to the reception.

Bernard Quimby and Torch were still a problem, so Rider had managed to get his own security team in place at the reception. Daniel was doubling as my personal bodyguard and my date since Rider still thought it too dangerous for his enemies to see him romantically involved with me. His hope was that his lack of personal attention to me outside of the bar would throw Quimby and Torch off my scent and bring the danger to him. I could understand his reasoning, but it still hurt.

We arrived at the reception hall without incident and stepped inside. The entire room was decorated in pink and silver, and I felt as though I blended right in with my light pink sheath and matching heels. My hair was slicked down with gel and I'd managed to avoid getting a lot of gunk applied to my face by my mother, escaping the dressing area under the church with just a coat of pink lipstick, a little eyeshadow in neutral tones and a swipe of blush. My eyelashes were already long and dark, especially since I'd turned.

"Are you thirsty?" Daniel whispered as he led me over to a table along the wall and held a chair out for me, waiting for me to sit before he took his seat with his back to the wall so he could see the entire room.

"I'm pretty good," I answered. "Rider made sure I was full before I left."

"Let me know if that changes." He spoke to me, but his eyes continued to scan the room. He was wearing a black suit with a black and pink striped tie to match me, but he looked adorably out of place with the rainbow colored hair and silver nose ring.

"Taking the guard duty seriously."

"Always." He groaned, and I followed his line of sight

to see my mother and grandmother approaching.

"Why are you sitting over here?" My mother asked, taking a seat.

"In my day, gentlemen pulled out chairs for ladies," my grandmother said, setting her purse on the floor as she took her seat.

"They still do *for ladies*," Daniel muttered. I gave him a gentle kick under the table and he grinned.

"Why did you do that to your hair?" My grandmother asked, wrinkling her nose as she eyed Daniel. He couldn't tell her it was natural because it wasn't possible to have naturally rainbow-colored hair in our realm, so he didn't respond. "And jewelry in the nose." She shook her head and turned toward me. "Where's that looker from the restaurant? The one with his own business? Did you blow that already?"

I inhaled deep and released the breath slowly, calming my nerves before I lost my temper. "He's unavailable. I brought Daniel as my date. We're very good friends."

She rolled her eyes. "Well, if you'd used that gift I bought you, you'd stand out more from the wedding party," she griped. "I spent good money on that and I know you haven't used it. I can tell." She stared pointedly at my chest.

"Or what I bought you," my mother added.

The pills and Jug-Jolter 2000 they'd ordered for me had arrived weeks ago. The guard Rider had on my apartment had informed him of the packages, and Rider had the guard place them inside my apartment. Apparently, the guard had a key, or a talent with locked doors. As long as he didn't go snooping through my underwear drawer, I didn't really care. "I don't think they work this fast," I said, not wanting to admit I'd never even opened the packages and cause more griping.

Terry the tiny rat-dog my grandmother toted with her everywhere yipped at me as if it detected the lie and wanted to call me out on it. I glared down at him and he burrowed down into the purse and farted. Daniel looked at me with raised eyebrows.

"It was the dog," I said.

"My baby has a delicate constitution," my grandmother said.

Daniel peered around me to look at the little Pomchi. It stuck its head out of the purse and growled at him. "Looks like a fuzzy chicken nugget," Daniel commented.

My grandmother gasped and grabbed her dog, settling it on her lap. "My little Terry is a precious angel, and he is beautiful. I suppose you prefer something mangy with a spiked collar."

The lights went down, and the DJ announced the newlyweds, successfully diverting my mother and grandmother's attention from poor Daniel. Shana and her new husband, Kevin, entered the room and a spotlight followed them onto the dancefloor where they shared their first dance as a married couple. They swayed together to a ballad, smiling as they looked into each other's eyes. Kevin didn't seem like a bad guy but he wasn't very good looking, with choppy blond hair, a stubby nose and eyes a little too big for his face. He was on the shorter side for a guy and a little goofy, but he had money and that's what mattered to Shana.

"That's not how she was dancing at the bachelorette party," Daniel whispered to me, and I snorted before smacking his arm.

"Isn't she beautiful?" my mother said. "And so in love."

I narrowed my eyes at Daniel and shook my head, warning him not to say a word. The corners of his mouth twitched and his eyes twinkled with devilish mischief.

"You could learn a lot from your sister," my grandmother added.

"Like the best positions to use in bathroom stalls," Daniel murmured.

"I'm thirsty," I said, grabbing Daniel's arm. I pulled

him from his seat and walked toward a punch fountain I saw near the back of the room. "What are you doing?"

"Having fun," he answered.

"Well, dial it back. It doesn't take much to get them going on a rant."

"Well, I'm sorry, but they're rude to you all the time. I don't like it."

"You sound like Rider." I stopped near the table and looked around. I couldn't actually drink the punch.

Shana and Kevin's official first dance as newlyweds ended, and they moved over to the cake. I sighed, looking at all the creamy white icing as Shana made the first cut. "Being a vampire sucks."

"You'll be able to eat again eventually," Daniel said. "You can always get Rihanna to do that thing again."

"She was nice enough to offer it that time. Rihanna normally charges for her services and she doesn't come cheap."

"Witches never do." Daniel smiled.

"What?"

"Nothing, just remembering the way you ate that cupcake."

I rolled my eyes. "It was a cupcake. I ate it. I don't know why you and Rider made such a big deal about it."

"Sweetheart, you damn near had a sexual experience with that cupcake. Hell, I nearly had one watching you eat it."

"Gross." I smacked his arm, earning a laugh in response.

"Danni Keller?"

I turned and stopped breathing as I came face to face with the only man I'd ever slept with prior to Rider. His name was Billy Thornburg, and we'd been in college at the time. He was my geeky lab partner and up until we'd slept together, I thought he was my friend. Our night together had been extremely disappointing, and the nightmare didn't end for me after that night because he'd blabbed to all his friends how I was the worst lay he'd ever had. His hair was still a dull brown and cut short. He still wore glasses but with less chunky frames, and he didn't look as geeky in a suit as he did in the T-shirts and khakis he always wore in school. He smiled and my stomach did a flip as I remembered the way he and his friends laughed at me. He hadn't even tried to deny the fact he'd told everyone what we'd done, or that I was horrible at it.

"It really is you. How have you been?"

I looked over his shoulder and saw two of his closest friends from college pointing at us. "I'm sorry. Do I know you?" I asked. I hadn't planned on pretending not to know him, but the question just slipped out.

His eyes widened for a moment and his cheeks pinkened. "It's Billy," he said. "Billy Thornburg. From college," he added after I just stared at him, frowning in fake confusion.

I shook my head. "I'm sorry, Mr. Thornburg. I was pretty focused on academics in college. I'm afraid I kept my head in the books and didn't really pay a lot of attention to the people around me."

He looked back at his friends, who had grown interested in the conversation, and his face developed more color. "You remember me," he said loud enough to make sure his buddies could hear. "I walked you home from Chub Porter's party and … stayed a while."

I felt Daniel's hand rest along my lower back, but didn't look at him. My eyes were burning, and I knew if I looked at him, saw any sign that he knew what this jackass was doing or how awful the memory he was trying to dredge up was for me, tears would spill from them and I refused to give Billy Thornburg the satisfaction. He'd had more than enough fun at my expense.

I shrugged. "Sorry. It doesn't ring a bell. Must not have been a very memorable night."

Billy's friends laughed, and Billy's face went from pink to red as he stepped toward me. Daniel's hand left my back and went to Billy's chest. "You're too close, bro. Danni, is this guy a problem?"

"I'm not sure," I said, careful to keep my face blank. "I honestly have no idea who in the world he is."

Rome, who was working security and had been watching us, moved in. "Is there a problem here?"

"Is there?" Daniel asked.

Billy looked between him and me and shook his head. "No problem."

Daniel and Rome shared a look, nodded to each other, and Rome moved away. Daniel grabbed my hand and led me to the dancefloor. He saw an elderly couple dancing and cringed before moving us a couple feet over.

"What was that about?"

"Old people creep me out," he whispered. "Most everyone in Imortia is immortal, so they don't get all old and creepy there. There's so many of them here."

I looked at the couple and laughed. "How is that cute old couple creepy?"

"They're all *doughy*, and they smell like ointment and old skin."

"You're ridiculous."

He looked over my head, and I knew he was looking at Billy. "I'm not totally sure what all that was about with that guy, but I can draw some conclusions. What I do know for sure is you just ruined that guy's night. Am I right in my assumption he deserved it?"

I sighed and focused my line of sight on Daniel's shoulder. "I lost my virginity to him in college. I, of course, didn't know what I was doing and the whole thing was awful, and he made sure to tell everyone that the very next day."

After an awkward moment of silence, Daniel tipped my chin so I had to look at him. "Was it his first time too?"

"Not according to him." I frowned. "Now that I've been with someone else, I wonder about that. He didn't really seem to know what he was doing either. He barely touched me, but after the way he told everyone I didn't have much for him to play with, I thought that was why."

Daniel shook his head. "It wasn't you, Danni. He didn't know what he was doing, failed to make the experience good for you, and decided to tell a version of the story that favored him before you had the chance to reveal how it really went down."

"How do you know that?"

"I know his type."

"I would have never said anything. He was my friend up until then, or at least I thought he was."

"A guy with a crushed ego can do some really shitty things. You were awesome. Acting like you didn't even remember him like that? That destroyed him, especially with his buddies watching. You just took all the credibility out of what he told them about that night."

I smiled. "I hope so. That mistake has haunted me for far too long." Not to mention, it had done one hell of a number on my confidence with men.

"Put it to rest and wipe him out of your mind. You're a strong, beautiful woman and a far better man loves you."

"Yeah, one who wouldn't even accompany me tonight," I couldn't stop myself from muttering. "He'd prefer I be here dancing with you. I'm not so sure what that says about our story."

"Danni, in this story, Rider is the king. You are his treasure, and I'm the dragon he's assigned to protect it. That's a pretty damn good story."

"Shouldn't I be the queen?"

Daniel looked over my head and stepped back, grinning as the air pressure around us shifted. "I don't know. I think it's possible she can be both at the same time?"

"She's my entire kingdom," Rider said, taking Daniel's place as the shifter left us. He was in a black suit with a black shirt open at the collar, a pink pocket square, and no tie.

"You came." I blinked back tears. "I thought you didn't want anyone to know about us."

"I didn't want my enemies to know about us." He brushed a light kiss across my mouth. "I have good reasons for that, but I don't intend on ever letting you go and forever is a long time to try to hide what I feel for you from the world."

"What about Torch and the remaining Quimby?"

"They're still out there, but we'll get them." He looked over my head and groaned. "I'm going to have to speak to your family, aren't I?"

"Yeah, but you can make the dog pee in my grandmother's purse like you did that one time. That's always fun."

He chuckled. "Should we get it over with now?"

"Later," I said. "I'm enjoying this dance. I'm so happy you came."

He smiled down at me. "I'll always be here for you. Besides, if I'm not careful, that dragon might think he can fly away with you."

"He wouldn't dare."

"I don't know, Danni. You have a way about driving men crazy."

I could see Billy Thornburg watching us from across the room, his hands shoved deep in his pockets, his eyes narrowed into slits. There was a time seeing him would have reduced me to uncontrollable tears, which would have given him power over me. He had no power over me now. I wasn't what he'd told people I was. His words couldn't hurt me, and neither could my family's. My sister had just married a man she didn't love to prove she could snatch up a man with money, and for all their criticizing me, my mother and grandmother were sitting at a table by themselves, judging people, and I was dancing with a gorgeous man who was willing to fight for me every day for the rest of his eternal life, a man who feared losing me. Being a vampire wasn't always fun, being a succubus came with even more issues, but I had to smile as I realized I was happy, and the people who'd put me down and made me feel inferior so many times weren't.

"Maybe I just drive you crazy," I said, looking into Rider's pure blue eyes, "but that's enough for me."

"Sorry to interrupt," Daniel said, skidding to a stop next to us, "but we have trouble."

TWENTY-FOUR

"What?" Rider immediately stilled, scanning the room with his eyes.

"Bernard Quimby and some men approaching from the front. We have an SUV waiting out back. I don't think you want to fight here with all these innocent humans."

"You're right. Let's go." Rider grabbed my hand and followed Daniel as he led us toward the back exit. Unfortunately, we had to pass my mother and grandmother's table on the way.

"Danni! Where are you going?" My mother asked, loud enough to grab Shana's attention. She was standing nearby, posing for pictures with friends.

"I have to run, Mom. I'll call you later!"

"Danni!" Shana called.

"I have to go," I called back. "Beautiful wedding! Congratulations!"

I sensed Rider's power around me and knew he was communicating with the members of his nest he had on security detail. "We have to hurry. Torch just arrived, and he brought a small army with him."

"These guys really want you dead," Daniel said.

"The feeling's mutual," Rider replied.

We reached the rear exit and Daniel stepped out into the alley first, scanning side to side for danger. I saw three SUVs parked outside the door, waiting. "Come on." He motioned us forward.

We'd just stepped out when I heard vehicles screeching to a stop at both ends of the alley.

"Shit!" Rider exclaimed, pushing me toward the middle SUV as the alley filled with men. One of them immediately started sweeping left to right with a flamethrower as he made his way deeper into the alley, determined to char everything in his path. "Get in and stay down!"

"Danni!"

I turned to see Shana exiting the door we'd just left through.

"Where are you going?" she asked, oblivious to what was happening around her, her narrowed eyes focused solely on me. "You can't just leave my—" Her eyes widened and she let out a cry as red blossomed across the bodice of her wedding dress and she fell forward.

"Shana!" I ran to her, catching her in my arms before she fell. Rider and Daniel dragged us both to the SUV, ducking as bullets zinged around us, and shoved us inside.

"Shit!" Tony said from the driver's seat, looking back at us as Rider slammed the door closed and jumped into battle. "Is that your sister?"

"Yes!" I cried, laying Shana across the backseat as I kneeled on the floor beside her. Blood gushed out of the hole in her chest. My own blood seemed to freeze in my veins, along with my ability to think. "What do I do?"

"Can you seal the wound with your saliva?"

I dipped my head toward the wound, but stopped before I made contact. "Wait. What if she's bleeding internally? Should I still seal the wound?"

"Fuck, I don't know. I'm a shifter. I get shot, I shift shape and heal." He looked around, searching the people filling the alley. "We need a witch or healer. I don't see any."

Something slammed into the SUV and I looked up to see a man sliding down the back window, leaving a trail of blood. All around us, bullets flew and people fought. I could sense shifters, vampires, and humans in the mix, but couldn't concentrate enough to pinpoint who was who, or who even belonged to our side. I couldn't see Rider or Daniel.

The door at my back opened and Rome leaned in with a towel. He pressed it to Shana's wound, staunching the flow of blood. I heard gunfire, screaming, and yelling all around him.

"What's happening?"

"War," he said, grimacing as he took in the amount of blood Shana had lost. It was pooled under her on the seat, dripping onto the floor, and some had smeared on the front of my dress. He glanced toward the front of the SUV and his eyes widened. "Holy shit."

I followed his line of sight and saw a huge dragon on top of the SUV in front of us. Daniel opened his massive dragon jaws and released a stream of fire, roasting everyone between the SUV and the beginning of the alley. The yelling outside grew louder, followed by the sounds of doors slamming and tires squealing.

"Looks like Daniel scared the shit out of what's left of the bad guys," Tony said, checking his side mirror. "They're getting the hell out of here."

"We got Quimby," Rome said, "and I'm pretty sure Daniel just torched Torch."

"How's Rider?" I asked, looking around. From my vantage point, I couldn't see him, but I didn't sense that he was dead, or even in pain.

"He's fine," Rome said, taking Shana's pulse. "He's fast and powerful. I can't say the same for your sister. Her pulse is barely there."

My heart stopped beating as my sister's life flashed before my eyes. She was spoiled rotten, and I'd spent most of our adult lives envying her beauty, but we'd had some good times together when we were kids before we'd cared so much about the way we looked or what the world thought of us.

The front passenger side door opened and Daniel climbed in. A second later, Rider opened the other back door. "Get in," he told Rome as he lifted Shana's feet and jumped in, pulling the door closed behind him.

Rome lifted Shana's upper body and slid in under her. Blood seeped through the towel, no longer gushing, as he rested her head in his lap. I remained on the floor, crying, knowing the slowing of blood was a bad sign.

"Get to the hospital," Rider ordered, taking Shana's pulse.

Tony was already speeding in reverse down the alley, the portion of it in front of us blocked by the carnage Torch and Daniel had left behind. We heard police sirens in the distance. Tony cleared the alley, threw the gearshift into Drive and floored the gas.

"She's not going to make it," I said, noting Shana's deathly pallor.

Rider met my gaze. "I'm sorry."

"You can save her!"

Rider made a small side-to-side movement with his head. "Not everyone can be saved the way I saved you."

"What?!" I stared at him open-mouthed as fiery hot anger burned through me. "Turn her! You can do it!"

"Danni—"

"Turn her!" I yelled. "Why are you just sitting there? Save her! Why aren't you even trying?"

"We can't save everyone," he said. "Someone like her isn't a good candidate for—"

"You sonofabitch!" I lunged forward, striking him with my fists. He blocked me, but I succeeded in connecting some shots. "You don't get to save me and let my sister die just because you don't like her!"

"Danni, calm down! It's not because I don't like her." He gripped my arms and held me away from him as best he could in the tight space. "I'm sorry, but I can't—"

"I'll do it myself," I shouted. My fangs descended as I leaned over my ghostly pale sister.

"No!" Rider yanked me away from her. "You're only half vampire and too young. You don't know what you'll turn her into if you succeed. You might even kill her faster."

I wrestled my way out of his grasp, oblivious to the others watching us fight as we sped toward the hospital that wasn't even going to do her any good if she was dead when we arrived. I didn't care about the others. I cared about my sister dying in front of me.

"Save her!" I screamed at Rider, beating his chest. "Save her or I'll never forgive you for just letting her die! She's my sister!" I broke down into deep sobs. "She's my sister. You can't let her die."

Rider stared at me, wide-eyed and gape-mouthed. No one in the SUV made a sound except me, heaving sobs as I sank down onto my knees on the bloody floorboard, too emotionally spent to hit Rider anymore. "I'll never forgive you," I whispered, my voice hoarse.

Rider growled a curse and plunged his fangs into Shana's neck, drinking what remained of her blood. He lifted his head to cut his wrist with one of his fangs and looked at me as blood pooled above the gash. "This could be the worst mistake I've ever made," he said.

"Please, Rider. She's my sister and she was shot because of us."

He closed his eyes, shook his head, and lowered his wrist to her mouth.

I sat in a chair in a small room in the basement level of Midnight Rider next to the bed Shana lay in, waiting for her to open her eyes. Rider leaned back against the wall on the opposite side of the room, staring down at the floor, his hands deep in his pockets. Both of us were still covered in Shana's blood and neither of us were talking.

"Are the restraints necessary?" I finally asked, looking at the steel cuffs holding Shana's wrists to the bedrails.

"Yes," he said softly. "She could wake up bloodthirsty and kill you."

"She wouldn't kill me."

"You don't know what she'll do," Rider said, looking me in the eye for the first time since he'd turned her. "Not everyone is meant to be turned. I know she's your sister, but she's selfish and conceited. These are not good traits for a vampire."

He wasn't lying. She was the ultimate snob, but she hadn't always been that way. "You barely know her," I told him. "You've only seen one side of her. Being stuck-up doesn't mean she's going to wake up a monster. She's my sister, Rider. Despite her flaws, she's my blood. She won't hurt me."

"Ryan was my blood," he reminded me.

"Shana is nothing like Ryan."

He looked at Shana and shook his head before returning his gaze to me, deep worry in his eyes. "For your sake, I really hope that's true."

ABOUT THE AUTHOR

Crystal-Rain Love is a romance author specializing in paranormal, suspense, and contemporary subgenres. Her author career began by winning a contest to be one of Sapphire Blue Publishing's debut authors in 2008. She snagged a multi-book contract with Imajinn Books that same year, going on to be published by The Wild Rose Press and eventually venturing out into indie publishing. She resides in the South with her three children and enough pets to host a petting zoo. When she's not writing she can usually be found creating unique 3D cakes, hiking, reading, or spending way too much time on Facebook.

Find out more about her at www.crystalrainlove.com